M000305057

All the Wrong Places

A Novel

Rebecca Fisher

Rebecca Fisher Books

Copyright © 2010 by Rebecca Fisher

Second Edition Copyright © 2014 by Rebecca Fisher

All rights reserved. No part of this publication may be reproduced, distributed, or transmitted in any form or by any means, including photocopying, recording, or other electronic or mechanical methods, without the prior written permission of the publisher, except in the case of brief quotations embodied in critical reviews and certain other noncommercial uses permitted by the U.S. Copyright Act of 1976.

Rebecca Fisher Books
P.O. Box 374
Santa Clarita, CA 91310

Visit our Web site at www.rebeccafisherbooks.com

All characters, events and locations portrayed in this book are fictitious. Any similarities to real persons, events or locations are coincidental and not intended by the author.

ISBN 978-0-9831569-2-5

Printed in the United States of America

Second Edition

Acknowledgements

The following have contributed a great deal to these pages both in spirit and ink, and to them I owe many thanks:

My God, for His Son, His patience with me, and His unfathomable love.

My first and faithful readers - for their willingness to read every last word and for encouraging me to write more.

My brother Ricky Udave and my sister, Justine Haeussler, for contributing their artistic talents.

Bill Santoro, for his formatting magic.

Tara Schiro, for her editing touch.

My daughter, Bailey, (Miss Page) "my world always shines whenever you walk by."

My daughter, Karis, for her contagious smile and her sweet spirit.

My husband, Jeff, my real life Oliver, for his unwavering support and faith in my love for words. Without you, there would be no happy ending to this tale.

Thank you. Thank you.

All the Wrong Places

Table of Contents

Chapter One

The Hillside

Sheets of rain fell, leading my car along a blind road. The rhythmic sound of the rain was soothing and combined with the fabricated heat, threatened a sleeplike trance. But memories of the day's surreal events were like a constant alarm, keeping me more aware than I would like. Each image brought with it a sickness in my stomach. I tried to shake them away, and it worked momentarily, but they inevitably returned.

The love songs on the radio were now the background music for the tragedy replaying in my head. It was epic in proportion, like in *Pride and Prejudice*, except the likely ending had Elizabeth settled for the shady Mr. Wickham.

It was the love dedication portion of the program, and I thought I might vomit in the passenger seat when the d.j. began reading the letters out loud. There's not a feeling more awkward than the embarrassment you have for someone else when they pour out their feelings in a letter mailed to a radio station. I wanted to call in and assure the writer that the undying love they felt would pass shortly, and that the real person would come out of hiding when there was no longer a need for pretenses. The thought of how this bitter truth had played out for me took me from self-pitying to thoroughly ticked off. I gripped the steering wheel tighter to suppress the rising emotions - remembering I wasn't alone.

Maddy had fallen asleep in the backseat, without the knowledge of the weight of the world now resting on my shoulders. I would do anything to protect her from our sudden change of circumstance and the harsh reality that created it.

She had shifted to one side, head bent toward the head rest, in an attempt to sleep comfortably. A once plush hippopotamus, now missing one eye and most of its stitching, was cuddled up in her arm. His name was Hippo, and he was her very favorite animal. One of those animals you bring with you everywhere because it seems to soothe them. It still soothed her.

I glanced back at her and fought the welling lump in my throat, crying vicariously through the rain so as not to wake her. My face ached as I tried to hold in the tears. My bottom lip was pushing out from the permanent frown. I always looked like a cry baby when I cried. I used to wish I could be an elegant crier, like in the movies – back of the hand to the forehead and no matter how long you cried, your makeup would be perfect and your eyes wouldn't swell and redden like Italian sausages. That wasn't me. I was a mess.

As the disturbing memories continued to replay, I began to realize that we had nowhere to go. The shock of the day was wearing off quickly now and reality setting in. I decided that before I had a complete meltdown, I would attempt a logical review of our situation.

To start, I didn't have a clue where I was going. I was simply following a winding highway – going only God and GPS knew where. Secondly, I had no one left to help me. In the last hour I had closed the door on any chance of familial assistance, and friends were out of the question as I no longer had any. Third, I was nearly destitute. I didn't have a single credit card to rent a hotel room with, and though there were sixty dollars in my purse from my unfinished grocery errands, it probably wouldn't be enough to rent a room anywhere in the state without the promise of filthy sheets, cockroaches and social deviants.

The logic was fading and the tears threatened a victorious return. Trying desperately to leave my emotions out of it, I moved on to possible solutions. I thought about what someone else in my shoes would do. What would I suggest they do with no friends, no family, and not much money? Every city has a shelter, right?

The image of Maddy sleeping on a stiff, green cot, next to a urine-soaked, dingy, smiling man with no teeth broke down the last bit of fight I had in me. I cried out in utter desperation, "Help me!"

A sudden chill came over me, setting off uncontrollable sobs. Everything I had been holding back for the last few hours was fighting its way to the surface with a vengeance. Every muscle tightened as the waves of heartache and panic searched for a way out. As I finally gave in, allowing it all to flow from my defeated emotional dam, a sudden jolt sent the car spinning at a dizzying pace.

Every emotion playing inside me was replaced with a fierce flood of adrenaline. I couldn't see anything through the windshield except the headlights flashing on ever-changing objects as we spun. The moment seemed endless. The screech of the tires on the asphalt triggered an automatic response. Without thought, my foot slammed on the brakes and I jerked the steering wheel against the spin of the car. Everything around me seemed to blur until we slammed into an unwavering structure and came to an abrupt halt.

I knew we were stopped, but *I* continued to spin. The breath had been knocked out of me by the impact, and all sound had been drawn from my ears. The silence was disorienting, but I was pretty sure by the rate of my heartbeat that I was still alive. It took a while before I could focus on anything through my blurred vision. My thoughts raced as I tried to catch my breath and figure out how much damage I was facing.

The realization of what I might see in the backseat hit me hard and furiously. My eyes shot back as I continued struggling to pull myself together. The volume of my surroundings and the ability to scream quickly returned.

"MADDY!" My voice had fought its way out before I could complete the terrifying images that shot through my mind. Maddy lay quietly holding Hippo, her eyes squinting in a dreary, dreamy fog.

"Mommy?" she responded in a confused daze. She lifted her head up, securely holding her hippo in her arms.

"Maddy are you okay?" I fumbled to unbuckle my seatbelt and carelessly stumbled into the backseat, freeing her from her seat and scooping her up in a panic - my arms trembling. "Maddy are you okay?" I asked again, desperate for a response that would quell my fears.

I frantically attempted a medical assessment, feeling around each and every bone - where they began, where they joined, and where they ended. She seemed so small and fragile as I held her in my lap. I ran my fingers over the slopes of her head, searching for any damage. There didn't seem to be anything wrong. Was it possible, with that impact, that we were okay?

She wiggled her head under my hands and looked up at me, confused.

"Mommy, what are you doing? I'm tired," she complained through a yawn. "Can I lie down again?" Maddy was a notoriously sound sleeper. I had once vacuumed the entire living room carpet with her baby carrier right in the center. She never budged. It didn't surprise me that the accident barely stirred her considering she had also succumbed, not even an hour ago, to a dose of acetaminophen. I had picked her up early from school because of a slight fever.

Pangs of guilt seized me. I stroked at her hair, determined to make things right.

Dozing off, she pulled Hippo in closer, tucking her hand around his body and into her chest. To provide extra security, she wrapped her other arm around him tightly.

The trust she put into the protection of that stuffed animal was so simple and so real. It seemed at the moment that it had more to offer her than I did. I so badly wanted to curl up with her and join in her peaceful sleep, trusting that everything would be alright, but I would have to settle for just one of us having it.

"Go to sleep, baby," I whispered. Her body soon lay limp with sleep. I gently leaned her head back on the seat as I continued to catch my breath. Fear had taken flight in my veins, and my heart raced to keep up. Trying to slow the pace, I took every other breath through my nose. I closed my eyes and tried to empty my mind of the swarming images.

The beating of the rain on the car seemed too simple a sound to follow such chaos, but I longed for simple. I tried to focus just on the sound of the rain and waited for my heart to slow.

The irregular rhythm of my heart had started shortly after Maddy was born and had grown steadily worse since. The doctors called it a tachycardia and assured me that it was unlikely I would die from complications. Doctors can be so very comforting. Unfortunately, the preventive medications I was prescribed to treat it caused a respiratory reaction, similar to an asthma attack, and with surgery as my only other option, I chose to just deal with it. But in stressful events such as these, the tripled rate of beats made it impossible to catch my breath.

I mindlessly stroked at Maddy's hair until my heart rate and breathing had returned to normal. I sat and waited for the next indicated step to present itself to me, but realized with heaviness that I was the only adult in the car, and at some point I would have to do something.

I peered through the back window to assess the situation. Above us the sky was black, filled with countless iridescent beads. Beneath us, a hill covered in ivy - our car propped upon it.

I slowly shifted my body from under Maddy and climbed back into the front seat. I figured I'd start with the basics and hope for the best. I started the car again and put it into gear. It wouldn't move forward, and it wouldn't budge back. The day's wrath was clearly not going to subside.

I peered through the fog-stained window, wiping my breath away with my sleeve. I could barely make out the shape of a building just atop the hill, and the outline of a large, lit sign bearing what looked like the shape of a cross. The sign revealed its age - a yellowed, fiber-glass cover framed by brick. I couldn't quite read the large, block letters to determine where we were. I had no choice but to investigate further than the driver's seat.

Though still dizzy and a bit nauseated, I turned off the car, put on my jacket, and climbed out into the cold.

It was pouring down now, and I had neglected, rather, never considered to pack an umbrella in my escape. It was merely drizzling when the day began, and I had come to truly love the feel of the light sprinkle on my face. I often laughed at the sight of others hiding under their umbrellas from such harmless mist. I found comfort in the smell of wet asphalt and the sound of squeaky shoes on linoleum. The rain seemed to change everyone and everything. It quieted the usually busy streets, replacing the fast-paced tension with the rhythmic wipers on the windshield and parting waters through the intersections. It was a change, and change for me was good, if only just wetter than before. It gave me the strong desire and hope to have more than the loveless, unfulfilling, and unfaithful reality that was my marriage.

This was real rain. The kind that won't let you forget as it pummels the top of your head. The winds didn't help matters either, and before I could close the door, my seat was soaked. I closed it quickly but quietly to avoid the litany of questions that are inevitable with a curious five year old.

Pulling the top of my jacket over my head, I knelt down to assess the damage. What little was left of the front tire was embedded in the ivy, and a large rock stood guard just behind the rear tire. I scooted through the ivy to the front and ran my fingers over the shredded rubber, which no longer covered the metal beneath. I had helped a couple of friends change tires in the past and convinced myself that it couldn't be too hard. I had a spare in the trunk. It wasn't impossible.

I moved through the pools of wet leaves toward the back. I glared at the rock standing firmly behind the rear tire. If only looks could move rocks too. Determined as always, I bent down, placed both hands on the rock, and pushed to test its hold. It was solid. I decided to push harder, judging by its shape that it couldn't be too deeply embedded in the ground. This time I stepped back with both feet, now in a runner's starting position, and pushed like our very future depended on it. In an instant, my right foot gave under the wet mush, and all of my weight landed my face on the side of the stubborn stone. In the sharp cold, the pain throbbed.

I sat in the ivy, since my clothes were already entirely soaked and covered in mud, and gently touched around my face. I winced at the pain. Pulling my hand away to assess the damage, I saw no blood. Nothing too bad.

Since it was painfully obvious that I wasn't going to get very far on my own, I decided to call information and get the number for a tow truck. They could surely pull us out. I forced out of my mind the fact that the service wouldn't be free, and even when the car was back on the road, we still had nowhere to go.

I crawled back to the door and slung my wet body onto the seat, shivering uncontrollably.

I searched through my purse looking for my cell phone. My fingers were so cold that they moved in stiff, slow motion. My mind wasn't moving much faster through the shivers. I had turned the phone off earlier, avoiding any possible contact with what was behind us. I held the power button down and waited for the sound. *Searching for network* flashed on the screen.

I felt sick at the thought of what I imagined coming. Of course I wouldn't have service. This day was determined to earn itself the ranking of "the worst of my life" without a single hopeful contender.

I had been so confident and sure about every choice I had made that day. It felt right, like for the first time I was on the right path, making the right choices for both of us. Was this a test of will? The challenge stirred up a new wave of courage. I *would* make this work. I would *never* go back.

My face and hands burned as they warmed. I would never go back, but I did need help. I looked again at the yellowed sign and at the mysterious building. Along one side there was a window warmed by an inside light. It glowed through faded curtains.

It was getting late. Could someone be there? I figured that if nothing else, someone in a holy establishment would feel compelled to help us somehow, perhaps give us shelter for the night. I did have the pathetic, lost, single mother appeal, and a tired, helpless child to boot. That was a cross on the sign after all, and from what little I knew of crosses, they carried with them the great burden of helping those in need. Though I didn't necessarily buy it, I would take help any way I could get it.

With no other options and a fierce determination to make my first claim on independence, I climbed back out of the car. I hurriedly opened the back door and pulled Maddy out and over my shoulder. I grabbed her jacket and placed it over her head. She squirmed a bit but didn't wake. My wet jeans provided some grip against her clothes, but my numb arms and fingers were finding it difficult to keep a tight grasp around her body. I didn't know how long I could hold on before I would have to set her down.

I looked to the building again, trying to decide what I was getting myself into. It didn't look anything like a church - too square and simple. There weren't any churchy ornaments or engravings. I hadn't been in a while, but I was sure churches didn't look or feel like this.

I forced my way up the hill, which was impossibly slick and steep. I could feel my shoes fill with cold water and my toes squish with each step. The bottoms of my jeans grew heavy as they absorbed the water from the leaves of ivy. My thighs burned from the climb. How long had it been since I'd walked at an incline holding a fifty pound weight around my neck and waist? I immediately regretted my lack of any consistent exercise. My body begged for air, and my lungs did all they could to keep up with what I sucked in.

We finally reached the top. I stopped to try and breathe through the burn in my legs and chest. I tried to encourage myself by declaring that no other kindergarten mother could have done the same.

Before us was the next leg of the journey - a large and empty parking lot.

With short but quick strides, I hurried across the asphalt until I reached what I figured was a front door. It was covered by a green awning - strands of accumulated water plummeting from the sides like miniature waterfalls - a shelter of sorts. Again, I wasn't picky and would take what I could get at this point, as it seemed an equal amount of water fell from me.

Large, dense shrubs lined the walkway lit by an old lantern affixed near the solid wooden door, shining the same yellowed color as the sign. It created a gloomy atmosphere, as if dark, rainy, and mysterious weren't enough. It seemed more like a door to a home than a church, but nothing concerned me more than the wet, biting cold, so I reached out and rang an archaic doorbell.

I could hear the faint sound from inside. What were the chances I would be lucky enough to get a response?

The adrenaline from the crash and the cold hadn't completely worn off, so I paced back and forth under the overhang awaiting an answer. Nothing. I rang it one more time without much hope.

I walked back into the rain to see if I could get a better look at the window on the side. Maybe if they could see who waited at the door they would be more likely to open it.

As I peered around the corner, the glow of the sign from the side of the building caught my eye. What I thought to be a cross were the deceptive designs of pine tree branches. I stepped in closer to read. Squinting through the rain, I mouthed the words out loud as I read the bold, black letters. *Golden Oaks Funeral Home.*

As the words sank in, a new feeling was causing the shivers. I gasped in and fought the growing scream, fearing what might follow if someone heard. I immediately turned to run and regretted having rung the bell twice.

Terrified at the thought of what lay behind that door, I started back out into the unrelenting showers. I covered the same amount of distance across the lot in less than half the time. Climbing down sideways to avoid the inevitable slip, I carefully but quickly made my way back to the planted car and fell inside. I closed the door and placed Maddy, who was now half awake, into the passenger seat.

"Where are we?" Her foggy eyes tried to make sense of what she saw. I must have looked alarming at best. I knew I was soaked. My skin must have been chalk white with fear and cold. I hoped I could lull her back to sleep without too many questions. She yawned. "Mommy? Why are you so wet?"

"It's okay, sweetie. Go back to sleep," I coaxed. I reached over and reclined her seat all the way. She pulled her knees up to her chest and shivered slightly. I tucked her jacket in tight all around her and started the car and the heater. Within moments she was asleep again.

Collecting my thoughts and my breath, I leaned my own seat back and closed my eyes, going over and over in my mind the events that led us to the top of that hill, hoping we were hidden from whatever lay behind that door.

Chapter Two

The Study

The memories of the events preceding our crash-landing came with a cutting pang of regret. Though I resisted, they replayed clearly on the back of my eyes.

We approached the familiar front steps, fifty paces beyond the white-gated entryway, along the rose-lined path that wound around and dropped off squarely in front of the oaken, arched door. I moved slowly, contemplating my choice to walk this path one more time. I couldn't shake the nagging feeling that I was making a big mistake. The feeling grew as I recounted my last visit six long years ago.

One wet brick at a time, I fit my feet into each rectangle perfectly, careful not to step outside of the lines. This was a habit learned early on.

With each step, I grew more densely saturated in the memories of this place and neglected to notice Maddy helping a snail along the recently rained upon walkway. Her little fingers delicately grasped its shell and walked it forward, speaking to it in a loving and motherly tone.

"Here we go little snail, doo, doo, doo, doo do." The nap on our drive over had given her a second wind of energy, and the sound of her voice was sure to sabotage my attempt to remain inconspicuous. I ditched my careful walk and quickly tip-toed to her.

"Maddy!" I hissed. "Put that down right now, and hold my hand."

My heart raced as I seriously contemplated my motives and the likely outcome of this visit. I was just steps away, and I still hadn't made up my mind. Maddy didn't know much about being secretive or indecisive, and she certainly did not know how to whisper. Everything out of her mouth had the same innocently shrill volume.

Why was I hiding? This was ridiculous.

In the midst of my turmoil, Maddy carefully explained to me the dire situation with the snail.

"He needed help mommy. He was never going to get to the door."

I sometimes wondered if she understood more than I gave her credit for. Would she pick me up with her little pincer grasp and carry me to the door if she could?

We eventually reached the front door where I stood still for a long thoughtful moment. Ringing the doorbell was such a simple yet nearly impossible feat.

"Oh, can I ring it, can I ring it? Please, can I ring it?" Maddy danced around in front of the doorbell, as if greeting it with a ritual before pushing.

"NO!" I growled. "Just wait a minute. Just wait."

Each ripple of flutters that came begged me to run. I turned to look out onto the landscape before me, hoping for a sign, or possibly a quick escape. But Maddy couldn't wait any more.

"Mr. Snail doesn't want to wait," she insisted. She reached for the doorbell, and before I even realized what was happening, she had rung it five times.

"Maddy, stop!" I gasped with horror, pulling her hand away.

Panic spread throughout me. My instinctive, gut reaction was to grab her, pull her down the stairs, and run. I looked around, choosing flight over fight, but saw no place to hide in the approaching storm. It was wet everywhere, rain coming down harder now, and I didn't think I could explain to Maddy why we were shamefully crouching behind a bush. I knew it was too late.

The door opened, and a friendly looking Hispanic woman stepped into the opening between past and present. I had never seen this woman before, but I knew exactly who she was. The "help" at the house had always changed every few years. My father never wanted *anyone* to feel too secure in their position. Sometimes he would merely fire them to get the others to work harder. Sometimes he would fire them because we liked them. He felt relationships undermined his authority and left too much room for an attitude of indifference.

She glanced to her right and to her left, trying to locate the ringer of the bell. She was pretty in a natural way, black hair pulled back into a sleek ponytail and dark features that made make-up unnecessary. I could tell that she was not going to give up the search anytime soon.

I was suddenly quite embarrassed by the fact that I was being so juvenile about the whole thing. I quickly tried to pretend that I was looking at some flowers on the side of the house. It didn't work for long.

"My mommy is hiding," Maddy announced. She pulled me forward and offered me to the woman who stood puzzled on the steps.

I tried to belittle Maddy's comment with a chuckle and a brush off with my hand, but the look on the woman's face told me she knew better. I forgot momentarily who she worked for. Who wouldn't hide?

"Hello! Please come inside. Mrs. Richards is waiting for you." The woman opened the large door into the entryway and stood at its side, waiting as I entered with trepidation. Her face was tolerant, warm, and welcoming - the required uniform of the estate. She must have sensed my unnerved hesitation, because she began to coax me in with smiles and an upside down wave - fingers pulling inward.

I used Maddy's shoulders as support as I walked into the room.

It felt cold and almost vacant with its vaulted ceilings and tiled floors. The smell was the same with a hint of Oleander, most likely cut fresh each day. White, or some shade thereof, was the color scheme. Every surface was uncomfortably clean and every piece of furniture and adornment perfectly placed. As always, it was beautiful in a disturbing and unwelcoming way. It was a place to exist, never to truly live.

I laughed, a laugh of bitter resentment, when I glanced at the antique sofa in the formal living room. It, like most of the house, wasn't meant to be enjoyed in the normal sense of the word. The punishments I'd endured learning that rule were many. Even *we* had been just carefully dressed ornaments for the perfect picture.

As Maddy skipped forward, past the woman, and did a small landing dance in the center of the travertine floor, I briefly recalled the carefree girl *I* once was. Determination rose in a wave of heat. Maddy would keep her innocence and individuality, and this façade wouldn't stop me from making it so.

I reminded myself of my one and only motive here. Ask for help for the sake of my daughter and be gone. I felt my insides harden as I tried to imagine myself impenetrable.

"Thank you." I nodded to the poor woman whose fate I knew better than she did. As resolved as I tried to be, I still felt ill at the sound of the door closing behind me, my fate sealing with it.

The woman smiled, bowed her head and left the room.

I felt trapped between the two sets of white-railed stairs that wound up each side of the room to the gallery directly overhead. Within just seconds, Maddy was swinging from one of the delicately hand-carved rails.

"Maddy, get down now!" I hissed. Not one minute had passed, and she had already broken at least three of the house rules. I could just imagine the lecture I'd get on raising a proper and respectful child.

I held Maddy's arms to her side and leaned over to explain the very basic rules, when I caught the familiar hint of brandy from behind.

"Hello, Casey. I'm so glad you came. I wasn't sure by your voice on the phone whether or not you would."

I stiffened and turned around, face to face with Evelyn, my mother. She was an attractive woman, always had been, and not just because of the expensive and well-applied make-up, or the perfectly draped, designer clothing, or even the classic, heirloom jewelry that decorated her skin. She was tall for a woman, about five feet nine inches. Her hair was a thick mahogany frame that lay perfectly at her collarbone, with a graceful curl at each end. Her eyes were blue and gentle, but meaningful. Her presence was always one of great poise. Of course that was merely her appearance, not my experience.

She approached me in a deliberate glide and with a look of bemused condescension, reached out to embrace me in the "appropriate" way.

"Hello, mother," I responded blankly.

I allowed the stiff-and-proper hug. Only pats on the back could have written it off more perfectly. The false intimacy brought on an instant wave of nausea. I never knew if it was the pretense of it or the complete emptiness I sensed from her, but it happened every time.

I instinctively stood back and held Maddy slightly behind me with a protective grip as Evelyn eyed her curiously. It seemed that she was holding back some emotion. Her eyes were red around the insides of her lids. I couldn't tell if it was the liquor or real tears.

She hadn't seen Maddy often in the last five years, only when she could sneak away without the chance of being discovered. She managed a visit to the hospital when Maddy was born and a few here and there when my father was on business, but it had become nearly impossible since he semi-retired. Aside from the pictures I sent to her "secret" post office box, she hadn't seen Maddy in almost two years.

I hated her for staying with him. And I hated that I had repeated that pattern. But my heart ached when I saw her taking Maddy in and realizing all she had missed.

"Well, hello, Maddy, aren't you all grown up?" she said admiringly. "I've seen so many pictures of you and have looked forward to this day."

She motioned toward Maddy, who was pulling away from me with great force. I held her tight, not sure that I wanted Maddy to experience the same cold and empty contact. Evelyn stopped and attempted to casually brush it off.

"Well, darling, it's quite alright. A hug isn't necessary. Why don't we move into the living room while we wait for your father?"

I had always been baffled by my mother's ability to maintain her stride after the three-shots of pre-dinner brandy, and wanted nothing less than to watch her controllably sip at her fourth. Her eyes were definitely glossed from intoxication and surrender, and her perspiration was beginning to carry the brandy with it.

Though I resented her checking out like this, I knew exactly why she did it and privately confessed that I would have too. Instead of drinking uncontrollably, I had run the first chance I got. Evelyn had nowhere to go - a sympathy I knew had led to the agreement to see me tonight.

I looked her over, my heart softening slightly. Whatever wishes or values she had once proclaimed had been belittled and chided into something only recognizable to her as childish notions. Though I had nothing more than the clothes on our backs and the very little that waited in our car, both of us knew that I had more hope, and it seemed that Evelyn was trying to protect that as well.

While I desperately wanted to give her a few moments of real human contact, I reminded myself of my mission and declined.

"We'll wait here." I tried not to say it in the permanently broken and judgmental adolescent tone that usually came with every conversation with Evelyn. Instead came the ever-terrified little girl speak that always manifested before a meeting with my father.

Before she could respond with her typical deep breath in and dismissive sigh out, the housekeeper appeared again.

"Mr. Richards would like you to wait in his study." Her English was slightly broken, but her voice was steady and soothing.

Again, the woman smiled and gestured toward the hallway off to the right. The way she looked at me made me think she felt sorrier for me than I did her. After all, it was *me* going into the study. This reminder brought on an episode of disorientation for a moment. Was I really subjecting myself to this again? Could it possibly have a happy ending? As I stood in my own little moment of doubt, Evelyn broke in.

"Dear, I'll take Maddy through the house and maybe show her where you grew up." She stepped in close to me, liquor mixing with expensive perfume. "Please listen to your father. He wants only the best for you."

Maddy ripped from my hold and flew into Evelyn's body, hugging tightly and beaming up with excitement. Evelyn stumbled slightly, not knowing how to respond to the rare expression of affection.

I went over her words in my head. He only wants the best for me? Well, we all knew that wasn't true. The doubt turned into certainty. Of course my simple request would be met with negotiation.

"Mother, I asked for a loan. I don't want *his* best for me. You said that wouldn't be a problem, and that's why I am here."

I reached for Maddy, but the housekeeper had gently taken ahold of my arm to lead me in the direction of the study.

"I'm not here to negotiate!" I insisted firmly. I was ready to violently shake the woman's hand from my arm when Evelyn pleaded.

"Just hear him out, Casey. Please!" she begged. The desperation in her usually controlled tone stalled me.

The housekeeper took this opportunity to put the nail in my coffin.

"Mr. Richards would like you to wait in his study." She began to suggestively pull me away from the nauseating scent emanating from Evelyn and from the only important thing left in my life - Maddy.

"She'll be fine. Please go and talk to him. It will be fine, dear. Go," Evelyn urged.

Evelyn turned Maddy around with a clown-like smile, followed by a pleading look back to me.

Watching them disappear around the corner seemed like an omen, like the next phase of his plan to physically separate me and Maddy from each other and, more importantly, from the judging eyes of his society.

With the woman close behind, I carefully stepped into the old interrogation room and again felt my fate seal with the lining of the door.

I shivered and held myself to keep warm. He liked to keep the temperature unbearably cold. It was one of his brilliant tactics meant to keep his target uneasy before attack.

I slowly walked the length of the oak cabinets that were built into the walls of the room, running my finger along the wooden divide. Memories rushed back of my innocent and unfulfilled longing to be loved and hugged by a man who expected everything I wasn't and couldn't be. Even though I knew that something in his make-up made it impossible for him to love, I hated him for withholding it from me. I hated him for setting me up for failure. I was doomed from the start to seek love in the arms of yet another man who didn't have it to give. But I refused to be Evelyn, the empty, drunk, and lonely woman in the other room. I left my husband that day to save myself, to save Maddy. Evelyn couldn't do that.

I made my way around the room to the chair on the opposite side of his desk. The chair's top reached my belly button rather than my forehead this time, but its cold repelling leather against my hand still personified him exactly. There was always a sense of loss in his presence - a useless and unsatisfied need to please him.

I fought back the welling lump in my throat, and the tears of anger toward him, and sadness for the little girl who stood here so many times.

I heard movement behind the door, and my knees became weak beneath me. I closed my eyes and prayed, desperately prayed, for the courage to stand my ground.

I turned to be sure to face him when he entered. I knew this would throw off the balance of power from the start. He would have expected to find me standing patiently with my head down, facing his empty chair.

I stood, as brave as I could be, awaiting his inquisition. He made no eye contact nor did he speak. His stride was slow and calculated. He stood momentarily, expecting me to sit. I didn't. With a dismissive breath, he took his seat.

He methodically lit his cigar, taking his time, and swiveled his chair to face a cabinet directly behind him. It was filled with hard-earned awards and plaques accumulated throughout his careers in the military and the law. Symbols of perfection - an unachievable perfection demanded of me from an age I could hardly remember.

This was how it always began - a silent comparison of the two unequal parties in the room. By now I would usually be hanging my head, but my perspective had changed a lot in the last few years, certainly the last few hours. I knew exactly what those accolades had brought him. They brought him nothing but the lifeless rooms outside that door, and the miserable woman who filled them. Though I had made plenty of mistakes, big mistakes, my experiences had bought me perspective. I had never felt more empowered.

A few endless minutes passed before he turned around and looked heavily upon me. The smoke lifted from the top of his head, seeming to carry his thoughts. The scent of judgment spread throughout the room, looming over me, not needing a single word.

I knew him well - the room, the scene, this same interaction on many occasions in my childhood. He was a commander, a tyrant who had been disobeyed and humiliated by an insubordinate inferior. He had sensed my desperation through the shaken phone call to my mother and confirmed it upon my first hesitant step into the entryway. He smelled my vulnerability and had laid out a clear plan of action long before I'd arrived.

His brows set low over his cutting, dark blue eyes, and were as perfectly framed as his entire dress. Everything pressed and everything shined - not a thing out of place. He was handsome, intimidating, and commanding. His presence was stunning. He had a way of drawing in my attention - his first move. He allowed the silence to set the battleground with each side preparing - him unmoving.

I planted my feet and prepared my argument. I looked down just briefly.

I don't know how I hadn't noticed it before. I was completely distracted by the cold and by my fear. But there it was. The folder sat purposefully in its place, lying in the center of the desk, facing my chair. It sat there deliberately, its contents carefully constructed to inform, persuade, and conquer. He knew that I saw it. He said nothing, but fixed his eyes on me, slowly inhaling the smoke, with his hands folded in front of his face.

I was enraged by his intimidating posture, by my weak submission into his control once again. I didn't need to look in the folder. I knew enough by its cover, *Brookford Academy for Girls*.

My whole life I had disappointed him, from my petty wants for play as a child, to my irrational and impractical decision to have Maddy and get married. The rage grew as I stood there, watching him sit with his game face on, waiting for me to break, while smoke passed over his fixed stare. I remembered his cold and matter-of-fact decision that I needed to have an abortion immediately. How he was infuriated by my sabotaging his plans for me to work at his firm, make him proud, impress his colleagues, be perfect.

My breath was growing shorter and this very big mistake becoming more lucid. I could still hear the echo of his harsh words as he presented me with calculated thoughts on the adoption process and annulment. And finally, I couldn't erase the cutting words of shame, of intolerance, of humiliation as he warned me not to come around with the child ever again.

I couldn't believe I was standing there again, to be insulted by another cruel proposition.

He sensed my unease and decided to strike.

"Casey, sit down!" he commanded. His words flew, but his body seemed plastered in the same position. I searched for the perfect words, the closing argument, the victory cry.

"Casey, *sit* down." His voice was growing hard and a bit concerned.

I closed my eyes and clenched my fists, thinking of the nothingness that lay beyond the front door. There was nowhere left to go from here, no one else to turn to. Maddy giggled from outside of the door. I could hear my mother scrambling, her voice faint.

"Maddy, honey, come sit down in here, please. Okay darling, Grandmom doesn't want to play hide and seek anymore."

Maddy giggled again.

I knew this wasn't the place. I had felt it all my life. It brought no comfort, no love, and no allowance for a life that could possibly bring the happiness I so desperately wanted to give to Maddy.

My concern for our future, even the next few hours, melted as unexpectedly as it had grown - turning into a determination unlike any I had ever known.

I nervously laughed, shocked by the peaceful and resolute feelings that overcame me so suddenly.

His face was molding into a glare of insult.

"What is it that you find so funny? Is it that you're alone with nowhere to go, with a child that brings nothing but shame to this family," he sneered, "or that you've come here once again to finally listen to something rational?"

He paused and waited. I was still in shock and absorbing the freeing feelings that had suddenly overcome me. He must have thought I was considering. He reached for the folder and started to explain.

"Now, in here you'll see that this academy offers more than…" I cut him off sharply and looked him in the eye with conviction and certainty.

"Father, I want nothing from you, nothing that you can give me. I made a mistake coming back here." With a mixed sense of strength and surprise, I turned and walked toward the door, knowing that I could never come back.

I felt dizzy, as though my feet weren't really touching the ground. Everything was moving in a fast forward pace. My face felt hot and my hands were trembling slightly. I turned to look at him one last time, to say goodbye.

He stood up from his chair, his hands pressed firmly against the desk, and his cigar burning between his fingers. "Casey! Get back here and sit down!" he growled.

I continued through the door, into the entryway where my mother was desperately searching for Maddy. My heart sank. Had she known about his proposal? It didn't matter. I had set us both up for disaster when I called. She couldn't help me from behind enemy lines.

I watched as she stood up and looked at me with great concern. I loved my mother, and my mother loved me, but she could never take the stand I just had, no matter her desire to help me.

"Maddy, let's go, honey," I ordered, using the *I'm serious* tone to make sure she'd come out quickly. I really didn't want Maddy present for the scene that would erupt soon.

"Casey, where will you go? Why don't you just hear your father out? Maybe there's a compromise," she pleaded, her voice shaky with the sound of heartache and fear. Her eyes were filling with tears, an uncommon sight to see.

"He has nothing for me…nothing. Maddy come out here now!" I looked around and found Maddy coming out from a closet beneath the stairs, grinning from ear to ear.

"Mommy, she couldn't find me, isn't it funny?" she giggled. Maddy ran to her grandma and wrapped her arms around her. "I love you, Grandma. When can we play hide and seek again?"

Tears streamed from my mother's face, which quivered as she fought to maintain composure. I was a little amazed, but felt an odd sense of release, a release that was a long time coming. My mother's tears were a needed sign that she knew everything *wasn't* quite right, something she could never admit out loud. My father charged out of the room and pointed his finger at Evelyn. I grabbed Maddy and pulled her behind me. Of course, she tried to peek around.

"I told you she was hopeless. She's an ignorant, hopeless fool, and *no one* can help her," he snarled.

He marched past us all and disappeared down the hallway.

"Who was that?" Maddy asked in childlike astonishment. "He was very, very mad!"

She moved behind me with a frightened look, arms wrapped around my leg. I picked her up gently and held her on my side as I turned to face my mother.

"Goodbye, mom," I said, sad to be leaving her in the situation.

Though it seemed too simple a statement to follow such a scene, it was all that I could gather. No words could begin to put together the puzzle of thoughts swarming my mind. I headed for the door.

"Casey, please call me. I'll help you in any way I can," she called after us. I could hear her walking toward us, but I was already out the door.

"I love you, and I *will*," I called back.

We walked out into the night sky. It was raining hard. I set Maddy down and pulled my jacket around to cover her.

"Where are we going? Can I go home now and play with my dolls?"

Maddy walked, holding my hand while trying to look at her grandma over her shoulder. She waved to her with an unknowing smile.

The horror of his proposition, sending Maddy to a boarding school as if she didn't exist, had sent me without regret, into the dark, drenched night, with nowhere left to turn.

Chapter Three

Hand-me-Downs

Maddy interrupted my dream-like memories and startled me awake.

"Mommy, where are we?" her voice asked drearily. She was still sleepy.

"We're just stopping for a minute, honey. Try to go back to sleep."

I set the heat as high as possible. It was getting later and much colder. I was completely soaked, and Maddy was beginning to shiver. She slowly sat up, peeked outside, and then nuzzled back into the seat.

"We're stopping on this hill?" she asked confusedly.

"Yes, honey, we're stopping on this hill," I said, as if it were perfectly normal.

I pulled her into my lap and wrapped her inside a hooded sweater from the back seat.

I couldn't form a logical thought beyond my frozen limbs. I waited for the heater to do its magic, and as our bodies slowly warmed, the rhythmic sounds outside tempted me to sleep.

My current dilemma began to play every which way through my mind, leaving me without a clue as to what to do next. I hoped that no one was around to hear the doorbell, and that the light inside was only a security measure. I was sure nobody lived in these places, but had seen who rested there - once when my grandma died and once for a friend of my father. The images of both made me shudder. I figured after I warmed up enough, I would do what I could to try and remove the rock again and replace the front tire.

I watched as raindrops gathered in agreement before making their voyage down the windshield. The shock from the day and warmth from the heater were slowly quieting my mind. Maddy was still, our calmed breaths were falling into unison, and I began to slip, without fight, into a serene sleep.

A loud knock on the window sent me into an immediate panic. My heart rate doubled and the adrenaline was back, pulsing through my veins. I could see a shadow outside of the door as it knocked again. I desperately reached for the lock button and hit it three times before hearing the click. I quickly set Maddy back into the passenger seat and scrambled through the glove compartment to find any sort of weapon to protect us.

A muffled voice interrupted my panic.

"Are you okay in there?" it asked.

I stopped and looked through the window, taking short, shallow breaths. A face was beginning to form through the fogged glass. A tall and slender man stood staring at me inquisitively. He looked sleek under his protective umbrella, wearing a black, stylish suit. He was quite pretty to look at with every piece of his hair fixed perfectly, and dark-rimmed glasses that gave his narrow eyes a sturdy frame. His complexion was pale with lips thin and red. His nose was pointed and accented his chiseled face.

We were locked in a contemplative stare for what seemed an eternity - me with a pen in hand, held to the right of my head as a threat, and the man, firm in his position under the umbrella.

"Do you need to come in and use the phone?" The accented voice struggled through the window and the rain.

I worked through my choices and settled on the fact that I really didn't have an alternative. I dropped the pen, suddenly feeling embarrassed by the thought of defending myself with a Bic. I scooped Maddy up and opened the door, starting in with rapid apology.

"I'll call a tow truck right away. I'm so sorry for this mess. I don't really know what happened," I explained breathlessly.

The man quickly placed the umbrella over the two of us, not saying another word, and began to help us up and out of the ivy.

The silence on our way back up the hill was painfully awkward. We were across the parking lot and back under the awning before he reached into his pocket, pulling out a set of keys. I struggled to find any words that might provide just a touch of relief. I could only come up with two.

"I'm sorry," I tried again.

He said nothing, but counted through his keys, quickly finding the right one.

"I'll get this taken care of and we'll be out of your hair before you know it."

The man simply glanced at me with an unsettling expression, and unlocked the door. I was longing for a large hole to climb into, and briefly considered abandoning all of my self-respect and calling my mother to beg, but the thought of another demeaning conversation with my father and the certain disaster to follow, sparked an anger inside that suddenly gave me the willingness to walk through the opening door.

"Come in," he offered with what sounded like attempted compassion to cover his aggravation. Without the window between us I could make out what sounded to me like a British accent.

He opened the door and walked us into an office directly off of a long, carpeted hallway. I was struggling to wrap my mind around the odd situation in which we now stood. I had no idea of what to do next. Each step forward brought me closer to that definitive reality.

Once inside the office, I gently placed Maddy into one of two armchairs next to the desk. They reminded me of furniture my grandmother used to have. They were upholstered with cherry red leather and lined with gold metal studs along the seams.

I was a little surprised but relieved that Maddy was still asleep. She was curled up peacefully, still clinging to her hippo.

The man interrupted my digression.

"The telephone is right over there." He stood in the doorway and watched me with curiosity.

I looked around and thought of whom I might call. I already knew the answer to that, but what would I tell *him*? I figured I could start with a tow truck.

"Um, do you have a phone book, or…" I nervously played with my fingers, wishing he would say something to make this humiliating experience a little less so.

He walked to the desk and began to finger through a rolodex. His long fingers flipped through each card gracefully. He looked up at me and noticing my absolute discomfort, gave me a somewhat soothing smile as he dialed a number and waited. He tried to hide the smirk forming on his face while he watched my every movement. I could only imagine what I looked like. He must have thought I was either totally pathetic or totally crazy. I felt like both. Someone picked up on the other end of the phone.

"Hello, Jim? It's Merman. I'm going to need your help. There's a car in the ivy…Yes, *in* the ivy…No, *ON* the hill." He paused and listened before continuing. "Can you do it tonight?" He paused again. "Jim, we need it out tonight, there's a service at 10 am…," his brows furrowed. "Okay then, first thing in the morning…if it's still here."

Merman hung up the phone and turned around in frustration, looking through the window at the anomaly on the hill. I began twiddling my fingers again.

"I'm so sorry. I'm sure there's someone else we can call," I suggested. I nervously fidgeted, waiting for a response. He was absolutely still as he stared out the window.

"You've managed to get yourself into a part of town where Jim is our *only* resource in these sorts of situations, especially at this hour." He seemed to have softened a bit and chuckled slightly when he looked back at the car.

I responded with a nervous laugh, not knowing what else to do. He looked at me, then at Maddy and then back at me. He laughed again, shaking his head.

"Can I get you a towel or a blanket, or perhaps some tea?" he offered, his voice now gentle.

His suddenly hospitable tone was comforting, but then frightening as I remembered where we were. A blanket? Tea?

"You have blankets and tea in these places?" I tried not to sound terrified or incredulous.

He gave another chuckle and approached me with an outstretched hand, "My name is Merman, Merman Patterson."

"Um, hello Merman, I'm Casey…Wheeler." I reached out hesitantly to shake and then immediately returned my arms to the tight fold I had them in around my chest.

"Well, listen, Casey - the two of you are clearly cold and wet, so why don't I grab some towels and tea while you make whatever calls you need to. Jim will have your car out first thing in the morning." He ducked out of the room, leaving me with some decisions to make.

"Yes, I'll call…whoever I need to," I called after him.

I thought about whom that might be, knowing very well there wasn't a soul.

I looked over at Maddy, who was still sound asleep, curled up in the chair. On the desk was a short clear glass with a bit of residue left over, and an ashtray that hadn't been cleaned in quite a while. There was an overwhelming dingy, cigarette smell that didn't quite fit Merman. He didn't seem the type to smoke, but then again I didn't feel the type who would be sitting in a mortuary drinking tea. I laughed at the absurdity of it, trying not to cry.

I looked around the room, hoping that a brilliant idea might hit me. Leaflets were stacked on the edge of the desk and had a picture of an old, smiling couple holding each other on the front. I picked one up and began skimming through it. *Pre-needs and plans for the future.* I wished that I had made some plans for the future. I had let Jerry take care of all the financial concerns and saved nothing for myself or for emergencies like this. My father had done the same my whole life, never allowing me financial freedom or understanding. Both men seemed determined to keep me as dependent as possible.

I walked to the windows, which were lined with mustard-yellow curtains at least thirty years old and housed dust the same age. I watched the rain and longed to go somewhere far away from my parents, from Jerry, and from my complete dependence. I wanted to start over and make a life for myself and Maddy, on my own, without the help of controlling, deluding men.

I took a deep breath to calm myself as the abnormal pounding of my heart started again.

"Get a hold of anyone?" Merman inquired. He had two towels, perfectly draped over his arms, carried a cup of tea, and had changed into a black smoking jacket, a matching pair of pants, and a cushy pair of slippers.

Despite the odd change, I found myself wanting to be in his warm and comfortable outfit. I squeezed my eyes closed to clear my mind of these thoughts that seemed so wrong to be having. I was quite confused by his new appearance and stared, uncontrollably. Where did he change? Why did he have clothes here? He paused and looked at the phone and then back at me.

"Casey?"

"Oh… well, no, not yet. Let me try someone else," I said, stalling. I walked to the desk and anxiously picked up the phone, placing a finger on the buttons, not pressing one.

"I'll just set this here and you help yourself."

Merman placed the tea on the desk next to me. He handed me a towel and watched me intently.

"Thank you so much, this is really kind of you. I'll be just another minute." I was completely hopeless at this point and struggled to keep my voice steady as it had a tendency to falter when my heart raced. I stared at the buttons as if they might give me the answer to all of my problems if I just waited long enough.

"Take your time. I'm here all night." At this he laughed to himself. I didn't get it. I didn't want to get it.

Noticing that I hadn't taken my eyes off the buttons, or pushed any of them, he interrupted.

"Maybe you should sit and collect your thoughts for a minute. I'm sure it'll come to you."

I looked up at him in a pause I couldn't shake. I wanted to say something, but I struggled to put the truth of the matter into words. As the reality of my situation became painfully sharp and clear, I dropped the receiver and fell into the chair next to me, sobbing. Crying never helped matters. I couldn't catch my breath.

"There's…no one…to call. I have no…one to call. We have…nowhere…left…to go." I fought to get the words out between sobs and gasps for breath.

I felt helpless and hopeless and utterly alone in the world. If not for Maddy, I'd wish for that rare, fraction of a percent likelihood of death that comes with my heart condition.

Merman, sounding shocked and concerned by my outburst of tears, and probably blue lips by this point, picked up the dangling receiver and placed it back on the phone.

"What do you mean? Surely you have a relative or a friend. Someone?"

His words burned through me and made the emptiness so much more sure and palpable.

I spoke the truth clearer this time.

"No one. There's…no one. No family…no friends…no place to go."

With this stated indisputably, the pangs moved through me without mercy. Though I tried to keep myself composed, for the sake of everyone in the room, my sobbing became louder and caused me to struggle for breath. He seemed startled and tried the next logical step.

"Well, we'll just get you a hotel room then. There's a decent place up the road," he said with a calming voice.

He put his hand on my shoulder and offered me the tea off of the desk. Mindlessly, I took the offered cup. I was going to have to walk him through the entire process that landed me here in the first place. I had already considered the hotel.

"I have no money. I left…with nothing…but some clothes, sixty dollars and Maddy."

I set the tea back down and reached for a box of tissue that rested on the desk. I was growing faint from the lack of oxygen. I put my head between my knees and tried to slow my breathing and crying. I was falling apart and felt horrible doing it in front of this poor stranger.

"Sixty dollars won't even…get my car out of that mess."

My eyes were beginning to swell from the tears, blurring the figures and the future before me. It felt like I had years of uncried tears waiting to come out. It was exhausting and yet a relief. In the middle of a sob, I yawned without control. I *was* exhausted. The day and the marathon my heart was running had worn me out.

Merman anxiously looked over at Maddy, who was beginning to shift around. I looked up to see him studying me, a hopeless mess in the antique chair of an old, haunted office. He nervously paced about, looking around the office and stopping now and then, shaking his head, having what seemed to be a silent argument with himself. He glanced back through the window, grunted a bit, and continued his pacing.

I felt horrible for dragging one more person into my mess. Having cried everything left to cry, I decided that Maddy and I would just sleep in the car until morning when Jim the tow truck driver could pull us out. I figured I had enough gas to be able to keep the heat going intermittently throughout the night.

I was about to tell him my final decision, when his eyes rested back on me with a look that told me he too had come to an arduous conclusion.

He hesitantly approached me and half mumbled, “I suppose if…if there’s absolutely nowhere…I suppose you two could stay here tonight.”

My residual sniffling and panting ceased immediately. I looked at him in disbelief…and horror.

“Here? What do you mean? Where? I can’t imagine…but this is a…?” I stuttered, trying to process what he possibly meant.

The smirk returned to his face as he watched me process. Did he mean here, in the office, in these chairs? I couldn’t imagine anything else. I didn’t want to imagine what else he could mean. The car suddenly seemed like a great idea.

“There’s actually an apartment here that I live in. I have a sofa bed that the two of you could sleep on,” he said coolly.

His voice had gained a conviction and even a hint of excitement that made me feel like he was really serious about his offer, and like he hadn’t had live guests in a long time.

He walked to the window and looked outside. I was frozen on the chair, completely speechless. My mouth stammered to find a response.

“Come on,” he argued “where else are you going to go? You can rest up tonight and plan your strategy tomorrow.” He folded his arms and waited for a response. I panicked.

“I’ll just change that flat and we’ll go,” I said resolutely.

I shot up and started to reach for my sweater that lay over Maddy, but he stopped me, gently taking my wrist.

"You might change that tire, but that boulder you've managed to plow over isn't going to move."

He let go of my wrist and leaned back onto the desk. His lip curved up into the smirk again as he seemed to wait for reality to hit me.

I walked to the window looking out at my fate. I looked back at Maddy and thought that it didn't seem like such an awful idea considering my only other option would be trying to sleep at a cold incline in the ivy.

He interrupted again with resolve and a bit of humor in his grinning voice.

"What kind of a boring life would this be if you didn't plow over boulders in the dark, pouring rain and land yourself in a funeral home once in a while?"

He seemed to find this very amusing. I'm sure the dead white look on my face told him exactly how comfortable I felt in a mortuary. How did anyone get used to this?

I looked at Maddy in the chair again and knew that I'd have to make the most of what we had in this very strange moment in time. I turned to assure him I had some kind of plan.

"We'll be out of here first thing in the..."

Before I could finish, he had taken my hand away from its reach toward Maddy.

"Come with me. We'll find you both something warm and dry to wear."

Something to wear? It seemed I had entered a parallel universe once I stepped over the threshold of this place. He let out a low chuckle in response to my gaping mouth.

"One more thing." He stopped and faced me directly. "You have to swear to me that you won't spread the word that we're offering hotel services or people are bound to come in flocks, and the local hotels will not be pleased with the competition."

I didn't know how to respond. He must have been kidding, but he continued to look me straight in the eye, as if waiting for me to draw blood and shake on it.

"Well, of course I wouldn't…" I began.

"Relax, Casey, I was kidding," he interrupted, regaining his more serious tone, "I think the rumor's already out, because people are dying to get in here." He was totally messing with me now.

I laughed nervously in response and decided that I'd need to loosen up a bit and try to see levity in the situation if I were going to sleep at all.

"We take what we can get around here as far a humor," he admitted apologetically.

At that I laughed out loud as he put his finger to his mouth, nodding toward Maddy.

We went down a long hallway with old, red carpeting. Along the wall was a small, antique table with more of the same pamphlets and a set of business cards resting nicely in its holder. A large, Victorian mirror faced us from the end of the hallway, through which I watched myself walk in my strange surroundings. I looked much worse than I had imagined. My normally wavy, brown hair was now much darker, soaked through with rain, and clung unattractively to my head. My usually clear, blue eyes were now red and puffy from crying, and the bleeding mascara reached down toward my red swollen cheek. Though I measured five feet, seven inches, the slight cower I stood in with my arms folded across my chest, made me look small and fragile, especially standing next to Merman, who stood well over six feet tall. I tried to stand up straight, to exude a little confidence. I managed to look a little taller, still fragile. I attempted to comb through my hair with my fingers and wipe the mascara from under my eyes. At second glance, it hadn't done any good, and it didn't much matter. I had more serious issues to worry about, such as my unfamiliar and eerie surroundings.

The lighting was dim, and there was an air of finality all about. There was absolute silence - even the rain had been muted. The smell was an odd combination of flowers and a chemical I couldn't place.

We stopped in front of a door just before the bathrooms. Merman pulled out the same set of keys from his pocket and unlocked it. Inside was a large armoire along with a vacuum, other cleaning accessories, stacks of stationary, and toilet paper. He opened the face of the cabinet, revealing drawers filled with neatly folded clothes of different styles and sizes.

"Now these are all clean. Just take your pick." He nudged me forward.

"What is this stuff?" I began holding things up one by one, not sure why they were there. They looked nice enough, but certainly not new.

"Well, let's just say nobody's coming back for them." He chuckled a bit under his breath and stared straight ahead at the collection.

I dropped the clothes and gasped, throwing my hand to my mouth to avoid screaming.

"You mean these are dead people clothes?" I choked out through my muffled mouth.

"They're clean, I assure you. I washed them myself. Just try to forget that they're *dead people clothes*," he said, rolling his eyes and making quotes with his fingers, "and pick something out. Think of them as hand-me-downs."

I could tell that he was enjoying my response to the whole idea. He tried to hold back a smile while I collected myself by closing my eyes and taking deep breaths in and out.

"You're soaking wet, Casey. Of course, it is your choice. But as for the little one…Maddy, is it? I'm sure you don't want her wet and cold all night." He was right. Her temperature was back down from the slight fever she had earlier that day, but wet, cold clothes would most certainly worsen her condition. That fact still didn't entirely ease my discomfort.

"Why do you keep these? I don't understand why you would want to keep these," I said in utter disgust and a bit of curiosity.

"Some people collect bugs, cards, magazines, soda can tops – I collect small pieces of people's lives left behind. It reminds me that they are people – that I'm doing something good in a place where it's easy to forget what's good," he explained. He seemed to know what I was thinking and shook his head, sad that he had to justify it.

"They are left behind, I don't steal them."

I cautiously fingered through the clothes, smelling a few of the items before choosing and closing the drawers. They did smell clean. Against my better judgment, I picked out a long, cream colored blouse, the color stained with age. It looked like it would serve fairly as a nightgown. There was also a medium sized long-sleeved shirt that I grabbed for Maddy. I was grateful that there weren't any her size.

There were boxes of jewelry, rows of shoes, and nicely hung suits and gowns. I struggled to separate the clothing from the dead bodies they once belonged to. After looking around and getting my fill of the macabre closet, he locked it up and we headed back.

With every other step back to the office, I cringed at the thought of wearing the clothes I held. The steps in between reminded me that my options were slim, and we would make it through the night with a story to tell at the end of it. I was sure that all of this violated some health code or another, but I was afraid to ask and wear out my welcome.

He smiled and guided me back through the hallway. I wasn't sure if I should be afraid for our lives or grateful. I wasn't sure if I should grab Maddy and run into the night or hug this strange man. I wondered momentarily if he was a serial killer, if he set up spikes in the road just for this purpose, or if he was just taking pity on a mess of a woman and her small child.

Despite my paranoid imagination, justified or not, I found myself walking very closely to him, which he seemed to find amusing.

We went back to the office where Maddy continued to sleep as I lifted her up into my arms. From there, we were back in the hallway and headed to what I imagined would be Merman's apartment. He found another key on his key ring, and before turning the knob he shot me a quick smile. His front door was off of the same red-carpeted hallway but opened into what looked like another world.

Candles burned from every corner, and the scent that filled the air was refreshing and soothing. The walls were decorated with posters from what looked like every Broadway play ever performed and many old black and white films. The floors were cherry hardwood and beautifully shined. A white leather couch stood apart from everything as if a centerpiece for the room. A coat rack held a red boa and an old Charlie Chaplin looking hat. The place was enchanting, and all of a sudden, his smoking jacket didn't seem strange anymore.

Chapter Four

The Great Escape

Merman made every effort to make us feel at home. While Maddy and I changed in his exquisite bathroom, he made up his sofa bed with sheets and all. I could hear them being shaken out through the door.

Maddy stood wobbly with her eyes closed and hands overhead as I changed her into her new pajamas. At least I wouldn't have too much explaining to do.

I could tell by the details he paid attention to in his decorating that Merman enjoyed his beautiful little home in this strange world. The paint in the bathroom looked like it had been done by hand with a sponge and a lot of care. The sink was an antique with an off-white porcelain bowl on a wooden, claw-footed frame. The floor mats matched the hand-towels, and the framed black and white picture of a romantic scene from an old movie was the perfect accent. I caught myself smiling in the mirror. The smile faded as I got a close-up version of what I had seen of myself in the hallway.

When I shuffled Maddy out of the bathroom, Merman was placing a fancy bottle of water on a side table next to the bed. I felt awkward, the two of us standing there in over-sized shirts, and hoped that we would get to the sleep part soon. I couldn't remember a time when I had looked forward to curling up in bed more than I did at that moment. My eyes had grown heavy, and my body was far beyond ready to quit on me.

"I hope that you find this comfortable for the night. I'll leave you two alone and let you know as soon as I hear from Jim." He kept his eyes down as he spoke to me, trying to avoid any embarrassment on my part, I assumed. He started to make his exit.

I felt like I had to make clear my gratitude to this warm, weird, and generous stranger.

"Merman?" I called after him. He paused and looked back, careful not to look directly at me in my archaic nightgown.

"Thank you, Merman. I can't thank you enough."

He smiled - eyes still away from me.

"Goodnight, Casey."

He was gone and in seconds I was soon in an unfamiliar bed, curled around Maddy's little body and drifting to sleep with the ever-haunting memories of our day.

The morning had been long, with an overcast gloom. My routine had been the same as any other Friday, but a sticky, restless, and inexplicable feeling sat in the most center part of my gut. My checklist was marked off almost completely, except for Jerry's dry cleaning and the grocery store. I had already posted up the art lesson flyers I'd made the night before, checked the post office box for responses from galleries and schools, taken an hour and a half to add a few paragraphs to the untitled play I had been writing for six months, and eat a sandwich from the deli.

I hated pickles, had specifically ordered *without* pickles, but was once again picking them out. I could still taste their trails in each bite.

I had long since grown tired of the weekly routine of busy work for Jerry, but complied to avoid the lectures. Rarely did his flyers receive a response, never did a school show interest, and the galleries would always respond in the same "not our style" rejection.

Friday was his "private tutor" day, and my stay-busy-with-an-endless-list day. He thoroughly explained many times over how it would be too distracting to have me or Maddy flittering about the house while he inspired young artists, usually from the junior college in the city.

Drizzle was forming a spotted sheet over the windshield as I sat in the deli parking lot. There was definitely a storm on the horizon. I smiled at the dark, looming clouds. There was something about the rain that brought me to a hushed calm. I enjoyed the quiet gray of the sky, the smell of wet asphalt, and the momentary pause of the unsettled feeling that came every time Jerry tutored privately.

I put the leftover pickle-tainted lunchmeat back into the plastic bag along with the crumpled napkin filled with limp pickle slices, and removed the crumbs one by one off of my shirt. I sometimes felt pathetic eating my lunch in my car like a homeless person, but I truly did enjoy the peaceful solitude.

I leaned back in my seat and closed my eyes for just a moment before continuing with the monotony of my day.

It was off to the dry-cleaners and then the aisle by aisle search for every single craving he had written down. On Fridays he was always very particular about ounces and brands, surely a distraction to keep me busy.

I started the car and began to pull out when a buzz from my purse broke my concentration. I rarely ever got calls. It made me nervous every time it rang. I opened it, seeing an unlisted number, and waited curiously to see who it would be.

"Hello?"

It was Maddy's school. She was sick, a fever around one hundred and she needed to come home. She had been curled up on a mat in the office for thirty minutes.

"Thank you. I'll be right there."

I hung up the phone and felt shamefully relieved, though slightly concerned. I looked forward to the end of each day when I could pick her up and be in sweet smiling, unconditionally loving company. It was the happy moment at the end of a day when Maddy would race from the rock under the tree with her friends and slam into my body with all of her force, squeezing tightly and giggling. Even though today wouldn't come with that same greeting, I looked forward to rainy days when I could pull her up on my lap and drift to sleep watching some old black and white TV. There was nothing quite like being bundled up in that soft, blue blanket listening to the rain outside.

Jerry's cravings would have to wait until tomorrow.

When I got to the office, Linda, the secretary, jumped up and waved through the window. I walked inside, greeted by the smell of freshly copied papers, and signed Maddy out on the designated school form. From a room in the back of the office came Linda, gently guiding a pale-faced and weary Maddy.

"Oh, sweetie, come here. I'm sorry you're not feeling well. Do you want to go home and watch movies with me?" I pulled her in closely and placed my hand on her forehead. Maddy nodded under the pressure of my hand.

"I checked it again before you got here and it's down around ninety-nine now. Tylenol works wonders," Linda stated proudly, standing with her hands folded on the counter.

Linda was very friendly and always paid extra special attention to Maddy. A few appearances by Jerry had given everyone reason to pity us.

"Thank you, Linda. I'm sure she'll be better by next week." I picked Maddy up, an increasingly difficult task at her growing weight, and covered her with my sweater.

"Bye, bye, Maddy. Feel better." Linda made a small, child sized wave at Maddy who was looking over my shoulder and trying to hide a smile.

We made it to the car with only a thin layer of drizzle covering us. I buckled Maddy in and shut the door behind me. The quiet was soothing, only the sound of little rain all around. As I sat in the car, preparing to start the ignition, a gnawing turning in my stomach disrupted my serene moment. I figured it was the pickle trails and started the car.

I knew that once we got home I'd have to quietly make my way up the stairs, hoping that Maddy didn't have to pee, and keep the television on low. I was home two-and-a-half hours too soon, and Jerry was serious about the quiet time during his private lessons. Sometimes I desperately wanted to collect all of our pots and pans and drop them right outside of the studio door, just to see what kind of art would come out of it. Sometimes I thought of throwing the pans into the studio, at his head. I never gathered the courage to do either.

As I approached the driveway, the turning in my stomach worsened, and my heart began pounding like mad. Despite the cold air outside, I was beginning to break into a sweat.

I paused before pulling in. The sudden and growing anxiety made my heart pound faster, and another flash of heat came over me. This felt like more than just bad lunch meat. I was anxious about something I couldn't put my finger on. I parked and looked back to find Maddy half asleep.

"Honey, we're here," I whispered while gently touching her arm. "Let's go sweetie, we'll be lying down before you know it."

Through the nauseating butterflies, I struggled to reach back and unbuckle Maddy's belt when I realized that I should probably make sure the coast was clear before bringing her in.

"Actually, honey, wait here for just a minute, I'm going to go inside and see where daddy is, okay?"

She nodded, though she was still only half awake.

I wanted to make sure he was still busy enough to sneak past so I didn't have to hear about my incomplete list just yet, or worse, hear about it in front of his student and Maddy.

"Okay, mommy," she said sleepily. She seemed fine with the idea and cuddled up with her hippo.

I managed to make it to the front door before I was stopped by another round of twists in my gut. I doubled over, trying to calm myself and catch my breath. I unlocked the door and walked inside.

There was music coming from inside the studio. He sometimes used music to inspire. A load of crap, *I* thought. I crept toward the studio door to make sure there was still inspiration going on, when I heard a noise, grossly familiar. It was a sort of moan, Jerry's moan, and then another, and a giggle, a girly giggle. The knot in my stomach was unbearable. My heart was racing as the reality hit me over and over with each disgusting sound.

I locked my hand around the knob, unsure of whether or not I wanted to see and know for sure, uncertain of what that would mean, or what I would do. Without my agreement, my hand turned the knob and threw the door wide open. I felt removed from my body, like my hand had a mind of its own. I tried to think of an explanation for such unexpected behavior when my reasoning came to an abrupt halt at the sight before me.

The young girl in the room shrieked, and Jerry turned in utter surprise, covered in paint. They were *both* covered in paint, naked on the floor. I was stunned and didn't know what to do next.

"Casey? Casey, wait. I know how this must look, but," he struggled to get up from the floor but was slipping in the paint as he tried to make his way. Green and yellow covered his feet, thighs, and butt. "Let me explain!" he pleaded.

I stopped looking at that point and turned to run, hoping that Maddy hadn't come in yet. I ran to the front door and saw Maddy in the back seat holding up her hippo, holding it in the same way I had held her at school. My heart ached, but not for Jerry, or even me. It ached for

Maddy and all of the questions she would have. I turned and ran to our bedroom, trying to find a bag in the closet. I was going to leave him.

"Casey! Casey, come here!" he commanded. I could hear his irritated voice, but it was at a safe distance. He was preoccupied with trying to console the naked and likely confused girl.

I grabbed at random clothes on hangers and reached in the drawers for anything that would fit in the duffle bag. I looked around in a panic, not able to form a logical thought. I was scrambling to think of what I would need to bring when I could hear his voice coming closer. I couldn't let Maddy see this. I threw the bag down and ran out of the room. I'd have to come back later.

When I entered the hallway, I was stopped short. Jerry was standing there with a false look of innocence on his face, naked and covered in paint. I started down the hallway.

"Casey, you don't understand. Casey! Stop and listen to me!" His voice turned from pleading to authoritative again.

I walked right past him and toward the door. He pursued me, trying to catch up, but slipped and fell on the hardwood floor behind me. I turned to see him lying there, so absurd. The girl's face peeked out from the studio. She looked no older than twenty and terrified. I felt sorry for her.

I walked out the front door and hurried into the car when I heard him growl, "Casey!" one last time from behind me.

I could think of only one place to turn as the rain began to build intensity. The thought of calling them to ask for help was almost too much to bear, but they were my last and only hope.

I awakened to the sound of an organ playing and a cloudy, gray sky peeking through the curtains of an unfamiliar window. It took a few moments for me to pull together enough information to figure out where I was exactly. My heart rate accelerated as I put the pieces and nightmarish memories together one by one.

The sickness in my stomach returned as I tried to shake them free from my mind. I couldn't decide which was worse – having spent the night in a stranger's apartment off of a mortuary or having nowhere to go after leaving my cheating pig of a husband and turning down an offer to rid of my daughter as if she didn't exist. As for the former, I tried to string together a perspective of gratitude. Though the events of the day had taken a morbid twist, fate had placed me in the hands of a generous, albeit odd, Merman. He had set us up nicely on what had turned out to be a very cozy sofa bed where, aside from the painful reminders in my dreams, I hadn't slept better in years.

I felt a shift next to me. Maddy opened her eyes and looked around in confusion. The very moment I had been dreading was finally here.

"Where are we, mommy?"

I hadn't had a chance to think of how I would explain this to her, but she was five and though she was growing sharper by the day, I could still get away with fudging the truth a little.

"We uh, rented a hotel room, honey," I said assuredly, and got out of bed quickly, trying to avoid any further conversation on the topic. She wasn't going to let it go that easily.

"But there's a kitchen…and someone left a bunch of their stuff in here."

"It's a different kind of hotel, but we're leaving soon so get dressed okay?"

She seemed satisfied enough with that explanation.

"Can I wear this shirt? It's pretty. Did you get it for me?" Maddy stood up on the bed and posed for me.

"No, no. That stays here. We borrowed that, too," I said, now frantically gathering our stuff. I wanted to make a quick and painless exit.

The organ was playing dreadfully depressing music, and Merman was nowhere to be seen. I hoped to quietly sneak out and maybe drop a thank you note later.

I got Maddy dressed and made up the couch. I looked around to make sure I wasn't leaving anything behind, grabbed Maddy's hand, and headed for the door. I reached for the knob and closed my eyes, dreading what might meet me on the other side. Slowly opening the door, I peeked out.

Nobody was in the hallway. There were voices far off, but quickly drawing near. I made a break for it. Holding Maddy tightly by the hand, I shuffled down the hallway toward the door, through which I had entered with such hesitation the night before.

The voices were getting louder the closer I drew to our escape. I could make out a conversation that was beginning to sound more like an argument. I couldn't help but stop and listen. I had an awful feeling that it was likely about us.

"What were you thinking, Merman? There's a goddamned car in the ivy, and that tow truck is blocking traffic. This service starts in thirty minutes. What are you going to do?" The man's voice was deep and extremely angry.

Thirty minutes? How long had we slept? Why didn't he wake us? Of all the terrible possibilities the morning could bring, this felt like the worst. I couldn't remember the last time I had slept until nine-thirty, and of course, the first time I did was the worst time I could have.

Merman sounded appeasing and calm, as if he knew how to diffuse this angry man.

"The car will be taken care of before the service begins, I assure you."

I could hear feet pacing back and forth on a harder surface behind a sliding door. Part of me wanted to run, quickly give the tow truck man all the money I had, and escape without having to face Merman and whoever that booming voice behind the door was. The other part of me wanted to stay and listen to Merman's confident voice. In the middle of my deliberation, he spoke again.

"They had nowhere to go. I couldn't just leave them out in the rain!" The pacing came to an abrupt halt.

"We are not a shelter, Merman. We're barely a business! Where are they? Get them out of here before I'm collecting complaints instead of payment!" he snapped.

Without warning, the large, middle-aged man opened the sliding door and walked right into me. I stumbled back and clutched Maddy close to me. He glared at me and snorted before storming off toward the office. He left a strong wake of stale smoke behind him.

I looked up at Merman. He stood on the other side of the sliding door in another hallway, this one more clinical with a heavy chemical odor and beige linoleum flooring. He quickly closed the sliding door, as if it hid something unspeakable.

He was so becoming in his black suit, and I felt a slight and unfamiliar kind of attraction to him. He had a warm smile spread across his face that made me feel at home. What an odd feeling. Nobody had taken me in like he had, not without an expectation of something in return. Would there be an expectation? Stopping my selfish ruminations, I started in with apologies again.

"I'm so sorry, Merman. We're leaving right now. Thank you so much for…" Merman interrupted me, pulling me closer to the doorway he stood in.

"Don't worry, that's just my Uncle Stanley," he whispered cautiously. "He's a grouch until about five o'clock when he's had enough whiskey to color the whole world happy."

He pointed out the front door, leading us in the right direction.

"Jim is here, and it sounds like he's almost got things under control."

A loud and persistent beeping sound was out of sync with the organ.

"So, where do you plan on going from here? Do you have a plan?" he asked with sincerity.

Merman looked down at Maddy, who was staring intently at him. He gave her a quick wink and looked back at me.

I hadn't really thought about what to do next. I'd have to go back home to get our things and demand money from Jerry. That was a start.

"I don't know what you're situation is, but here's my card. You can call me at this number at any time." He handed me a business card and looked again at Maddy who was still staring at him.

"Mommy, what kind of hotel is this?" A smirk appeared on Merman's face as he looked back at me, tilting his head to the side, curious to hear my answer. I laughed nervously and avoided the question with a goodbye.

"Thank you for everything, Merman. We'll be fine. Take care. Come on, Maddy."

I turned toward the door, but before I made it outside, Merman had stuck his hand out to Maddy.

"It's a pleasure meeting you, Madame."

He took her hand and bowed. Maddy giggled and curtsied, waving goodbye as I led her outside toward the hill of ivy. There was something very comfortable and natural about the interaction. Maybe I was in shock. Maybe I was delirious with hunger. Maybe it was the sweetest and most normal thing I had ever seen.

When we reached the bottom of the hill, our car was out of the ivy and on the street with what looked like two new tires intact. My heart sank when I realized that now I would have to come up with money for the tires. We would never get out of here. I tried to imagine the cost as I hesitantly approached Jim.

"You must be Casey." Jim reached out his grease stained hand to shake mine and then laughed, pulling it back. "I'm sorry. Sometimes I forget how filthy I am. Well, your car is ready to go." He handed me the keys and turned to walk toward his truck.

"If you could just give me the bill, I'll pay you what I can now and come by with the rest later. I…" I felt horribly uncomfortable with the situation "I only have sixty dollars with me right now."

He stopped and turned around, waving me off dismissively.

"It's no problem. Merman insisted on using their auto club card for the tow, and I happened to have a couple of extra tires just lying around. Besides, the chapel here brings me a lot of business, what with their vans and hearses and such. It was no trouble at all, miss. You take care now and be careful out there." He grinned and shook his head. "I haven't seen something like this in quite a while." He nodded toward the scar I'd left in the ivy.

I didn't know what to say or do. I wasn't used to unconditional help like that. I was instantly skeptical, but thoroughly relieved. I looked back up at the mortuary just as confused as ever. How could I repay this?

It looked like a crowd was beginning to gather in the parking lot. Mourners. I shook off the eerie feeling that traveled down my back.

"Thank you," I called after Jim as he got into his truck. He waved back at me and pulled away.

I put Maddy into the car, knowing that I had bigger problems to face without the hope of much of anything unconditional from Jerry.

Chapter Five

Final Straw

I pulled up to the house and suddenly felt like I was on enemy territory. I took a deep breath and closed my eyes, trying to come up with strong words and cold, careless comebacks. Images from the past overwhelmed me. I indulged them, hoping they would give me the courage I needed to see this through.

I remembered when we first met, and how he had dazzled me with his predatory charm. I was nineteen years old and desperate to leave my sheltered and oppressive home life. I did find him attractive once, though the thought of him now made me physically ill. He had the rugged surfer look – shoulder-length, sandy blond hair, sparkling blue eyes, strong hands, a deep and enchanting voice, and always the right words to say. I had been charmed, and it was all downhill from there.

I scrolled through my memories and landed on a short period later - about a couple of months from when we started dating. I was unexpectedly pregnant, and when Jerry got a look at my parents' home and inferred wealth, he thought marrying me would guarantee him something. I was too terrified *not* to marry him. Little did he know that my father wanted nothing more to do with me.

My mother did help us get a house, unbeknownst to my father, but soon after, Jerry would be duped, as he had called it, when he found out my father had all but disowned me. Had he ever found out about the abortion or adoption that my father had planned, he would have been on board without question. He would have even found a way to swindle some money out of it too. Thank god I managed to keep him in the dark.

I thought that I was somehow protecting Maddy by staying. It seemed that Jerry and I both settled. He took advantage of a live-in servant and philandered about arrogantly, while I lived in my own little world with Maddy. For the most part, I stayed out of his business and he stayed out of mine.

Maddy interrupted my survey of the past.

"Mommy, I'm hungry," she said, cocking her head to the side and sticking out her bottom lip. It was past ten, and we hadn't eaten a thing since the fast food in between stops the night before.

"Okay, honey, one sec." I rifled through her lunch bag and found a fruit roll that she had left over from school. "Here you go. Just stay in here and eat that, and we'll get some breakfast as soon as I come back."

Her eyes lit up at the sight of it. I never let her have candy for breakfast, and she knew this was a rare exception. She grabbed it quickly before I could change my mind.

"I want to come inside and play," she announced, taking off her seatbelt.

"No, Maddy! You stay in here this time, and I'll be right out."

I took the fruit roll back and opened the wrapper. Her eyes smiled again in anticipation. I gave it to her along with a kiss on the forehead.

"Well, can I play in my room later?" she asked.

"Yes, you can play later, honey," I promised, with an amendment. Luckily, she missed the omission of her room in my response.

I got out of the car and slowly walked up to the door. I felt sick thinking about the paint everywhere, and that girl. Every step closer made me want to run away that much faster, but this had to be confronted sooner or later. I preferred sooner since I was still on a little bit of a high from all of the boldness I had conjured up in the last twenty-four hours, and I would need it as Jerry was a master manipulator, much like my father.

I closed my eyes and took another deep breath. I pictured his cold and uncaring eyes and the smug smile he'd display when he knew he had me where he wanted me. I shuddered at the thought. I wouldn't let him get that far this time. I stood, squarely facing the beginning of an end.

I didn't know if I should knock or just open the door. This was my house after all. But the last thing I wanted was to walk straight into a reenactment of the day before. I realized then that I felt no sense of jealousy whatsoever. I didn't care who he had in there with him. I didn't care that he found physical fulfillment in the arms of another woman. I was glad though that the arms were no longer mine. I laughed at this revelation and wondered how long I'd felt that way. I could hardly remember *not* feeling that way.

Disgusted and emboldened by the memories, I knocked three solid times to give whoever was inside fair warning. I paced back and forth on the patio, mulling over the reality of the last six years and trying to muster up some courage out of the rage that was flooding me.

Jerry opened the door and quickly put a phony, regretful look on his face. He was only half-naked this time, wearing only long, board shorts. He enjoyed himself far too much. I stopped and braced myself.

"Jerry, we need to talk," I began.

"Come inside, baby," he coaxed, taking a step toward me.

"No, we'll talk right here." I stepped back a bit and folded my arms, hoping to appear strong.

Jerry stepped further out onto the patio and waved to Maddy in the car. She perked up and waved back, chewing on her snack. This had been the extent of his interaction with Maddy for the last five years, though she adored him with that familiar and unfulfilled need to please. I was grinding my teeth at the thought of the cruel, inherent pattern.

"I'm so sorry, Casey. I know I blew it. We were just doing some experimental art and one thing led to another. I love you," he said, as though he were reading from a script.

He reached out to hug me, and I pushed him off. I couldn't remember the last time he used those words to get something. The insincerity of it caused an involuntary gagging sound to spill from my mouth.

"Ugh! I don't care about what happened…yesterday, or the time before that, or the times before that - I'm done. I think we've both been done for a while now." I looked him dead in the eyes to make sure he knew I was serious.

He chuckled antagonistically.

"Don't say that. Just come inside and we'll talk it over," he said with his smooth and charming tone.

He stepped toward me again, and I defensively stepped back. I actually felt that his touching me might provoke something wild, something I hadn't felt before. I spoke quickly, not sure what to make of what I was feeling at the moment.

"There's nothing to talk about, Jerry. I'm leaving you. Maddy and I are leaving."

He laughed dismissively again.

"Where are you going to go, Casey, to your parents?" His tone had changed from pleading to mocking. "Your mother called last night to see if you had come home. I guess that didn't work out."

For a second I saw a flash of red. My vision actually blurred, and a rush of adrenaline coursed through me. What was this?

He must have thought I was wavering because he kept on.

"Where are you going to go? How are you going to support yourself? You don't work," he pointed out mockingly, not really caring for an answer.

"I can do it," I growled. "I've just never had the chance. I gave up everything for your pathetic career."

His eyes hardened for just a flash and then softened again quickly.

"You gave up everything because you got knocked up, doll. My pathetic career is what saved your ass. You can't do it on your own, baby. You don't know how. You've had someone spoon-feeding you your whole life." He laughed and leaned against the door. "There's a big bad world out there, that'll eat you right up."

My vision wavered again, and my heart rate picked up. It seemed that every sound and every sight, even in my periphery, were very clear. I felt like I was on the verge of attacking, of fighting for my life. I tried to pull myself together, to say something sensible.

"Give me what's left in our savings and I'll leave you alone for good. Remember, Jerry, the money my mom gave me? I won't even come after you for the house. You can have it." I hoped that giving him the bigger prize would be a sure victory, a sure escape.

I was wrong.

"You think I'm going to make it that easy for you? I'm sure the courts will see it a little differently, babe. Who's been paying for this house? Who's the one with a job?" he asked laughing. "You think I'm going to pay you to leave me? Listen to you. I think it would be in your best interest to stay and try to work things out. Look at her out there, Casey. She's eating candy. Is that her breakfast? Is that how you plan on supporting our child? You're nearly unemployable, you're putting our daughter's health and safety at risk, you have nowhere to go and…who knows, you may start up drinking again. Like I said, babe, the courts might see things differently."

I was enraged. That euphoric, strange feeling returned, and I had trouble not going for his throat. He couldn't be right. I had some rights.

Didn't I? I hadn't even had a sip of alcohol in over six years. I was scrambling for an argument now.

"You leave then. Go live with your teenage bimbo. Go launch your illustrious career. Just leave us alone."

Jerry laughed uncontrollably, holding onto the door frame for support. In between gasps for air, he would look at me and start again.

"I'm not going anywhere, but you're welcome to stay. I hope you don't mind my little flings here and there. It's art, baby, and it's in your best interest to stick around."

It was the final straw. I snapped and pushed past him, both hands directly in the center of his chest. He stumbled back and hit his head on the door. I growled as I stormed past him through the entryway.

"You have no idea what's in my best interest, and as for raising "our" child, I've done a pretty good job on my own for five years." I glared back at him with hatred. "I wonder what the courts would think about a deadbeat dad who doesn't know one detail about his child's life, let alone the dirty, cheating, drunk husband part."

I heard a slight gasp from behind me, but I couldn't tell if it was the shock from my threat, my sudden empowerment, or him finally getting his wind back from my surprisingly hard blow. I headed into different rooms, gathering as much as I could fit into the two bags I could find. I put them by the front door and went in search of another bag. He was following behind, but keeping a safe distance. It made me laugh that he seemed…scared.

"Let's not fight, Casey. Here's a little money." He reached into his wallet, pulled out twenty dollars, and held it out to me as I stormed past him into the kitchen and rummaged through the cupboards. "Go get yourself a nice breakfast and think it over, okay?"

There was no food. I hadn't finished my errands the day before. I stopped to pull myself together and plan something. I grabbed the money from his hand.

"I want the money in the savings account, Jerry." I stood firm and stared him down.

"Don't be stupid. You belong here. We have a family." I ignored him and continued my search for snacks.

"You're not leaving me, do you understand?" His innocent and pleading tone turned once again into a threat as he grabbed my arm a little too tight and pulled me to face him. His eyebrows furrowed and a frightening darkness came over his face. I wavered momentarily and then regained my conviction, pulling my arm out of his grip and stepping back a few feet for safety.

"I'm taking the money out today. There's plenty in the checking account to get you by for a while."

I turned, and he followed me through the house as I collected anything else I could think of and placed it all into a suitcase that I found on a shelf in the closet. I headed for the door at a determined pace. His sudden aggression in the kitchen had me a little worried.

"You're not getting that money, babe." He walked after me, but I got into the car and backed out before he could say another word.

"Are we going to get breakfast now, mommy?" I hadn't realized that she was still out of her seat when I'd pulled out in a blind fury.

"Get your seatbelt on, honey. We'll get breakfast, but I have to stop by the bank first." I didn't know how he would stop me from taking that money out, but I didn't put it past him to try.

The drive to the bank seemed to drag on at a torturous pace. I was in a race against time…and Jerry. I was trying to go over in my head all the ways he could keep me from getting that money out when a memory as sharp as a sword pierced through my center.

I recalled the day we set up the account, how his name was listed as the primary account holder for credit purposes. I felt ill and hoped against hope that this small detail would either be overlooked by some young and mindless bank teller, or irrelevant.

I pulled up in front of the bank that I regularly deposited checks into. I realized that I had never *withdrawn* money, one of many stipulations enforced by Jerry where money was concerned.

I sat for a minute, feeling almost like a criminal as I prepared to go in and ask for what I almost already knew the answer to. I wasn't sure how helpful the mom with little girl act would work when the little girl was tired, hungry, and reminding me of it every other minute. I felt a gnawing sense of doom, the same sense of doom that I had approaching both my father and Jerry the day before.

I unbuckled Maddy and started into the bank. I was simply going to fill out a withdrawal slip with Jerry's name, as I did with the deposits, and hope that the response would be with the same indifference as every other time I had come. *I* completely understood the difference in the transaction, but I was hoping *they* would miss it.

There were three people in front of me in the line and four busy tellers. Two looked like they hadn't graduated from high school long before they applied, but the other two seemed a little more practiced. There were also two managers who looked over the shoulders of the tellers when necessary. I prayed I would get one of the kids who didn't need help counting out money.

I watched with immense anxiety as each customer before me was placed at a window. My eyes shot back and forth trying to determine which transaction would finish first. The young teller that I was hoping for was helping a little old woman who needed him to repeat every question more than once. The older, experienced teller had already helped two customers in the same amount of time.

The person in front of me stepped up to her window with what looked like a simple deposit.

"Mommy, I'm hungry," Maddy whined, and then decided to hang very heavily on my leg.

"Maddy, sit still!" I hissed. "We'll be out of here in a minute."

I grabbed an extra deposit slip and a pen from my purse desperately trying to distract her so that I could pay attention to the ensuing race ahead of me. She sat on the floor and then readjusted, laying belly down.

My heart was pounding again. More than anything, this arrhythmia was inconvenient. It had never been this bad before, but I had been in a haze of denial for a long time. Maybe this is what reality felt like.

I was silently screaming at the old woman to shut up and take her receipt. The teller was trying to repeat, one more time, that he was thankful for her business and wondered if she needed anything else. As she paused to listen and consider his proposition, the other teller had finished up her transaction and glanced up to count the number of customers in line.

She glanced up and down the line once and then slid a thin "closed" sign in front of her window. My heart rejoiced, and I nearly laughed out loud in relief with hands raised in the air, until I heard the old woman say,

"Dear, I can't read this here, would you mind telling me what it says?"

I could have strangled her right there, but I focused on the objective at hand. I heard a loud beeping noise directing me to a window. I looked up, and my heart sank when I saw that a manager had taken over the available window. I thought for a moment about letting the man behind me pass me by, but I figured it would be better to get it over with. The woman smiled and gestured for me to step forward.

Maddy didn't forget to remind me that she was hungry twice on the way to the window. I squeezed her hand on the way, more for my own personal comfort than to quiet her. I handed the woman the slip as discreetly as possible and awaited my fate.

She casually, but with lightning speed, typed in more numbers than I could have possibly written on the slip. After a minute and endless key strokes, she broke the news.

"Honey, the amount you put on this withdrawal slip is not in this account. It looks like a transfer was made from the savings account back into checking." She waited for my response, prepared with an answer before I asked.

"Well, can I just take it out of the checking account?" It seemed reasonable, though I knew the likely outcome.

"It looks like the primary account holder has to sign for any withdrawals from the checking account."

She began to look at me speculatively and could tell that my circumstances were not the norm. My heart sank, and I didn't know what to do next. It felt like everyone in the bank was waiting for me to decide. I could hear a foot tapping from behind us. I wanted nothing more than to break that foot off and beat Jerry to death with it. She interrupted my bloody fantasy.

"Honey, you can take what's left in the savings account." I looked up in shock, wondering what he would have left in the account for me and why. Did he have a change of heart? Was he trying to make it right? Before I could give him any more credit she asked,

"Would you like the forty dollars that is in the account?"

Forty dollars! He left me forty dollars? Now this was more like the Jerry I knew. Even more insulting than the twenty he handed me at the house. I was on the brink of total madness. My face was surely flushed because it felt like I had suddenly developed a high fever. I was sweating and almost panting. The woman looked a little concerned, so I tried to respond as normally as if forty dollars was what I expected to find in the account.

"That would be fine, thank you." She had me out of there with my forty dollars in less than twenty seconds and a line full of nosy and impatient customers behind me.

We sat in the car eating our fast food while Maddy watched a movie on the portable DVD player I took from the house. It was a welcomed distraction, giving me time to figure out my next move. I was a few dollars over one hundred thanks to our fast and cheap breakfast. We had technically missed the breakfast menu by five minutes, but the woman working the window took pity on us when she saw me nearly well up with tears upon hearing the news.

I was usually able to think more clearly with food in me, and had already called five hotels in our area. Even the budget priced hotels would cost me more than sixty dollars, leaving us with a little bit for food and still nowhere to go the next day. I decided to buy a newspaper in hopes of finding a miracle and was suddenly hopeful that we would be taken care of somehow.

I flipped through the newspaper, sitting in the car outside of a liquor store, looking for anything that was better than a shelter. I remembered reading a story once on a convent that rented beds to abused women and children for five dollars a night. I knew it was in the Bay area, but had no idea where.

Five dollars a night would get us by for a while, at least until I could find a temporary job and get us a small place near Maddy's school. I had seventy-four dollars and thirty-two cents left after the cereal bars, beef jerky and apple juices I bought for snacks. Grocery shopping in a liquor store has its limitations.

In theory, the money I had left could buy us a week in one of those places, not counting food and gas. I was sure that if I could make it that long, I could haggle another couple of weeks somehow. I was surprised by my composure at the thought of all of this, but reminded myself that this was a matter of survival and it could be a lot worse.

There was nothing in the newspaper about any convents. I opened my cell phone to call information, but the battery was dying quickly. I wondered how long before Jerry cut off the service entirely. His name was on that account too. It began to dawn on me how every part of my life had Jerry's name on it as primary something or other. A chill came over me at the thought of having nothing of my own.

With a sigh, I got out of the car and walked to the payphone, something I hadn't used since my high school days. I lifted the receiver, with my sweater covering my hand for protection, and dialed zero. The smell was worse than the worst kind of bad breath. The black receiver looked oily, and I was afraid to let it touch my face. I waited for the voice of the operator while Maddy carefully walked an imaginary tightrope along the sidewalk next to me.

The voice was there.

"Yes, um, I need a number for a convent in the San Francisco area." I wound the metal cord around my index finger as the operator searched.

"Which convent ma'am? I have multiple listings." She sounded perturbed and somewhat skeptical of my inquiry.

Multiple convents in San Francisco? There was obviously a whole lot I didn't know about this town. I tried to think of the name.

"Um…I don't really know. Could you give me the names of convents with the word sisters in it?" I remember the word sister in the article I read and hoped there weren't too many.

Without a beat, or much personality she responded, "Again ma'am, I have multiple listings under that name."

She clearly was not going to help me out with this. I was momentarily more irked by her lackadaisical attitude than my current crisis, but I needed her on my side for now.

"Could you please give me the first five numbers?" I heard her chagrin through the receiver.

Without warning, the numbers came flying at me. I scrambled to grasp my pen and write the numbers, or as many as I could keep up with on my newspaper. I tried to keep my balance while using my leg as a table. I only got three down, but I was too afraid of this woman to ask her to repeat them even though, as her job required, she asked, "Is there anything else I can help you with today?"

"No, thank you very much." I hung up the phone and walked back to the car to look for change. I prayed, hoping it would help my case in this instance in particular, that one of the three convents was *the* convent I was looking for.

The first two that I dialed were no's. That dreadful sense came over me as I dialed the third and final number. Someone picked up.

"Hi, do you offer shelter to women with children and nowhere to go?" I didn't know how to ask and felt absurd as the words came out for the third time.

"Yes, we do…" I cut her off before she could finish. I was elated at the news

"Oh my Go-, I mean Gosh, this is amazing. I never thought-," then it was her turn to interrupt.

"Yes, we do, but we're all full, dear. I'm sorry we couldn't help. Maybe you could try another, though we all seem to be quite full these days. I wish you God's blessing." She hung up.

God's blessing? I thought the convent would be the place for that. Although, the last time I prayed for help, I ended up in a mortuary.

In desperation, I looked through the paper again, hoping for anything. I scanned through the job postings, looking for something immediate, something that would give us temporary housing, something miraculous. When I was about to give up, I noticed an ad at the very bottom of one of the pages under "Earn Your Keep". It read:

> "Family owned funeral home seeks professional and responsible individual to perform simple office duties and help care for the home after hours. Room and board will be provided as well as a small salary, to be arranged upon hire. Please contact Merman, at The Golden Oaks Funeral Home for more details."

"Oh my gosh, oh my gosh!"

My mouth hung open in utter disbelief, which slowly turned into a smile.

Of all the irony! Of all the possibilities! I was frightened for a moment that I was actually considering calling, but excited at the opportunity it presented. It was perfect. We'd have a place to live, and I could make some money. It would just be temporary until I could save to get an apartment and a real job. It wasn't too far from Maddy's school. I realized that I had little experience to offer any position, let alone one that had me running for my life in the cold, wet ivy just last night, but this had to be a sign. It seemed my life's gravitational pull had suddenly shifted toward a place I never would have imagined, and in which I had never slept better.

I scrambled through my purse to find Merman's card. The number was different in the paper. The last person I wanted to talk to was Uncle Stanley, so I opted to use the number on the card. I walked past Maddy, who was now conducting class to an audience of parked cars, and dialed the number. There was no answer.

"Maddy, honey, get in the car. We've gotta go."

Chapter Six

The Interview

I pulled into the parking lot of The Golden Oaks Funeral Home. This was a welcomed change from where I last planted my car. My face flushed at the memory.

People were leaving the building, crying and holding each other, dressed in black. I thought for a second that I too might break down and cry, but I quickly collected myself, knowing that this would be something I would *have* to grow accustomed to if I got the job.

I wondered how they did it and remained sane. I remembered Uncle Stanley's drinking habits and attributed them to his inability to live soberly in his environment. The obvious parallels with my mother were painful. I understood Stanley and Evelyn, but Merman seemed so…content and settled. I thought that perhaps I could be that way too.

I spotted him standing at the door as people exited the mortuary. He looked genuinely compassionate. I watched as he offered his condolences and waited patiently for them to exit.

All of this was a stark contrast to what I remembered of the mortuary staff at my grandmother's service years before. They had been completely indifferent to our suffering and had the nerve to joke it up with each other about one thing or another when they thought we weren't looking. I remembered questioning their humanity. I hadn't thought about it once until now. I never thought I'd have to. I guessed that Uncle Stanley was their future when they had nothing left to joke about.

Merman didn't notice my car in the lot. I wondered if it looked much different to him sitting in a proper space. I decided to wait until everyone was gone to approach him. I was actually enjoying his calming presence as I imagined the family was.

"Mommy, how come we're at that different kind of hotel again?" Maddy asked.

As frustrated as I was by the interruption of my gaze, I knew I'd have some explaining to do at some point in the future and felt terrible about not having much of an explanation just yet.

"We might stay here again, sweetie."

I hoped that answer would spare me the third degree. To seal the deal I handed her a piece of gum from the liquor store.

"Will that funny man be there?" Maddy popped in the gum that barely fit in her mouth.

I laughed at her innocent and quite accurate observation.

"Yeah, that funny man will be there."

I watched as the last couple got into their cars and left. We got out and walked to the ominous door from the night before and rang the bell. I already had my argument and rebuttal prepared until Merman opened the door and looked at me in happy bewilderment.

The happy part is what got me. I half-expected anger or irritation at the least, but happy never occurred to me. My heart fluttered at the welcome.

"Is everything okay?" he asked in a half-whisper, stepping outside and closing the door to avoid Uncle Stanley.

He certainly handled things much differently than I expected. From the very first moment, he seemed to override any frustration or concern with some underlying kindness and curiosity. I struggled to place the feeling that overwhelmed me, but couldn't.

"Everything's fine." I paused, considering again what I was about to ask, and dreading the likely response. "So, I was looking through the paper today…and I saw a great job opportunity."

Merman allowed me to continue, but wore a hesitant look as if he already knew.

"See it would be perfect for me…well, us, because I'm looking for both a place to stay and a job." I waited to see how he would respond, but he stood still with the same expression of concern. His eyebrows were furrowed and his arms were folded across his chest.

"I can do anything I set my mind to, Merman. I graduated with honors you know." I had no idea how that applied to this situation and could tell he wondered the same as a brief smirk crossed his face.

I desperately thought of the skills I did have to offer here, guessing of course at what I would really be doing. "I can clean. I love flowers. What do you think?"

He stood staring at me for a few moments. Every time I would start in with another qualification, he would silence me by putting a hand up and then return to his contemplation. Finally, he responded.

"Uncle Stanley will never go for this." He was pacing and talking as if to convince himself, not me.

"I'll do whatever it takes. Just give me some time to learn," I pleaded.

I was following him, trying to keep up as he paced back and forth across the same five feet of pavement. Behind me was Maddy, now playing a follow the leader game. I felt desperate, as if suddenly I would give anything to be back inside that mortuary.

"I have nothing else."

It was the truth, and all I had left. He stopped and turned, looking at me over the top of his dark glasses.

"Do you have a resume?"

My heart rejoiced at his consideration just before it sank. I hadn't had a resume in six years. Jerry had refused to let me get a job, stating that he preferred me barefoot and pregnant. I knew he didn't like or really mean the pregnant half of that, but the indentured servant part was as real as anything. He expected me to be at his beckon call, barefoot or otherwise. He felt owed, entitled, and deserving.

"No, I don't have a resume," I answered dejectedly.

We both stood in silence for a minute. I knew I was under-qualified to say the least.

"On what basis am I hiring you then, Casey?"

His head was tilted and his eyes very serious. I didn't know on what basis. *I really need this*, wasn't going to suffice.

He continued his deliberation, stating all of the reasons it would be impossible.

"Uncle Stanley's going to look for every reason to say no. He'll even *make up* reasons."

He was pacing back and forth again, obviously unnerved. I knew it was a long shot, but I had to try one last time.

"Please, Merman."

I looked him in the eye and tried hard to let him know I was genuine, not pathetic. I could tell that my pleading pained him greatly. Maddy began playing follow Merman again.

"Why do you walk like this? You're silly." She giggled and skipped to my side.

He stopped, mid-pace, and laughed at himself.

"I don't know, Maddy. I guess I *am* silly."

He concentrated for a few moments, and the look of distress slowly turned to a half smile. The same smile from last night as he offered us a place on his couch. It looked like a child making up their mind to do something very sneaky and very dangerous.

"I'd love to have neighbors, though. It's so bloody lonely here."

I grabbed his arm and shook him in complete excitement. He interrupted me with all seriousness.

"I'll have to work on Uncle Stanley, but I think I can at least buy you some time until you can prove yourself useful around here." He put his finger to his chin and held his elbow with his other hand. After a moment of thought he said sneakily, "I think we can make it work!"

I clapped my hands together and giggled with relief. Maddy giggled too. And that ended the interview.

When the coast was clear, and Uncle Stanley started on his Scotch, Merman whisked us quickly past his office and into his apartment. It felt different in the light of day and in dry clothes. I thought that I should feel immense guilt for imposing in such a way, but I didn't. I realized that the feeling I wasn't able to place earlier was not a feeling, but a lack of one. I didn't feel like a burden. I felt welcomed and wanted. I laughed at the irony. I felt like an unwanted burden in my own home with my husband, but completely safe and welcomed in a creepy mortuary with a stranger. None of it made much sense, but it felt very right.

I was truly excited about the possibilities ahead. Jerry was wrong. I *was* going to be able to do it. I had secured shelter and a job, much more than I could have hoped for in one day, and as long as Maddy and I were together, I knew that everything would be okay.

Merman left momentarily and returned with a stack of papers.

"There are some forms you have to fill out to make this legitimate. Don't worry about some of the information - we'll get creative where we need to. You're not a felon are you?" He smiled as I paused in surprise.

While I filled out endless forms, Merman invited Maddy into his kitchen to help him make peanut butter and jelly sandwiches, apparently one of his favorites. When they were done, there were a dozen perfectly cut flower and heart shaped sandwiches before me.

"Try one, mommy," Maddy urged, as she pointed to one shaped like a lily.

She watched closely as I usually found a way around eating anything she made, but I had seen that Merman was watching the process carefully as well. I took a bite and made a sigh of satisfaction, to the great pleasure of them both.

When I finished the paperwork, feeling very concerned about the references and last address sections, Merman took his turn at them. He assured me that neither would be a problem since he was responsible for the hiring and firing for the most part. I nibbled nervously at a tulip shaped pb&j, worried that he would find something that would end this impossible reverie.

After a few minutes of checking boxes and entering data, he stood up.

"I will take this to Uncle Stanley and settle the deal."

I looked at him as anxious as an interviewee could be, but he seemed very convinced it wouldn't be a problem.

"He'll put up a fight, but he'll see it the way I do soon enough, like it or not. He trusts me."

I nodded and swallowed hard on the last bite. I wished I could take him at his word. After all, this was the second time he had saved us.

"I'll be gone for a few hours, talking with Uncle Stanley, finishing up business and closing up shop. You two are welcome to anything and everything here. I have plenty of old classics for you to watch if you're interested."

He showed me to a book case stocked full of classic films, restored and enhanced on DVD. It couldn't have been any more perfect. It was starting to rain again outside, and I wanted nothing more than to snuggle up with Maddy and sleep to the sounds.

He was gone, and we were soon wrapped up in a blanket, drifting off to the sounds of pitter patter outside and background music on the screen

Chapter Seven

Home Sweet Home

When I awakened, the light through the windows had all but disappeared. The sun was setting, and the DVD menu was replaying over and over. I sat up, still a little groggy, and turned the television off. We must have slept for a couple of hours. The triathlon of a day had drained me completely.

Merman was nowhere to be seen, and I wasn't sure what to do next. I considered sneaking out to the car to get our bags, but as I snooped about, I found them sitting neatly by the door. I smiled, feeling warmed by his thoughtfulness, and looked through the mess I had thrown in.

More than anything, I wanted to brush my teeth. An unpleasant film coated each and every one. Maddy and I had brushed over them in the liquor store bathroom earlier that morning, but the smell of never cleaned and liberally used toilet made our attempts quick and ineffective.

I grabbed my toiletries and headed for the bathroom, hoping to clean up before Maddy woke up. I looked in the mirror and was shocked by my appearance. My hair was a mess, and I had developed dark circles under my eyes. I quickly washed my face, brushed my teeth, and brushed out my hair. It would have to do. I hoped that a good night's sleep, the security of a place to live, and a job would make me look and feel human again.

Maddy giggled from outside the door. When I opened it, I found her sitting up with her fingers in a Chinese finger trap. Merman was next to her showing her how to get them out.

"Mommy, I have a trick."

She showed me her fingers stuck and then showed me how to get them out. Merman seemed pleased by her excited response to his gift, and Maddy seemed so proud of her accomplishment that I had to give the appropriate oohs and aahs. What I really wanted to know was how things had gone with Uncle Stanley and whether or not I would have to carry our bags back to the car. Merman seemed to comprehend my anxious posture.

He winked confidently. "You're in. Now you try it!" He held out a finger trap.

I was so relieved and elated that I succumbed to the multiple requests by both for me to ensnare my pointer fingers. We did it over and over, and Maddy couldn't get enough of Merman pretending he couldn't get his out.

While we played, Merman told me how he had convinced Uncle Stanley to give me a chance at the job.

As he had predicted, Uncle Stanley put up a pretty big fight. He described the different shades of red that had passed over Uncle Stanley's face throughout the debate. He had a very dramatic yet entertaining way of retelling events. He even acted out Uncle Stanley's gait and many different faces and voices. Maddy was in near hysterics by the time he was done. I was more than a little nervous about running into this man who clearly didn't want us here.

"Casey, it's going to be fine. Just stay close to me, and he'll leave you alone. On another note, I guess you'll want these."

He smiled a clever smile and dropped a set of keys in my hands. The excitement was overwhelming. In my hands were the keys to our new home. With the job came the apartment upstairs.

"Can we go see it?" I asked.

I felt like a child, having something of my very own for the first time. I couldn't keep myself composed, and he seemed just as excited for me.

"How about now?" he asked, with a smile that hinted of excitement.

He led us out the door and back down the hallway toward the infamous closet from our first visit. Just beyond the closet was another door. We walked through to find a set of stairs. It didn't seem like they were used very often as they housed more dust than the rest and carried a musty smell of loneliness. The stairway dropped us off right in front of another door. This one had a peep hole and a brass door knob.

"Welcome home, ladies."

He bowed and winked again at Maddy. She curtsied and giggled.

"Would you do the honors, Madame?" He gestured toward the keyhole.

I unlocked the door, and we all walked in. It was pitch black, but Merman quickly found a light.

"There's already electricity?" I exclaimed with surprise.

Merman laughed at my excitement.

The floor plan was the same as the one below, but completely empty and without the homey feel that Merman's apartment had. It smelled like it had recently been cleaned, and the carpet had lines from a vacuum. The proud smile on Merman's face told me he had something to do with the recent preparations. I was slightly embarrassed to think that he had done all of this while we slept on his couch.

The carpet and paint were very simple and neutral, and everything begged for color and creativity. The possibilities were endless. I was completely and totally in love with it. I couldn't contain myself. I hugged Maddy and Merman together and jumped up and down.

"It's perfect!" I squealed. "It's more than I could have ever thought to hope for."

I felt so proud and so grown up. I was so wrapped in jubilance that I had forgotten one minor detail.

"Mommy, what is this place?" Maddy asked, looking around.

I forgot that I hadn't given her an explanation beyond hotel.

"Maddy, this is where we are going to live for a while."

I waited for her response, terrified that she would be sad.

"Is daddy going to stay at home?" Her tone was very matter of fact.

The pain in my heart made me wince for a second.

"Yes, honey, daddy is going to stay at home." I felt sick.

She seemed to think hard about something.

"Do we get to see Merman every day?" She watched me carefully for an answer.

I didn't know what to say. I didn't know if seeing *us* was part of his plan. As I fumbled around with words, he interrupted.

"Everyday, until you get sick of me! Pinky promise." He stuck out his pinky, and she didn't miss a beat. Her face lit up and she sealed the deal with a thumb press.

I don't know why I trusted him implicitly, but I did. It seemed that Maddy did too. I closed my eyes and prayed, which was becoming a habit, that this wasn't too good to be true, that Maddy and I were going to be okay, and that the grotesque realities of the job wouldn't do me in.

I looked around at our vacant little home and felt at peace.

Merman cleared his voice.

"Of course…you can stay with me until we can furnish this place. I'm sure we can find some good stuff soon. I know of a couple of shops."

I didn't miss the "we" part of that statement. My eyes welled up again, another new habit.

"Merman, I don't know how I can ever repay you for all that you've done for us." I really did feel that there was no way.

"There will be no repaying of anything. You work here, remember?" He winked and gave me that sly smile again. "As for tonight…we have plans."

While Maddy and I showered, something we both desperately needed, Merman cooked an amazing dinner of chicken stuffed with something delicious, a salad with blue cheese and blackberries, and home made mashed potatoes. We ate together at the table, an event that never occurred with Jerry, and Merman questioned Maddy about school and friends.

I thought for a moment that I should feel concerned by this suddenly intimate relationship, but it felt so natural. I was grateful that he kept the questions light with me. I didn't know if I was ready to talk about everything that had transpired in the last couple of days. I was actually trying to avoid thinking about it altogether, mostly because I didn't have a clue as to what I was going to do about Jerry.

When Maddy seemed to be out of steam and stories, he turned to me.

"Tomorrow we're here alone, so I'll show you around. By Monday you should be able to get by enough to keep Uncle Stanley off your back."

"Mmhmm," I muttered in response, dreading the very thought of Monday and being shown around.

I tried not to think about my new job and what it really entailed as I tried to get my dinner down. Jerry was nothing compared to Uncle Stanley and dead people. Merman was watching me with concern. I smiled and got Maddy talking. I didn't want him to regret his decision. I'd have to just suck it up and make it work.

After dinner, he entertained us with one of his favorite classics, *Gone with the Wind.* On occasion he would say the lines with the characters. I wondered if he saw me in Scarlet, stubbornly independent and reckless. I couldn't give myself that much credit.

Before the movie had ended, Maddy was sound asleep.

"I guess it's time for bed," I whispered with a quiet chuckle as I pointed to Maddy.

"Get your rest, because tomorrow is a new and busy day," he reminded me. "I'm guessing you're terrified of what's out there and what you'll be doing for a living?" he asked with a knowing grin.

"Just a little," I lied.

He laughed, low and quiet. "I won't lie to you, it's likely nothing that you've done or seen before, but you'll survive. I'll see to that."

"I'm counting on it," I informed him.

After our adieus, I soon drifted to sleep imagining how our new little home might look with a little bit of time and love.

Chapter Eight

Duties

I awoke Sunday morning to sunshine peeking through the blinds and classical music playing softly somewhere in the apartment. Though I felt rested, the sick feeling in my stomach and ache in my heart was left over from my dream. Jerry and my father had teamed up and starred in it. Through some odd circumstance they had managed to take Maddy and my new life out from under me, leaving me in a desperate search. In the end of my dream, I was driving in the dark rain trying to find the Brookford Academy for Girls and *my* girl.

I felt my pillow and it was damp with tears. I knew that these would continue until I had dealt with Jerry and ended things officially.

When the agony subsided, it was replaced by a feeling of dread. It was the day that I would venture out into the world of undertaking, and though I had recently proven determined enough to take on anything I set my mind to, I didn't wholly trust my gag reflex. All of my life I had suffered from a weak stomach when it came to gruesome sights, sounds, and smells. It also acted as an alarm, telling me when something wasn't quite right. The burdensome arrhythmia served as an effective back up alarm. Though I hadn't recognized it at first, the pain and breathlessness as I approached the house and Jerry's studio that day had been a warning screaming *Do Not Enter*. I don't know what good could have come from heeding that warning. I *needed* to see it that time. I had felt for a long time that things weren't right and that we would one day have to find a way out. The visual and colorful confirmation had been the impetus - the starting point.

That kind of pain was no longer my concern as I hid under my pillow. It was now the concern of looking death in the face, in all its gruesome wonder. I had seen plenty of death on t.v., but I sensed that in person it would be much more difficult. I pulled the pillow down tightly around my head, hoping for just a little more time.

I was briefly calmed at the thought of not having to go through the entire experience with Uncle Stanley watching. I knew Merman could forgive my queasy outbursts, but Uncle Stanley would be taking notes and waiting for a reason to send us away.

When I finally came out of my cave, desperately in need of a trip to the bathroom, there was a familiar looking cup of tea placed on the table next to me. I watched the steam rise and the tea bag swirl, smiling as I remembered when this was first offered me and the confusion I had felt at its existence in this place. I mostly remembered how kind and gentle Merman had been in spite of what a mess I was.

I didn't see him. He must have snuck the tea in while I was hiding. I awakened Maddy and went into the bathroom to clean up and get dressed for the day. By the time we came out, Merman had already started preparing something in the kitchen.

"Good morning, ladies. Any special requests for the kitchen?" He was wearing a chef's hat and looked absurd.

Maddy giggled. "He looks funny, mommy."

"I think he looks very professional," I teased. "How very nice of you to offer, Merman. I would actually feel much better about all of this if I could pitch in a bit." I didn't want to be taken care of any more than I already was, living on his couch, begging for a job, and eating his food.

"Be my guest." He waved a hand across the kitchen counter and bowed out, but not before setting the chef's hat on the counter and gesturing for me to put it on.

"No thanks, I think I actually cook better without a hat."

"Mommy, put it on. Please!" Maddy begged and giggled. Merman shrugged as if innocent in the whole affair.

I whipped together blueberry pancakes and eggs. Merman had a surprising selection of foods to choose from.

When we finished eating, I joined him in the kitchen to clean. He broke the news while we washed dishes.

"Uncle Stanley decided to come in and catch up on some work in the office." He paused and waited for a reaction. I had none besides silent terror.

"He's *never* come in on a Sunday, and though I told him it wasn't necessary and might make things harder, he insisted and promised to stay out of the way."

The calm I had managed to claim during breakfast had quickly abandoned me. I tried to hide my discomfort as I dried each dish to a shine, but I had never been able to fake much.

"Look, Casey, I'll be honest, he's here to watch you. This business is his life. He's managed to maintain ownership and keep it afloat through a nasty divorce and a handful of recessions. He's leery of newcomers and has very little tolerance for error, which is why I've hired you to do the simple things around here, for now anyway. And even though he would like to prove me wrong about you, he is also very curious." He watched me dry another fork to perfection as I struggled to hide my anguish. "The good news is there's not much you can mess up today. I'm just showing you around." His tone was encouraging, as if he believed everything was going to work out splendidly.

Splendid seemed like a stretch considering all the messes I had created in just a few short days, the results of which had landed me on Merman's couch. But my only choice was to make it as ridiculously splendid as I could and show Uncle Stanley he was wrong about me. More than that, I didn't want Merman to regret his decision. How I would manage all of that I wasn't quite sure.

I set up a play date for Maddy, a once implausible feat, now not so difficult since word had quickly gotten around the school that Maddy and I were on our own. It has been my observation that word gets around quickly, in fact, spreads like wild fire, amongst classroom mommies. I was grateful such "word" was working in my favor this time. Support from women that I could, in one way or another, consider my peers was more than encouraging. Feeling alone in the world doubled the agonies of life and made the pleasures less enjoyable.

This particular play date was absolutely necessary as I was a probationary employee, and Uncle Stanley would be in "gotcha" mode, scrutinizing and evaluating my every move. Besides, I wanted to see for myself what lurked beneath the floor-boards of Golden Oaks Funeral Home before I let Maddy step foot beyond Merman's front door.

I followed Merman through the hallways, in and out of closets and through the reception area, walking so closely behind that when he turned to face me we collided. I was more than intimidated by every inch of death-like creepiness surrounding me, and I secretly wanted to cling to his arm. Instead, I walked right on his heels. He was patient, only letting a smirk slip before continuing. With a gentle yet business-like disposition, he explained the necessity of such work and the goodness behind the services they offered to grieving families.

He sadly acknowledged the skeptical and bitter accusations of scandalous profit in times of loss, so frequent in the funeral business, and explained that on his part at least, he hoped their efforts helped more than they hurt. He admitted that the business was riddled with profiteers and cold, careless wretches who took advantage, at every turn, of the grieving. He hoped that *their* business would be known for the contrast to such stereotypes, but knew it was a nearly impossible feat.

Being a business, they too had to worry about overhead and cost, and though it seemed a miserable practice to him, they always made mention of the higher valued caskets, plots, and services. Some families felt compelled to provide the very best for their departed, while others felt insulted and angered by both the suggestion and their inability to partake of it. It was an emotional business, and those in it found ways to survive. Some hardened their hearts to it, others medicated themselves through it, but some tried merely to be a light in the unequivocal darkness of it all. The latter was most assuredly Merman.

As I listened, I knew that he was an exception, that he did care for the comfort and well-being of others, and that it was this very characteristic that had saved me the night before.

After the solemn history of undertaking, Merman went over some of the basic duties of the job I was to begin: vacuuming the chapels, filling the pews with tissue boxes, documenting all of the flowers for each service, controlling the organ music from the house stereo, and other menial tasks. Up to this point, everything mentioned seemed more than manageable. I imagined no struggle at all, but this would soon change.

When he saw that I was comfortable with the chapel and the tasks involved with the services, he led me through the sliding door, down the clinical hallway, and squarely in front of a well-sealed door. I remembered how he had quickly closed that same sliding door the day before, seeming to hide whatever was beyond it. This very memory caused the hair on my arms to stand straight. I imagined Frankenstein's monster, the ghost of Hamlet's murdered father, the vampire-like lunatic locked in the tower of Thornfield, the wailing and haunting Catherine on the moors. I had spent way too many hours in the pages of gothic romances. Their supernatural horrors paled in comparison to the realities of the embalming room.

I followed Merman into the bright, clinical room, still tailing him like a toddler. There were two white slabs in the center and some odd looking machinery. There were hoses attached to the slabs and drains at the bottom leading into the floor. Everything was extremely sterile and thankfully, very empty. I had begun feeling dizzy as soon as we started down the hallway, but now I was chilled and hyper-aware of my surroundings. The room was ice cold and filled with finality. I inched closer to Merman for warmth and comfort.

"This is the embalming room. This is where we restore beauty and prepare our friends for their long journey."

He had taken on the tone of a television narrator, probably to ease my discomfort. I tried to mask my disgust with a nervous laugh. I had a small understanding of embalming, but the name in conjunction with the equipment in front of me brought on a barrage of grotesque images.

"Don't worry, you get used to it. We all get used to it. Pretty soon you'll walk in here like you walk down the cereal aisle."

Merman walked toward the slabs and hopped up on one. He looked at me with concern, noticing my expression of hesitation. I still hadn't gotten past his labeling of the dead people as "friends", but the more I got to know Merman, the more I believed this to be an honest assessment of his.

He continued, "Now you'll be helping me a little bit in here, doing things like dressing our friends and maybe applying their make-up if I'm running behind…" I hadn't moved an inch since the mention of my actually working in here routinely, and the horror-struck expression on my face felt permanently set. He finished his sentence but cut short, "…which tends to happen when the fog rolls in. Casey, are you alright?"

I didn't understand what he meant by make-up and fog, but what I couldn't ignore was the violent churning in my stomach. The blood rushed from my head, and it was all I could do to keep myself upright. I tried to fight against the rising wave of nausea, but from much experience I knew it was futile.

I ran to the bathroom, which thankfully was right off of the main room, as the inevitable quickly approached. I made it to the toilet and gagged uncontrollably for minutes on end. I could hear Merman laugh, although he tried to do it quietly so as not to offend me. I waited out the last of the heaves and rinsed my mouth for a few minutes more in an attempt to collect myself.

I came back out feeling quite dizzy and humiliated. There was no hiding it now, no point in trying.

"I don't know if I can do this, Merman. I mean look at me, I'm puking, and there aren't even any "friends" here."

I sat on a small stool near the door and put my head in my hands. The chapel I could do, even collecting the cards filled with broken hearts and endless grief, but this, I didn't think I could ever get used to this. He hopped off of the slab and approached me consolingly.

"Oh come on. We'll get through it. We all feel a little… strange at first, but I promise, you do get used to it."

I tried to remind myself of my goal and gather up some resolve. The life behind me was where I intended to leave it. I *could* lead a happy and productive life, put together with any scraps I could find along the way, but it was obviously going to be in a way that challenged my very nature at every turn. I laughed at the irony. Caving to the "easy", submissive life had left me miserable, and the road to happiness was marked by impossible feats, one after another. But I wanted it desperately.

I tried to stand up and quickly lost my balance. Baby steps then. Merman caught me with one arm around my waist.

"Alright, that's enough in here. Let's go get some food back in you."

He lifted me gently by the arm and guided me through the door.

As the day passed, Uncle Stanly had followed as inconspicuously as he possibly could, being as large as he was. When I would unwittingly catch him around a corner, he would make a *hmph* sound and walk away. As Merman walked me back through the building, Uncle Stanley followed us quietly, but by this point, I couldn't care any less.

The week went by slowly, and luckily, the fog hadn't come. Merman tried to explain this phenomenon to me. There seemed to be some correlation between the fog rolling in and the number of "friends" who arrived. He said they imagined it to be the creeping hand of death, and it usually swept over the retirement homes and hospitals. He admitted the silliness of how it sounded, but couldn't deny the truth in it. That was all I could get out of him as he could tell that I was easily spooked.

Maddy had gone back to school and though it was a bit of a drive, I enjoyed learning my way around the small town on the opposite side of the bay. There were dozens of little stores formed along the willow-lined streets. They had few if any customers, and I wondered how they could afford to stay open.

I passed by an auto shop and noticed Jim working outside, covered head to toe in grease and surrounded by parts and rusty, junk cars. I waved, and he smiled, waving back. I still felt indebted to him for the tires. No one had done anything so kind for me before, with the exception of Merman. I thought of Merman and was warmed by a great sense of content.

I spent the week learning my job and avoiding Uncle Stanley whenever possible. I was adjusting to the nauseating smells and eerie silence, but still got shaky when I heard strange and unaccounted for whispers, running as fast as I could to find Merman. I always had a gnawing sense that I wasn't alone as I walked the hallways. When I ventured to mention this to Merman, he quickly returned to his work and stated that it was easy to let our imaginations get the best of us in such a place. I could tell his posture and tone were saying something entirely different and that at some point, I would hear more about this.

There weren't any "friends" or services planned for the week, so I spent my time following Merman around and trying to "get used to it" as best I could. He was patient and forgiving when I would occasionally run to the bathroom holding my mouth as he explained the machinery and processes in the embalming room.

I was introduced to Eddie, an on-call driver who picked up our friends as they passed on. He was short and stocky and full of untamed energy. He seemed to be moving in some way or another at all times. His hair was always in disarray and his clothes much the same. There was something certainly mysterious about him, as if he was waiting for some fantastically wayward adventure to present itself to him. He was ready and awaiting any and every little errand that Merman might have for him. It seemed that he wasn't surviving at all, that he actually liked what he did.

I also met Celia, a thin but clearly-able-to-hold-her-own girl about my age who acted as a receptionist of sorts. She handled a lot of the paper-work and scheduling. She was eclectic to say the least. Her hair was shoulder-length, black, and arranged with hold in every which way possible, but it somehow didn't look messy. It reminded me of old hairstyles from the forties. She wasn't classically pretty, but every feature of her face was bold, and her eyes were magnetic, especially when they looked at Merman. I was curious about their relationship as her attraction, when they made any contact at all, was undeniable. Her dress was a modern vintage style and made her look like she came straight out of one of Merman's films. I wondered if she knew of Merman's antique preferences.

The sudden realization of this energy between the two of them pricked a slight and surprising twinge of jealousy, but only momentarily. The feelings I had for Merman weren't romantic. I hadn't even considered the possibility until I saw him from Celia's perspective. He was undeniably handsome and generous. I could be myself with Merman. For reasons I didn't entirely understand, he accepted me, chaos and all. I felt at home with him, but not in love. Celia, on the other hand, seemed like his perfectly matched puzzle piece, and I had only exchanged a few words with her. I decided I would find out more when I had him alone.

I received a much kinder welcome from Eddie and Celia than I had Uncle Stanley, though Celia watched me with curiosity. She asked once if we were comfortable on Merman's sofa and when I thought we might be moving into our own apartment. The jealousy had clearly pricked her too. She was still kind though, in a way that hinted at her confidence.

As the days moved on, I focused on learning everything I would need to know for an upcoming service. Our nights were filled with music, movies and dress up, with Merman picking characters from his favorite films and likening Maddy to them with hats and boas and jewelry from the closet. He would help her memorize his favorite lines, and they would act them out brilliantly. I watched, applauded, and laughed like a good audience member.

Merman cooked the most extravagant home-made meals I'd ever tasted, all while donning what he explained was his nana's old apron. It was pale yellow and slightly worn around the edges, though well-kept and finely decorated with a large, pink pig sitting on its hind-legs, proudly wearing a chef's hat. I couldn't help but laugh every time it caught my attention. He would just look back in confusion and ask, "What?"

Feeling far too taken care of by Merman, I insisted on helping in the kitchen. Though I couldn't yet contribute to the groceries, a dependency that made me extremely uncomfortable piled up with the rest, I was determined to pitch in to earn our keep, so to speak. He obliged, dubbing me sous-chef and putting me on "chop-chop" duty, a duty consisting of…well, chopping up ingredients.

In another week, I would be receiving my first paycheck, and I would be able to hunt around for furniture for our apartment and start to repay Merman with some home-cooked meals of my own. I needed just about everything but figured we could get by with the minimum. Of course, Merman kept an open invitation to his sofa bed until we had what we needed, and I gratefully accepted, determined to make our imposition as brief as possible. Every couple of days or so, Merman would come home with a lamp, a rug, or some other kind of decoration. He swore that he had found them out on the street or claimed that they had been left to him by one of the "friends", but some of them were new, and I had a feeling he was making his own personal contributions. This didn't help with my feelings of being the worst kind of leech, but it made me adore him even more. We kept the collection upstairs, and it had soon grown to include even a painting and some dishes.

The two of us, three if you count the two square feet of wall Maddy worked on, painted the apartment my favorite shade of olive green in the living room, a vanilla white in the kitchen, and the happy, light pink Maddy picked out for her room. We added some faux finishes inspired by Merman's bathroom, and in no time at all, we were finished. Knowing that the place was all mine, every inch, made it difficult not to sleep on the living room carpet with a blanket that very night.

As for the permanent sleeping arrangements in our one-bedroom apartment, I decided I would sleep on a fold-out-couch in the living room, similar to Merman's, and let Maddy have the bedroom. It made me feel a little better about the strange lifestyle I had imposed on her. Yet, aside from the guilt I felt about taking her away from everything she'd known in her short little existence thus far, Maddy seemed to love our new life and didn't mention the house much except for an occasional longing for her toys and neighborhood friends. This was easily remedied with play dates, which were certainly easier to come by these days.

By the looks of the apartment, we would be able to move in soon. We just needed bedroom and living room furniture. I sat in the middle of the empty living room and looked around, full of pride and gratitude. I still couldn't believe how much had been given us in just a matter of days, and the fear of what could be taken still lingered.

I lay on the carpet and stretched out, looking through the open window and pondering the unknown before me.

Chapter Nine

A Wedding

By the end of the week, a new friend had arrived. Merman hadn't needed me yet, and I gladly avoided the embalming room. I prepared the chapel and cleaned the bathrooms, feeling proud of my completed tasks. When Maddy wasn't in school, she followed me around and tried to help in any way she could.

"Is this a church, Mommy?"

I looked around and thought of how to explain the dark circumstances in which we were now living.

"Well, kind of, sweetie. Do you remember MacGuyver?" I asked, recalling our cocker spaniel. Maddy nodded sadly. "Well, when MacGuyver died, remember how we buried him and said some prayers?" Again, Maddy nodded. "Well, this is a church where people do just that, but for other people when they die." Maddy looked up curiously.

"Then the dead people are here?" she asked simply. I was surprised at her nonchalant manner in asking this.

"Well, yes. They come here for a bit, and then they get buried. Like MacGuyver." I tried to explain.

I was becoming uncomfortable with the discussion and feeling that I wasn't doing a good job explaining. Maddy's questions were bringing forward the reality that I was now raising my daughter in a mortuary, a fact easily forgotten when we were together in Merman's apartment. I knew how it would look to the outside world and felt sick at the thought of being deemed a negligent, unfit mother.

"Honey, does it bother you that we are living in a place like this?" I was feeling desperate and sad, wishing I had asked her this before.

Merman entered the room, and when Maddy saw him, her eyes lit up.

"No, mommy, I like it here." She ran to Merman, quoting in a semi-southern accent, "But Rhett, where will I go? What will I do?"

Merman replied in full character, "Frankly my dear, I don't give a…hoot!"

Maddy curtsied, and Merman applauded then picked her up and swung her around. He looked at me and gave me a comforting wink, and it suddenly didn't seem so bad anymore.

After Maddy had gone to bed and I had cleaned the kitchen to a shine, I plopped myself next to Merman on his white, leather sofa, carrying a bottle of wine and two glasses. He filled them both and casually started a very solemn and unexpected conversation.

"So where's Maddy's dad?"

I froze, speechless for a moment. I dreaded the very thought of Jerry. The mention of his name, or even reference to it, filled my chest with an anxious fire and instantly doubled my heart rate. I knew the time would come when it was only fair that I explain our situation to Merman. I felt awful that I hadn't already, but the fact that I didn't have a plan made talking about it unbearable, like a suspense novel without an ending.

"Oh, he's around." I shifted uneasily and picked up a weekly entertainment magazine from a pile on the coffee table.

"Hmmm…around huh? Not around enough, it would seem."

"It would seem so," I deflected.

"Are you going to tell me the story or am I going to have to start a fire and smoke it out of you?" he teased.

I caved. "Fine - But you have to promise that no matter what I tell you, you won't think less of me."

"I couldn't possibly!" he stated with his right hand in the air as a sworn oath.

"Wait, you couldn't possibly think less of me, or you won't hear the story and judge me, leading me to believe you think less of me?" I asked for clarification.

He laughed after he understood my interpretation. "You're being ridiculous. We all have our stories. Now let's have it!" he demanded playfully.

"It's a shameful story, Merman, of a young and foolish teenager."

I was stalling now, but as I went over the details in my head, I was embarrassed to relive them in front of him. He took my hands in his and looked me directly in the face.

"What is this, story time? Is that the opening line?" he teased. "Look, whatever it is that brought you here, I'm thankful for it. There hasn't been this much life here – ever."

"Fine, I'll tell you, but when I'm done, I have some questions of my own."

He seemed lost on what I could possibly want to know, but I interrupted.

"It started with a chance encounter at a friend of a friend's house when I was nineteen. My friend and I ended up there after a night of drinking, dancing and near arrest – it was the beginning of my rebellious stage. Wherever trouble lurked, I would find it. When I walked into the house, there he was, sitting in the dark, watching some 1980's horror film by himself.

"After I cleaned up my friend, who had vomited on herself in the car, I came back into the living room to find him waiting there for me holding a pillow and blanket. He suggested neither of us were in any condition to drive, and that we were welcome to stay. I remember thinking it was the sweetest gesture anyone had made before. Now," I admitted, "I can see that it was quite a pathetic measure of romance. If you ever met my father, you would understand that I didn't have much to go by in the way of courtly love, and the bar was set pretty low. Anyway, I had been so enamored and desperate for attention that we quickly began dating.

"He was an artist, getting gigs in movies doing make-up here and there. I didn't find out until later that they were adult films, and he was powdering butts for a living, but he aspired to work on make-up in major films and sell his sculptures and paintings. I had started to notice that his art was usually very dark in nature, but I was so enamored with his charm and intensity, that I didn't pay much attention to it. I didn't mind that he was broke and barely getting by, because I had come from money and wanted anything that was completely different from my father. Money had never bought me happiness before.

"After several months, the reality of who Jerry was began to wear on me. The darkness at his center and his increasing selfishness were too much to ignore anymore. He was possessive, checking my cell phone when I used the bathroom and demanding that I not see my friends anymore. Early on, it seemed like a worthwhile sacrifice, but when things came to a head, I had alienated friends whom I desperately needed. None of them wanted to see me if he was around, which in the end meant I never saw them.

"After he met my parents and saw their evident wealth, he became even more clingy and possessive. I knew why, and it made me sick.

"One night, after he had plenty to drink and was becoming belligerent, I decided to break it off with him before things got any worse. I was going to tell him the next day, fearing his drunken response. He tended to get a bit rough when he drank, and I didn't want to give him the bad news and risk a scene. I woke up sick to my stomach, and after an hour of intermittent vomiting, it became frighteningly clear."

I paused and waited for Merman's jaw to drop open or for him to cringe away in disgust, but instead, he just leaned forward anxiously and said, "Then what?"

"Well, I sat on the bathroom floor for a while before I worked up the courage to take the pregnancy test I'd bought. I followed the instructions step by step and waited. The stick felt like it weighed three hundred pounds as I held it in front of me, waiting. I didn't need to see it, I already knew."

I waited, but no judgment passed over Merman's lips. In fact, the only emotion I saw in his eyes was sorrow. It looked like empathy, like he somehow knew my story well. I wondered at his response, but continued with my story, as he said nothing.

"I called him up to meet, feeling doomed and trapped with no real good choice to make. When I told him, I remember vividly the eerie smile that came over his face, as if this news gave him what he wanted. *I* was devastated and *he* was excited. I remember thinking that he had probably meant for this to happen. Within a week he had proposed. He thought this would guarantee him some kind of financial reward, but he didn't know my father.

"My father, in the meantime, made every effort to convince me to have an abortion, even organizing an intervention with adult and child psychologists. He brought them in to discuss my selfish and reckless behavior and to convince me that the best decision for all involved would be to rid of it once and for all. It was humiliating. I had nobody to really support me, nobody on *my* side. Everybody wanted me to clean up the mess or wanted to use the mess to manipulate me into something.

"When all was said and done, my father swore he would wash his hands of me and told me not to come to him for anything if I planned on keeping it. He dared me to see how far I would get in life without him, to see how well some bum like Jerry could provide for me. The thought that my father was right about Jerry made me furious and ashamed.

"When I told him of Jerry's proposal and told him I was seriously considering, he decided that he would try negotiating. He was notorious in the legal world for being one of the most ruthless and insidious litigators and probably assumed he could handle *this* little problem. He proposed that if I would stay out of sight while I was pregnant and follow through with an adoption that he would take care of all expenses and see to it that my position in his firm would remain open for when I finished law school. He was obsessed with the idea of me following his path in law. I was a disappointment from birth. He had wanted a son, and after me, my mother wasn't able to have anymore children – so it was all up to me, and I've never ceased to fail him.

"In the midst of the emotional chaos and war between Jerry, my father, and myself, I was growing clearer and clearer about one truth. I knew that the life inside of me was something significant, something worth fighting for, something that gave me a purpose. I could feel it growing, and I felt an overwhelming sense of protection over it. It was part of me, and I couldn't kill the one thing that made sense of my world, no matter how inconvenient it was to everyone else. I was absolutely sure that the selfish and cold world of my father had nothing to offer me but the eventual lifeless and broken spirit of my mother, who by the way, didn't have the courage to stand by me through any of it.

"I decided that of all my options, marrying Jerry was the best way I could protect this baby and try to build something for *it* that I'd never had. I couldn't imagine at the time that I could do it on my own, so I went with what I knew – life dependent on a cruel and controlling man. It was the same old story with a different cover. There were many omens along the way of the cruel similarities between Jerry and my father, but I hoped, desperately hoped, things would be different and get better when we were settled.

"We were married, and the wedding was small, with no one there but a witness at the courthouse. We had no money and only the room he rented in a house he shared with his womanizing, drunken friend. I tried to remain strong and positive, but things were beginning to look hopeless. Jerry's excitement over what he thought would be a lucrative investment was soon dashed when I explained that my father had cut me off. His rampage lasted weeks, and he claimed that I had duped him into marrying me. I was too dejected to remind him of his plot to extort money out of this and of *his* begging *me* to marry him.

"He threatened an annulment, an option I'd myself considered, and he would have followed through with it had I not received a call from my mother just a few weeks after the wedding. She wanted to meet and talk, but swore me to secrecy, as this would have been considered mutiny by my father. We met for tea, and before we even took a sip, Evelyn passed me an envelope. It held twenty thousand dollars in cash - a wedding gift of sorts. She wanted to see me safe and happy. She had even set up a meeting with a realtor to help me find a home. The only catch was that we had to move away, where my father could never find out. There was a nice little neighborhood on the opposite side of the bay from my parents. Evelyn had hoped that it would be far enough away from my father, but close enough that she could still visit.

"We met with the realtor and found a cute little house. My mother handled all of the paperwork and actually enlisted the services of a lawyer for some of it. She told us not to worry about the fine print, and since Jerry was happy enough about a free house, we both signed without reading a thing. She made such a large down payment that our mortgage was easily paid for with Jerry's inconsistent art work." Merman held his hand up for me to pause while he considered something.

"So you don't know why your mother hired a lawyer to draw up paperwork?"

"She said it was standard real estate and loan paperwork."

"And neither of you read it?"

"No." I had no idea what he was getting at.

"Do you know where that paperwork is?"

"I think my mother has it. Why?"

"Do you know whose name is on the property?"

"Well, it doesn't really matter does it? We bought it *after* we were married, and he's the one who's been paying for it." Jerry had been sure to remind me of that.

Merman nodded in agreement, but still looked like he was searching for the missing puzzle piece.

"Please, go on," he prompted. I had lost track, ruminating over his questions and their implications.

"Well, the last six years have been the same loveless, abusive fiasco. I haven't spoken to any friends or family since, with the exception of my mother, who keeps in contact once in a while. Any new friends that I made through Maddy's school would be subjected to the same monitored relationships by Jerry, so I keep it simple with play dates and school functions. It's just been me and Maddy for the most part. My days consisted of Maddy and all of her school activities, completing any to-do list Jerry would concoct, and sneaking in some writing here and there." Here, Merman interrupted me.

"Writing? What kind of writing?" He seemed truly interested, and I suddenly felt embarrassed.

"Oh, nothing serious. I eventually gave up on all of my half-done stories and plays, and they collected dust in a secret, hidden folder in the cleaning closet where only I went. Jerry made it impossible for me to write or do anything purely for myself. When he would sense that I was getting too involved with something, he would come up with some big project that needed all of my attention. Between Jerry's lists and Maddy, I didn't have time. I used to dream of finishing a play or a novel, publishing it and sneaking away with Maddy in the middle of the night." I laughed to disguise the tears welling up. I was so sad for the time I had wasted.

"Well, you managed the sneaking away part!" He gently squeezed my hand in encouragement. "So what pushed you over the edge?"

"Ah, to the dramatic ending," I teased. "Well, it had been getting worse…or maybe I was waking up to how bad it already was. Jerry spent as little time as necessary with Maddy, calling her *my* job, and he hadn't sold many paintings or sculptures since we moved in. He made money by giving art lessons to kids and clueless college girls. Even though the math didn't add up, I decided I didn't want to know where the rest of the money came from.

"So many nights Jerry came home reeking of alcohol or completely stoned on something, all the while denying bold faced that he was on anything. He would claim the sky was green, and even though I knew it was blue, I had begun to question my own sanity.

"On one occasion, when Maddy was just beginning to walk, Jerry was so drunk that he grabbed her by the arm, just a little too rough, and pushed her away when she toddled over to him for attention. She cried in pain and sadness at his response, and he only yelled over her, warning me to shut her up before he did something himself.

"I made a silent oath that night, to Maddy and myself, that I would never let him close enough to touch her again. To make good on this promise, I made sure we had plans on his drunken nights, sometimes just driving around until he passed out, and filled our days with activities. Eventually, we were living completely separate lives. We rarely saw each other except for when he needed me to take care of business for him. We didn't even sleep in the same room anymore.

"That's about the time that his tutoring business picked up. He had so many young girls in and out of the house that I lost track. I knew there was a good chance he was messing around with one or all of them, but I decided I didn't want to know. I decided we could stay out of each other's business, and one day I could just leave without him even noticing. The idea of escaping was in the forefront of my mind, but I was terrified that I had nowhere to go.

"Like I said, I think I woke up. The ugly reality of our life was painfully clear, and it had gotten so bad that I began to get knots in my stomach on my way home from errands, not knowing what to expect when I arrived. If Jerry was gone when we got home, I would anxiously await his return, and the headlights from his car as they shined through the windows would make me sick to my stomach. I couldn't stand being near him. I couldn't stand what I was living in anymore.

"I was so ashamed of what I had allowed to go on and ashamed to admit I had known Jerry had been unfaithful for a long time. I knew it, but I had never *seen* it until just about a week ago when I walked in on his "experimental art".

"Experimental art?" Merman asked as he tried to hold back a laugh.

I painted the scene of Jerry slipping and sliding naked through the hallway.

By the end of the story, we had finished off the bottle of wine and were laughing uncontrollably at the thought of naked Jerry.

"Green and yellow, huh?" Merman was in tears.

"I swear I saw butt prints leading out of the room." I could hardly catch my breath, and the alcohol was making the jokes worse by the minute.

"He's such an ass."

We were both hysterical and more than a little tipsy.

After we had laughed ourselves into exhaustion, I sat up and wiped the tears.

"If I didn't think I'd walk in on another circus, I'd break in and get all of our stuff."

"It's not really breaking in when it's your house, Casey." His suddenly serious expression took me by surprise.

"He'd never let me near the house without trouble," I said, trying to dismiss the topic.

"What if he's not there to cause trouble?" he pressed. His voice was growing more serious and calculating. He groped at his chin as he thought.

"No way, Merman! I just want to start over. Move on."

"No, I think you want to avoid a real confrontation because you're afraid he'll win."

I fumbled over my words trying to respond to this. He was right. I was avoiding having to face Jerry again. I was avoiding his abusive comments and his manipulation. I was avoiding giving in.

"I think that we should take a van and go get your stuff this weekend." He was standing now and pacing back in forth in thought.

"Merman! What if he's there?" I was panicking now.

"What if he's not? We'll wait until we're sure he's gone."

"So the two of us are going to unload the house?" I asked sarcastically.

"Are you kidding? Eddie lives for things like this! And Celia would love to be a part of espionage! We even have walkie talkies here. Eddie and Celia can case the joint while we wait in the van." He was laughing with excitement.

"Merman, you can't be serious!"

He stopped pacing and stared me down.

"I am dead serious! Maddy will have her entire room upstairs by Sunday."

This argument and his intensity took me by surprise.

"Why are you helping us?" I demanded, my voice sounding more desperate than I expected. But I wanted to know. I needed to know. There was no obvious explanation for why Merman took us in as family and would now risk a quite possibly awful confrontation with Jerry.

He paused for a moment, as surprised as I was by my question. He looked down and shook his head, contemplating his answer.

"You and Maddy, you were a disaster that night, completely soaked through, lost and totally loony thinking about sleeping in your car to survive the night. But you were together. You were clearly running from something, but you brought her *with* you. You see, Casey, I was left behind. When I was Maddy's age, my mom didn't take me with her when she decided to run. I didn't have what Maddy has in you. So, I couldn't help but want to help you. I knew it was stupid, but it didn't matter. I liked you for the simple fact that you were there, together, trying to make the best of it. And everything I've learned of you since just confirms that. So," he concluded, clapping his hands together, "let's leave it at that and settle this business about your things."

I didn't know what to say. I wanted to hug him. I wanted to know more. I also cringed at the idea of his proposed breaking and entering. But he was right. Why should Maddy suffer because I am a chicken? He took my pause as compliance with his plan.

"I'll let Eddie and Celia know the plan tomorrow, and we'll head out after we close. You said Jerry likes to get out and wet his whistle, right? I'm sure he'll be anywhere but home tomorrow night."

I hesitantly nodded in agreement.

"You should get to sleep. Your very first service is tomorrow. Don't want to screw that up or there won't be enough whiskey in the world for Uncle Stanley." He patted me to let me know he was joking, but he wasn't. Tomorrow was the real deal. No more practice.

"Alright. Goodnight." He hugged me and went to bed.

After a long hour of imagining the break in and the impending funeral, I began to doze off. When I thought about the hours of talking, I realized that this was the first interaction with a man that was loving and sincere, where I could be who I was without judgment or expectation. I also realized I hadn't gotten my question in about Celia.

Chapter Ten

A Funeral

I awakened in a sweat with my heart racing. It was still dark outside, but after that dream there was no way I could fall back to sleep. Each time I started to doze off, the images started up right where they left off.

I was standing in the back of the chapel, and the pews were mostly empty. I looked around at the people sporadically seated throughout the chapel. It took me a moment to realize that they were all impossibly beautiful and young girls. I was immediately curious as to who was in that casket, and who would draw a crowd like this.

I casually made my way along the outside of the pews, pretending to check the tissue boxes.

I didn't recognize any of them, but the blond hair of the girl in the front pew caught my eye. It was very long and very straight and triggered a memory that brought the aching in my stomach front and center. I doubled over, trying to catch my breath - and then I saw it.

Clutched in her hands was a small, tattered and light blue, stuffed hippopotamus. It was Maddy's Hippo. The aching turned to violent fury when I recognized the girl from Jerry's studio holding *my* Maddy's Hippo. The urge to tear out her throat was overwhelming.

I moved along the pews, trying to get closer without drawing attention, though I knew in just a moment the scene would be out of control. As I maneuvered to the front, I was overcome with the need to laugh when I saw her hair streaked with green and yellow paint.

The humor only lasted a moment, and then I put the pieces together. Why would she be here? Who would she be here for? My attention suddenly shifted to the casket at the front of the room. It was up a few steps so I couldn't see inside. I decided that I would pretend to adjust the flower stands and move in closer.

The sickness returned in waves with every step. I worked my way through the flower arrangements until I was there – looking right down over Jerry. He was dressed only in board shorts, and he too was covered in green and yellow paint. This didn't make me laugh, because the knowledge of the cause of death hit me like a frying pan in the forehead. I had killed him, and with a frying pan. The circular marks were there on his forehead - the brand name barely visible between his eyes.

My knees went weak, and I lost my balance, but Merman was behind me, out of nowhere. He led me away, acting as normal as possible, but when we got outside of the chapel he had a creepy grin spread across his face.

"Relax, it's all over, Casey. Maddy's whole bedroom is upstairs now."

I was a murderer. The thought of Jerry dead by frying pan had crossed my mind so many times, but the reality of it shot a jolt of electricity through me, waking me with a shock that had me sitting straight up in bed.

It took me a few minutes to catch my breath and calm down. Dawn was breaking, and in just a few short hours I would be working my first funeral service. I shuddered and tried to think of other things to distract myself.

I started with the next indicated step. It always calmed me down when I planned. The first thing on the agenda was getting Maddy to her friend's house for a play date since she couldn't, nor did I want her to be around the service.

Luckily, since I had left Jerry, the staff and other mom's at the school had huddled around me and seemed excited and eager to help. A lot of them already knew a little bit about my life with him and couldn't wait to see me get out. I had been able to arrange for play dates with their kids and Maddy for when I had to work nights or weekends, and they all promised to plead ignorance should any of them run into Jerry.

The calm I had achieved by planning through my day was lost when I got to the part after the funeral service – the part where we broke into the house, and I possibly killed Jerry. It was useless, so I decided to just get up and get the day over with.

I had gotten back to the chapel just in time, after dropping Maddy off for her play date. I rushed into the chapel half an hour before the service was to begin and re-checked every pew for tissue and made sure the stereo was still ready to play.

I scrambled to get the flowers set up as Uncle Stanley followed close behind. He carried with him the stench of cigarettes. His suit jacket barely made it around his waist, and the rolls from his neck fell over his collar. I was finding it difficult to break my focus from these fascinating folds of flesh under his chin, when he caught me.

Ignoring his intimidating stare as best I could, I continued with my duties, making mental checks as I completed each one. I tried to avoid looking at the casket that was propped in the center of all of the flowers, but an overwhelming curiosity forced my eyes directly upon it. As I suspected, it wasn't Jerry.

The woman inside was sleeping, or at least it looked like she was sleeping. Her skin had a waxy, translucent quality to it, and the nauseating, chemical death smell grew as I stepped closer. Merman really had done her up well. Her hair and make-up were perfectly set, and I thought for a moment that she looked a lot like one of the women on a movie poster in his apartment.

People began to fill the chapel, sobbing and talking quietly amongst themselves. I couldn't help but feel like crying myself. It was so…sad. They looked like they truly loved and missed her. The tears began to well up, and as I turned around to excuse myself, Uncle Stanley was standing directly behind me. He looked at me condemningly as I wiped the tears from my eyes and walked to the back of the chapel.

The service began, and there were quiet sniffles throughout. I desperately tried to pull myself together, remembering Merman say *there won't be enough whiskey in the world for Uncle Stanley* if I messed this up.

I *was* very emotional, but it seemed silly that I was struggling to get control of myself. I considered what was wrong and realized that with everything that had happened in the last two weeks, I hadn't allowed myself to really feel anything or process through it. I had kept it together as long as I could, but it was starting to come out now.

A young man got up to say something nice about his mother in the casket, and as he choked over his tears to get through his first words, I teared up, and a whimper escaped my lips. Merman looked up in shock from across the room. Uncle Stanley hadn't noticed yet.

"What's wrong?" Merman mouthed to me.

I wiped my eyes and mouthed *I'm sorry*, but I had started something much worse. An older woman, who had come in late and was standing in the back, moved close to me and put her hand on my shoulder. She was consoling me as if I were a part of the family.

"We all loved Bertie dear, but she's in a better place now." The woman began hugging me and gently patting my back.

Merman froze, and then hesitated back and forth not knowing what would be better, going along with the scenario or whisking me out of the room.

Uncle Stanley stormed out of the chapel. Merman looked at me in frustration, raising his hands in the air as if giving up on the doomed situation. He left to go after Uncle Stanley, probably to try and diffuse him. I followed after as quickly as I could without upsetting the woman who was still clinging to me in comfort.

I made it out of the chapel and through the hallway when I realized they were headed toward the delivery door in the back. Merman looked confused as he tried to keep pace with Uncle Stanley, until he heard the very loud buzzer. I wondered who would be delivering flowers now when the service had already begun. Uncle Stanley rushed to the door to stop the persistent sound from disturbing the service.

When the door opened I could see the outline of a man standing in the doorway, looking around and taking note of his surroundings. The churning in my stomach came on fiercely when I saw the shoulder-length, wavy hair resting nicely on one of Jerry's fitted white t-shirts. He had black sunglasses perched atop his head, and he was chewing gum.

"Hey, man. How's it going?"

He looked back and forth from Merman to Uncle Stanley with a smirk. Neither moved or said a word but waited for some sort of explanation. I stayed around the corner, praying that he would disappear. How had he found me? I went over and over in my head all of the possibilities.

"I can't believe I'm about to ask this, but is there a gal named Casey staying here?"

He had one arm up on the doorway and was leaning lazily. Uncle Stanley shot Merman a harsh glance and stormed away, luckily in the opposite direction from me. My knees were wobbly, and I felt as if my executioner stood at the door, and Merman was my only hope of escape.

"Who are you?" Merman's tone hinted that he already had an idea, but wanted a formal answer. He took on a defensive stance, like my protector.

"Well, I'm guessing by your answer that she *is* here. I'm Jerry, Casey's husband."

He reached out his free hand, still leaning on the doorway and smiling through his unshaven face. Merman's entire body tensed up, but he carefully reached out and shook his hand anyway.

"I'm Merman. Let me see if I can get her for you." He turned and headed right toward me.

He nodded his head to the right, trying to get me to move further around the corner. When he reached me, he looked me in the eye, his brows furrowed with concern.

"What do you want me to do, Casey? Do you want me to tell him to leave? I can make him leave with one phone call."

His arms were now on my shoulders, trying to get a response out of me, but I was frozen in fear. I didn't know what to do. I *never* expected this. I had intentionally avoided this very moment, even the very thought of this moment.

Merman shook my shoulders. "Casey! What do you want me to do?"

"I'll go talk to him," I decided, with great hesitation.

The words came out in a weak whimper, and as soon as I spoke, the gut wrenching ache returned and doubled me over again.

"Casey, forget it. I'm going to tell him to leave."

Those words were everything I wanted to hear, but I knew that it had to be dealt with eventually. Jerry would keep coming, at the most inopportune times as possible, to get what he wanted. I had to end it now. I was bracing myself against the wall, trying to think through the panic.

"No! I have to do this," I insisted.

Merman's teeth were grinding harder as I spoke, but he yielded.

"Just go out there and tell him to leave you alone, and if he won't listen to you, I'll tell him myself." His eyes were narrowed, and his long arms were folded across his chest.

I nodded, weakly.

"I'm going to try and assess the damage with Uncle Stanley. I don't know how much he saw of your…well, your outburst in the chapel before Gerardo over there started in with the buzzer. I'll be right back."

I laughed at the nickname for Jerry, but it came out as a frightened whimper.

I looked at Merman for a minute, trying to gather as much courage as I could from his intensity, and then walked toward the back door.

Jerry was still leaning in the doorway, looking around and flipping his air. He began to laugh as I approached hesitantly.

"Baby, what are you doing here? I followed you from school a few times last week. Is this where you're shacked up now?"

His laughter enraged me.

"What do you want, Jerry?"

"I want you to come home." He stopped laughing and put on the face of repentance.

"Jerry, it's over. You need to leave now."

I grabbed the door to close it, but he put his shoe in the way to block it.

"Stop it, Casey." His voice and face hardened. "You and Maddy are coming home."

I was slightly frightened by his vicious tone and angry expression. I had never pushed this hard for anything, and it had obviously rattled him.

"You're not listening to me. It's over. I'm done. I'm moving on, and so should you."

Again, I tried to close the door, but this time he pushed it open with his hand. The force of the door made me stumble backward slightly, but he didn't seem apologetic at all.

"You're making a big mistake. You know some people might consider this an inappropriate and harmful environment to raise a child in. You should think about that, Casey. Someone might start asking whether you're fit to be a parent." His calculating smile returned, and my blood seemed to boil just beneath my skin

"You wouldn't dare!" The disorienting and violent feeling I'd had before I shoved him at the house had returned and doubled.

"Wouldn't I?" he challenged.

He was leaning on the doorway again, with a wicked smirk.

"Maddy's happier here than I've ever seen her before. She doesn't even ask about you, Jerry. What might some people think about that?"

He didn't seem bothered at all, like this was just a game to him, a game that he wanted to win. He leaned in toward me, narrowed his eyes, and clenched his teeth.

"Get your ass out here right now, Casey, before I take you out myself."

I was shocked and a bit concerned by his threat. I instinctively took a step back, and he began to reach for me through the door.

Before I could respond, Merman came from around the corner, walking forcefully toward Jerry. Jerry didn't move from the doorway, but perched himself in a defensive position, ready to fight. I was horrified, trying to imagine Merman fighting anything. Jerry was a thug and would make sure he left an impression. I couldn't stand by and watch that happen. I wouldn't let Merman sacrifice anything else for me.

I started to turn to put myself between Jerry and the oncoming Merman when, out of nowhere, Eddie was running down the hallway, just feet behind Merman. His run was impossibly absurd. He looked like a cartoon character, like he was trying to imitate the Road Runner in slow motion. I heard Jerry spit out a laugh and take one step closer. Eddie came closer but didn't slow down. He ran right to the doorway and let out a loud shriek just inches from Jerry's face. Jerry stumbled back in confusion, and Merman slammed the door.

We all stood there quietly for a few seconds. I was in shock, trying to wrap my mind around what I had just seen. Eddie looked as if he had just done something as normal as taking in a flower delivery. He dusted of his hands and bowed himself out. Merman's eyes were on me, waiting for my reaction. From outside, Jerry's muffled voice was yelling. I leaned my ear to the door to listen. Merman did the same.

"Don't get too cozy in bed at night, baby, 'cause I'll be watching you. You will come home to me, one way or another – in one piece or as many as it takes. The only thing separating us is a door, Casey. Don't you think I can get through a door?"

Shivers ran up my back, and my knees buckled beneath me. I had never had my life threatened before, but this sounded real. I didn't know what Jerry was capable of anymore. I listened again, but he was gone.

I was terrified and nearly hyperventilating. The irregular palpitations of my heart hit me hard. I suddenly felt like I had run up ten flights of stairs. I couldn't catch my breath, and I was starting to see black spots.

"Are you okay? What's going on?" Merman asked with concern.

He looked truly worried, and I could only imagine how I looked as I struggled to get air into my lungs. I was a mess enough without heaping a heart problem onto it. I had made the mistake of thinking it would be one more reason for him to have turned us away. Now I realized I should have told him.

He helped me to the floor.

"I have a…little…heart problem. I'll be…fine."

His eyes bulged, and he tried to get me to sit.

"A *little* heart problem? Is there such a thing as a *little* heart problem? I think I need to get you to a hospital."

That was the last thing I needed. Where would Maddy go?

"I'm fine…Merman. I just…need…a minute." I tried slowing my breaths, concentrating on the sounds as they went in my nose and out of my mouth.

"Seriously, Casey, let's go." He tried to get a hold of my arm, but I batted him away with what little energy I had left.

"I've seen…them all…Merman. I'm fine. It's…him I need…to worry about." I pointed toward the delivery door like a drunken person. I felt so weak, much worse than I had with any previous episode. I panicked for a second, wondering what would happen to Maddy if I suddenly died of heart failure.

"Relax, Casey, relax. He's not getting anywhere near you while we're here." He ran his hand along the top of my head and down the back of my hair. He was kneeling on the floor next to me where my life was taking a frightening turn before me.

"What have I done?" I barely choked the words out. "Look at what I've…gotten you into." I was so ashamed of the mess I had created, knowing what Merman would have to deal with later.

"Casey, please. I'm a big boy. The only thing you've gotten me into is some 'splainin to do with Uncle Stanley." He tried to do a Ricky Ricardo impersonation. It made me smile, but it couldn't melt the ice that was forming all over me. I was trembling.

"I need a minute…to get it together. I'll be back…in the chapel in a minute." The least I could do was put on a good show for Uncle Stanley and hopefully get us through his first glass of whisky.

"Forget the service, Casey, just go back to the apartment and relax. I have a feeling that it would be better if you lay low for the rest of the afternoon."

The shame came back like a heavy blanket. It couldn't have gone any worse. I imagined there was probably no way for Merman to get me out of this one, maybe not even himself. I wondered how much of the altercation was heard from inside the chapel.

Merman started to help me up, and I could tell that I was still in shock. I could barely hold myself up, and as I tried to speak, my words were weak and broken. My heart rate had slowed back to its regular rhythm, and I was left feeling like those people who are wobbling their way to the finish line of a marathon.

"I'm sorry, Merman." I leaned against his shoulder for support. The idea of this being the end of the road here was too much. If Uncle Stanley had his way, I'd be out of here by morning.

"Just go rest. I'll take care of this." He pointed me toward the hallway that led to his apartment, and after making sure I could stand on my own, he headed in the opposite direction toward the chapel.

I started off toward the hallway, and just before I turned the corner, I caught a strong whiff of cigarettes not far away. I peeked around the corner to see Uncle Stanley storming his way in my direction, probably looking for Merman.

Without a plan of where to hide, I turned and ran down the hallway and slipped into the first door I came to. I landed in the hallway that led to the embalming room. I carefully and quietly closed the sliding door and slowly slid down the wall as my emotions got the better of me again.

I didn't know if Jerry was serious, but I knew he had never had to fight me on anything like this before. I had never seen him pushed, so I had nothing to compare it to. I thought about him trying to take Maddy from me, and it sent shivers up my spine again. The thought was terrifying.

I looked around and tried to imagine what people would really think about the lifestyle I had Maddy living in. Didn't love and happiness count for anything? Wasn't this far better than the home she had before?

As I compared the two scenarios and flashed back to Eddie shrieking at Jerry, and the shock on Jerry's face, I laughed through my tears and grew confident about my decision. The people we were surrounded by were certainly odd, but they weren't threatening my life, and they truly cared about my daughter. There was no comparison.

I heard Uncle Stanley pacing about in the hallway, muttering under his breath what sounded like profanity. With nowhere else to go, I quickly but quietly slipped into the embalming room. The noise the door made was infinitesimal, and I was pretty confident that I had gone unnoticed.

Considering the current circumstances, I didn't care that the poor, waxy woman had been in here an hour ago. I didn't care that the smell was nauseating. I closed the door behind me and put my face in my hands, quietly contemplating through silent tears.

I didn't notice right away that I wasn't alone in the room. There was a man on one of the slabs in a gown. Eddie must have picked him up in the middle of the night.

When I saw him lying there, I was startled. I hadn't actually seen any friends in this room before. The startle turned to a tragic sadness as I realized he was very young, maybe thirty. And he was beautiful.

He drew me in.

Without a second thought, I was inching closer to him. The emptiness that had surrounded me when I approached the woman in the chapel was not present. I felt his life pulsing around me, as if he were still there.

He had dark, cocoa brown hair and perfectly shaped features. His soft, pink lips and smooth tanned skin were inviting. I was mesmerized and couldn't stop staring. He truly didn't look dead. I marveled at what I thought was the best make-up job I had ever seen. He didn't even look waxy like the poor woman in the other room. My respect for Merman's artistic talent doubled.

I moved closer and circled the slab in a trance. His muscular arms rested at his side, and I followed the length of them up to his neck, which I had an unshakeable urge to touch. I wanted to feel for a pulse and the stubble just below his jaw line.

I wanted to know his story, know everything about him. I was shocked by the instantaneous connection I felt. I reminded myself that he was dead, and the sadness replaced the attraction momentarily, but I didn't want to leave.

I worked my way around the other side of the slab, taking it all in. I noticed that he was wearing what looked like a hospital gown. I went over in my head all of the possibilities that could have led him here. There weren't any obvious injuries.

The curiosity was overwhelming. I wanted to look more - see if there was any trauma underneath his gown that would explain his cause of death. It was on backward, with the opening in the front. I looked around the room and back at the gown. I felt like a criminal as I contemplated peeking underneath it – just to see. It was too tempting. I slowly reached out and began to lift the opening when the body shot up with a gasp.

I screamed in horror and jumped back. He yelled in shocked response. We both continued to scream at each other until I ran from the room, terrified, and smacked into Merman in the hall. My momentum almost took us both to the ground.

"Merman, there's a dead…there's something…he's alive." I couldn't catch my breath, or explain what I had just seen. I was sure that I had just seen his ghost and offended him so deeply that he had risen from his body in protest. Either that or Eddie had taken the wrong body from the hospital without checking for a pulse first.

I was in shock again. My hands and feet were frozen, and I was so dizzy that I had to slide down the wall again to keep myself from fainting. Merman looked at me, entirely perplexed, and then opened the door to look in. He came back out, kneeling down to put both hands on my shoulders to calm me. He looked like he was trying to hold back a smile, or even hysterical laughter. Was he insane? Was I insane?

"Casey….," he could no longer hold back the laughter to finish what he was going to say. "Are you okay?"

I nodded since I didn't have the words. It took him a minute to contain himself, which was infuriating me. What was so funny?

"Casey…that was Oliver."

The new and confusing information lessened the anger slightly, but now I was mortified, feeling like I was on the outside of a really bad inside joke – and I still didn't get it. Merman could tell.

"Oliver works with us on the weekends when we have friends."

I was growing more flustered and embarrassed at the thought of what I had done. I was attempting to look at the naked body of someone

I would have to face every weekend for who knew how long. And then, I was furious again.

"Why was he on the…why was he wearing that gown?" I wasn't able to clearly state my questions before Oliver stumbled out of the embalming room in khaki pants and an unbuttoned shirt, barely on. I was so humiliated that I couldn't look at him. I literally hid my face in my hands, between my knees, like a child. I could see his untied shoes cautiously approaching me, and I just wished I could be in a casket. This day was *never* going to end, and it apparently wasn't going to get any better either.

"I'm sorry for that back there. It must have seemed…um, kind of strange," Oliver offered apologetically.

He paused, seeming to wait for my response. My head felt like iron, so heavy that I couldn't imagine ever lifting it. I knew my blood was circulating again because the heat in my face had intensified when he began speaking to me. I couldn't just sit there and ignore him. I'd have to stand up and try and live through the humiliation. I adjusted myself to stand, and Merman quickly helped me up.

"I'm Oliver." He nervously reached out his hand to me.

I didn't know what to say. He was more beautiful standing there in front of me than before when I had…I remembered again, with great agony, what I had been ready to do, and the rush of blood hit my head again. The anger returned, and I felt like a fool. Why had he been lying there…in a gown? He continued to patiently hold his hand out in front of me, but I only glared at him and walked away.

I heard Merman burst into laughter as I turned the corner. I hurried into the apartment and grabbed my purse and keys, desperate to leave and only too happy to get Maddy early.

That night, after Merman encouraged whiskey and smoothed things over with Uncle Stanley, he came into the chapel where I was collecting cards from the flowers, and Maddy was pretending to be a speaker at an important gathering.

"You doing okay?" he asked. I looked up with a lingering blush and continued with my task. "Well, it couldn't get any worse than today, right?" He walked over and hugged me, and after a little stubborn resistance, I sank into his arms. He chuckled and then stood me back as if to address an important issue.

Chapter Eleven

Espionage

"So, Eddie and Celia have the vans and walkie talkies ready to go. Maddy can stay in the car with Celia." Merman listed off as he paced about doing a mental checklist.

I couldn't believe what I was hearing, but he was dead serious as he spoke. I pulled him aside to avoid Maddy overhearing.

"Merman! You can't be serious. After today, can't you tell that Jerry is more than ready for a fight? He *wants* one!" I reminded him.

He looked past me as I talked, obviously still planning.

"Merman!" He took his hand down from his chin and looked at me in confusion, having heard nothing that I said. "He'll kill me!" I whispered forcefully.

He waved his hand dismissively and exhaled, frustrated by the interruption.

"He's not killing anyone, Casey. He's just a bully, and like most bullies he's mostly talk. Besides," he looked at me with a sly smile, "there will be four of us and one of him."

He wasn't taking this as seriously as he should, and it was starting to irritate me.

"Five of us," I corrected him. "No one was available for a sleep over." I nodded toward Maddy. "I can't bring her, Merman." He ignored me, pacing back and forth.

"She's safer with us anyway," he concluded. "Wouldn't you rather her be with us than wondering if she's safe the whole time?" I considered his logic. It was frustratingly sound. I would rather her be safe, with us close by. But I couldn't stand the thought of her being there if Jerry showed up. He interrupted my thoughts. "She'll stay with Celia in the van. It will be fine." Celia had come in and nodded in agreement.

"This is ridiculous, Merman!" I tried again. Again, he ignored me.

"Do you have black clothes? We don't want to stand out."

"Merman!"

"Casey?" He stared me down, and I could tell that he would have a quick response to anything I threw at him. "We're going to *your* house, to get *your* things. She'll be safe with us there. What is the problem?" he challenged, with a slightly perturbed tone.

Now I was the one pacing and panicking.

"We have plenty of stuff upstairs already. I don't want anyone getting hurt over this," I confessed, hoping for a take back on the agreement I had made the night before. I knew I couldn't bear to see someone hurt, and with a little booze in Jerry, it was more than likely. My only hope was to convince Merman of it before he had us all in the van.

He tilted his head to the side and contemplated his question carefully before he asked. A dark look came over his face, which made goose bumps rise all over me.

"I've been living around death most of my life. Do you think I'm afraid of Jerry?"

I tried to swallow over the lump that was growing in my throat. I hadn't seen or ever expected this side of him.

"I've known a few Jerry's in my lifetime, suffered enough by people like him. But when you've looked death in the face and accepted its inevitability, people like him," he said through his teeth, "make people like me want to set things straight in the world, show him his proper place in it."

Again the lump grew, and again I wanted to know more about Merman - the little boy Merman who I guessed had been hurt many times over. The darkness that had come over his face passed, and he was sweet Merman again, but I would never forget it.

I'd had the same thought as him though- that in light of death and even Uncle Stanley, Jerry was nothing. Merman watched as I gained conviction and surrendered to the plan.

"So go get changed and we'll meet in the garage." He gave me a wink and it made me feel better. I trusted him, my dark knight.

Maddy and I were dressed head to toe in black. I felt ridiculous and terribly negligent for involving Maddy. I tried to convince myself that she was better off close to us and that Jerry was holding *our* things hostage and that we were simply on a rescue mission. I liked that version of reality, and I didn't seem to be the only one who believed it either. When we stepped into the garage, everyone was buzzing around getting ready.

Eddie was over the top, as seemed usual for him, with black paint under his eyes and a face mask ready to go. Celia was also dressed in black and was testing out some wireless headset connected to the walkie talkies. Eddie kept saying "testing, testing, testing" over and over. She was toying with him and pretending she couldn't hear him, though he was five feet away. I tried not to laugh out loud.

Merman wasn't kidding about Eddie. He *did* look like he lived for these moments. Celia seemed more businesslike, while enjoying her teasing. She acted like this was just another part of the job, but I suspected it was more of a favor for Merman. Her eyes followed him as he loaded the van with dollies and flash lights. She lit up every time they made eye contact.

I wasn't sure how I would feel about them when I saw it for myself, but I was surprised to feel happy. I caught Merman smiling to himself a few times, and I knew he felt the same way for her.

As Maddy and I waited through the preparations, I scanned the garage. It was huge, almost the entire length of the building. There were two vans, two hearses, a fancy town car, and still room for a delivery dock. Aside from the size of it, it was just a normal garage - nothing too mortuary-ish about it. But tonight it felt a little more sinister with all of the plotting involved within its walls.

Eddie was now involved in some sort of warm up routine as he punched and kicked at the air and practiced what looked like the attack moves of a pouncing cat. Again, I tried not to laugh, but Maddy was not as successful. Eddie heard the giggle and stopped, not because he was insulted by it, but because he had been interrupted and now had to start from the beginning.

Celia was with Merman, doing some kind of inventory check off of a list that he held. When they were finished, Merman stated loudly enough for everyone to hear, "We're ready. Let's go."

"Yes!" Eddie exclaimed as he pulled a fist into his side. The adrenaline flowing from him was contagious. I suddenly had butterflies.

"Mommy, where are we going?" A stab of shame shot through me. What was I doing?

"Maddy," Merman was kneeling down to her eye level, "we're going to get all of your toys and bring them back home!"

"Really?" Maddy jumped up and down and then hugged Merman. Of course *she* wouldn't see anything wrong with this. He glanced at me and seeing my discomfort, furrowed his brows at me.

"*Your* house, *your* things, remember?" I took a deep breath and nodded.

"Yep."

It took us no more than 30 minutes to get there with Eddie and Merman leading the way and Celia keeping pace. Maddy and I sat on the bench seat with her. I preferred her sober presence to Eddie's maniacal twitchings.

We pulled up the street and parked in the shadows of the tall trees, about four houses up. I could hear Merman through Celia's headset, asking whether or not I could tell if he was home. His car wasn't in the driveway, but it could have been in the garage. He usually kept all the lights on when he was home, and it looked dark inside, except for one light coming from the kitchen.

"I can't tell for sure."

"She's not sure." She waited for a response.

"You're up." Merman's voice was calm and deliberate. Celia unbuckled her seatbelt.

"I'll be right back."

The plan was for Celia to ring the doorbell and pretend to be selling restaurant coupons. The hope was that she wouldn't have to go through with the whole façade, but she had her lines down perfectly just in case. If he was home, we'd wait a while to see if he left and come back another night if need be.

If he didn't answer, Eddie was prepared to scale the back wall and check every window for signs of *the target*, as he had called Jerry. It made me nervous. I thought our furniture was the target. Maybe my dark knight was darker than I thought. Maybe my nightmare was a premonition, and I was merely an accomplice, but Merman had promised that if Jerry was home, we would leave as planned.

If all was quiet, then I would first try my key, which I was sure wouldn't work by now. If and when it didn't work, I would use the sliding window by the dining room. The handle was broken, and I could wiggle the lock loose. This was something I had learned on tutoring days when Jerry wanted to keep me out. I doubted he knew about it.

Merman had mumbled something about another plan, but I didn't want to know, so I stopped listening.

We watched as Celia approached the front door and rang the bell. I cringed at the thought of having to watch Jerry harass Celia like the pig that he was and feared that this might give Merman an excuse to go after *the target*. She rang the bell about three times in a few minutes, and there was no response. She headed back to the van and hopped in.

"Eddie, you're up." She spoke lightly into the earpiece. I could hear Eddie respond because he was nearly yelling.

"I told you to call me night hawk!"

She giggled and responded, "You're up night jock." She turned it down before he could respond.

We all laughed as "night hawk" conspicuously ducked and weaved across the street and paused behind each tree with his night goggles on. He made it to the back wall and awkwardly stumbled over it.

The laughing stopped. I was suddenly terrified about a possible altercation and what that would mean for the rest of us. It seemed like Celia was thinking the same thing. I wondered if she resented me for putting her…and Merman in this situation.

"Thanks for helping, Celia."

She didn't respond right away. She seemed to think over her answer first.

"Merman wants to look after you. He doesn't like seeing people mistreated. He's kind of sensitive about injustice in the world. But there's definitely something about you that…" She stopped and looked out the window contemplating. "I'd do anything for Merman…and it seems like Merman would do anything for you."

I could hear the disappointment in her voice, but she had it all wrong. Merman had just taken pity on me, and by all means he was unusually generous, but I saw the way he looked at her. She smiled and shook off whatever she was thinking.

"I'm glad to help, Casey."

"Celia, it's not like that. I'm just a charity case. I'm certainly thankful for that, but that's all it is, I swear. Besides, I'm still married to Geraldo in there, remember?" I teased.

She smiled at the joke, but I could see her confidence waiver.

"I've seen how he looks at you, Celia." I leaned forward to watch her expression.

"Really?" she asked with a hint of longing in her voice.

It was obvious that whatever it was between them, it hadn't been confirmed on either end. I was going to have to get to Merman and figure out why he was stalling with this. I'd answered all of his questions. It was his turn.

"Really!" I confirmed.

She shyly looked down and away, but I could tell she was happy about this news. We were quiet for a few minutes, and I was getting unbearably nervous about Eddie slinking around. We hadn't heard a thing from him. I decided to keep the conversation going to distract us.

"So how long have you been working with Merman?" I had broken her thoughtful gaze.

"Oh, about six months." Her answer seemed to bring back the uncertainty, as if something should have happened in that amount of time. Six months wasn't long though, and Merman was very old-fashioned. I doubted dating a co-worker was high on his list or easy to get past Uncle Stanley with just a little liquor.

"What about Eddie?" I asked, attempting to change the subject.

"He's been here for years. All he needs is a bell tower, and he'd never leave." We both snickered, but quietly because Maddy was beginning to fall asleep.

I had an idea.

"I want you to come over for dinner with us. How about tomorrow night?" I plotted.

She shook her head. "I don't know, Casey. I don't want him to think…"

I cut her off. "He won't think anything. You're *my* friend and I'm inviting you."

She gave another shy smile at my use of the word friend.

"It's been six months, Casey, and he's never invited me over. It would just be awkward."

"Merman's done enough saving. It's time someone saved him…from himself. He just needs a little push in the right direction. I'm sure he's just nervous about Uncle Stanley, but he's getting a lot of practice with that, thank you very much." I bowed to her, and we both laughed again, but were interrupted through her earpiece.

"It looks like no one's home. You're up, Casey." She winked and reached into a backpack to grab something. "Merman wants you to have these with you." First she handed me a flashlight and then some piece of electrical equipment I had never seen before.

"What is this?" I almost didn't want to know.

She shook her head and laughed. "It's a taser."

I gasped. "What do I need with a taser?" Before I finished the question, I already knew the answer.

"Merman said something about Gerardo." She smiled and fought back a laugh.

"Oh."

She took it from me and held it away from her to demonstrate.

"Just hold it up to him and pull this trigger right here."

She made it seem so simple and harmless. I had seen what they did to people the one or two times I had watched *Cops*. I shuddered at the thought but figured it would be better than a frying pan.

Both vans backed into the driveway, and I heard Merman's door close and the back of his van open.

"Okay, Casey," Celia started to review the plan, "I'll be out here with Maddy and Oliver, and…" I jumped when I heard his name and flushed with embarrassment.

"Oliver!" I turned my shout into a whisper when I realized he was getting out of Merman's van. "What is he doing here?" I insisted in a panic.

He must have gotten into their van while we were all loading. I remembered wondering what the hold up was about. Merman probably snuck him in, knowing that I would protest.

Celia laughed and shook her head. "I heard about what happened earlier. Be honest with me, Casey, were you trying to get a peek at his peter?"

"Oh my gosh! So that's the rumor going around? I'm a perv? I can't get out of this car! I can't see him again!"

She couldn't stop laughing, and I was contemplating using the taser on myself.

"No, that's not the rumor, but that's what I would've been looking for."

"So what is the rumor?" I asked. Maybe it was a little less humiliating than her version.

"Well, the way he tells it, it's all his fault and he's the one embarrassed. But when he mentioned you messing with his gown, I drew my own conclusions. I don't blame you, he's a looker."

"Celia, I wasn't…" she put her hand up to stop me.

"I'm not judging, sister, just let me have my version. Now, Merman and Eddie will be loading up with you, and Oliver will be on the lookout with me. I'll let you know if I see Cherry Garcia out here." She waited for me to move. "It'll be fine, Casey. Go." She patted my shoulder and gave me a nudge toward the door. There was nothing I wanted less than to see Oliver right now.

When I got out, Merman was waiting with an impatiently excited look across his face. I glared at him, and he apparently knew why. He fought back a guilty smirk and put his arm around me.

"He wanted to help, Casey. Give him a break. He feels bad."

I looked over and Oliver was keeping himself busy and out of my way.

"I guess," I conceded.

I figured that if he was willing to show up to this circus, he didn't think I was a total loser yet. Why did I even care? He was undeniably gorgeous and proved to be a smidge heroic by showing up, but…

Merman interrupted me. "Are you ready?" He grabbed my arm and practically dragged me to the front door. "We don't have all night,

Casey. As much as I'd like bury Jerry a piece at a time over the next ten funeral services, I'd rather just get your stuff and go." He smiled to let me know he was half joking.

"Ugh! I don't even want to know what you're talking about! And what is *this*!" I pulled out the taser, and his laugh in response was sinister.

"I really am trying very hard not to pre-plan his funeral, Casey. It would help me out if you would cooperate. *That* won't kill him, but *I* might if he touches you."

"Well, he's not here, so take it." I pushed it toward him, but he pushed it back.

"He's not here *yet*. Let's go."

Chapter Twelve

Shocking

The thought of Jerry coming home in the middle of this operation was making me jumpy. We got to the front door, and to our surprise, my key worked, though it took a few tries because my hands were shaky. The whole thing seemed too easy, but Merman chalked it up to Jerry's fatal arrogance. His choice of words were beginning to concern me.

"He doesn't think you'd dare, Casey," he concluded.

"Whatever. Let's go," I replied flatly.

It was too late to analyze Jerry's behaviors. We were in, and I quickly gave directions around the house. Merman went straight to Maddy's room, while Eddie and I went to mine. Merman had stocked up on boxes, and our objective was to box and move as many of our personal things as we could in an hour, though my idea was to take as little as possible so that Jerry wouldn't notice anything missing right away.

Eddie started putting the nightstand on the dolly.

"What are you doing, Eddie?" I snapped.

"Merman says everything goes."

"What?"

He ignored my outraged burst and kept loading up everything he could…lamps, pictures, toilet paper, pills out of the medicine cabinet. Jerry *was* going to kill me. I ran to find Merman before this went too far. He had already taken apart Maddy's bed and was rolling it out toward the door.

"Merman, this is crazy. He's going to know I was here!"

"Yep." He shrugged me off and kept rolling.

"Were you there when he threatened my life? Did you forget about that part? And that was before I robbed his house!"

"Keep packing, Casey." He rolled right out of the door.

"So this is it then. It's war," I yelled after him, but it was really to myself.

I was numb and a little dizzy. It was worse than when I walked out on my father. My father couldn't take Maddy from me, but Jerry would try. I stood frozen in the living room, going over all of the possible acts of retribution he might come up with. I snapped out of it when Merman shook me.

"It's always been war, Casey - you're just starting to fight back. Are you going to fight back? Aren't you done yet?"

It didn't take long for the answer to come - I *was* done. The bomb had been dropped – might as well loot the place.

"You're right. I want my grandma's china hutch and the flat screen in the living room."

"Whoo!" Merman yelled.

He hugged me fiercely and looked at me with excitement and admiration. It felt good.

After forty-five minutes, we had packed up more than half of the house including dishes, hangers, and even the food out of the fridge. I didn't want it, but Merman was determined to make a point.

"Well, I would say we divvied things up pretty equally here. Jerryatrics can enjoy his half…for now."

I was too exhausted to read into that one.

We headed toward the door, with a high I had never known, and I was prepared to leave and never look back when, like in a nightmare, Jerry's voice pierced through me. We ran outside to see him walking toward the house and swearing, obviously drunk.

"Who the hell are you?" He stood on the sidewalk and looked around at the vans and then at me. "So you're back – and you brought your friends to watch."

With that, Merman walked toward him violently. I was terrified of seeing him get hurt.

"Merman, NO!" I ran to him and grabbed his arm, trying to pull him back.

"What are you going to do Mer-Man? She's mine, and I'll get her if I have to go through you."

Jerry took off his shirt and threw his watch and wallet to the ground. I wrestled with Merman but quickly let go and grabbed for the taser as Jerry approached.

Before either of us could react, the van door flew open and hit Jerry hard. As he stumbled to catch his balance, Oliver grabbed around his throat and held tight. Jerry fought and jerked as we all watched, stunned.

After about ten seconds, Oliver laid him down on the ground, clearly unconscious.

"That's awesome!" Eddie leaned over Jerry, shaking his head. He then proceeded to attempt a super high five with Oliver. Oliver's disinterest coupled with Eddie's eagerness, made for the most awkward high fiving I'd ever seen.

"He'll be out for a few minutes, so we'd better finish up." Oliver glanced at me with a look of concern. "Are you okay?"

"I…I'm fine. Thank you…I mean for stopping him like that." Seeing Jerry on the ground was still surprising…and oddly satisfying. "What about you? I mean, are you okay?" The way he held my gaze made me feel a little wobbly. I had to look away.

"I'm fine. But *he'll* have quite a headache when he wakes up. What do you want to do with him?" He was asking me, but Merman decided.

"We can't leave him in the driveway like this. Eddie, help me pull him inside."

Eddie happily grabbed one arm, while Merman grabbed the other and pulled. They pulled his limp body all the way up the driveway, over the front step, and through the door. As they passed the threshold, we heard a thump and then a chuckle as Merman said, "Oops."

Celia laughed out loud, and Oliver seemed to be trying to hold his back. He cleared his throat and straightened his face when he saw that I was still shocked over the whole scene. When Jerry woke up, there would be hell to pay, this I knew for certain. I didn't know what to do exactly, but I wanted to leave things as cleaned up as possible. It was getting messy.

I followed in after Merman, with Oliver close behind.

Merman and Eddie had left Jerry in the middle of the half empty living room and were checking around to make sure we hadn't left any blatant evidence of the rest of them being there. I was becoming paranoid and started frantically wiping down doorknobs and drawer handles with a towel.

"Casey, what are you doing?" Merman stopped me mid-wipe. "The FBI won't be involved here. You can leave the fingerprints."

I was beginning to have another episode of palpitations as the hard reality of the night began to sink in. I looked at Jerry, sprawled out on the floor, and I suddenly couldn't catch my breath. It was too late to undo any of this.

"What are…we going to…do? We can't…leave him…here. He's…going …to…KILL…me!"

I couldn't get a complete sentence out without gasping for air. I started to feel faint and lost my balance. Merman grabbed under my arms and helped me to the floor, uncomfortably close to Jerry. I was beginning to see black spots again as I tried to look closely at his face to see if he was still alive. Oliver was kneeling in front of me, holding my face with both hands.

"Casey, I need you to breathe through your nose. Take a deep breath." I could hear him, but I was definitely losing my vision as the black spots filled the scene before me.

"Casey, breathe with me. Breathe in…good, now breathe out." I was trying to follow the rhythm of *his* breathing. It was all I could hear anymore. His gentle hands held my face, and then one moved to my wrist, keeping time. My breathing started to slow, and I could smell him, the musky and insanely sexy smell of cologne and sweat. I could feel the warmth of his breath, and I knew he was just inches away. I didn't want to move, and not because these episodes drained me of all energy, but because I wanted nothing more than to stay right there, with Oliver close enough to breathe in.

"Casey? Are you okay?" Merman was right next to me. "Oliver, we have to leave before he wakes up."

Hearing his name made me more alert. I opened my eyes to his looking intently at me. He was still inches away, and my heart was fluttering again. He smiled gently and took both of my hands to help me up. We stood there, looking at each other, him helping me get my balance, me overwhelmed with desire and a rush of blood to the head.

"Do you feel dizzy?" He leaned in closer, furrowing his brow as he checked my eyes.

I felt something, but it wasn't just dizzy. I remembered we weren't alone and looked over to see Merman, Eddie, and Celia staring at us. That was enough to snap me out of it. Celia had a smile across her face that told me I would have to talk about this moment the entire ride home, and Merman tilted his head to the side with a sly smirk. I took my hands out of Oliver's.

"I'm fine…I'm sorry. Let's get out of here." My breath still fought to catch up with my heart, but I wanted out of there before Jerry woke up and struck back.

We all headed for the door in awkward silence, and then I remembered the sliding door. I wanted to cover all of my tracks.

"I'll be right there. I just have to make sure the door is closed." I hurried back through the living room, carefully maneuvering past Jerry to check the door. I secured the latch and looked around one last time before heading out. I moved as quickly as I could past his body, but before I made it halfway, I felt a tight grip around my ankle. I screamed out in shock and tried to pull away, but landed hard on the floor. It was Jerry, and he was pulling me toward him to get a better grip. The look on his face was one of sloppy fury.

"Where do you think you're going, doll?" he slurred.

He pulled harder and had me halfway under him. He reeked of liquor and sweat. I struggled to pull away, but even though he was drunk, he was stronger than me. He grabbed for my arms, but I pulled one away and reached for the taser in my jacket pocket. I yanked to get it out while I kicked as hard as I could. He was too heavy, and there was no way I would get him off of me. I held the gun to his neck and pulled the trigger. He froze up instantly and started jerking.

I scrambled to stand up, and Oliver and Merman were suddenly at my side, as shocked as Jerry was. Merman looked down at my hand, which was still clinging to the taser.

"Thank god!" he sighed.

I looked down to see my knuckles white from the grasp I had on it. I dropped it to the floor and waited for a resurgence of the palpitations to follow the shock. I had just tazed my deadbeat husband after robbing my house. I tried to think of all the reasons why this *wouldn't* land me in jail with some lumberjack of a cellmate.

Eddie came running in holding a bottle and whispering to Merman.

"What do you think, Oliver?" Merman showed Oliver the bottle.

"I found it in her cabinet." Eddie glanced at me with just a hint of remorse.

"Combined with the amount of alcohol I'm assuming he's had tonight, the Ativan will keep him out 'till morning. Another bonus is that he probably won't remember most of what happened tonight."

"We're going to drug him too? We're all going to jail, you know this right?" I argued in a panic.

Merman and Eddie chuckled, and Oliver, once again, turned his head so as not to laugh in my face.

"Casey, he won't remember anything. And what is he going to do, tell the cops that his wife came home and took her stuff? This," Merman held the bottle up and shook it, "is the best find of the night." If I had any adrenaline left, I would have wrestled him to the floor, but as things stood, this looked like our best option.

"Put it under his tongue." Oliver instructed Merman on the proper administration of the Ativan that I had left over from a trip to the dentist. I was beginning to wonder about the amount of medical knowledge he had and why he was wasting it, on weekends, at a funeral home.

Merman and Eddie pulled Jerry up into a chair and leaned him over to one side so he wouldn't slump forward. Merman squeezed his cheeks together to get his mouth open and put the pill under his tongue. He cringed at the smell emanating from Jerry's mouth.

"He's rotten!" he gagged out, looking away to catch his breath.

Eddie was back with a glass, which he had just finished the contents of, and placed it in one of Jerry's hands on the armrest.

"It's whiskey." He wiped his mouth with his sleeve and stood back to observe his work.

"Nice touch, Eddie. He's going to be putting the pieces together for a while." Merman slapped him on the back. "Well, it looks like our work here is finished. Shall we?" He motioned toward the door.

I was more than ready to leave. The night left me drained, and all I wanted to do was safely sleep it off while Jerry remained in a drug induced slumber.

Celia was in the car, impatiently waiting to hear what had happened. Maddy was asleep across the seat and all of our belongings loaded in the vans. Merman quickly filled Celia in, and we were on our way.

The drive home seemed to go by quickly, and I had many questions I wanted answered. Celia had been driving with a grin on her face for five minutes. I knew what she was thinking, and I wanted to avoid the subject.

"How does Oliver know so much about medicine?" I inquired. I thought I'd start with something simple. She looked bored by the question.

"Oh, he's a doctor." Bored. I was clearly going to have to pry this out of her.

"A doctor who volunteers at a mortuary and lies on embalming tables in a gown? What's wrong with him?"

"Nothing much, he's just troubled by death and trying to get over it so he can have a life."

"Do you always speak in the abstract?"

"Do you always fall in love with strapping young doctors while your husband lies unconscious on the floor after you've tazed and robbed him blind?"

"Stop it! What are you talking about?"

"You stop it," she said, teasingly pushing me. "I thought you guys were gonna make out right there next to Jerronimo."

"I was in shock, Celia!"

"Whatever you want to tell yourself, sister. The rest of us will just camp out in reality while you take your trip down De Nile river."

"Very clever! Can we please drop it?" I pleaded.

"I'm already pitching my tent." She held up her hand in surrender.

"Ugh!" I turned on the radio to prevent any further discussion on the topic and to avoid remembering how much I wanted him to kiss me.

By the time we pulled back into the garage, the shock had worn off, and I was so exhausted that I had fallen asleep in the van during the last ten minutes of the drive.

Oliver opened my door and woke me right up.

"I'll carry Maddy to Merman's place, and you two can go to bed," he whispered softly. "You need to get some sleep. I imagine you're pretty exhausted after that episode back there." I was suddenly embarrassed. Did he mean the episode with Jerry or the episode of palpitations that brought me to my knees? His tone hinted that he knew exactly what was happening with me. I was exhausted. It exhausted me every time it happened.

He helped me out of the van and reached for Maddy. I didn't want him doing anymore for me. I was feeling sheepish enough, and I certainly wasn't going to let everyone unload *my* things while I rested.

"I'll get her – *and* I'll help unload," I insisted emphatically. "This is all of my stuff after all," I paused through a yawn. "I know this because Merman has reminded me at least five times tonight."

He pulled Maddy from the bench seat.

"Looks like I beat you to it. You can lead the way."

He waited while I stood, stubbornly contemplating a comeback. Celia giggled from inside the van. Lovely.

"Goodnight, Casey," Merman sarcastically called from the other side. "We can handle this."

I wasn't sure *I* could handle the awkward silence as we walked to the apartment. It was awkward because I kept remembering Oliver's breath and smell and eyes, and it was giving me chills each time I thought about it. Even worse was that I had no idea what *he* was thinking. He could be thinking that this poor pathetic wretch of a woman is rapidly losing her mind, or that Maddy should be taken from her for ever having talked to a guy like Jerry, or that he really wants some Lucky Charms when he gets home. It was maddening not knowing.

I had to concentrate while I unlocked the door, because I could feel his eyes watching everything I did. I had performance anxiety. It took me three tries.

I reached for Maddy, but he gestured toward the inside. To be somewhat useful, I quickly made up the sofa bed, and he gently placed her down. I pulled off her shoes and left her dressed, figuring she'd be comfortable in her black spy sweats. I tucked her in and wondered what I should say and how I could end the evening with some dignity left over.

I stood up to speak, but before I could say anything, Oliver took my hand. For a second I thought he was going to make some kind of romantic gesture. It caught me by surprise. I pulled my hand away and gasped.

"Relax, Casey. I'm just checking your pulse. Come a little closer." He smiled softly at my awkward response while he held my wrist and counted on his watch. His hands were strong but gentle and soothingly warm against my cold skin. I wanted to feel them on my face again, which had quickly changed from a pale cold to a mortified pink. My heart started to speed up.

He looked up at me, first with concern and then with a shy smile. "Come closer and look straight ahead."

He covered my eyes with his hand and held it there for a few seconds. I could smell him again. He uncovered them and looked closely…too close. He was just inches from my face again. My heart sped up even faster, and though I tried to hide it, my breathing was audible. He smiled again. He was having too much fun with this.

"Have you ever been seen for this, Casey?" he asked.

So he was going to discuss medical issues with me? I had to even the playing field somehow, so I hit below the belt.

"So you're a doctor, huh?"

"Yes. I am," he said plainly - not the response I expected, but I wanted to know why he stiffened at the question. I wanted to know everything, but he was determined to get an answer to his own question.

"How long has this been going on?" he persisted.

I really didn't want to talk about another one of my problems.

"For a while. I've seen doctors, and they don't seem to have much to offer. But it hasn't killed me, so I'm guessing it's made me stronger."

He smiled, but still seemed concerned.

"You seem very strong to me." He stared at me in silence for a long moment. I was speechless, either from the train wreck of a day or because I couldn't quite comprehend my feelings well enough to express them. "I hope I will have more than this one time to get to know you, to make up for our first meeting."

The thought of spending time with him again, or better, that he was thinking of spending time with me again, was triggering high school style excitement. I couldn't seem to conjure a response.

He spoke before I had to.

"You seem fine to me." He gently lifted up my hand, with his fingers still keeping count on my wrist. "Just exhausted I'm guessing." And then he let it go, and my hand fell limp at my side, longing for him to hold it again.

I didn't want him to leave. What was happening? This was completely irrational. I had gone from a cheating husband, to living in a funeral home, to breaking and entering, to assault with a deadly weapon to…what? Falling in love with a doctor who naps on embalming tables for therapy? I forced out a response.

"I *am* a little tired. Um, thank you… for everything tonight."

"I'm actually happy I could help. Good night, Casey." He walked to the door.

"Good night." I called after him, suddenly frustrated that I hadn't said more when I had the chance.

I didn't sleep for a while. I listened to the furniture being moved up the stairs and replayed the scenes from the night over and over. But these weren't scenes of tasers and struggles on the floor with Jerry. These were perfect scenes of Oliver close enough to kiss.

Chapter Thirteen

The White Couch

Sunday closed my first official week, and as I looked back on the entirety of it, I hoped that the worst was over - but I knew it was highly unlikely. All I could think about was Jerry waking up to a half-emptied house in the state we had left him. I wondered if the Ativan had worked and how long it had taken him to figure out it was me. Mostly, I wondered how long before he sought revenge. I had perpetual butterflies and was startled by every noise. I tried to stay focused on my work.

There was talk in the office of the fog rolling in, and as Merman had tried to explain before, it had an uncanny way of carrying in new "friends". Oliver was there to assist with the high volume of intakes.

Every time our eyes met, a thrill shot through me that was so intense, I had to look away. I tried not to look too often, but I was growing addicted to the emotions that surged through me when he was near and dreaded the longing that I felt when he wasn't. In the meantime, I tried to make myself useful.

The sky had grown dark and the office busy with commotion. Since the majority of the work was beyond me, I sat with Maddy on Merman's white leather couch and watched *Casablanca* as the rest of them finished up outside. Our TV wasn't set up yet, and Maddy loved Merman's movies and his couch. I knew she really just liked being around *him,* and so did I.

He came in to check on us and partake of the dinner I had made. I had earned a promotion in the kitchen that night and was very proud of the roasted salmon recipe I had mastered with one try. I hoped that in small ways, over time, I could give back a little of what he had given me. In the spirit of giving back to Merman, I also made enough food for Celia, who I had made sure to invite.

The table was already set with a collection of fancy place settings and decorations Merman had stored away. They were antiques and apparently belonged to his grandmother, with whom he had lived in England. He grew very nostalgic when we pulled them out. When I pried, he promised that he would tell me his whole story when the busy evening was finished. I was going to hold him to that. He was a master at avoiding any conversation that had to do with him.

He didn't even flinch when he passed by the dinner table, which was surprising considering I had four place settings rather than the usual three. For a second, I wondered if he hadn't noticed, but then I heard him rummaging through the box in the kitchen.

"What's the matter?" I asked as I hurried into the kitchen to make sure he wasn't putting one away.

"Oh, nothing," he said with a sly tone. He had that sneaky smirk on his face again.

"What?" I asked, confused and a little scared to find out.

I hadn't told him about Celia yet, so I wasn't sure where he was going with this. He obviously had something planned. He pulled out another place setting and put it on the table.

"Merman, I already counted out four. I invited Celia."

"I know you did." He just grinned as he adjusted things on the table. He was taunting me with his silence.

"Merman..."

Just before I could finish, someone knocked on the door. I was relieved and excited that Celia was coming, but suddenly terrified to find out what Merman had done. I hoped that it was just Eddie, but knew better.

Merman smiled and went for the door. When he opened it, Celia stepped through, looking more beautiful than I had ever seen her. Merman even looked dazzled for a moment. He took her hand and kissed it. I wanted to shriek with giddiness, and then...I saw him.

Oliver stood in the hallway just outside the apartment door. He too looked beautiful. He was dressed casually, in jeans, but wore a dark green sweater that made his hazel eyes stand out from across the room. That inconvenient and debilitating switch on my heart was flipped, and I had to try and make my breathing look natural and not like someone climbing Mt. Everest.

I envied women who could hide their physical attraction with a simple smile, or even pretend to be indifferent. My heart was a megaphone screaming, *you make me lose my breath when you walk into a room.* I looked at Celia. She seemed perfectly normal, even though I knew she felt just like me, with the man she was hopelessly attracted to standing just feet from her.

My discomfort must have been obvious because when Merman looked over to me, he had to try and hide his laughter and pleasure at my surprise. He shook Oliver's hand.

Maddy was thrilled about the company. She ran over and hugged Celia and Oliver.

"Mommy, are they going to eat our sandman?"

Everyone laughed.

"S-A-L-M-O-N, honey. Yes, everyone is going to eat our salmon."

"Maddy, did you make us dinner?" Oliver asked with surprise and delight and then winked at me.

Maddy beamed and nodded. I just tried to steady myself. One stupid wink, and I thought I might lose my balance.

"Casey," Oliver greeted. He smiled and walked my way.

Merman and Celia played along with some movie lines that Maddy was trying to repeat from *Casablanca.*

"How are you feeling? You look a little faint."

He took my hand and tried to check my pulse. That didn't help matters. I pulled it away.

"I'm fine. I just have an unpredictable heart. The knock on the door startled me." Merman laughed at me from behind us. I would have to kill him for that later.

"Well, shall we?" Merman directed everyone to the table and conveniently arranged the seating so that I was next to Oliver.

"Can I help you in the kitchen, Casey?" Merman offered.

He smiled and led me by the arm. As I pulled the salmon from the oven, Merman took the salad from the refrigerator while whistling the old tune of "Matchmaker", from *Fiddler on the Roof.*

"Merman!" I hissed at him and kicked his shin.

"Ouch!" He laughed. "I thought we could use some music."

"I'm just trying to do for you what you won't do for yourself!" I whispered.

"Me too!" He winked and took the food to the table.

"I'm still married!" I tried to whisper back, but he pretended not to hear me.

Dinner was pleasant with light talk about how crazy business had gotten overnight and how hilarious Night Jock was with his night goggles. Every once in a while, Oliver would comment on how delicious the food was, and everyone would respond in agreement. Merman and Celia would smile at each other sweetly when their eyes met, and Oliver would clear his throat in response to the silence on my end.

Maddy broke the monotony.

"Merman, are you and Celia going to get married?"

Both of their eyes shot up, and Celia's face went red. Oliver choked on his bite of food. Normally, I would say something like *that isn't a polite question*, but I was thoroughly enjoying the moment of revenge. Who would have thought that Maddy would be my greatest weapon in this little dinner battle? I did feel awful for Celia. Merman was going to have to be very careful in his response.

"I don't know, Maddy."

So he was going to play it safe.

"I think that you should marry Celia, and Oliver should marry my mommy."

The weapon was turning rogue on me.

"Maddy, you're being silly. Eat your salmon," I redirected.

This time Merman was enjoying the moment. Oliver seemed to be enjoying it too. He had a grin from ear to ear, which he tried to hide by drinking his wine. I wondered what that meant.

"Then can I have dessert?" Maddy bargained.

"Yes, then you can have dessert."

"Okay!" She said with excited determination, then immediately changed her focus to the food on her plate.

Everyone giggled at the ease with which she could be distracted.

After dinner, Celia helped me clean up while Oliver and Merman pretended to get their fingers stuck in the finger trap again and again for Maddy's amusement. As mortified as I had been, I was glad Merman invited Oliver. If only I wasn't married to a moron.

I noticed that no one was readying to leave, and dinner was all I had planned. Afterward, I intended on taking Maddy upstairs and leaving Merman and Celia alone, but with one quick glance, I knew that Merman had other ideas. The edges of his mouth curved up into that same mischievous smile – as if Maddy's proposal wasn't bad enough. I dreaded what he would try next.

He went into kitchen and came out with an array of candy, from licorice to assorted chocolates, and informed us all that the movie of the night would be the 1944 version of *Jane Eyre*, "the story of a passionate, complicated and fated love," he dramatized with a deep narrative voice to enchant us.

We all laughed, though I knew he was still attempting to make me squirm. I could tell that his taunting hadn't been lost on Oliver either, who seemed to tolerate it with humor. Having him aware of the fact that Merman was attempting to force us together made the situation doubly awful.

Before I had a choice of where to sit, Maddy chimed in.

"Mommy, can I lie down on our sofa with my blanket?"

If Maddy took up the pull-out, there would only be room left on a small spot on the leather couch next to Oliver.

"That sounds perfect Maddy, and your mommy can sit on the couch with us!" Merman encouraged her.

She smiled and snuggled herself up comfortably. I glared at Merman, after which all I could do was look at Oliver with an apologetic and mortified expression. He returned the same.

The four of us sat perfectly still throughout the movie. Merman had us situated closely together, with no room to wiggle without some part of me touching some part of Oliver. I remembered sitting like that with friends during movies, but this was entirely different. I could hardly concentrate on what was happening on the screen.

Every time we would touch, even just knee to knee when attempting to get comfortable, my heart would start its rapid pulse, and I would feel a rush of warmth in my face. I wondered if he felt anything similar, even though I was sure his heart was perfectly healthy. During the passionate scenes with Jane and Mr. Rochester, it was all I could do to act completely detached from the storyline, as if I didn't feel the same sitting next to the tall, dark, and mysterious stranger beside me.

Halfway through, I was having a hard time holding my head up and tried to rest it on one side of me or the other without touching him. After a while of me trying to get comfortable, he leaned over and whispered in my ear.

"You can lean on my shoulder and not have to marry me."

His breath was electric and pulsed through me in a way I had never felt before. I wondered if he knew what he was doing to me. I was terrified by how physically drawn to him I was. Could I lean on his shoulder and not totally fall for him? I looked over to see him holding up a Boy Scout pledge, two fingers held up on his right hand. It made me laugh. He patted his shoulder, and I caved.

I don't remember the rest of the movie. I closed my eyes and took in every smell, sound, and pulse around him. He was warm and stoic, careful not to move an inch or disturb my resting head.

At some point, I fell asleep and was awakened by a loud ring. It was Merman's phone. Everyone on the couch sat up in alarm. Maddy didn't budge.

"It's probably another pick up." Merman announced. He went and answered it. Celia got up and stretched.

"I think I'm going to head home," she said through a half-yawn. "Thanks for dinner, Casey. I'll see you both tomorrow." She collected her purse and sweater and walked toward the door.

When Merman had finished taking down instructions, he met her at the door and took both of her hands. For a moment they both just looked at each other. I tried not to stare, but it was better than watching a movie. I was so happy for both of them.

Merman interrupted the pause. "I'm glad you came," he said to her softly. She shyly smiled and agreed. He looked to us on the couch. "We should do this every Sunday!"

"Next time we should rent a *Bourne* movie," I suggested with sarcasm. He playfully glared at me, but Oliver and Celia laughed.

Merman walked her out to the front, and I sat up, awkwardly shifting my hair and clothes into place. I looked over at Maddy. She was fast asleep.

"Thanks…for the shoulder," I whispered and quickly looked away since looking into his eyes was hard to do without physical repercussions.

"Anytime," he whispered back. His smile was so genuine and intoxicating. I was going to have to get a grip.

"I'd better get Maddy to bed." I got up and looked around, deciding what to leave behind for the night.

"Will you let me help you?" He gestured toward Maddy. I knew that the more time I spent with him and allowed him to get closer, the more complicated things would become…but at the moment, I just didn't care. I wanted every minute I could get.

"That would be nice."

He carefully picked Maddy up while I collected all of her toys and her blanket. We passed Merman in the hallway and whispered goodnight. He was beaming, and I hoped it was because of Celia.

We quietly climbed the stairs and entered my new home. It felt so still compared to Merman's apartment, and I quickly decided that the next dinner would be upstairs since I was now completely furnished, except for one of four feet to my coffee table. It had been left behind, and I had no intention of rescuing it.

We put Maddy in her bed and tried to close the door without making noise. Halfway closed, the door squeaked, and we both snickered quietly at our failed attempt. I walked with him to the front door, wishing that there was an ethical way to keep him. He turned and looked at me fixedly until I made eye contact.

"I had a really nice time tonight. Thank you for dinner. It was amazing." He leaned in and kissed my cheek. He lingered for just a second, and for the first time, I sensed that he felt the same way. I could hear his breathing in my ear, and it was slightly uneven, like mine. I felt like I was in a dream, at least the one that had unfolded in the last week, and every part of me was alive. I considered grabbing him and kissing him for hours outside of my door. But that little moment would have to do.

"You're welcome." I managed to get it out breathlessly. "Goodnight."

"Goodnight." I could see him smiling as he walked down the stairs.

I closed the door and took a deep breath, trying to commit to memory every last second of the evening. As I lay in bed, I replayed each scene again and again with the theme of *Jane Eyre* in the background. If after all of the complications thrown in their way, Jane could have Mr. Rochester, then maybe I could have Oliver too. The only problem was that my lunatic ex was not locked in an attic, and the chances of him throwing himself from the top of a tall building were slim.

My dreams continued to play tug-of-war, some with an endless and passionate kiss and others with struggles to escape Jerry as he fought to pull me back down to the ground.

Chapter Fourteen

Harold

Monday morning, after taking Maddy to school, I would have my first actual work experience in the embalming room with "friends" in it. There were three services for the week, and Merman had asked me to try and help with the dressing and make-up.

While I walked to the car with Maddy, I couldn't shake the opposite extremes of emotions that lingered from my dreams, coupled with the miserable idea of waiting a week to see Oliver again and wondering when Jerry might strike back. I had Maddy buckled in the back seat and the engine started before I saw it.

I couldn't tell what it was through the frosty windshield, so I got out and looked closer at the object sitting on the hood of my car. It was the missing foot of my coffee table. I panicked, trying to reason through how it got there. It was possible that Merman or Eddie or someone found it in the garage. But they wouldn't leave it on my car, out in the open. My heart raced and my stomach turned. Underneath it was a yellow piece of paper, weathered from dew and frost. It was hard to tell how long it had been there. I reached for it and unfolded each fold slowly, terrified to read what was on it. The handwriting was unmistakably Jerry's. It read,

YOU FORGOT THIS

I looked around, afraid he was hiding in the parking lot, but no one was there. I got in the car, locked the doors and drove away as though he were right behind me – adrenaline and fear pumping the gas.

When I got back, I was grateful to see Eddie in the front, messing around with some hose attached to the wall. He made a gesture with his hand that resembled a wave, without once looking at me. As strange as he was, he wasn't afraid of Jerry, and that gave me comfort as I walked through the parking lot.

"Hey, Eddie. Seen anyone lurking around the parking lot? And by anyone I mean Jerry."

The name made him stop and look up.

"Not unless he's turned into a large rodent with a mask and long tail."

"A raccoon?" It was difficult to keep up with his cryptic riddles.

"Came running across the lot from the ivy. I hosed him down." He laughed to himself. "It was awesome."

"We're talking about a raccoon, right?"

He rolled his eyes. "Yes."

"Well, I found this sitting on the hood of my car this morning." I showed him the foot of the coffee table and the damp note. He snatched it out of my hand and examined it closely – smelling it, turning the paper every which way, and even tasting it.

"Eddie, seriously? Is the taste going to tell you anything?" He ignored me.

"Looks like Jerry left it here," he concluded.

"Right," I said, impatiently waiting through his analysis. "So you haven't seen him then?"

"Is he a large black rodent with…," he started, but I cut him off.

"I get it, Eddie, you saw a raccoon." I headed toward the door and heard him behind me repeating what I had said in a childish, mocking tone. He reminded me of a boy I knew in kindergarten - a squirrelly, booger ridden, five year old boy. He would repeat everything I said in that same way. It was the first and only time I had been sent to the principal's office. I had slugged him after having had enough of him one day. I had learned my lesson and would spare Eddie a bloody nose, no matter how tempting.

Remembering the morbid work I had ahead of me beyond that sliding door, I took a deep breath before entering. I had to regroup when I saw Oliver working over one of the slabs. I was momentarily confused but completely content. He turned when the door closed.

"Hi," he greeted, smiling excitedly. I wondered if I had starred in any of his dreams, as he had become the focal point of mine.

"Hey. I thought you were just a weekend warrior," I teased. It seemed easier to talk to him after overcoming last night's inconceivable temptation, and I felt a little more confident in my ability to withstand his charm. Just a little bit more.

"Yeah, I offered to stay and help out for the week. They're pretty busy, and my schedule is free. Besides, I promised Merman I'd keep an eye on you in here." He smiled, and I knew it was probably true. Merman knew my likely reaction to a "friend" on a slab and probably thought having a physician handy wasn't a bad idea.

"Speaking of, where is Merman?" I wanted to show him the foot of the coffee table and the note. More so, I wanted to give him the *I told you so* lecture about Jerry's impending retaliation.

"He's meeting with a family in the front."

I thought about showing Oliver, but decided to avoid dragging him any further into my drama. To calm myself, I played through Merman's likely response. So Jerry knew. So what? There was nothing he could do about it. I even got the missing foot back, so his intended threat turned into a blessing. I set the items on the counter, hoping

Oliver wouldn't notice. He glanced at them, then at me, and decided to leave it be.

"Today, it's our job to get these three dressed and ready." He held out his arm to show the three "friends" he spoke of.

I tried to hold back a gag at the thought of touching them. The smell alone was almost too much.

"This is Harold." He walked over to the first slab. "Harold, this is Casey." We both laughed.

He handed me a picture of what I assumed was Harold.

"Is this the same person?" I wasn't sure because they looked completely different.

"Yep. Minus the soul. They never look the same, but Merman comes pretty close with the makeup."

I could attest to that, although Merman always put his own retro spin on their appearance.

"Harold is eighty-eight years old and died from complications of pneumonia. He was in a nursing home because his wife, Hazel, could no longer care for him herself and couldn't afford in-home care. I met her this morning. She's still in love with him. She gave me his suit and a pair of cufflinks and told me to take good care of him while he was with me. I promised I would."

I was starting to get teary but he continued as if this was a necessary part of the process.

"He was a pilot in his younger days, fought in World War Two, and spent the rest of his life collecting and re-selling old airplane parts. He has three children - Robert, Sally and Catherine. I met them too. They seemed like good people." He paused thoughtfully and continued.

"And here we are - charged with the task of seeing him off with some dignity."

I imagined Harold and Hazel in love, and my heart broke. I wiped at the emerging tears as discreetly as I could.

"Knowing that these were people, with family and a history is the hard part," he said. "The part that never gets easier for some of us. But I think it's good. I think it keeps us grateful for every minute and unwilling to let life slip through our fingers." He watched me, looking for something, it seemed.

"Merman told me this was all pretty hard for you. He told me about you grieving with the family in the last service," he said, trying to hold back a smile.

"Yeah, luckily Uncle Stanley was distracted by Jer…Jerry." That anxious fire in my chest returned at the mention of his name. The image of him standing at the delivery door threatening me gave me goose bumps, and the idea of him lurking around the place made it worse.

"Don't worry about him. Nobody's going to let him near you…or Maddy." He put his arm around me. I really wanted to be comforted by his reassurances, but I wasn't. I did enjoy his touches though, so I just smiled and nodded.

"Well, we should get started in here. We'll just get them dressed, try your hand at make-up and fix whatever hair they have left." He nudged me trying to keep it light.

"I'll let you start," I said, hoping to put it off as long as possible. I figured it might be easier to watch first and see if I could hold it together before I jumped in with both feet.

Luckily, they already had their underclothes on when I came in. A thoughtful gesture on Oliver's part, I assumed, because I knew they didn't start out that way. He began with Harold's pants and gestured to me when he had moved on to his shirt.

"Here you go." He handed me a pair of gloves, which made me feel a little better, and then a white dress shirt that was unbuttoned in the front and cut straight up the back. I looked at Oliver in confusion. "It makes it easier to get on. You'll see. Start with the right arm and then I'll lift him up a little so you can move it under him. That way he'll be hugging me and not you!" He smiled, and I threw up a little in my mouth.

I put on the gloves with true procrastination, making sure each finger was in place. I couldn't even take a deep breath to prepare myself, as I was already trying my best to keep from vomiting.

I tried to maneuver the sleeve over Harold's hand without touching him and was successful. I was relieved that I might not have to touch him at all if I was careful. I got it up to his elbow, and Oliver stopped me to lift Harold's body off of the slab. I quickly walked around the head of the slab and with the precision of a nuclear physicist, pulled the shirt under his body and through to the other side without touching him once. Putrid smells and all, I was pretty proud.

I started to work the other sleeve with the same no-touch approach, but realized halfway up that I would have to hold his hand to get the sleeve past his elbow. With dread, I touched his hand and was shocked for a second by the stiff cold.

"It's weird the first time. You'll get used to it," he assured me and smiled with encouragement.

"Everyone around here keeps saying that, and I'm still waiting." He nodded in amused agreement.

I struggled to lift Harold's arm and after a few tries, determined that he wasn't going to go quietly.

"Yeah, sometimes you have to tug a little harder than would seem natural."

I looked up to see Oliver watching me with amusement, but when I caught him, he quickly straightened his face and cleared his throat. I pulled harder and harder, trying to maneuver the arm into the sleeve. Oliver seemed like he was going to lean in to help a few times, but I was becoming determined about getting that sleeve on, so I waved him off.

Just as I gave a final tug, there was a loud snap. I gasped and dropped Harold's arm, looking to Oliver in horror. He laughed a little and walked to my side of the slab to assess the damage. I waited, sick to my stomach, for the bad news.

"You broke the poor guy's arm." He nudged me jokingly. I was horrified and disgusted.

"This is so bad. Uncle Stanley's gonna kill me." I stepped back from the slab to avoid causing any more damage.

"It happens. Don't worry. Sometimes they're a little stubborn. As long as they are dressed for the service, no one really cares how they got that way." He put his hand on my shoulder to brace me. I didn't understand why at first.

"You look really pale. You should sit down."

I was tired of being told to sit down, and I was tired of my weak physical disposition.

"I'm fine. Let's finish Harold up."

Oliver didn't argue.

Since Harold's arm was now pliable, I got the sleeve on easily. Oliver scooted the other side up at the same time and then tucked the loose pieces of the shirt under Harold's back and into his pants.

"Ta da!" Oliver clapped for me, and I felt a very odd sense of accomplishment.

I buttoned Harold up and tucked the front in. I then moved to his tie, remembering the lessons my mother gave me for one day when I might need to help my husband. I had watched her help my father without even a simple thank you. I knew I wouldn't be getting one today either.

"He looks great! Nice work with the tie." Oliver commended me again. "Wanna try some make-up?"

"Sure, why not? When in Rome, right?" Except this was more like Dracula's Transylvania, but either way, it applied.

"Right," he agreed with a smile, and in a way that had my heart skipping again. I walked over to the counter so that he couldn't see me lose my breath. I gathered a box full of different make-up items and set them on a tray next to Harold.

I tucked a wash-cloth in around his collar so that I didn't stain it with foundation and spent about ten minutes trying to pick out the right color for his skin, settling on something between the photo and the opalescent, bluish man before me. I began to apply the foundation to the cold, thin skin and was surprised that the fear and disgust had mostly worn off. I became so focused on the job that the unnerving realizations of what I was doing came only intermittently.

When I got to his lips, I had to look closely as I noticed a white substance on their surface and a wire poking out from between them. The gagging sensation came on again, and I had to step away from the table.

Oliver had been working on another friend and stopped what he was doing.

"What is it?" he asked with concern. He walked over and looked around for what might have sickened me. I pointed to Harold's mouth from a few feet away.

"His lips. There's something on them, or in them." I gagged again at the thought of it.

"Oh," he smiled while he explained, "we put lotion on their eyelids and lips to keep them from drying out, and sometimes we have to wire their mouths shut." He reached down and pushed the wire in with some kind of metal tool and then reshaped Harold's lips.

"That's disgusting." I shook off the information that I shouldn't have asked for. He chuckled.

I was so happy, despite the morbid setting, to spend more time with him. Everything about him dazzled me, the sound of his voice and the light in his eyes especially. I focused on finishing Harold's make-up to ground myself.

"Don't forget his hands." Oliver pointed to Harold's hands and smiled waiting to see my reaction. I had never thought about covering up hands, but it made sense. They were bluish too.

We put his jacket on together, and I combed his hair to match the picture, all except for the very back of it since that would require I lift his head, and no one would see it anyway.

I stood back and admired my work, which seemed more than decent to me. Oliver nudged me in approval and suggested we leave the final touches to Merman.

I moved onto the next friend, who Oliver informed me was named May. He told me her story, or what little he knew of it since no family had come, and helped me dress her before leaving me on my own to do the make-up.

There wasn't any choosing to do. May had picked out a foundation, blush, eye shadow, and a lipstick to be used for this occasion. We were told that she had insisted we use only her make-up and clothes that she had picked out. She had even sent rollers to be put in her hair after it was washed. It was clear that she was a very particular person, and that wasn't going to change simply because she died. I wondered if I would rather know I was dying and do as May had done, or leave it up to the Merman's of the world. I figured that I wouldn't really care at that point and got to work on May.

The time flew by, and Oliver and I both went out of our way to pass by each other as often as possible. I looked forward to his encouraging nudges and his chuckling at my discoveries and partial gags, and found myself praying for some way to be with him without dooming myself to judgment for eternity.

As my thoughts drifted and my hopes grew, Merman suddenly walked in holding a large envelope and a concerned look.

"This is for you." He handed it to me and waited next to me while I opened it. It looked official, and though I had no idea what it was, I knew it had something to do with Jerry. I read through the initial few pages of court documents and then quickly flipped through, page by page, in horror. Jerry did strike back and with my worst nightmare.

"Merman, he wants to take Maddy from me!"

Chapter Fifteen

Mr. Linden

Merman and Oliver tried to console me with reassurances that Jerry didn't have a chance at getting Maddy. I wanted to believe them, but I couldn't see through the terror of the possibility. As I suspected, Merman didn't seem too concerned about the items Jerry had left me, though I heard the two conversing about when he might have come and how secure the building really was.

After nearly fainting during another episode of uncontrollable palpitations, Oliver conceded to Merman's suggestion of a glass of wine and a bubble bath once I'd recovered.

I couldn't sleep much at all that night, and the few times I drifted in, I was awakened, desperate for breath from nightmares of Maddy being dragged away from me.

Monday morning, after taking Maddy to school, I made my way down a two-lane road with a scrap piece of paper clutched in one hand and the steering wheel in the other. I attempted to decipher the directions scratched on the paper, match them with the addresses on the buildings, and keep my eyes on the road all at once. Needless to say, there were many unhappy drivers illegally crossing the double yellow to get around me.

Merman had given me the number and address of a local family law attorney who Uncle Stanley had known for more than thirty years. He said that Uncle Stanley had, by his own volition, called and put in a good word for me. He also warned that I not mention the favor to Uncle Stanley, even to thank him, or he would surely deny it flatly as he didn't want to be known as the generous type. The thought of Uncle Stanley doing anything to help me gave me a bit more hope in humanity.

I parked on the side of the road and looked across at a very aged office building holding the address I had been looking for. It was one of many little business spaces that lined the street, all of which were of varying colors and designs. Though separate, they were built so closely together that they appeared to form one single stretch of construction, giving it a small-town and very unique personality. Even the government buildings were extravagantly designed, with large sprawling entrances and well-kept lawns. This particular building was two stories high, with the same early twentieth century architecture, a steep set of stairs to the entrance, and coated entirely in white paint with blue trim.

I grabbed the ominous envelope to take in with me and was once again gripped by fear. I quickly decided to pray before I started the next part of my journey. I figured that something or someone in the universe had provided us with shelter, food, work and friends, albeit in the unlikeliest of packages, and I had nothing else to put my hope or faith in and everything to lose. I closed my eyes and tried to focus on being grateful and sincere.

"I just want to start by saying thank you." I spoke out loud, trying to make sure I was heard, just in case anyone was really listening. "I never expected so much when I left that night." The sound of my voice was strange and lonely, and I felt like an idiot…but I was desperate. "Thank you for Merman and the job and the apartment and Oliver and Celia and Eddie. Thank you for keeping us safe from Jerry." This list could go on, but my appointment was in three minutes. "I'm hoping that whoever is in there waiting to meet me was put there by you, and that he will help get me through this mess. Please let me keep Maddy. Please don't let him take her from me." I listened, but there came no response. I didn't expect a burning bush or a tap on my window by a heavenly angel, but I hoped my prayer had done some good. I hoped even more that my past mistakes wouldn't be a consideration in the decision. I stopped before the tears could begin and started on my way.

The nearest crosswalk was fifty yards away and jay walking wasn't an option with the amount of traffic passing by. Small as it may be, this was downtown and the hub of business in the area.

So, I would be late then. Usually the idea of being late would stress me into an episode, but considering the weight of the rest of my problems, I figured they could just suck it up and deal with it if they didn't like it.

When I opened the door, an old sleigh-bell, loosely hanging from the top, rang. The smell of the office sent me into an unwelcomed flashback. I was suddenly tense and rigid and as uncomfortable as I was standing in my father's study. It smelled like the lingering smoke of a cigar and of shelves filled with books on law. My predisposed hatred for lawyers and resentment for my father had my fists clenched. I hated how they manipulated, hated how they twisted words and the truth, and I hated their cold and warped perspective of the world.

I had momentarily forgotten that I was standing in a stranger's office, about to beg for help. I could only hope that the characteristics I despised could be used to my advantage for once. I chanted a few times "he's not my father, he's not my father…" in an attempt to keep my focus and composure.

I looked about the room for anything that might confirm my hopes. The disarray was in stark contrast to the impeccable order of my father's office. Nothing matched, and nothing seemed to have a designated spot. There were stacks of files all over the top of a desk in the reception area, and behind the desk were two large, black filing cabinets that seemed to glare at the rest of the room with their sheer size.

Next to the door was a tall green plant that looked slightly under-watered and completely out of place. The office emitted a vibe of functionality, and anything decorative seemed forced and awkward. Aged, brown blinds covered the windows, and I found myself enchanted by the particles of dust floating in the air through a few stray beams of light sneaking through their slats.

A woman walked out of what I assumed was the lawyer's inner office and eyed me up and down. Her appearance made me desperate to laugh out loud, but I resisted. She wore a short, black skirt and a tight pink top that matched her high heels. Her hair was matted into a mountain that formed around her head, held by at least half a can of hairspray. Her fingernails were unnaturally long and painted the same shade of hot pink, and her make-up was painfully overdone. She was a caricature from a really bad 1980's glam video. I admired her obvious efforts as she sat herself on the edge of the desk.

"Can I help you honey?" Her words found their way through her smacking gum. Classy. I immediately questioned this lawyer's ability to help me at all, but I was already here, so what the heck.

"I'm here to see Mr. Linden. I'm Casey."

The woman looked me up and down again before hopping off the desk. "Oh. Are you his eight-thirty appointment?"

Um, obviously!

"Yes," I replied flatly.

She scoffed a bit and looked at the clock. According to the indignant look on her face, three minutes had set back his entire schedule. There wasn't another soul in or around this office.

"I'll let him know you're here." She went into another room and closed the door. I sheepishly sat in one of the seats and nervously flipped through a magazine on the center table. So much for them sucking it up! This was not the way I wanted to start things off. I hoped that Mr. Linden was nothing like his secretary and could look past a few minutes.

The door opened, and a stout and balding man came out with a genuinely welcoming smile. His shirt was one button off, all the way down and haphazardly tucked into his slacks. Again, I questioned his credentials. He approached me and introduced himself, holding out his hand.

"Hello, Casey, I'm Donald Linden, but you can just call me Don." I shook his hand and caught the scent of the cigars that had put me into that frightful flashback of my father.

"Let's just head into my office and see what we're dealing with here. Thank you, Vivian." Vivian watched me with judgmental curiosity as Don walked me into his office and closed the door.

Before I accumulated a bill that would have me in debt for years, I decided to get the subject of money over with. "I appreciate you meeting with me, Mr. Linden."

"Please, call me Don," he interrupted.

"Well…Don, before we start, I have to tell you that I don't have a lot of money. Actually, I have very little of it." It had only been a couple of weeks since I had become the keeper of my own money, and I already hated the trouble it caused. I had recently learned that everything in life was contingent upon money. He seemed to listen while pondering the circumstances, so I continued.

"I can make payments as long as it takes. I just…I really need help right now."

His pondering ceased, and he flashed his sincere smile again. "Well, Casey, I've known Stanley for a long time, and let me tell you, he doesn't speak highly of many people. If *he* thinks you're trustworthy, then I do too."

What was this? Uncle Stanley spoke highly of me and thought me trustworthy? I felt a rush of giddy fulfillment. I guessed it was what acceptance felt like.

He continued, "I usually require a twenty-five hundred dollar deposit and charge two-hundred and fifty an hour, but…" My heart sank as a wave of nausea came over me at the impossible figures he was proposing. Not in a million years could I ever afford that, and just maybe in that many years could I pay it off. I began to collect my things and prepare my humble exit.

He held up his hand and continued again, "But, what little I've heard about you inspires me to want to help you out. You seem like a fighter, and better yet, for a good cause. I don't like seeing good people bullied around. It's sort of a pet peeve of mine. I've done many pro bono cases fitting that very description. My compensation comes in the form of seeing justice done…and I'll admit, making the other side squirm in the process. Let's just see what we're up against, and we'll talk money later if it ever comes to that."

I was relieved but suspicious. Ever since I crash landed into Merman's world, I had met more generous and caring people than I knew existed. Deep down, I had always suspected that most everyone was selfish and out for themselves.

He interrupted my wordless contemplation, "So, were you served any papers?"

The reminder of the portentous papers that had brought me there snapped me back into reality. I reached for the envelope.

"This was delivered to the funeral home yesterday."

"Was it served directly to you?"

"No, Merman brought them into me." I hadn't a clue what that meant.

"Hmmm…, well that could buy us a little time for a response. I may use it, I may not. Nevermind, let's see them."

I handed them over and he matter-of-factly flipped past the first couple of pages and then stopped to read more thoroughly the pages that had me falling to my knees in terror the day before. After a few minutes, I couldn't hold back my questions anymore.

"What does it mean?" I couldn't wait while he read the whole thing. It was fifty pages or more, and I wanted to know my fate as soon as possible.

"Just give me a minute, and I'll tell you." I could hardly sit through his vague grunts and sighs. I tried to calm myself by breathing intentionally and focusing on the good things of the last couple of weeks. Oliver kept popping into my mind.

Eventually, he closed up the documents, rubbed his eyes under his glasses, and looked at me carefully.

"Well, Casey, he says that he wants Maddy. He's willing to let you have visitation with her, but he wants it supervised, paid by you of course, and not until you've completed six months of counseling and alcohol rehab, since he claims you are an abusive alcoholic. He wants the house, since he's been the sole earner paying for it, and because it will be Maddy's primary place of residence. He wants you to pay him alimony and child support now that you're working consistently, which he claims he is not. He also claims that you have Maddy in a dangerous environment, where you neglect her well-being by feeding her unhealthy food, subjecting her to situations that are inappropriate for her age, and are more than likely drunk in her presence on a regular basis. He's made claims in here about violent behavior, threats on his life, infidelity, and drug and alcohol abuse." I could hardly contain myself. I had already read all of it, but hearing it again stirred up the rage. I did want to kill him, and there would be no threats about it.

"But those are things *he* did! Not me! He can't get away with this, right?" I was on the edge of my seat yelling. I looked at him, begging him to tell me that I was right.

"Well, are you a raging alcoholic?" he asked in all seriousness.

"No!" I paused and thought back to the night I met Jerry. "I mean, I had my wild moments as a teenager, but I'm no alcoholic. That's Jerry's specialty." I knew I could have just stuck with no, but complete honesty seemed like the best way to go with Don.

"I didn't think so. And I'm going to assume the rest is just as inaccurate."

"Yes, they are all lies, and they are all exactly Jerry," I confirmed, waiting to hear how he planned on setting this straight.

"Well, I'm not surprised," He said, leaning back in his chair and folding his hands behind his head. "Have you ever heard of projection?"

"Projection? Um, I think so." I hoped he wouldn't ask me to define it.

"The best way to protect himself is to accuse you of his very own behaviors before you accuse him. It's a very common behavior, and most of the time it's subconscious, but when you're dealing with sociopaths or scummy lawyers, it's usually intentional. Sometimes people even accuse the other person of projecting to hide the fact that they're really projecting and want to preempt the accusation of projecting." He sighed after the lengthy description. "But that's an entire course on psychology and neither here nor there. Right now it's your word against his. The best place to start is to write down your version of life with Jerry and Maddy - everything you can remember. Don't leave a thing out, and we'll decide what we use and what we don't. More important, is pulling together solid evidence that is not hearsay, such as witnesses, documents, dates, and the like. I'll take care of discovery, which includes finances, criminal records, and so on."

My mind raced, trying to think of what I would write and anyone who might be able to attest to the lifestyle, habits, and characteristics of the real Jerry. Having an action plan had actually started to calm me a bit.

He continued, "Take your time and write down everything you can remember, including dates, times, and every detail." I nodded, still scanning my memory of incidents and images over the last six years. "This is going to get ugly, Casey, make no mistake about that. He's going to lie to get what he wants. It would help me to know what he's really after, because if what I've gathered is correct, he doesn't really want Maddy."

"He doesn't want Maddy. He doesn't care a thing about Maddy. He wants control...over me, and he'd sacrifice her in a second to get it." I knew it was the truth, but it wasn't something he could have anymore. I would fight to the death for it.

"Well, work on your statement and I'll start on discovery. Try and have that to me by the end of the week so that I can prepare a response to this nonsense." He gave me a reassuring smile, but I knew that he saw a real battle coming.

"He has everything Mr. Lin…I mean Don. He's kept my name off of everything from the start. I can't even get money out of the bank. That part will be pretty easily discovered." I felt like such a fool. The lessons from this just seemed never ending.

"Things aren't always as real or important as the other side will make them seem, Casey. Let me do my job and you work on your statement." He stood up and walked around the desk to gently pat my shoulder. I collected my things and headed toward the door. He followed.

"Things have a way of working themselves out, and I'm here to help them along a little. If I've learned one thing in the last thirty years of this dirty work, it's that the bad one's get theirs in the end. This will work out - you just need to have a little faith in the process. Now, there are some papers you need to sign so that I can let these folks know you have representation and that they'll be dealing directly with me. You let me know if he comes anywhere near that funeral home again or if he harasses you in any way. I'd love nothing more than to file a restraining order." He patted me on the back one last time and handed me off to Vivian.

"Thank you, Don. Thank you!"

"No problem!" He went back into his office, and I could hear him shuffling through papers as Vivian began handing me some of my own to sign. As I read through and signed, Vivian busied herself with bubble gum popping.

When all was said and done, I headed back across the street feeling like I had taken another step toward independence. My hatred for Jerry was turning into a fiery determination. He wasn't going to take anything from me, except for maybe a harsh awakening. I would win this and never look back.

Chapter Sixteen

The Response

For days, I took notes, summarized events, researched dates, times, phone numbers, addresses, and was running on pure adrenaline. I wrote during breaks, after work while Maddy ate a snack, napped or watched movies, and late into the night while she slept. Merman reviewed my writing and added details that he knew or language that he thought was more convincing, as he found mine a bit too passive. In between, I worked.

The week was packed with services, starting with Harold that Tuesday. I thought that since I knew so much about his family and had worked on him personally, that I would be uncontrollably teary, but I worked through it without emotion since all I could think about was the response. I got a lot of work done in a little amount of time so that I could get back to writing. This seemed to please Uncle Stanley, though he didn't know my true motive. I was on a mission.

Memories swarmed me - memories that I had carefully stored away for good. The inventory of my life over the past six years brought forth so much shame. I felt so far removed from the person I had been years ago. The desperation, the helplessness, the willingness to do anything to avoid conflict, the abusive environment I subjected Maddy to - it all came to the surface and caused immense grief and profound self-evaluation.

This is what I had run from that night.

It wasn't Jerry, it was myself. Jerry could have been any name or face. This epiphany turned my world as I had believed it to be, upside down. I wasn't a weak, helpless victim. I had perpetrated these acts against myself. I was responsible for my circumstances. This truth was shocking and painful, but very empowering. Since I had created it, I alone could change it. I would only be a victim if I chose to. Maddy would only suffer by my mistakes if I allowed them to continue. Though my intentions the night I fled were elusive and chaotic, it had been my subconscious first grasp at change. It was a powerful and spiritual enlightenment and left me hopeful.

I wrote about how I had raised Maddy on my own, how he had refused to participate from the beginning in basic things like feeding, bathing, or even diapers because, he said, he hadn't wanted her to begin with. I wrote about the nights when she would cry and cry and how he threatened to shut her up himself if I couldn't do it- how he never attended a ballet recital, a class play, a teacher conference, or a doctor's appointment, and not because he worked, but because he considered it my job. But that was the small stuff compared to the overall sense that he didn't know her or care to know her. She interacted with him like she did the mailman or the cashier at the grocery store - they'd wave or say hi, and she'd wave back. That was it for five years.

I wrote about his drinking, and how I was careful to keep us away to avoid his fits of rage because of how rough he had gotten with her when I didn't. There were the countless young girls and women in his studio and his shady, thug friends who made quick stops at our house for reasons I didn't know. But this wouldn't be enough, Don had made that clear. I needed more.

I called Linda at Maddy's school and asked her if she would be willing to write an affidavit about her experiences with Jerry at the school. I also asked her teachers to do the same. They were all more than willing to help, as they had been concerned by his behaviors in the past - for instance, how he would possessively question them about the times that I had come in to help in the classroom and about what I did there and who I did it with - or the one and only time he came to a school function completely drunk and hitting on every female in the room - or the pictures Maddy would draw of him with an angry face holding a beer. Finally, I asked Merman and Eddie to write about the confrontation at the delivery door and the night at the house. Oliver and Celia both offered to do the same.

The more I wrote and researched, the more confident I became in the fact that Jerry didn't have a thing going for him in this case. Aside from his ridiculous accusations, I couldn't think of a thing, and yet, the fear loomed. He wouldn't give up easily, I knew that. I wondered how far he would take it and what he had up his sleeve. I couldn't even imagine that our life at The Golden Oaks could be bad enough to lose Maddy over. And still, I was frightened.

It was two o'clock in the morning when I finally finished putting everything together. After endless revisions and additions, I decided to be done with it and hand it over to Don.

I turned the lights off and started to get comfortable on the pull out when a loud crashing sound came from downstairs. I sat up startled, and when I heard nothing but silence for a few minutes, I assumed it was Merman working on something and tried to go to sleep. I didn't know if I was becoming paranoid, but I was hearing strange noises that I couldn't place with what I normally heard downstairs. I was getting a little scared and decided to check it out myself rather than lie there in frozen fear.

I left the apartment and locked the door behind me out of habit and extra precaution should Jerry be lurking about. I slowly crept down the stairs trying to listen for the sounds, but heard nothing. I opened the door at the base of the stairwell to the quiet and completely dark hallway except for the light inside of Uncle Stanley's office. I remembered the night I crashed and that light coming through the curtains into the rain, calling me in like a lighthouse to the lost and weary boat. I was really getting scared and decided to call out for Merman.

"Merman?" I called out in a loud whisper. I don't know why I whispered since we were the only ones there.

He didn't respond, so I crept to his door and turned the knob.

"Merman?" I whispered again, this time a little louder as I was growing more and more frightened. His apartment was empty and quiet. I figured he must have been moving about the embalming room and garage, so I made my way down the hallway with trepidation.

I passed the small chapel and noticed that the top section of May's casket was closed and the bottom was opened. I realized that it must have slammed shut and that's what I'd heard upstairs, but I didn't understand why the bottom was open, unless Merman hadn't closed it yet. I considered leaving it alone and running to find Merman, but I didn't want Uncle Stanley storming around about it in the morning before the service, so I quickly went in and opened the top again.

After I propped it open and checked that it was secure, I ran out as if something were chasing me. I made it halfway down the hallway when I heard it slam again. I froze where I was, trying to talk myself down from the terror I was starting to feel.

"Merman?" This time I said it out loud, my voice growing shaky. Still, there was nothing.

From behind me came a whooshing noise, as if someone had walked past me. Goosebumps rose all over me, and I turned, terrified to see what might be there. All I caught was a passing shadow in the mirror at the end of the hallway. Without another thought, I ran full speed to the garage where I prayed I would find Merman.

I opened the door and called out loudly, "Merman?"

There was no answer. I noticed that one of the pick-up vans was missing. Merman or Eddie must have left to pick up a friend. Just as I started to close the door and head into the embalming room, I saw another passing shadow on the side of one of the vans.

"Who's there?" I barely choked out over the lump in my throat. No one answered, but I heard the whooshing sound again and ran as fast as I could, this time with the idea of locking me and Maddy in our apartment with the taser until morning. As I turned the corner, I slammed into a body and screamed.

"It's me, Casey. It's just me." I knew the voice before I had the courage to look up. It was Oliver. I was relieved, out of breath, and a little embarrassed.

"I was hearing noises upstairs, so I came down. I thought I saw someone in the mirror over there. Were you in the hallway a minute ago?" I was talking really fast, trying to catch my breath.

"No, I was in the embalming room," he said as he held both of my arms. I didn't realize that I was shaking. "We got two more in tonight, so I came to help out."

He sure was helping out a lot lately. I wasn't complaining.

"Well, I saw someone in the garage too. Who's here right now?" I asked, trying to collect myself.

"Eddie is probably who you saw in the garage. Come on." He led me back to the garage I had fled from.

"Nobody answered me in there! Is he trying to freak me out?" I was considering punching Eddie to make myself feel better.

"Who knows what Eddie's up to." He opened the garage door and called out.

"Eddie?" No one answered. "Eddie?" He still didn't answer.

I grabbed Oliver's arm and held on tight. He looked at his arm and grinned a little before heading into the garage. We walked in between the cars looking around for any sign of Eddie.

I could hear the very faint sound of music coming from somewhere in there. Oliver must have heard it too, because he was slowly making his way toward it. We scooted behind the town car expecting to see him kneeling on the other side, but there was nothing.

"Eddie!" Oliver said it louder this time. We crept behind the remaining van and peeked around the side. "Eddie!"

Someone touched my shoulder and without thinking, I turned around swinging my arms to fight off whatever it was. Unfortunately, it was Eddie. He looked stunned as I beat on him and realized who he was. He had headphones in his ears, and I could clearly hear the music to "Heartbreaker" by Pat Benatar. I yanked them out of his ears so he could hear me yelling at him.

"You scared me to death!"

He cowered, covering his head with both arms. "What did I do?"

"Why were you creeping around the hallways? You're freaking me out!"

He stood up confused. "I've been in here for the last few hours…rockin' it. Heartbreaker…dream maker…" He put one earpiece back in and was playing air guitar while he squealed the words.

"Is Celia here?" I yelled at him. I prayed that he would say yes because there was something or someone in that hallway with me.

"Nope, she left a long time ago. Dream maker…love taker don't you mess around with me…" He was useless. I punched his arm one last time.

"Ow! What was that for?"

"For scaring me!" I walked back toward the door and heard Oliver snicker behind me. When I turned back, Eddie was rubbing his arm.

"I need to know what that was out there or I'm not going to be able to sleep tonight," I implored.

"Well, let's go check it out. I've seen stranger things here. I think they like to linger until their services are over," he said nonchalantly.

"What are you talking about?" I hoped he was kidding, but he sounded serious.

"Wouldn't you want to stick around to see how you're remembered?"

I supposed I would. The thought of it was depressing since there weren't many people who would come to my service.

We passed the small chapel, and I pulled on his shirt. "May's casket slammed shut. That's what I heard from upstairs. I came down and opened it, and when I walked away, it slammed shut again."

He seemed curious. It did look peculiar, with only her feet showing, like a bad joke. He went over and propped it open again. We both stood back and waited. Without any apparent cause or force, the lid slammed shut again.

"That's interesting." He went over and started to lift it again but met resistance.

"I can't…get it open. It's like something's pushing down on it." He let it slam shut and stepped away. "Okay, May, we'll keep it closed. I'll tell them in the morning."

Suddenly the lights in the chapel flickered and went black for a second. I grabbed his arm again and stood as close as I could.

"Don't worry," he whispered, "I think she just wants to be left alone." We both stared at the casket, with the wrong end open.

"Should we leave it op…" Before I could finish, the bottom half slammed shut too. "This is creepy."

A dark and deep voice spoke from behind us, sending chills up my spine. "Don't take it personally, Casey."

I turned around ready to punch again. The lights flickered and went back on. Merman was standing there chuckling. I punched his arm too.

"Ow! Geez, Casey, lighten up. I was just saying it's probably not because of the make-up job you did on her." He rubbed his arm, making me consider my actual strength.

"Were you messing with the lights?" I held my arm up to punch again.

"No, *they* do that." He pointed to the casket. "Don't worry though, they've never bothered me in my apartment, and I'm sure they'll avoid the hike up the stairs."

"Are you kidding me?"

"No." He smiled, still rubbing his arm and looking at mine. My other arm was still locked around Oliver's.

"Sorry!" I let go and stepped away, embarrassed.

"Don't be sorry." Oliver just smiled and folded his arms.

Merman thankfully changed the subject.

"Did you finish the response for Don?"

"It's as done as it will ever be." I couldn't help but feel like it wasn't enough, but I was so tired of reading and editing and thinking about it.

"Great. Let's send it."

"Right now? It's almost three in the morning!"

"What, are you afraid of waking his fax machine?" he mocked. I rolled my eyes, too tired and shaken to fight back.

"Well, I think I'm going to head out," Oliver said, then turned to me. "So, I'll see you tomorrow then…I mean, there's still a lot to be done," he added, clearing his throat.

The excuse was for my benefit, I assumed, since he didn't seem to have the same reservations about the situation as I did.

"It doesn't matter to me why you come, so long as you do," I said timidly. "I wouldn't have made it past one sleeve on Harold without you," I added to prevent myself from sounding too sentimental.

"And Harold might have two broken arms instead of one," he teased.

"Harold might have needed a closed casket!" I added.

"Well, then I'll look forward to more misadventures in the embalming room tomorrow," Oliver replied, running his hand gently down my arm.

Before I could respond, Merman interrupted.

"Okay, love birds - we have some papers to fax before sunrise."

Oliver and I both rolled our eyes.

"Goodnight," we both said in unison and laughed.

Then Merman rolled *his* eyes.

Oliver left, and Merman and I printed out the response for the fax. We watched as it was sent page by page, and looked at each other in thoughtful silence when it finished.

The response encapsulated a chapter of my life that I wished to be freed from. It was out in the world now, transmitted over phone lines, in the hands of someone who knew how best to use it to gain me that freedom.

Merman took the copy, then my hand, and led me to the delivery door. He turned over and emptied a garbage can that sat on the side of the mortuary. He gave me the response and a lighter.

"Go on. This part of your life is over. You've gotten it all out. You even let someone else read it so it doesn't hide inside of you anymore like a sick secret."

I took the lighter and closed my eyes, praying that Jerry would go away like the curling ashes of the paper.

We watched as the flames grew and consumed my past. I saw the light in Merman's eyes and in the light was me. I looked different in the red glow of the flames.

Chapter Seventeen

The Small Chapel

I awakened to a feeling of levity I didn't recognize. I was grateful for it, and said so in a brief prayer before getting up and ready for the day. I didn't know how I felt about religion, but I knew that none of what had happened was a coincidence. I also knew that the weight that had been lifted was due to letting it all go and trusting that there was something much bigger than me out there, and I was willing to say thank you for it. Besides, I was going to need practice in trusting and letting go before the court date rolled around.

Maddy's school was handing out flyers for their annual fall party - a western round-up. Apparently they had sent them home a couple of weeks before, but I hadn't been great about checking Maddy's backpack for school flyers lately. Between running away, taking up residence in a mortuary, robbing Jerry, and filing a response in a divorce, I had missed the flyer for the round-up.

They had a limited number of tickets left and were pushing to sell out before the big event that Friday. I took one and left it in the passenger seat of my car with other discarded papers as I was not planning on attending.

When I entered the chapel, Oliver and Merman were explaining to Uncle Stanley that it was probably best to leave May's casket closed to avoid any startling incidents when the family came. He grumbled something and headed my way. As he passed, he struggled to make what I assumed was some sort of friendly smile. It didn't suit him, but I felt honored to receive it. Things were definitely starting to look up.

We waited most of the day for visitors to come and see May. I understood that day why some services were held in the small chapel and some in the larger one. No one came to see her until an hour before closing when a tired looking man in his late thirties entered quietly and asked Merman where May Sheffield could be found. Merman pointed him toward the small chapel.

When he entered, he stood before the casket for a while without saying or doing anything. There was one arrangement of flowers next to her, but otherwise, nothing. He looked extremely troubled.

Merman left me alone to assist the man if necessary, but was confident that he wouldn't need much from me. I tried to be as discreet as possible in the back of the room.

I watched May and who I assumed was her son, and considered the differences between people who end up in the big chapel versus those in the small one. At first glance it appears that those who draw crowds led happier, fuller lives. But at times it was very clear that most of the people in that crowd merely manufactured a sudden and deep attachment to those who have passed, making the loss all about themselves. It begs the question, how many true relationships existed in that chapel? How many of that crowd really knew, really grieved over, and really loved the person in that casket? Though May had only one visitor, it was clear that he grieved over her and loved her no matter the differences they might have had.

After a long while, the man turned to me. "Has anyone come to see her?"

I was startled by his question and afraid to tell him the truth. I paused before answering.

"Well…no. Not yet." I felt awful for him. It was the lonely scene I had imagined for myself the night before. But that night I had gained perspective. I knew at least four people who would be there for me when I died, and that was better than an entire crowd of insincere mourners.

"And just these flowers were sent?" he asked regretfully, pointing at the sole arrangement.

"Yes, and whoever sent them must have loved her. They're beautiful." I knew they were from him.

"And did I ask that the casket be closed? I don't remember." He seemed lost, not knowing what to do, as if he had done it wrong and wished he had done more. I wished Merman were there because I didn't know what I was supposed to say to that.

I chanced it.

"I think she wanted it closed." It was as close to the truth as I was willing to get on that topic. He shrugged as if my answer was good enough. He sat down in one of the chairs in the front and put his head in his hands.

"I didn't know what to do for her. We barely talked at all anymore." He looked up again, at the casket with its one floral adornment, and shook his head in his hands again. "I thought she might have had friends in her retirement community." He sounded like he was crying, but it was difficult to tell with his head buried. My heart broke. I sat next to him and hesitantly patted his back. When I touched him, he broke into sobs. I handed him one of the tissue boxes from another chair.

"I'm so sorry for your loss." I held back tears and tried to repeat the line I had been told to use in these situations. But it seemed meaningless, so I added to it, knowing this kind of contact was far outside of standard procedure.

"I think what you did for her was perfect." He didn't interrupt, so I continued, hoping to comfort him with what little I knew of his mother. "I only spent a little time with her here, but she seemed like the kind of person who liked to keep things simple, like she wouldn't want a big fuss made over her and definitely wouldn't want to be showing off in her casket...even though she was a beautiful lady." His crying stopped, and he laughed a little.

"It sounds like you knew her better than I did."

"Well, from what I can tell, she knew what she wanted and wouldn't have it any other way."

"That sounds like my mom. You're very kind. Thank you." He handed me back the tissue box. "Would you mind sitting with me for a few minutes? I know it sounds strange, but if she's still here, I want her to see that she's not alone."

I agreed and fought back the desire to tell him that she was probably there at that very moment. We both sat back in our chairs and listened to the music playing through the speakers.

After a while, he stood up.

"Thank you very much. I never thought someone like you would be somewhere like this." He seemed to think about what he meant by that, as did I, and attempted to explain. "I mean, you're young and personable and…, well, attractive." With that awkward addition to his summation of me, he quickly tried to recover. "You just seem like a *normal* person, not someone you'd meet at the friendly neighborhood mortuary." He emphasized the word normal, which made me laugh. Little did he know. "Anyway, it was very comforting…not being alone."

I was embarrassed but flattered by his complements.

"I'm just glad I could make this a little easier for you…and your mom." With that he looked back toward May and approached her casket. He placed his hand on top of the pink, silk-lined steel that she lay in.

"I'm just going to spend a minute with her and say goodbye."

I nodded and stepped out, leaving him to find closure with May. I understood at that moment what Merman sought to do there. He tried to reach out to people in one of life's darkest hours and shine a little light. When I opened the door, Merman was leaning against the wall with a proud look on his face.

"I think you're a natural, you know. I knew there was something about you from the first night I pulled you out of that ivy."

I playfully hit his arm.

"Stop it. Were you listening the whole time?"

"Not the *whole* time." He smiled. "It feels good, doesn't it? To make it just a little bit easier?"

"Yeah, it does."

Merman finished up May's service so that I could pick Maddy up. She had gone home with a friend for a play date after school. Relationships were blooming all over the place ever since Jerry was out of the picture. Moms offered to help me all of the time and even started including me in emails for possible moms' nights out, all of which was made possible by setting up an email account of my very own. I was beginning to feel like I fit in, and I truly loved it.

When we got home, I heard a group gathered in Merman's apartment, talking. Merman pulled me inside when he caught me trying to slip past his door.

"You're the guest of honor! Where do you think you're going?"

"What are you talking about, Merman?"

He was always up to something that would likely embarrass me. When we went inside, they all stopped talking and raised glasses. It was the usual crowd – Celia, Oliver and even Eddie, who seemed completely out of place and anxious to get back to work. Merman handed me a glass of champagne and Maddy a plastic cup with apple cider.

"Here's to a fresh start, lasting friendships, and burying the past where it belongs." We all raised our glasses.

"Here, here!"

We toasted and drank, and despite the unwanted attention, I felt like celebrating too. I felt amazing, empowered, and surrounded by love. I thought of the small chapel and how I'd be perfectly content looking down on that room filled with these five people.

Maddy interjected. "Will you come to my party at school?" Maddy held the flyer that I left on my passenger seat and was waving it around. Merman grabbed it.

"A party? I love a good party!"

"It's a round-up." Maddy pointed out.

"I see that, and I have the perfect hat for it too!" He turned to Celia and started in with a terrible southern accent. "Would you join me at the hoedown, little lady?" She giggled and replied with the perfect impersonation of a southern bell.

"Why, I'd be honored, sir. There aren't many hoedowns in these here parts."

"It's a round-up." Maddy corrected.

"Yes, it is, Maddy, and I can't wait to go!" Celia took her hand, spun her around, and curtsied. Maddy followed suit.

I looked to Oliver, knowing that I was about to ask him on what Merman was going to harass me endlessly about as being our first date. But I surprisingly didn't care.

"Would you like to go to a hoedown, Oliver?"

"Round-up, mommy!" Maddy insisted.

"Well then, would you like to go to a round-up, Oliver?"

"I thought you'd never ask! I'd love nothing more than to go to a round-up with you." I filled with waves of electricity at the "with you" part of his response.

"Eddie, you wouldn't mind staying behind and taking calls would you?" Merman asked.

"Do bears sh-" he paused and looked at Maddy before correcting himself. "Do bears poop in the woods?"

"Why yes, they do, my friend," Merman confirmed, slapping him on the back.

Maddy giggled, and the rest of us joined her after a brief and awkward moment of delayed shock and relief at Eddie's almost slip of the tongue.

We all moved to the table to eat the Chinese food that Merman ordered. I had grown dependent upon any good luck and blessings I could find, the promises in the fortune cookies included, and I had quite a collection after everyone's contributions. I was glowing with utter content. I looked around the table at everyone eating, talking, and laughing. It felt like a real family.

It was in such serene moments that the terror would clench me unexpectedly. It had been days without as much as a word from Jerry, but I knew he was plotting his attack. I didn't know when, and I didn't know how, and it threatened every worthwhile moment of my day. It took every ounce of will I had to stay present throughout the evening, and before I knew it, time had quickly passed.

We all began to part ways for the night, but before I could make it to the door, Merman held me back.

"Are you excited about tomorrow night?" He nodded toward Oliver and winked with a teasing smirk.

"You know what? I knew you were going to go there with this. You can think whatever you want. I'm going to a round-up with my friends and, just to remind you, I'm still married, as much as I might hate that fact."

He rolled his eyes and waved me off dismissively.

"You are officially, almost divorced, Casey."

"You are absurd, *Merman*." I said his name sarcastically to add emphasis to my claim.

"You are resisting the inevitable. I understand your being cautious, but if you blow it with him, I will personally punish you for an eternity."

"What are you talking about? What is the inevitable, I'd like to know?" I didn't want to know since there was nothing I could do about it anyway, and at the same time, I was desperate to hear what I thought he might say.

"If you can't tell that that man over there is falling in love with you, then you are denser than I thought." It was everything I wanted to hear but only added to the frustration.

"And what am I supposed to do about it, Merman? I'm not even finished cleaning up my first mess!"

"Who says it's going to be a mess? I think he's waiting for you to go through whatever you need to go through before you're ready to move on. I'm not telling you to marry him and make babies, just enjoy it and stop fighting it!"

"Speak for yourself." I nodded toward Celia.

"Oh, don't worry about me. I'm enjoying every minute." He folded his arms and grinned from ear to ear.

"Tell me everything!" I knew there was something going on, but I hadn't had a chance to get the details. "Do you *love* her?" I dragged the word out to tease him a little. He covered my mouth and gave me a stern look.

"I enjoy her immensely." He was being his proper self. I rolled my eyes. "And…" he conceded "I can see myself loving her."

"I knew it!" I couldn't contain myself, and it came out as a little more than a whisper. Oliver and Celia stopped their conversation at the door and looked. Merman glared at me.

"Sorry. It must be the champagne," I announced. It didn't seem like Celia had heard, but Merman was acting as if I had revealed top secret intelligence.

"Okay, goodnight, everyone," Merman said abruptly. He shuffled me out of his door a little more forcefully than usual.

"Geez, Merman!"

He paused his glare momentarily to wink at me quickly and then shut the door.

It was just the four of us in the hallway.

"Well, goodnight, guys," I initiated. "Maddy looks like she's ready to sleep for a week!" She was barely able to hold herself up anymore.

"I'll see you tomorrow." Oliver took my hand and squeezed it. Excitement pulsed through me again, as did the gnawing reminder of the past I needed to get in order before I could have a future.

Oliver walked Celia to her car as I put Maddy to bed and lay there thinking of the school round-up. I was restless and finding it impossible to sleep.

I wondered if Merman was still awake and decided it was the perfect time to learn a little bit about what made my elusive rescuer tick. I called from my dark kitchen, standing barefoot on the cold tile. With the first ring, I felt a little remorse at calling so late.

"Yes," he answered coolly, obviously still awake.

"Hi," I said through a giggle, feeling a little mischievous.

"Is that why you called? To say hi?"

"No, you brat. I want you to come upstairs and keep me company. I can't sleep." There was silence for a moment.

"I'll be right up." He hung up and was at the door in less than a minute.

"Did you run or something?" I asked as I let him in.

"Yes, I ran the full fifty feet."

"You are so ornery!"

"Is that how you treat your guests at midnight?"

"Just come in."

I pulled out some wine that was left over from a previous dinner and began to pour two glasses, hoping it would encourage a lengthier and less reserved conversation. He was immediately skeptical.

"What are you up to Miss *I can't sleep*?"

"I don't know what you're talking about." I handed him a glass and, he gave in with a shrug. "So I think you owe me some details on a few things."

"Oh, do I owe you?"

"Yes, you promised."

"Okay, what do you want to know that you haven't already announced to the entire staff of Golden Oaks?"

"She didn't hear me," I reassured him.

"Right," he said rolling his eyes.

"It makes me happy that you're so happy. Just don't screw it up by being your proper self." He started to argue, but I cut him off. "Spill it, Merman. I want to know every detail from the time you took your first breath to the time you pulled me out of that ivy."

"Oh, brother. Fine, but don't blame me when I bore you to sleep."

I folded my arms and refused to say another word. He took a sip, considering where to begin.

"Well, as you can guess I was born in England, a town called Brighton. I was much older before I gathered details about my parents, but never really knew either of them. I have very faint memories of my mother and never met my father. As I've heard it, I was conceived when my mother was only seventeen years old, with some dodgy character she'd met while aspiring to become a musician. My nana talked her into keeping me and promised to help with whatever we would need, so long as she dropped the rat, as she referred to my father."

"Who's your nana?" I asked, wanting to keep up with every small detail.

"My nana is my grandmom, Casey. Would you like me to continue?"

"Yes, I would like you to continue, touchy."

"Right. Well, my mother agreed, but continued to see him on the sly. I was only a year old when she decided to leave with him. She was going to put me up for adoption, but my nana insisted I be left with her. So…she left me."

As he spoke about his mother, I sensed resentment slip through his attempts at indifference, and I easily pictured him as a little boy, wondering where his mother was and why she didn't want him. My heart broke for him. Who wouldn't want Merman?

He continued, "She came back on occasion, wanting to see me, wanting money. Nana would give in to her every whim to avoid a scene. To protect me, she insisted my mother not tell me who she was and introduced her to me as Mary, though even at five, I knew exactly who she was by the way they spoke about me. When I was younger, I desperately wanted her to stay - wanted her to want me enough to stay - but as I got older, I would refuse to see her when she stopped by for her self-indulgent reunions. I hated her for leaving me, even though she left me with the most loving human I've ever known.

"My nana gave me everything she could afford and raised me with the values she had tried to give my mother. She taught me music and the significance of tea time." He smiled nostalgically. "She even taught me how to cook. Everything I know, everything worthwhile anyway, I learned from that amazing woman."

I suddenly understood why he wore her apron and kept what little he had left of her. I understood his love of old movies and retro fashions, and I was grateful that he'd had her.

"My mother did me a favor by leaving, even though she left a bit of a hole in me. I would have missed out on so much. So for that selfish deed, I am forever grateful, and I told her so the last time I saw her.

"She'd come looking for me when I was about twelve. She was haggard and obviously scarred by a hard life of drinking, drugs, and the rock and roll life she had chased. She told me that she'd made a mistake by leaving me for him, that from the start he'd gotten her involved in a lot of bad things and cheated on her without end before finally leaving her. He'd been arrested a couple of years before she came to me, and she had been trying to get her life together since.

"It was then that I told her it wasn't a mistake - that it was the best thing she could have done for me, and though I was happy she was getting her life together, I wanted nothing to do with her. I felt that if I let her back in, I was being disloyal to my nana and setting myself up for disappointment. She begged and promised that she would make it right, and that childish longing for acceptance and love from my mother took over. I told her I'd give her a chance.

"For my sake, my nana agreed to let her live with us again, and things were going really well for a while - long enough that I let her get close. She told me stories about her life and spent every afternoon teaching me how to play the guitar. I was finally happy to have her back and no longer waited for her to leave.

"It had been about a year of her living with us when I came home to find all of her things gone. The rat had gotten out of jail and come for her again, and she went with him without a fight. She left me a note telling me that she was proud of the young man I had become, and knew she was doing the right thing for me. Looking back, I can say that she was right, but back then it destroyed me. One more time, my nana picked me up and loved me through it – teaching me that there's a blessing and an opportunity in everything.

"A month after I graduated from high school, my nana had a heart attack and became very weak. Uncle Stanley came to help take care of her. He had moved to the U.S. when he graduated from college and started this funeral business, but he came back on occasion when I was growing up and took a liking to me, as he had never had children of his own. He was bitter toward my mother for abandoning both me and nana, and refused to let her near the house when she found out about how sick nana was.

"It wasn't long before nana passed, taking with her the only real love and dependability I'd ever known. I didn't have a job to keep up the house, let alone take care of myself. I was completely lost. Uncle Stanley offered to bring me back with him and give me a job and a place to live. There was nothing left for me there, so I came with him. I've been here ever since.

"I'm glad," was all I could think to say. "Not for the rest, but that you're here."

"I'm pretty glad myself. Now, is that enough, nosey?"

"That's enough…for now."

He rolled his eyes. "You're relentless." He got up and stretched. "Well, if you're done with me, I'm going to go to bed. I've just lived a lifetime in less than an hour."

"I'm done with you. Get out of here." I pushed him toward the door.

He turned before leaving.

"You are everything my mother couldn't be. I get a lot out of watching you love Maddy. I can't imagine you crashing anywhere else but my hilltop."

"Me either. I just hope I can do as good a job as your nana."

"She'd be proud. I am." He winked and closed the door.

I was glad to know him a little more, but my heart was broken for that little boy in Brighton. Everything he did began to make more sense to me. I understood why he kept Celia at a distance, why he helped a lost and struggling mother in the middle of the night, why he hated Jerry - Jerry the rat. The parallels in our lives were amazing. It couldn't be a coincidence that I'd landed here.

I drifted off considering what nana had said – that there were opportunities and blessings in everything, and I knew she was right. Like a butterfly, I would have to squeeze myself out of my cocoon, as painful and arduous as it might be, so that I could fly - and I would look back at that cocoon with gratitude…one day.

Chapter Eighteen

The Round Up

The next day there was a lot of work to be done. There were three new bodies to prep for services. Oliver was there as promised and took every opportunity he could to help me, teach me something new, or even just nudge me for encouragement. In the same place that once had me on my knees gagging over a toilet, I was now falling in love. It was happening, and there was nothing I could do about it. Half of the time I tried to heed Merman's advice and just enjoy it, and the other half I spent analyzing the possible ways it could end terribly. I knew deep down that if I didn't identify and resolve the repetitive patterns of my father and Jerry, I would inevitably repeat them. That wasn't something I was willing to do, especially with Oliver. I had gained a lot of clarity about my part in my past, and it was a good beginning. My choices would determine my future. I decided that with Oliver right beside me, just for the moment, I would choose to enjoy it, nothing more just yet.

Halfway through the day, Merman came in with an interesting smile on his face.

"Never in my life have I seen such a sight." He laughed a bit while Oliver and I waited for the punch line.

"Vivian is here with some papers for you to sign." My stomach turned at the mention of her name, not because she was an odd bird, but because it sent me back into the terrifying world where Jerry threatened to strip me of all happiness. My fear must have been obvious because Merman stopped laughing.

"This is good, Casey. Things are moving along, and from what I can tell, it's Jerry who should be frightened right now. You just need to sign some papers and get to a hoedown milady!" His horrible southern accent made me laugh and his summary of the circumstances made me feel a little calmer.

"We'll come with you. No one should have to go through an encounter with Vivian alone." He was right. She scared me with her wild attire and fiercely perfected glares. But really, I couldn't look at those papers without someone at my side.

The three of us walked down the hallway and into the office where Vivian awaited my signature on documents that were the equivalent of launching a missile into the enemy camp. There would surely be retaliation.

She was wearing a different color short skirt and tight top with matching shoes, and her hair was still in the same position. It was obvious that she liked to color coordinate. It was oddly impressive and reminded me of when I was thirteen - listening to and emulating Madonna. Her attempts at being sexy worked well I guessed, on a particular kind of man.

When we entered, she was adjusting her hair and shirt in the window. She straightened up when she noticed us.

"Mr. Linden wanted me to get these to you to sign as soon as possible." She handed me a stack of papers.

I leaned against the desk and began to read. Merman stood next to me and read along. It was a skeleton of my response, muscled up with a lot of legal jargon and a much harsher tone. Merman seemed delighted by the additions. I was shocked.

"This is going to really flip him out!" I flipped through to the last few pages.

"It's perfect," Merman responded, eagerly leaning over to read the end. We were asking for everything, including a psychological evaluation to determine whether or not Maddy should ever be subjected to a visit with Jerry without his receiving intense drug and alcohol rehab, parenting classes, and anger management classes. Don recommended, as was custom, to divide all assets equally, starting with the bank accounts, which he requested be frozen and divided immediately as well as the liquidation of all property. He concluded with the request that Jerry's half of the assets be used to pay all legal expenses and any remaining debt. It was a lot more aggressive than I could have ever been, and it frightened me a little.

"Sign it, Casey. What's the problem?" Merman was forcing a pen into my hand. I just stared at the papers hesitantly. "The war began long ago. It's time to invade and conquer."

I looked up for a second to ground myself in the moment and noticed Vivian throwing herself at Oliver. She was talking to him about something I couldn't hear and touching each button of his shirt down toward his belt. I suddenly felt jealous and tried to get her attention away from him.

"Where exactly do I need to sign, Vivian?" She shot me a glare and strutted over, pointing to the very obvious "sign here" stickers.

"Oh, thanks." I wasn't sure what to think about what I was feeling, but I wanted to make her leave before she could even look at him again. Oliver looked a little embarrassed.

Vivian turned back to him. "So why don't we get a bite to eat tonight, honey. I'm starving, and you look scrumptious." She was running her finger down his sleeve. He pulled away and laughed uncomfortably. I tried to focus on signing the papers and not stare with envy, but I couldn't help it. Merman stood back, looking amused by the sudden and strange triangle.

Oliver flashed an astonished look at me and then suddenly seemed to have come up with a way out.

"Well…actually, I already have plans tonight….with Casey." Vivian turned and shot a vicious glare at me again.

"Really, the sheets aren't even cold!" She grabbed the papers from me and looked through them. Merman was unable to completely hold in his laughter, and I was frozen in shock over her haughty flirtation and cattiness. "Did you sign everything?" I nodded - stunned. She abruptly walked out, swaying her hips down the long hallway.

Merman completely lost it, slapping the desk and laughing hysterically. "That was awesome!"

"Oh shut up, Merman. This isn't good. She's supposed to be on my side!" I turned on Oliver. "Why did you have to say you were going with me?"

"Well, I am, aren't I?" He looked confused and apologetic.

"Yeah, but now she's angry with me and carrying my response!"

"Relax, Casey. What do you think she's going to do, take it over to Jerry because she can't have Oliver? Listen, maybe she'll stumble into a black and white comic book, run into a flock of seagulls and realize love bites on her way back, forgetting all about you and Oliver." Merman was laughing hysterically again.

"Yes, Merman, she's going to time warp back to the eighties and take my response with her! You're ridiculous."

"Fine, I'm ridiculous, but you need to go get ready for the ball, Cinderella. We'll finish up out there and meet you and Maddy downstairs in an hour." I rolled my eyes and left to prepare for the round up and what I hoped would be a vacation from the drama of Jerry.

We all met outside of Merman's apartment wearing our array of cowboy and cowgirl attire. Oliver looked gorgeous as usual, wearing a button down plaid shirt, jeans and cowboy boots. Merman went all out with a leather vest, chaps and hat. Celia rivaled him with a similarly extravagant outfit. Maddy and I both wore jean skirts, white blouses, boots that I found at a vintage store, and pigtails tied off with red ribbons.

Everyone was excited to be dressed up and going out, and spent a good amount of time admiring each other's costumes before heading to the cars. Merman said he'd forgotten something inside and would meet us out by the car. When he came out, he had two cowboy hats for Maddy and me. Though I had been irritated with him earlier, it passed with the reminder of how generous and loving he was to both of us.

On the ride there, he played what he called mood music. It was a lot of old country music that was easy to recognize and had us all singing along.

The school parking lot was packed full, and the campus had been completely transformed into what looked like an old western town with bales of hay, hitching posts with cardboard horses, old wooden business signs, and even a little petting zoo at the entrance. Maddy was delighted and ran ahead of us to her teacher, Miss Lindsay, who was running the zoo. She asked if she could stay and help with the animals while we walked around, and Miss Lindsay was happy to keep her. She promised to keep an eye on her and then walk her to us when she was finished with her shift. I was a little nervous about leaving her but figured she would be safe with her teacher.

The four of us bought our tickets and went inside.

The Saloon was offering fruit punch moonshine, cactus rings, and cattle burgers, while the town bank was trading money for game tickets. The blacktop had been converted into a dance floor with a decent size stage for the band that was playing.

Celia and I were hungry so the guys went and got food while we watched a cowboy lasso some kids who were brave enough to run around in his rodeo. It was the first night out that I'd had since before Jerry, and I was overfilled with giddiness even though it was an elementary school function.

Since the line for food was long, Celia and I went to have our pictures taken in front of an outlaw backdrop, using some of their gun props to spruce it up. When we came back to the table, Oliver and Merman had returned with two trays full of food and drinks.

I looked across the yard to see if I could wave Maddy down so that she could come eat and also because I was beginning to have that gnawing, anxious feeling in the pit of my stomach. There was no real reason that I could see to feel anxious, but I did, and I wanted her close by. I spotted her and waved my arm to get her attention. Merman grabbed it and pulled it down.

"She's having fun. Let her stay. Her cattle burger and moonshine will still be here in fifteen minutes. Just enjoy your night out on the plains of the wild, wild west." He tried his accent again.

"That accent is absurd, and I just feel nervous having her out of sight." I was holding my stomach as it twisted.

"Are you afraid she'll be held for ransom by the child lassoing cowboy over there?" He made a very serious and concerned face as though he'd get up and wrestle the cowboy himself if I were that worried about it.

"I don't know what I'm afraid of - my guts are just twisting, which usually happens right before trouble."

"There's no trouble to be found here. Look, there's the sheriff's station right there." He pointed over to one of the booths that had the sign Sheriff's Station hanging over the top. The principal was dressed up in an old sheriff's costume and looked hysterical with her fake moustache.

"You're right - she looks like someone you don't want to mess with."

"So should I spike the moonshine fruit punch?" He winked at me, but I had a feeling he'd find a way if I agreed. I pushed him, and he pretended to fall off of the bench, threatening to report me to the sheriff. He had a knack for cheering me up.

We ate our cattle burgers and cactus rings and enjoyed the bustle around us. As we were cleaning up, the band began to play. Everyone was migrating to the dance floor to watch or dance. Merman stood up and took his hat off.

"Well, hello, pretty lady. Would you do me the honor of joining me on the dance floor?" We all laughed at his accent, though I had to admit, it was getting better. Celia agreed and took his hand.

"We'll be back quicker than you can tie a hog." They headed off to the dance floor. Meanwhile, I couldn't stop looking toward the entrance for Maddy. For a moment, I couldn't see her, and a shot of terror ran through me.

"It's okay, I see her. She's coming over here with Miss Lindsay. They're walking by the bank." Oliver had put his hand on my back and was pointing to where they were, clearly sensing my fear.

"Oh, good. Thanks. I'm just a little nervous tonight." I was more than a little nervous. For some reason I was completely on edge. Maddy skipped up and gave me hug, talking as fast as she could about everything that had happened in the last half hour. We waved to Miss Lindsay and watched while Maddy scarfed down her food so that she could go and play more. Oliver told her that the best eaters chewed at least ten times with each bite. We laughed as she concentrated on her chew count.

Renee, one of the moms that I had recently befriended, approached our table with enthusiasm.

"Hi, Casey, how are things going?" She was acting overly friendly and sort of silly. She kept looking at Oliver, and I could tell that she wanted an introduction.

"Renee, this is Oliver. Oliver, Renee." They greeted each other and shook hands.

"Have you had a chance to do any dancing tonight? The band is great." She kept looking at Oliver with a big and silly grin on her face. I knew that he probably got this all of the time, and I hadn't noticed before since I'd never seen him outside of the mortuary but for the crime scene at Jerry's.

"No. Not yet. Maddy's working on her cattle burger right now. Maybe later." I was hoping she'd leave before she embarrassed me and herself further, but instead she winked and carried on.

"Well, James would love to sit and eat with Maddy. You two should head out to the dance floor." Her son, James, was picking his nose while staring off toward the cowboy in his rodeo. I looked at Oliver, and he gestured to me as if it were my choice. "Oh, they'll be fine," Renee insisted. "We'll finish eating and then I'll take them to the pony rides."

"Oh, mommy, can I go? Please?" Maddy had barbeque sauce all over her face and had stopped mid-chew to beg.

"That's very nice of you to offer, Renee." I was a little embarrassed about the idea of dancing with Oliver, let alone to country music and it's notoriously cheesy love lyrics, but I didn't want to disappoint everyone, so I agreed.

"We'll be right by the ponies when you're done." She winked at me again and then shooed us away. Oliver stood up, put his hand out, and then led me to the dance floor.

He walked me to the center of the stage, took my right hand, and twirled me around once. I nervously laughed at the unexpected formality. He pulled me in close and wrapped his other arm up and around my back. We were eye to eye and my heart was racing. He watched me for a second and smiled, then led me into the song. He was a very good dancer, whereas I just tried not to trip over him. We somehow found our rhythm together, and beyond the nervous pattern of my heartbeat, I was completely content.

The song ended, and we all clapped, though I hoped it hadn't stopped for good.

"You were great." He was trying to compliment me, though I knew he was just being nice.

"It's not exactly hard to follow your lead. Where did you learn to dance like that?"

"My mom taught me, actually. It's the one thing I have to remember her by. We used to dance together in our living room all of the time." Just then, the music picked back up, but this time it was a slow song. He held his hand out as an offer, and I took it. This time he pulled me in a little closer and we were almost cheek to cheek. His smell overwhelmed me. I felt dizzy and dreamy as he moved me around the floor. I was glad that he couldn't see my face because it wouldn't have been hard to read. I couldn't imagine the moment ending. I couldn't imagine wanting to be anywhere else, with anyone else. I closed my eyes, rested my head on his shoulder and let myself be lost in the moment.

"Mommy!" Maddy's voice pulled me out of serenity and into a full blown arrhythmia with the unusual desperation it carried. I stepped away from Oliver and looked up to see Jerry standing there holding her hand in the middle of the dance floor. If it weren't for the irregular beats, I wouldn't have known my heart was beating at all. I certainly wasn't breathing. I was taking note of every possible exit in my periphery, but my eyes were glued to his hand, which held Maddy's.

"Isn't that sweet?" He kneeled down to Maddy's height. "Look Maddy, your mom is dancing with some stranger instead of watching you." He made a tisk sound and an evil, but sloppy smirk. He was obviously intoxicated, and Maddy looked scared. I wanted his throat. Renee came running up with a horrified and apologetic look on her face.

"I'm sorry, Casey - he just came and took her from me."

"Let go of her, Jerry." I stepped forward ready to fight if I had to.

"But she's my girl." He pulled her close to him, and she tried to pull away.

"You're hurting me, daddy, and you don't smell good." Just when I thought it was going to turn into a massacre, he let her go, and she ran behind me. I looked her over to make sure she was fine.

"Celia, take her out of here, please," I implored, desperate to remove Maddy from the hostile scene.

"Okay, come on, Maddy, let's get some ice cream." Celia whisked her away before Jerry started in again.

"So you think you can beat me with your lawyer and your lies. You're gonna wish you hadn't started this. Even if you win in the end, I don't need a courtroom to beat you. Everywhere you go, I'll find you. Everywhere you go, I'll find her." He pointed after Maddy, and Merman and Oliver both stepped in front of me at the same time. Merman looked like he was ready to lunge at him, but Oliver held him back.

So Vivian had served Jerry the papers, and he came looking for me here.

"I think it's in your best interest to leave and stay away from both of them." Oliver's tone was calm but firm. By this point, almost the entire dance floor was stopping to watch.

"I don't know who you think you are, but you need to stay out of my business. This is between me and her." He stepped a little closer to Oliver, who didn't budge.

"Well, now it's between you and me. So if you have anything else to say, you can say it to me. Then you can leave, or I can walk you out if you'd prefer." From what I had seen before, I felt fairly confident that Oliver could and would walk Jerry out without a fight. Jerry jeered at him.

"Who is this guy?" He looked around and laughed sarcastically. "Isn't this cute? Pointing fingers at me and you're having your own little fling. You always were a tramp. So you want a piece of my wife, huh?"

"It's time for you to go, Jerry." Oliver carefully approached Jerry, who looked indignant.

"If that's how you want it, tough guy, then bring it." Jerry swung at Oliver, and within seconds, Oliver had Jerry's arm hiked up behind his back with him completely submissive on his knees. Jerry was swearing, but I could barely make out the words through his growls of pain. "Let go."

"Are you done fighting?" Oliver's voice was still as calm as before.

"Yeah, let go, asshole!" He could barely talk through the pain.

"Are you going to leave without a scene?" Everyone had crowded around and was waiting to see what would happen.

"Screw…you!" He was struggling to breathe. It was oddly pleasing to see Jerry so powerless. It's how I had felt for so long.

"I can't let go until you agree, Jerry."

"Fine. Just get off of me!" Oliver let him go, and Jerry got up and shook himself off. "This ain't over, bitch." Oliver stepped toward him, and Jerry flinched before making his way back to the parking lot. As I followed him with my eyes, I was startled by who I saw standing next to one of the school buildings. It was Vivian. Merman and Oliver saw her too. Merman looked at me, dumbfounded, with his eyes wide.

So she had gone to Jerry with the papers and then she'd brought him here. But how had she known to come here? I was so confused and infuriated. I'd had a bad feeling about her from the beginning. I watched as she followed Jerry toward the parking lot.

Oliver turned to me. "Are you okay?"

"Yeah, I'm fine." Words couldn't describe how I felt, so I kept it simple.

"Okay, stay here. We'll be right back." He and Merman followed Jerry and Vivian out into the parking lot, and I looked for Maddy and Celia. They were sitting by the faux sheriff's station eating ice cream. Maddy seemed to have recovered just fine. I sat down hoping to recover myself, but in an instant we were surrounded by people whose dramatic tones and explicit questions threatened to disrupt the calm. I moved them away from Maddy and endured their inquiries alone.

"Oh my gosh, are you okay?"

"He always creeped me out, Casey. I'm so glad you left."

"I'm glad your boyfriend put him in his place!"

"Just let us know if we can do anything to help."

"You poor thing. How awful it must have been to live with him!"

"Who was that hottie that had him on the ground?"

I couldn't even get a word in. They were talking over me at that point. It was pointless to try and explain that Oliver was not my boyfriend. They were practically planning my wedding shower…or their own.

I was still spun by Vivian. It was Friday night, so there was no way for me to reach Don to tell him that we had been compromised. The old feeling of not being able to trust anyone in the world came back tenfold. I was trying to go over all of the scenarios that would make sense of what she had done. If she expected to keep her job, then she must have at least served Jerry the papers. I knew I wasn't going to solve the riddle that night. I would have to find some way to make it sanely through the weekend until I could talk to Don.

Chapter Nineteen

Oliver

Once Jerry was far from the scene, the police arrived.

"I'm glad there wasn't a *real* emergency," Miss Lindsay scoffed, concerned with how long it took the police to arrive. Everyone was huddled into one group or another, speculating like the nosy neighbors who come out in their pajamas and watch as a house burns down.

The police took statements from multiple people who claimed they had witnessed Jerry's drunken and hostile behavior. I was surprised that Jerry was losing control so progressively. I never thought he would respond to all of this with drunken, public assaults, but then again, I had never stood up to him, or anyone, like this before. I imagined life as he knew it had been flipped upside down, and apparently Jerry didn't do well upside down.

"Did you call them?" I asked Miss Lindsay. I was curious, as were the police, as to which of the present witnesses had called. So far no one had taken credit.

"No, I didn't even notice him until people started gathering around the dance floor," she muttered, looking as caught up in the drama as everyone else.

I left, totally unnoticed by Miss Lindsay or the others, and made my way back to our group of incident "victims", as we had been recorded in the police report. We sat at a table and watched the spectacle, laughing at some of the rumors that were beginning to spread. One woman swore she had seen a gun, and another one was pretty sure it all started with Jerry trying cut in for a dance with me.

It was starting to get a little cold for the skirts we were wearing, and when the excitement had died down, we decided that we'd had enough entertainment for one night. We walked past the crowds of people with their questioning stares and pointing fingers, and loaded into the car. The drive home was quiet for some time, with Maddy asleep under my arm. Merman broke the silence.

"I hate to say you're right, but you were right!" I knew exactly what he was talking about. "But I should have known. Anyone who uses that much hair spray is likely to suffer rare side effects such as attending a round-up with a drunken lunatic."

"It just doesn't make any sense," I jumped in - relieved that someone else was still thinking about the fact that Vivian had shown up. "I mean, I didn't really know what she would do, but I didn't expect that! How would she even know about the round-up? And what interest could she possibly have in Jerry? And why would she do this to Don?" I was hoping someone had some insight, but nobody had much of an answer.

Oliver assured me that Vivian or no Vivian, Jerry was knitting quite a noose to hang himself with in court. Celia seemed to think that the two were a perfect match and hoped that maybe, with all of the gum Vivian chewed, she would blow a bubble big enough to carry them both back to the crazy town they came from. Merman couldn't wait to meet Don outside of his office Monday morning to get some answers. I felt relief at Merman's inclusion of himself in the Monday morning scenario. I couldn't begin to imagine how that was going to go down.

We came home to Eddie in a whirl. He had received two pick-up calls in the last hour and had just returned from the first.

"Oliver, do you think you can stay tonight?" Merman asked. The fog has come back with a vengeance." I dreaded another sinister and humiliating matchmaking plot.

Oliver didn't put up any resistance to the idea. "Sure. No problem."

I figured I would make my exit before Merman took it too far, and get Maddy to bed since she was a heavy sleeper and could no longer stand on her own. I was actually looking forward to plopping myself down on the couch with a glass of wine and a good movie. Oliver next to me would have been better, but it seemed he would be busy.

Just as I started to head off and say goodbye, Merman changed the course of the evening.

"Great. I won't need you for another hour or so. Eddie's in the embalming room getting things started. I'll send him home when I get back, and we'll finish up in there."

To my surprise, Merman wasn't pushing for holy matrimony that night, just providing an interesting twist. I was relieved, but wondered what Oliver was going to do in the meantime. I didn't waste a second.

"You're welcome to come and kick your feet up at our place." Just after I said it, I was afraid I had crossed the line and terrified that he wasn't really interested.

"Are you sure I wouldn't be in the way?"

"No! Of course not. I'd love to have you." Did I actually say love? Well, there was no taking it back.

"Then I'd love to come and kick my feet up with you." He smiled contentedly.

Merman walked away, yelling down the hall, "I'll be back in a couple hours."

"I thought he said an hour," I pointed out.

"Me too, but are you surprised? He's been trying to get us alone for a while now."

I didn't know what to say in response. We were both well aware of Merman's intentions, but discussing it suddenly felt awkward. I wasn't sure whether to drop it or make a joke about it. It seemed like anything I said would make me appear either indifferent or presumptuous.

I tried for something unassuming. "I'm not surprised at all. Sometimes I think it's sweet and sometimes I want to strangle him."

We continued to talk as we walked up the stairs.

"I think Merman really cares about you. He can be a little over the top, but he means well. I'm actually flattered that he thinks you would be interested in me."

He had it all wrong. I couldn't believe he would be interested in me! I was in the middle of a quarter-life crisis with a psychotic ex-husband and just beginning to turn a new leaf, let alone carrying a five year old child in my arms.

"Me? Are you serious? I can't believe he thinks you would want anything to do with the drama that swirls about me daily! I do think you're amazingly generous for helping me the way you have though, and I feel a little bad about getting you involved, but let me just say that seeing Jerry crying uncle on the ground was quite thrilling! You have to tell me where you learned that." I was talking too fast, but I was so nervous. I hoped to change the subject before I got my foot too far down my throat.

"Casey," he said seriously. He wasn't laughing at my Jerry joke, but was intent on looking me in the eye. Every time he looked at me like that, I felt like one of those collapsible toys, where you push from the bottom and they go completely limp.

"Yes?" I swallowed over the lump. His intensity made me nervous about what he might say.

"It's too late for me. I've been wholly and hopelessly bewitched by you, and I'd be willing to try for an eternity to make you to feel the same. But I will never ask for more than you have to give, and if a friend is what you want to be, then I will be your friend."

I was totally speechless - in a daze - waffling between wanting to give in and considering the likely disaster if I did, let alone the fact that he just pulled a line from my favorite movie of all time.

"I don't know what to say." I searched for the words that might summarize the blitz of thoughts swirling my mind.

"You don't have to say anything," he stopped. "I just wanted you to know, and I don't expect anything in return. Besides, we should get sleeping beauty in her bed."

"But I want to say something," I said, still grasping for words. "I'd be lying if I told you I didn't look forward to seeing you each day, or that I find it difficult to stand when you look at me like that, or that I felt something I've never felt before when you held me on that dance floor." I'd said it. There was no longer the need for pretenses, just honesty. "I don't know what the answer is, but I know that when I stumbled in here, I was lost, and I've been trying to find my way ever since. I'm making choices about what I want and who I am, and it feels amazing!" He listened earnestly. "I like who I am today, and I love who I am with you, but between my father and Jerry, I know that I must have some remaining knee jerk reactions when it comes to men, and I want to make sure this isn't a knee jerk reaction." I paused to see if he understood, or if I merely sounded like an existential feminist to him.

He looked relieved, maybe that I felt the same as he did. "I completely understand what you're saying, and we have time to figure this out. It doesn't have to be tonight."

"But we don't have forever. That's something I've learned here. I want to look back without regret." I felt free to tell him everything. There was no holding me back anymore. "Give me a just a minute."

I unlocked the door and walked Maddy into her room, placing her in her bed. My heart was pounding as I considered what I was about to do. I spent a few seconds trying to catch my breath and then popped into the bathroom to look myself over. My hair was still in pigtails so I took them out and combed through it with my fingers. I brushed my teeth and pinched my cheeks for a little color, though I knew I wouldn't need that shortly. I looked at myself from every angle and finally concluded that it wasn't going to get any better. When I walked into the living room, he was still standing by the door. I walked over to him and took his hand. I put it to my heart and let him feel the double pace.

"This is what you do to me." His response was hard to read. He almost looked sad about the revelation. "I don't mind when it's for you."

"Casey, I…" I cut him off because I had more to say, and I didn't want to lose my nerve.

"Just let me finish. I don't want to believe that what I feel for you is fleeting or part of a repetition of dysfunction handed down to me by my parents, but I want to be sure. I figure if I keep working on me that it will all fall into place naturally." He nodded. "Having said all of that, I want to ask you to do something for me."

"Anything. I'll do anything for you." He seemed sincere, but I'd wait to judge after I laid out my plan.

"Will you kiss me? Just once, and then I want to make a promise to myself that the next time we kiss, all of this mess with Jerry will be behind me, and I will be starting fresh, pursuing my dreams and standing on my own two feet…"

Without missing a beat, and before I could finish my sentence, he stepped in toward me, moving me nearly up against the wall behind us, and took my face with both hands. He looked at me for a moment before pressing his lips to mine. I melted into him, taking in every movement and every sense. He reached behind me like he had on the dance floor and pulled me in closer. He was gentle even though the passion stirring up was fierce. I was completely consumed by him, and I couldn't tell anymore where his lips and body stopped and mine began. I felt an electric heat all over, and thought I might lose myself entirely. I wanted more and more, and I didn't know how to stop. I had never felt this way or imagined anyone *could* feel this way. It took me by surprise. I ran my fingers through his hair and pulled him in closer, at which point he pulled his lips away from mine.

"Casey," he breathed.

"What?" My eyes were still closed, and my lips were reaching for his.

"Just one kiss?" He leaned his head back far enough to look at me.

"Right." I confirmed. "So why are we talking right now?"

He smiled, then held my face once more and pressed his lips against mine in a way that told me the moment was coming to a close. I pulled him in closer, not wanting it to end.

"Casey, I don't want to break any promises tonight, but if you keep pulling me like that, it's going to take more strength than I think I have to resist."

He was right, and in an instant, all of that passion was replaced with frustration and longing. I suddenly felt like there was nothing that could get in my way from finishing things up with Jerry - mercilessly and thoroughly.

I let go of him and leaned against the wall. He did the same. We both laughed quietly as we caught our breath. As I replayed the kiss in my mind, I was shaken by chills. He laughed again.

"Me too." That's all he had to say, and I understood.

"Well, how about a movie and a glass of wine?" I offered, to change course before I dove back in. We both laughed at the simplicity of the suggestion in comparison to what had just happened.

"I'd love that." He took my hand. "Is this okay?"

"Yeah, that's okay." He held my hand to his heart this time, and I could feel it beating hard. I returned the gesture and we both smiled. I had never been so happy, and I had never looked forward to a lifetime before.

We sat with our wine and had a dvd in the player waiting to be played, but I was more interested in him.

"So what are you doing here?" I asked. He looked at me quizzically, and I realized that could have been taken any number of ways. "Not here with me! Here, at Golden Oaks." He laughed at me teasingly, and I playfully pushed him.

"So, no one's told you?" he asked, seeming truly surprised.

"Well, Celia says that you came here to find life through death, or something philosophical like that." He laughed slightly at the simple summary of what I could tell was a more complicated story.

"Yeah, it's something like that. So you know that I'm a doctor." I nodded, not wanting to interrupt. "I'm actually a surgeon, or was a surgeon at a hospital in the city. I was one of the youngest surgeons on staff, studying under one of the greatest surgeons in the state. I had it all, or one might think from the outside looking in."

I nuzzled into the couch, getting comfortable for the story I had been waiting to hear. He sank in close to me and looked afar, pondering for a moment before he continued.

"I spent most of my time there for nearly six years, working forty hour shifts, napping in the call room and eating all of my meals in the hospital cafeteria. I couldn't imagine anything else. I have a home, but I was rarely there. My refrigerator stayed empty, and I hired a housekeeper just to keep the place aired out and in working order. It was kind of absurd now that I think about it, but it's what most of us do. It's all-consuming work in residency.

"Things had become rather routine, and I found myself gliding in and out of the OR on a daily basis and growing somewhat callous. It was becoming less and less about the patients and more and more about successful surgeries. I hadn't experienced one patient loss, mostly due to the nature of the cases and also sheer luck, or so I thought. One might think a record like that would be an accomplishment that would build confidence, but over time I was beginning to grow more and more anxious, knowing that it was only a matter of time. I had seen the impact that death had on some of my colleagues, especially their first.

"For weeks, the fear and anxiety was growing, and I noticed that I was becoming careless in surgery under the pressure. Each patient that came into the room was a potential loss for me. My attending recommended I take some time off, but I didn't want to give in like that. I thought the best thing to do was to push through, and I convinced him that I would be fine.

"One morning, we were assigned a patient who had been in a car accident - the driver had already died, and he was barely hanging on. By the time he arrived in the OR, he had lost a substantial amount of blood through severe trauma to his torso and head, and brain damage was of great concern. He was very young, maybe eighteen, and I knew that his chances weren't good.

"We worked for hours trying to repair extensive damage, but nothing had improved. I was becoming obsessed, trying every way I could to stop the bleeding and repair the damage, when suddenly, his heart stopped. I tried everything I knew to bring him back, but there was no use, he was gone. After three minutes of manually pumping his heart, my attending pulled me away and called the time of death.

"I couldn't accept, despite the overwhelming facts of the case, that nothing could have been done for him, and I was becoming convinced that my self-produced anxiety was the cause. I couldn't understand why I had become so overwhelmed with the fear of death when it's a daily occurrence in my profession. I was a wreck and my attending insisted I take a leave of absence and seek counseling before returning, which I did.

"He referred me to a therapist, who after a week had me convinced he was a quack. I never believed in therapy and certainly never thought I would be sitting on a couch talking about my fears. He concluded that I needed to face my fear of death in order to overcome it. It seemed like a diagnosis I could have concluded on my own for free, but when he told me his recommended solution, I almost fell over. He admitted that it was outside the realm of traditional treatment, but felt confident that it would have me back on my feet in no time." He paused and smiled to himself as he seemed to reflect on that very day. He took a sip of wine and looked at me.

"Just making sure I haven't bored you to sleep."

"Are you kidding? So what did he want you to do?"

"Well, he said he had an old friend who owned a mortuary and suggested I work weekend hours there to directly confront death. It was experimental, but he figured that if I saw enough deaths that were out of my control, I could possibly accept that there was only so much I could do and that the rest was up to God or fate or the universe or whatever I believed in. I didn't know what I believed in, but I knew something drastic needed to happen because I was completely lost. So I agreed."

"You must have thought he was crazy!"

"Of course I did, but I was willing to do anything at that point, and they weren't going to let me come back to the hospital without clearance from the therapist. I knew that if I did nothing, it would eventually ruin my career and the life I had been working to build for so many years." He stopped and smiled at me.

"What?"

"Well, I had been working here for a month, doing the embalming since I was knowledgeable about anatomy, and I had developed a sort of meditation when the room was empty where I would get into a hospital gown and lie down on one of the prep slabs to experience what death might feel like. I know it seems weird, but being here had given me an entirely different understanding of death. I wasn't afraid of the death of others anymore, but I was suddenly afraid of my own, so I imagined myself as one of the people that come in here, lying on a slab, being prepared for a service, and it brought me an odd sense of peace about it. It's just part of life, and it's not good and it's not bad, it just is. This is what I was doing when you found me."

I just stared in amazement as he concluded his story. He had been through so much and was trying to find peace just like me. All of a sudden, the thought of what I was going to do before he had jumped up and screamed that day was now reviving the humiliation. After a moment of silence, Oliver broached the subject further.

"So…you were going to look at my…I mean, were you really?" He was beginning to laugh, and I was mortified.

"Well, I thought you were dead and…"

"And you wanted to see a dead man's…"

"Okay, okay, stop, it was really nothing, I mean, I'm sure it's really something, I mean…" I was floundering, and he seemed to be enjoying it.

"Keep it coming, this is getting better every second." After a minute of torturing me, he changed the subject.

"Now it's your turn. What are you guys doing here? I mean…how did that happen?"

I really didn't want to talk about Jerry. The thought of him infuriated me and reminded me that there was much work to be done before I could have this amazing man sitting before me. But he had told me everything, and I felt I owed him the same in return. So I decided to briefly describe the events that led us there that night - the paint, my father, the crash, Merman, the ad in the newspaper, and Uncle Stanley.

As I spoke, he gazed at me sweetly. I could tell that he was following my every move. He watched my lips as I spoke, my hand as I nervously pushed my hair behind my ears, and he seemed amused by the way I became fidgety when I noticed him looking at me.

"You're amazing you know," he said when I was finished telling my story. "There aren't many people in this world that would give up everything and start over."

"You did," I reminded him. He smiled shyly and gestured in agreement.

"I think we're all working through our messes," he said "and the best thing we can hope for is someone to trudge through it with us. Someone who makes it all seem worthwhile at the end of an awful day and makes it even brighter on a beautiful one." He put his hand on mine.

"That sounds perfect," I agreed.

We didn't speak after that. We just sat on the couch with our heads resting on the back of it, looking into each other's eyes. Our fingers played together, and every new touch set my heart up again. I was growing sleepy and my eyes heavy.

"You can go to sleep," he whispered.

"Don't leave," I whispered back. I barely had the energy to speak anymore.

"I won't," he promised, running his fingers through the top of my hair. I don't know when, but I drifted to sleep with his eyes on me.

I was awakened by a gentle knock on the door. Merman opened it and whispered loudly, "You ready, Oliver? It's gonna be crazy tonight." Seeing us sitting together and the obvious connection, he quickly bowed out of the room. "I'll see you in a minute then."

"Oh, Merman. You've gotta love him." We both laughed.

"I'm glad we had a chance to tell our stories. I'm looking forward to the day that I can scoop you up and kiss you again." He leaned forward and put his forehead to mine.

I breathed him in one last time that night, and through the pounding of my heart, I could hardly whisper the words, "Me too."

Chapter Twenty

Shady Business

The weekend flew by with services on both days, filling up both chapels. I didn't even flinch anymore at the morose and gory details of my job and was beginning to feel a great sense of purpose in what I was doing.

There was a nagging question weighing on my mind about Oliver, but there wasn't a moment to ask him until Sunday night. We were all gathered at Merman's for our weekly family dinner and while cleaning up, I asked him.

"I was wondering how long you plan on staying here," I queried with trepidation, dreading the thought of him leaving. "I mean, I assume that you'll want to get back to the hospital at some point."

"I'm actually starting back at the hospital next week, on a limited basis. I'll really just be acting as a fill in, and I'll be here the rest of the time." He paused before continuing. "As for the future, I don't know anymore. I thought I'd be done here a month ago, but then…I met you, and I can't seem to leave."

"Am I the only reason you've stayed this long?" I didn't like the idea of holding him back no matter how much I enjoyed being near him.

"I'm here because it's the happiest I've been in a long time. As for medicine, I've officially completed my residency, and the world is my oyster. I figure I have a while before I have to make any big decisions. What about you? How long are you here?" He too seemed to be looking for more answers.

I wasn't expecting that question. I had no idea. I laughed nervously as I really didn't have an answer.

"I haven't thought about it. I've really just considered myself lucky to be here at all. I guess a lot hinges on how things turn out in a couple of weeks in court. Anything could happen."

"I don't think you have anything to worry about. You have an army of people on your side, and Jerry seems determined to bring himself down," he reassured as he pushed my hair behind my ear.

"God, I hope you're right."

Merman walked up and joined in the conversation.

"He's right, and I'm sure we'll get some interesting information tomorrow morning. I bet Don's going to turn purple when we tell him about Vivian. Do you think it would be tacky to take a picture of his reaction?" he asked. Oliver and I both responded at the same time.

"Yes, Merman!"

"Fine. You're a couple of party poopers, you know that?" He dismissed us with a wave of his hand.

We eventually parted ways after I had milked the night for as much time as I could, dreading the restless hours ahead.

I could hardly sleep with all of the possibilities swarming around in my chaotic mind. Though I felt more and more confident each day, the idea of losing Maddy seemed to creep up and haunt me in the darkest and loneliest of hours when there was no way to escape it.

My eyes were still open when the sun came up, and the churning in my stomach set in with the sounding of my alarm. I rolled over and took a deep breath before starting the day.

Merman and I dropped Maddy off at school and headed straight to Don's office. We were there early and had to wait outside until he came.

"What do I say?" I asked Merman nervously. I didn't know how to tell Don.

"You just tell him what his lovely Vivian has been up to and ask where we stand now," Merman said flatly. Before he finished his sentence, Don came walking up the street and didn't seem surprised to see us there.

"Hello, Casey, Merman. Come on in," he said coolly as he opened the door. He seemed far too casual and almost expectant in his tone. Merman jumped right in.

"Did you know that Vivian was moonlighting as a spy for the enemy?" he asked with a hint of accusation.

Don smiled and chuckled at Merman's description of Vivian. He took off his suit coat and casually placed it over the back of his chair before sitting down and gesturing for us to do the same. Merman and I both looked at each other perplexed, but complied.

"Vivian's no spy - at least not for the enemy," he said assuredly. We both remained puzzled, so Don continued.

"Vivian is good at what she does. She found Jerry at a bar he frequents, and served him with the papers. Apparently, he didn't take it well and was already pretty intoxicated. She followed him, hoping she could call him in for drunk driving or catch him in some other compromising situation that might help us. And I hear that she did," he said proudly.

"So she didn't tell him we were at the school?" I was beginning to feel a little bad about misjudging her.

"Of course not. Jerry already knew about the round-up. She saw the flyer in his truck on the way into the bar. When she realized where he was heading, she called the police and stuck around to make sure things were handled."

"So *she* called the police," I said out loud to myself, putting the pieces together.

"She's flippin' brilliant! A little shady, but brilliant!" Merman nearly shouted.

"Well, Merman, a little shady business gets the job done sometimes. Jerry's done much worse, wouldn't you say?"

"I *would* say!" While they continued to talk about how brilliant the plan had been, I was still trying to review the details of that night in my head.

"I'm glad you came this morning, because his lawyer has filed an emergency hearing with the court. They filed it Friday before the close of the day, and it's been scheduled for tomorrow morning at eight o'clock. They're hoping to get temporary custody until this battle has concluded." I couldn't believe what I was hearing.

"Tomorrow? And he wants to take Maddy tomorrow? This can't happen, Don. Tell me this can't happen!" My heart was racing again, and I felt like I might fall to the floor.

"Relax, Casey. Unless the court finds that Maddy is in imminent danger with you, they won't do much more than assign minor's counsel, which is a lawyer for the child, who investigates each side and reports their findings to the court. Besides, when I present the judge with Friday night's police report, I doubt we'll have a problem. I'm also going to request that the accounts be frozen tomorrow and that the balance as of *your* last transaction be split, and request that the sale of the property be forced immediately. There are some benefits to this emergency hearing, Casey. In fact, this may help settle the case much sooner."

I was overwhelmed with information and anticipation. "So what do I need to do?"

"You just need to show up at the court house tomorrow morning. I'll do the rest." Don gave me a comforting smile and labored to lean over his desk to pat me on the hand. "It's going to be fine."

"Do you have any more espionage in the works?" Merman was so excited he could hardly contain himself.

"Well, now, Merman, that's something I wouldn't tell you today, is it?" Don chided teasingly. Merman took that as a yes and hugged me hard.

"This is going to be great, Casey, you'll see," Merman insisted.

I wasn't so sure about that.

I had a difficult time getting through the day of work. We had one remaining service to prepare for the following day. Apparently, Uncle Stanley had arranged for Merman to be with me in court and was going to cover the service himself. He still wouldn't say anything to me personally, but I truly appreciated the gesture.

I prayed more than ever that day, for calm, for faith, for protection, and mostly for victory. In utter powerlessness, I turned it all over and acknowledged that whatever happened would be the right and perfect thing for now. That resolve lasted about a minute, the rest of the time I was a complete wreck. I couldn't bear to think of losing Maddy in less than twenty-four hours, but I tried to turn that over too. I tried to convince myself that no matter what happened, we would be okay.

Toward the end of the day, Merman approached me in the chapel. I had been setting up the flower arrangement while Maddy played teacher at the pulpit. It was amazing how well she had adapted.

"You look like you need to get out and have a good time."

"And what do you have in mind, Merman?" I answered with tired sarcasm.

"Well, there's someone here to see you in the front," he said with a hint of playful excitement.

I couldn't imagine who it could be, but was too caught up in the anxiety surrounding the next day to really care.

"Are you messing with me, Merman? Because I'm not up for it right now. I'm freaking out!"

"I know you are, so why don't you just go to the front and quit giving me such a hard time!"

He wasn't going to let it go, and I was too tired and terrified to argue with him. I wearily walked to the front entrance and staggered backward upon seeing Oliver standing there, beautiful as ever, in a dark suit and a tie.

"Hi there," he said in his deep and enchanting tone.

He approached me with a vibrant bouquet of flowers.

I was so happy to see him and suddenly felt like a frump wearing the same thing from that morning. I took the flowers and breathed them in.

"They're beautiful, thank you," I said shyly.

"I thought we could go out and get something to eat…just talk and forget about tomorrow for a few hours?" Considering his attire and preparation, I assumed that he was taking me out whether I liked it or not.

I looked down at my clothes and over at Maddy, feeling totally unprepared. Merman jumped in.

"Maddy, Celia, and I are going to stay and watch movies. You should go get ready," he insisted.

"So, what do you say we meet down here in half an hour?" Oliver asked, leaving room for negotiation. Before I could reply to him, Merman interrupted again.

"That would be perfect. You two just go and have a great night, and we'll be here with Rhet and Scarlet."

I rolled my eyes at Merman for answering for me. I appreciated his loving interference, as silly as he was.

"Thank you, Merman. Oliver, half an hour would be perfect," I agreed.

I walked down the hall with the uncomfortable feeling that I was being watched the whole way. I could hear Merman behind me saying with a tone of pride, "Huh, how about that?"

Oliver responded, "Merman, one of these days she's going to strangle you, and I'm not going to try and stop her."

They both laughed as I hurried up the stairs before I had to hear anymore.

I spent the entire half hour showering, trying to pick a decent outfit that might compare with his sleek suit, and staring in the mirror before changing again. I settled on a little blue dress that fell just above my knees and hung far enough off of my shoulders to reveal the entirety of my neck. I hadn't really dressed up in so long. I stared in the mirror, looking sideways and turning around. Not bad. A pair of heels completed the outfit.

I put my flowers in a vase and looked at them, knowing that like Oliver had said about himself the night before, it was too late for me. I was in love. It was going to take every bit of strength I had to stay focused.

The night was cold - a true Northern California fall, and along with the nerves, it was causing me to shiver. The drive to the restaurant started off quietly. This was our first official date, and I was analyzing that fact a bit too much. The committee in my head was in a full blown argument over the morality of it all. One side maintained the position that I was still married and should be careful about how I proceeded with Oliver, while the other side argued that I had lived under other people's rules and expectations all my life, and I wasn't going to let something amazing pass me by to continue that tradition. I concluded that I would do my best to honor the promise I'd made to myself and beyond that, I would just live in the moment.

Oliver would occasionally look over to the passenger seat and flash a lovely smile - though I could tell he was unnerved by my silence.

"Are you cold?" he asked with concern. He reached for the temperature control.

"Just a little," I admitted through chattering teeth. I couldn't hide the tension in my shaky voice. He adjusted the heat.

"Is that too hot?" He looked over again, seeming eager to please.

"No, that's perfect. Thanks." This time, I tried to give him a reassuring smile and reached up to take his hand away from the controls.

"You seem shaky. Are you okay?"

"I'm just cold and a little terrified about tomorrow and even more terrified about not being able to keep my promise," I admitted in all honesty. He laughed.

"There will be no promise breaking tonight. I promise," he teased. We both laughed. "I would be terrified about tomorrow too. He's threatening the most important thing in your life. You wouldn't be human if you weren't terrified, but I can tell you from an outsider's perspective that you really have nothing to worry about besides worry, and that's why I'm here. I'm going to help you try and forget about tomorrow. I don't think you'll find it difficult," he enticed.

"Really? Why's that?" I played along.

"We have a long evening ahead of us, and I think you'll be too busy to worry." He was being intentionally vague, and it worked - I was curious.

"So are you going to tell me about all of these things that will keep me so busy that I couldn't possibly have a moment to think about one of the most dreaded days of my existence?" I prodded.

He smirked. "No, I can't. I'm sorry. That's the first part of the plan." He looked at me, smiled slyly, and looked away.

"I get it. I'll be preoccupied with trying to figure it out. Okay, I can play."

He smiled and changed the subject. "Do you want to listen to some music?"

"Sure," I conceded.

He was right - all I could think about was what we would be doing. It was only five-thirty, and apparently it would be a long night.

"What do you want to hear?" He began flipping through the stations.

"Anything is fine. Is there a station that broadcasts the night's events?" I joked.

He laughed. "Hmmm…I don't think I get that station in this car. How about this?"

He stopped at an oldies station, playing a love song I recognized from when I was young. I couldn't remember the name, but the melody brought me back twenty years.

"I love this song," I said excitedly, trailing off into a memory.

I remembered my mother in one of her happy moods. She used to turn the music on and let me sit on her bed while she got ready to go out to one of my father's business events. It was one of her favorite songs and one of my happiest memories of her. Those days were long gone.

"I do too. My mom and I used to dance to this. It was her favorite." He carefully reached over and placed his hand on mine. "Is this still okay?"

It didn't take much to get my heart racing again.

"It's okay." It was more than okay, it was amazing.

After a while, I noticed that we were on a highway lining the ocean. It was so serene. The sun was close to setting, and the birds seemed to dance to its farewell. If this was what the night had in store, I knew that Jerry would be the last person on my mind. At that moment, I just wanted to know more about Oliver.

"So do you and your mom still dance?" I had a feeling by the way he spoke of her that she had long since passed.

"No. She died when I was just fifteen. I miss her a lot but I'm glad I had the little time that I did with her. She was an amazing woman. Very strong…like you." He looked at me and smiled, carrying a deeply nostalgic weight beneath it. "She died of ovarian cancer. From the time that they found it to the time that she died was only six months. I was so afraid of losing her because she was the only person in the world I could trust. I didn't have much of a relationship with my dad. He was very busy working most of the time. He was a doctor too. Funny how that works, isn't it?"

"Yes. My father's a lawyer and had very big plans for me. Obviously those didn't work out!" We both laughed. "I'm sorry, Oliver. It sounds like she was a wonderful person and left a lot of her with you."

"I'm glad I can share pieces of her with you, for instance a whirl around the dance floor."

"I liked our whirl. I could do that again."

"We might." He winked at me.

Just as I thought I could stay in the car all night, with the harmony of our touching hands, we pulled up to a restaurant and parked. He quickly got out, walked around, and held his hand out for me to take. Together we walked up the steep hill and into the restaurant.

It rested on the cliffs over the ocean. Every wall of the room was lined with glass overlooking the beautiful view. The lighting was dim, and music played softly in the background. Glasses hung from their slots above the bar in the center of the room, creating a reflective shimmer all around with the light from the sunset.

Everyone looked content, their voices creating a low murmur of conversation all about. He gave his name, and we were quickly whisked to a table overlooking fiercely crashing waves and what remained of the setting sun. I watched as the waves violently hit against the cliffs, and then I followed the water out further and further until there was barely a ripple on the horizon. I longed for the ripple in the setting sun. Today I was a wave.

"What are you thinking?" he queried.

I sighed. "We're so removed from the chaos down there. It's sort of beautiful chaos from up here."

"Life is all beautiful chaos when we can step back and see where it's landed us. It's hard to see that being tossed around," he said, looking out to the scene below.

"It *is* hard to see that," I agreed.

He walked me through the menu, and I took my chances on their special of pan-seared fish. I was feeling adventurous.

As we ate, we discussed everything from life in the hospital to my love of writing. He tried my fish, and I ate half of his steak, apologizing when I realized. I was content in his company though painfully and passionately longing for more.

After dinner, he stood and once again held out his hand to help me up. I wasn't used to such chivalry, but I liked it.

"Time to move on to our next stop of the evening," he said.

I checked my watch to find that two hours had passed, though it felt like minutes. There was no better news than there was more to come.

"I can't imagine more than this. This was beautiful."

"Well, you'll have some time to wonder," he said, smiling as I took his hand.

We drove a short distance into the city, and I became excitedly curious. The city was buzzing with traffic and people crossing streets. I looked around, trying to guess where we might end up. He was enjoying this, I could tell. After guessing wrong numerous times, we finally parked in a very busy parking structure underground.

Once out of the car, he put my jacket over my shoulders and squeezed them tightly, looking at me with excitement in his eyes. I melted again, and tried to hold my footing.

"Close your eyes," he said.

"What?"

"Just close your eyes." I did as he said, not knowing what to expect. "Do you trust me?"

"I trust you," I said with great confidence.

"Good. Now take my hand." I took his hand as he wrapped his other arm around me. We began to walk.

"Oh my gosh, Oliver, I'm going to trip doing this!" I argued, feeling terribly vulnerable.

He laughed. "I thought you trusted me," he challenged.

"Fine. You're doing the stitching if I fall!"

"I happen to be very good with sutures," he teased.

We walked slowly through the parking lot, with people giggling as they walked by. I heard a woman say, "look how romantic, honey. How come we don't do that kind of stuff anymore?" I thought I heard the man sigh. I felt badly for him. It would be hard to top someone like Oliver.

As the sounds doubled in volume and lost their echo, I knew we were outside. Horns honked, whistles blew, people passed by with their shoes clicking and conversations trailing away, and I stood safely in his arms. We stopped, and chills shot down my back when I felt his warm breath an inch from my ear.

"We're here," he whispered. Again, I had to concentrate on keeping my legs firmly planted as the warm pulse shot through me.

"Okay," I whispered back, barely aware of my surroundings.

"You can open your eyes."

I opened them, and it took a second for the blur to clear. In front of me was an old and richly ornamented theatre. I had seen it in the city before, but never been. My mother had gone on a few occasions with my father and told me of the vibrant colors and rich architecture of the building. Above the theatre a banner stretched across its length and read *Les Mise*rables. My heart skipped with excitement. I had read the novel and always wanted to see it performed. I wondered how he knew and then he interrupted.

"I know how you love stories, and this is one of the better ones I've heard." I turned to him with an uncontrollable smile. "I'm glad you like it," he said smiling. "Let's go."

I had all but forgotten Jerry existed. I was in heaven, or what I imagined to be the closest thing to it. I took Oliver's hand with ease and we began crossing the street. I watched people's faces as they passed, some happy, some indifferent, all strangers…but one. It was only for a flash, but it was unmistakably Jerry. The hatred in his eyes as he stared made me cry out loud. I saw him grin before he disappeared.

Oliver turned, stepping between me and whatever I had seen. I couldn't breathe, or move.

"What was it?" Oliver tried to look me in the eye, but I couldn't stop staring at the spot Jerry had vanished from.

"Casey?"

"Jerry…" was all I could mutter.

"Where is he?" Oliver looked every which way and turned to me. "He's gone. Casey, breathe." He took my arm and led me to a bench on the sidewalk.

Again and again my wave crashed against the rocks. It was all I could envision. I was terrified…and then, I was angry. I wouldn't let Jerry keep me tangled in his quagmire of control forever. I would force my way out to the quiet calm. I took one last deep breath.

"He *is* gone, and we should go in before we miss the show," I said, my voice still a little shaky.

Oliver looked at me as though I were crazy. "We don't have to stay."

"Yes," I nearly yelled. "Yes, we do. *I* do." He nodded and then pulled me in close, crushing me against him. "I won't let him take this," I whispered.

"Neither will I," he promised.

Watching the chaos, misfortune, and relentless love in the play, I realized that the only thing in life and certainly in love that is guaranteed is conflict. It's how we face the conflict and with whom we face it that makes it livable or entirely miserable.

When the curtains rose, I could barely contain my tears. Oliver hugged me beside him and kissed my forehead. "I take it you enjoyed it?"

I laughed through my tears. "Yes, I loved it. Look at me, I'm such a girl!"

"I love that about you," he teased back. "Are you ready for more?"

"You've got to be kidding me! You are about to ruin me for life. How will I find pleasure in anything again?"

"I'll make it my life's work," he promised.

We made our way back to the highway along the Pacific Ocean. I didn't know where we were going, and I didn't care, so long as it meant more time with Oliver. He pulled over along the side of a road off of the highway and asked me to wait. He got out and opened his trunk while I sat in the quiet car, full of ecstatic new love and fighting the growing fatigue from the long and emotional day.

He was gone for a few minutes, which had me wondering excitedly again. My door opened, and he knelt to the ground, gesturing for me to swing my feet out of the door. I looked down to see that his shoes were off and his pants cuffed up to his shins. His jacket was gone, probably in the trunk, and his sleeves were rolled to his elbows. He was the sexiest man I had ever seen, cuffs and all. I complied with his request, and one at a time, he slipped my heels off and placed them in the back.

"This way." He led me onto the sand.

The beach was dark and still but for the washing rhythm of the waves breaking on shore and the moon brightly shining a pathway to the sea. By my watch it was nearly midnight.

"Maddy," I said, suddenly remembering. I had lost all track of time.

"I called Merman when we were at the theatre and told him we'd be home within the hour. Maddy's asleep and everyone's fine," he assured me.

"You have it all figured out don't you?" I said playfully.

"Not all of it," he replied thoughtfully.

When we had walked toward the shore several yards, I could see by the moonlight the outline of a blanket in the sand, and as we drew closer, a picnic basket on top. He pulled out a bottle of champagne and two glasses.

"A toast to living in the moment," he offered.

"I can definitely toast to that."

He poured the champagne, and we sat with our toes in the sand, living in the moment. We watched in humble awe of the scene before us.

"There's one last thing…for the night that is," he said, reaching into the basket. He pulled out a small cd player, pressed play, and pulled me up - perfectly into the dancing position he'd had me in the night before, but this time we were eye to eye, close enough to hear each other breathe, close enough to kiss.

He danced me through the sand, to the song that brought us both happy memories. If the sun happened to rise, I wouldn't have noticed. No promises were broken that night, but a confirmation made.

Chapter Twenty-One

Omens

A persistent knocking on the door awakened me from a deep and much needed sleep. It was just after one o'clock in the morning before I had both myself and Maddy in bed, and nearly two before I actually slept, as I couldn't stop replaying moments of the evening - some including frightening flashes of Jerry in the city.

I couldn't see a clock, but it was still dark outside, with just a hint of morning gray. I sat up, feeling delirious and not sure that I was really awake. The knocking started again, so I shuffled my way to the door and peeked through the hole. It was Merman.

"Are you crazy? I'm dying in here!" I opened the door, grumpy and desperate to lie back down.

"There's somewhere I need to take you before we go to court, so, can you be ready in the next forty-five minutes?" He waited for a response.

"Merman!" I said, totally irritated, but totally ready for anything that might bring a positive start to the day. "This better be good!"

He was pleased and showed me so with a smile full of teeth.

"I don't think I can top last night, but I think it'll be worth it," he teased, winking.

I rolled my eyes and shut the door on him. Feeling sick from a lack of sleep, I lay back down and almost dozed off when another knock shot me back up. I stormed to the door and readied myself to tear Merman's head off.

I opened the door, as messy as one could possibly look in the morning, to Oliver standing in front of me - holding a cup of coffee. I was mortified and even more so by the fact that he was neatly dressed in a suit. I hid behind the door.

"Merman thought you could use a cup of coffee," he said through a laugh.

After accepting the fact that I couldn't very well hide behind the door through our conversation, I stepped back out into the doorway.

"How do you look so chippery?" I snipped.

"I've been working these hours for years," he said with a soft smile. "I had time to take a quick nap and change before coming back. I'm helping Uncle Stanley with the service while you two go take care of business."

"Oh," I said, thankful for his help and sorry for the snipping. "Thank you."

He handed me the coffee, and I took it, desperate for anything that would wake me up.

"You look beautiful by the way. You shouldn't go hiding behind doors," he said, teasing.

"You must be crazy. I'm a disaster. But I appreciate your generosity."

"Well, I could look at this disaster for hours and feel confident that I'd never seen anything so beautiful." Everything he said was beautiful and very hard to believe. Most compliments I had received from men were dripping with insincerity and came with expectations. That was never the case with Oliver. I didn't know how to respond, so I sipped at the coffee. Luckily, he broke the awkward silence. "I really wanted to come and tell you that I'll be thinking of you today and that everything will work out fine."

I wasn't grumpy anymore, but I was finding it very difficult to keep my hands to myself. Standing there, with lingering thoughts of our evening, I felt as though we had never parted. Still less than lucid, I had to pull myself together to respond. "You're very sweet." I rested my head on the doorway, barely able to stand up.

"In just a few hours you'll be back here sleeping again," he comforted, gently running his hand over my head and down the length of my hair.

"Then I'll look forward to that," I forced through a yawn. His touch tingled and made it harder to want to really wake up.

He left me to my morning and with a better start than I could have hoped for. I met Merman downstairs with a sleepy Maddy, and we started on our way.

"Should I even ask?" I questioned, as Merman drove us through a residential neighborhood.

"You can ask all you want," he challenged haughtily.

"So long as you have me to court by eight, I'll play along."

"Are you kidding? I can't wait to see the look on Jerry's face when he's handed a restraining order," he whispered, looking back to make sure Maddy was still asleep.

"It will probably be similar to the look on his face in the city last night," I recalled with disgust.

"What?" he almost shouted.

"Shhhh…" I reminded him. "He must have followed us. It couldn't be a coincidence. He made sure that I saw him, gave me a creepy and twisted grin, and then disappeared." The thought of it made me shiver.

"You need to tell Don this as soon as we get there," he insisted.

"Jerry's allowed to be in the city, Merman."

"Not after what he pulled Friday night. Trust me, Don needs to know." He furrowed his brows to let me know he was serious.

"Fine, I'll tell him. Relax and keep your eyes on the road, would you?" He rolled his eyes before putting them back where they belonged.

We drove down a street lined with beautifully colored trees ready to drop their leaves. The homes were aged and charming, with yards full of green grass, flowers, and the occasional picket fence. Families were getting into cars and starting their days as the sun began to break overhead. Halfway down the street, Merman pulled over and parked.

"We're here."

We woke Maddy up, though she resisted for a while, and walked along a stone path that led through the yard of a large and neglected house. It looked less cared for than the others on the street. The paint was fading and chipped, and the grass nearly dead. The porch held an old wooden rocking chair that begged for company. The windows were darkened by years of dirt and in them hung very familiar looking, yellow and dusty curtains. The only evident source of life came from the large tree in the front yard. I immediately felt sorry for whoever lived there.

We followed Merman up the path and through a gate that opened to the backyard. As we passed along the outside of the house I heard a shuffling noise and immediately grabbed Merman's arm.

"What was that?"

He didn't answer, but kept walking closer to it.

"Where are we, Merman? The last thing I need right now is an arrest on my record!"

"We're fine. I happen to know the owner, and so do you," he said with a grin. I went through the rolodex of names that might fit, and blanked. "I needed to stop by to pick up some paperwork for the office and figured I'd bring you along." The shuffling noise grew closer and interrupted my train of thought. When we rounded the corner, the source of the noise made its appearance. It was a very large, pink pig.

"Oh my gosh!" I was completely startled by its size and more so by its presence in the yard.

Merman laughed again. "That's Sandra."

"It's a pig, mommy. Can I pet it?" Maddy asked, jumping up and down.

"Sandra? Odd name for a pig. If it's okay with Merman, you can," I said, keeping my distance.

"Of course, come here." Merman squatted down and petted the pig with Maddy. "She's named after Uncle Stanley's ex-wife, and just like her, she's been living off of him for years."

"This is Uncle Stanley's house?" I asked in surprise.

"Yep."

"And he was married?" I said with more surprise yet.

"I know. Imagine that!" I looked around a well-kept yard filled with all sorts of life. I couldn't believe it. It just didn't seem to fit Uncle Stanley, though I knew nothing about him save the few words he'd ever spoken to me and his brief appearance in Merman's history.

"Stay here. I'll be right back." Merman entered the house through a back door, leaving the two of us to the miniature farm and its animals. Maddy was still fascinated with Sandra and busied herself with introductions.

Merman returned, smiling at my lingering shock. He took my arm and faced me toward the back of the yard. "*That's* why we're here."

There was a large, wooden coup in the back corner of the yard. I could tell by the wiring that it contained chickens.

"He has chickens too?" I laughed.

"He's not very good with people, but he loves animals. He has a cat inside, and somewhere out here is a huge turtle."

I was having a hard time picturing Uncle Stanley being affectionate toward anything, and here he had a virtual farm in his backyard full of animals with names. I wondered which one was named after Merman.

"I'm afraid to ask, Merman, but why are we here for chickens?"

"Well, I have a lot of time on my hands - or *had* I should say, until you two came along," he winked at Maddy, who was busy petting the pig "and when I'm waiting for calls or in between services I like to read, about everything." I was waiting for him to get to the point, and still completely at a loss as to why we might be there. He continued, "Just the other night, I was reading about the Roman generals and the omens they believed in…"

I interrupted him, worrying about time. "Chickens, Merman, chickens!"

"I'm getting there. Are you in a hurry for something?" he teased. "So before a major battle, they would throw seed at all of their chickens. If they ate it, the generals were guaranteed a victory, but if they didn't, a deadly defeat was on the horizon."

"Are you telling me that we came here to feed chickens?" I said, slightly irritated.

"That's exactly what I'm telling you. Come on." He headed to the coup and opened it. Nothing moved.

"I'm not superstitious," I said flatly, folding my arms, though I suddenly feared the outcome. He opened a large bucket filled with chicken feed.

"I know, but after reading that article, I thought it would be bad luck not to do it. This is a war, after all. It couldn't hurt to have the birds on our side."

"Speaking of birds, you're an odd one."

"That's very clever, now throw some." He held the bucket out.

I peeked into the coup. Still the chickens hadn't come out.

"What if they don't eat it, Merman? Should we flee the country?"

"Well, the Romans threw the chickens overboard when they wouldn't eat. We could behead and eat them."

"That's great. I'll bring one to the judge."

"Just throw the feed," he urged. Part of me was afraid to – afraid that they wouldn't eat, and Jerry would take Maddy.

"This is absurd! I can't believe we're here!"

"Would you rather be pacing back and forth at the courthouse?"

"Sleep would be nice," I argued.

"Just throw it, Casey!"

"I'll do it, mommy!" Before we could stop her, Maddy had a hand full of feed and had scattered it across the yard. I watched and waited, in fear of a ridiculous superstition. It was silent for a long moment and my heart sank. Now what?

Then, Maddy began to clap her hands in excitement as we heard the clucking begin.

Suddenly six chickens were scouring the yard for feed, as if they hadn't eaten in weeks. I was so relieved and so happy, that I laughed out loud and clapped along.

"To victory," Merman cried dramatically.

"To victory," I repeated.

He closed up the bucket of feed and stood with his arms folded. "So then, today we win."

"You are a nut, but I hope you're right."

"Alright, let's get you to school little farmer," Merman said, picking Maddy up and swinging her around onto his back. Maddy loved the idea of being a farmer.

"Can I come and pet the pig again, mommy?"

"We'll see, babe."

"So long, Sandra," Merman called out with genuine friendliness before leading us back out to the car. Watching the pig as we left, I hoped to learn more about Uncle Stanley and Sandra and considered the odd satisfaction I would get from a pig named Jerry.

After dropping Maddy off at school, we made our way through the city and to the courthouse. My stomach had been churning all morning, and it somehow worsened when we reached the parking lot. My heart was racing. I was terrified.

I held myself to keep from shaking and breathed deeply through my nose to slow and quiet my audible breaths. I was completely gripped by fear. This wasn't just Jerry anymore, this was the law. One judge would now determine the future of my life with Maddy, and I could only hope that whoever it was, they would see through Jerry's phony accusations and hate filled motivations.

As we walked to the entrance of the building, Merman rubbed my hands together between both of his to try and warm me. I couldn't tell if I was shaking out of fear or the morning frost. With every step into the courthouse, I lost a little more control over my body. My legs felt wobbly, and I got a little light headed on occasion. As we approached the security, my hands changed from frozen to clammy.

We filed one by one through the metal detector where I stood nervously while the security guard ran a wand up and down the length of my body. I suddenly felt like a criminal. Looking around, I wondered how many real criminals were there and knew of at least one – I just hadn't seen him yet. I collected my things out of a small wooden box on the security conveyor belt and waited for Merman to make it through.

We quickly located the courtroom on the directory and made our way up the stairs to the third floor. Despite the beautiful architecture on the outside, the inside of the building was old and everything a various shade of beige. The cold, hard surfaces of everything there were decorated with codes, warnings, and an intentional lack of welcome. There was no comfort to be found on its hard, wooden benches or from the unemotional and ever suspicious security. Everything about it reminded me of my father, which made me shudder all the more. He lived in courtrooms for most of my life and always pictured *me* in them most of mine – just not this way.

Most of the people there sat quietly and waited, like me, for some courtroom door or another to open. Some seemed unaffected, as though this wasn't their first or last visit. Others seemed as terrified as I was. I wasn't planning on coming back too often. In fact, there was little I wouldn't do to avoid it.

It was a quarter to eight, and I wanted time to speak with Don about his game plan. I was surprised by the relief I felt at his appearance around the corner. He approached us with a calm demeanor that conflicted greatly with my shakiness. I could only assume his calm came from years of walking these very hallways, along with the simple fact that he wasn't the one losing anything today.

"We're all checked in. It shouldn't be long now."

"I'm glad you knew to check in. I'd be standing here at closing time," I joked.

"That's why I make the big bucks," he teased back.

"Do you have the police report from Friday night?" Merman asked with great concern, not interested in our banter. Don leaned in to quiet the conversation.

"Vivian is on her way with it now. We had to wait until this morning to pick up a copy." He turned to me in all seriousness. "Casey, I can't tell you that this will be a slam dunk, because you just never know with these judges. What I can tell you is that the judge will be hard pressed to refuse you a restraining order and hand Maddy over with so many witnesses to his hostility."

Merman interrupted before I had a chance to respond.

"Jerry was stalking her last night too!"

"What happened?" Don asked, while pulling out a notebook of yellow-lined paper. "Tell me exactly."

I told him the whole sordid story about Jerry being near the theatre and how he waited to make sure I saw him before giving me his creepy and threatening smile and disappearing.

"But he's allowed to be in the city, right? I mean, I can't prove that he was there to stalk me, can I?" I desperately hoped I was wrong.

"It's about building a case. Along with this report, it's not going to look good for him. I'm going to press for an evaluation before our next scheduled hearing and hope to keep him away from both of you in the meantime." It all sounded reassuring, but before I could get my hopes up, he continued.

"He's making the same claims about you, Casey, but without the evidence. Still, the judge will have to give due diligence to all of the claims in order to ensure the safety of Maddy. Jerry could request that Maddy stay with a neutral party until this is resolved, and the judge may consider it."

"What's a neutral party? Is that going to happen?" The possibilities were terrifying, and I could hardly catch my breath through the panic. I wanted to find Jerry and kill him before we went in for our hearing. I was already planning possible ways to flee the state.

"It could be a family member or the foster care system. It's only a possibility, but I'm going to fight to make sure that doesn't happen."

"Foster care? Please, Don - tell me you have a plan to keep that from happening!" I was shaking again and sick to my stomach at the thought of Maddy with a foster family.

"I don't need a plan, Casey - I have evidence that Jerry is a threat to Maddy's safety and well-being. He's done himself in. I just want you to know that there are endless possibilities in there and endless ways of dodging them."

"Maybe you shouldn't tell her *all* of the possibilities," Merman suggested with a bit of irritation.

"You're right," Don agreed apologetically. "In reality, I think this will turn out well."

As Merman consoled me and Don backpedaled on his already voiced concerns, I looked up to see Jerry rounding the corner with a man, who I assumed was his lawyer. I felt a knee-jerk panic and then a blind rage. He was dressed up in a suit, with his long hair combed back neatly. He was ready to perform. When he saw me, he winked and smiled. I jumped slightly, as though I might follow through with the murder plan, but Merman held me back. They had both seen him, too.

"Casey," Don stood in front of me to block my view "you need to avoid all contact with him. He will do anything to provoke you and prove his accusations true."

That sounded like Jerry. I hated that he was so cool and calm. I hated that he was dressed up and faking it. But more than anything, I wondered if he knew about the police report. I couldn't imagine he would be so calm, knowing we were going to show him for what he was.

"I'm going to use the restroom before we get started." Merman had to pry my hands from his arm to leave. "Just stay here with Don, and don't even look his way." He waited for me to nod in agreement before leaving.

Don and I waited on one of six benches on the second floor of the courthouse. Jerry and his lawyer lingered by the stairs on the opposite end. I couldn't help but look over as they occasionally laughed at something they were discussing. It was making me crazy.

"Do they know about the report?"

"What report?" Don said with a smile.

"The police…" he covered my mouth.

"There's no report here…yet. I'll inform them of it when it comes."

"Why are they laughing it up over there? Do they have something we don't know about?"

"It's all for show, Casey. He's all about control, remember? He wants you to think he has it. Now, quit watching him!" he commanded.

Just as he said this, Jerry's lawyer began to approach us.

"Hi there. Bill Oxman - representing Mr. Wheeler." He reached his hand out to Don, who shook and introduced himself in return. I instantly hated this man for no other reason than he was with the enemy. He nodded his head toward the door, gesturing for Don to leave and speak with him alone.

Don turned to me and patted my shoulder. "I'll be right back. Stay here." Without a choice in the matter, he left me alone on the bench.

I quickly and repeatedly prayed that Merman would be out of the bathroom soon, as Jerry's lawyer walked with Don through two glass doors and into a breezeway. I felt vulnerable sitting alone, trying not to look at Jerry, who I knew was looking at me. I was still shaky, and my mouth was becoming increasingly dry. I decided to get a drink of water from the fountain that was safely located between the men's and women's restroom.

I tried to walk with confidence, knowing that I was being watched. Leaning over, I focused on the water touching my lips and quenching my impossibly dry mouth. If I lingered long enough, Merman would be out to stand by me. As I drank, sip after sip, I waited to hear the comforting sound of the bathroom door swinging open. Instead I heard a voice in my ear that sent chills right through me.

"So this is how you want it?" Jerry whispered in my ear.

I shot up and took two steps backward. I didn't know what to do…or what he was talking about? He had started this whole legal battle, not me. For every step I took back, he took one toward me. "We can end this right now, Casey. You give me everything I want, and I'll leave you alone," he said through a sinister chuckle. I tried to remind myself through the fury that he would give anything to have me blow up right there in the courthouse. I continued to back up toward our bench, as if it would provide me unquestionable safety.

"Stay away from me, Jerry," I tried to say firmly.

His face turned to stone, and his eyes to fiery slits.

"Nothing will keep me away from you, doll. Everywhere you go, there I'll be. Remember? Just like last night with your boyfriend." He continued to back me into the bench.

"Jerry, get away from me!" I said louder, hoping someone would hear. As luck would have it, not a single officer was near to help. The people in the hallway didn't even seem to notice. I was backed up against the bench with nowhere left to go without pushing past him.

"You think you're going to just move on and forget about me? I won't let you forget about me. I'll be the last face you see." Before I could think about fighting my way past him, Jerry was being pulled backward.

"She asked you politely," Merman said through a growl "to stay away from her." He had Jerry by the back of his suit jacket and had pushed him a few feet back. "I'm sorry I left," Merman said, looking me over to make sure I wasn't hurt. At this point, people were beginning to watch and whisper.

"I don't know what you're talking about, man. I was just having a little chat with Casey here," he said with a wink at me. Merman stood between us until Jerry sauntered off to his spot by the stairs.

"Where did Don go?" he asked through gritted teeth.

"Jerry's lawyer took him outside to talk."

"A total set up!"

"You think?" I asked in honest surprise. Don came back in rolling his eyes.

"No, I know." Merman confirmed.

"Well, they're willing to settle this whole thing if Casey will agree to give Jerry the house, put Maddy in a boarding school, and pay him both child support and alimony. Basically everything he asked for in the order, except he's willing to drop the whole rehab issue in exchange for giving him full custody. He was just wasting my time and trying to see how we would respond."

"Well, when you left her here, Jerry took the opportunity to harass her a little more," Merman said in anger.

"Huh. I figured as much. Did anyone see?" Don asked suspiciously.

"You figured?" Merman said, gritting his teeth again.

"Casey's a big girl, and there is security all over this place. So what did he say?"

"He just told me to give him everything and that he would be following me all of my life. The basics," I said sarcastically.

"And then I had to pull him off of her because he was breathing down her throat!" Merman added, still irate.

"Good," Don responded casually, writing it all down on his notebook. "Well, it looks like it's time to go." The doors to the courtroom were opened by the bailiff, and I immediately went limp again.

Don had us sit in the back row of a tiny courtroom. It was nothing like the fancy, dramatic courtrooms on t.v. It was the same dull color as outside with four rows of seats on each side for people awaiting their hearings. A waist high, wooden dividing wall with a swinging door allowed access to the front, which consisted of one long table, four chairs and microphones. Beyond that was a raised wooden platform for the judge, the stenographer, the clerk, and a witness box. Altogether, the courtroom was no bigger than an average sized living room. I was surprised by the simplicity of it all. It was purely functional, like the rest of the courthouse.

Jerry attempted to sit directly in front of us, but Don interceded.

"Would you mind sitting on the other side? I think your client has harassed her enough this morning," he said politely, as if a host speaking to a diner at a restaurant.

"I'm sure I don't know what you're talking about, but we'd be happy to oblige if she can't control herself near my client," the lawyer responded with a snide smirk. Don simply nodded with thanks and sat down next to us.

"I told you it would be ugly. They are not going to fight fair, because they have nothing to lose."

The courtroom busied with lawyers checking in and people finding seats. After a few minutes, the bailiff called the court to order and a very short, Asian woman came out in a black robe. I was shocked by her size in comparison to her power. She wore a very stern look on her face, which was framed by a black bob-cut of hair and glasses. Her name was Felicia Oto, and she was prepared to change lives.

She called case after case about child support, visitation, problems at school, evaluations, and one restraining order. I began to grow more confident as I could see she had great distaste for nonsense and manipulation and seemed to be able to sniff it out.

One woman had thrown a fit at a bowling alley and slapped her ex-husband in front of a crowd. The small and scraggly mother of two argued that her ex had instigated the whole situation and had abused her for years. I waited for the judge's response on the edge of my seat, as if her verdict would predict the day's outcome. Without hesitation or emotion, she issued a restraining order. The woman, who represented herself, yelled and cried about how unfair it was. The judge ignored her complaints and asked if she needed to be shown out of the courtroom. I looked to Don, who simply winked at me in acknowledgement.

Another couple had simultaneously enrolled their child in two different schools as they disagreed on where he should attend. This had resulted in their child attending a different school with each parent. The judge was disgusted and ordered that the couple go outside and agree to one school before the close of the day in court, or face serious consequences. I wondered how that was going to turn out, until I heard our names called out loud. My stomach dropped.

Don walked with me to the swinging door and situated us on the right side of the long table. The judge had gone to her chambers after the last hearing to review our case, so we all sat down and waited. I could hear Jerry chuckling again with his attorney, but this time I was too terrified to care. I looked at the microphones and wondered what might be said in them this morning and who would be picking Maddy up from school as a result of it.

When the little woman came back into the courtroom, we all stood up. She sat down, ready to do business. She began by summarizing the requests of each side and asked that both of our lawyers introduce themselves.

During all of the formality, I suddenly realized that Vivian had not yet arrived with the police report. Through utter panic, I tried to convince myself that Don had it under control, but what if he didn't? If we didn't have proof, what would happen to Maddy?

After introductions and summaries, Jerry's lawyer began.

"Your honor, my client fears that the respondent has their daughter in an environment that is not suitable for a child. They currently live in a mortuary, at which the respondent has worked merely a month. Furthermore, he is concerned that her violent and unpredictable behavior threatens the child's very safety. She physically assaulted my client at their home and apparently threatened him in the halls of this very courthouse. Until a proper psychological evaluation can be performed, and the child's safety ensured, my client requests that the child live with him."

I couldn't believe what I was hearing. I was enraged. He was twisting everything around, and it sounded awful. I prayed that Don would straighten him out before they led me from the room in handcuffs. I looked over to see Jerry leaning forward in his chair with a phony concerned look on his face. The judge looked to Don.

"Mr. Linden?"

"Your honor, despite what the petitioner would have you believe, it is he who is violent, threatening and unpredictable. Just four days ago he showed up, intoxicated and belligerent, to the child's school and verbally assaulted my client before physically assaulting one of their friends. There is a police report…" Before he could finish, Jerry's attorney burst in.

"I object, your honor. We aren't aware of any police reports. I was never provided with a copy of such." The judge glared at him.

"Whether or not you were aware of it isn't my concern, Mr. Oxman." She turned back to Don. "Do you have a copy of this report Mr. Linden?"

"I do, your honor." Don turned around and nodded to someone. I looked to see Vivian in the back of the courtroom, now strutting up to the front. She waited as the clerk took the report from her and gave it to the judge.

Jerry sat up stiffly and glared in my direction and then at Vivian. Apparently, he didn't know about the report or that he had been duped. From the look on his face, he must have thought that if enough accusations were thrown around without proof, the judge would consider it all hearsay, and I would lose Maddy, as a precaution, until the next hearing. It seemed he was very wrong.

Oto read carefully through the paperwork and then stared down at Jerry.

"There were over twenty-five eye witnesses to this assault, Mr. Wheeler. What do you have to say to this?" She turned to the clerk. "Make him a copy, please." The clerk disappeared through a door.

Jerry's attorney fumbled around for words. "As I've said, your honor, I haven't heard of or seen this report…" Oto interrupted him.

"I wasn't speaking to you, Mr. Oxman. I was speaking to your client, and a copy is being prepared for his review."

Jerry stiffened again, and his attorney quickly leaned in to discuss the sudden change of events. The clerk returned with a copy of the report and handed it to Jerry. He and his lawyer flipped through the pages and decided on something. He started in with his charming voice.

"It was all a misunderstanding, your honor…" She cut him off sharply.

"It seems very clear to me and everyone else who was there."

He cleared his throat and sat up straight. "She was antagonizing me…" he started, pointing in my direction. She cut him off again.

"That's not what the report says." She waited, but he didn't respond. He silently flipped through the report, looking for a way out. "I take it you have nothing to add." She turned back to Don and gestured for him to continue.

"Your honor, it was in fact Mr. Wheeler who threatened my client in the hallway. Mr. Patterson, who is present in this courtroom, had to pull him away from her as his aggression escalated." I felt relief and vindication as Don laid out the truth and noticed out of the corner of my eye that Jerry could hardly contain himself. He was gripping the ledge of the table as if to break it off and kill me with it. He shot a glare my direction that gave me instant chills. Don continued, "His behavior has become increasingly hostile, your honor. He has threatened her at her place of work, left menacing notes on her vehicle and just last night, followed her to the city and repeatedly threatens to continue this behavior. We plead with the court for a restraining order to protect my client and the child until further notice."

"Granted," she said flatly. Jerry growled from the other side of the table.

"We also request the assignment of minor's counsel to review the facts of the case and report to the court, with the petitioner forwarding the costs."

"Granted. Minor's counsel will be chosen by Mr. Linden and the costs forwarded by the petitioner."

Jerry's lawyer jumped in. "Your honor, you haven't even..." She turned to him coldly and cut him off.

"I've heard all I need to hear. Now I would advise you to sit quietly until I address you again." He sat down sheepishly and Don continued.

"We request that Mr. Wheeler submit to random drug and alcohol testing and attend both anger management and individual counseling between now and the next hearing."

"Granted; though I am extending the counseling to a minimum of six months and twenty-four visits. Proof of enrollment shall be provided to the court within fourteen days of today."

"Your honor!" Jerry's lawyer stood up in total frustration.

"Mr. Oxman, I am seconds away from holding you in contempt. The evidence shows that your client is not only dishonest but has committed grievous and increasingly dangerous acts of hostility toward Mrs. Wheeler and those around her. Do you argue that?"

"I would argue that this was a one time, harmless event..."

"It clearly is not a one time event. There's a witness to that in this courtroom."

"My client being in the city at the same time as Mrs. Wheeler proves nothing, your honor, and I feel that the actions taken against him by the court are quite severe."

"Mr. Oxman, Mr. Wheeler may be in the city or anywhere else for that matter, whenever he wants, so long as it is not within five hundred feet of Mrs. Wheeler or their daughter. So far as the severity of actions against him is concerned, it does not match or exceed the severity of his own. Your client may argue his case after an evaluation by minor's counsel, random drug testing, and counseling. Before that, I don't want to hear another word from you until I ask."

After a moment of silence and the judge wringing her hands, she turned to Don.

"Is there anything else, Mr. Linden?"

"Yes, your honor. My client asks that their joint accounts be split equally and the sale of their property forced immediately. I have a receipt showing the balance as of the day she left. Mr. Wheeler transferred all funds into their checking account, to which she does not have access."

"Granted. The accounts provided to the court will be frozen and divided equally as of Mrs. Wheeler's last transaction. Mr. Oxman, your client is to provide Mrs. Wheeler and the court with information regarding the twenty three thousand dollar balance of said accounts and an explanation for any missing funds beyond the monthly bills that have been recurring over the last twelve months. Regardless, eleven thousand and five hundred dollars of that balance will be transferred to Mrs. Wheeler via Mr. Linden in the form of a cashier's check within fourteen days from today. The joint property shall be listed with a realtor of Mrs. Wheeler's choosing within thirty days from today. Is there anything else, Mr. Linden?"

It seemed as though there couldn't possibly be anything else. We had won…everything. The relief was surreal. I was floating in my chair, completely detached from reality. But Don had more.

"Your honor, we ask that full custody be awarded my client temporarily, without visitation for the petitioner and that my costs be paid for by the petitioner."

"Since the restraining order will prevent Mr. Wheeler from being near the child, it is only logical to award, temporarily, full custody to Mrs. Wheeler. Do you have a statement of your fees, Mr. Linden?"

"I do, your honor." Don handed the clerk a copy of a bill that I wasn't aware of, then turned and winked at me.

"The petitioner will pay to Mr. Linden three thousand seven hundred and fifty dollars, within three months and after the division of assets. These rulings are in effect immediately and without change until further order of the court. Mr. Linden, you will type up this order and file it with the court immediately." Don agreed. "I will set the next hearing for…"

Don interjected. "Your honor, we would like to request a hearing no later than eight weeks from today."

"And you think minor's counsel will have a report by that time?"

"I do, your honor."

"Okay, I will set the hearing for December 20th. Mr. Linden, you and your client are free to leave, and Mr. Oxman, your client must stay to be served with the restraining order."

And with that, it was over. Don lifted me by the arm as I seemed permanently frozen to the chair. I looked up to see Jerry fuming and clenching to the arms of his chair with white knuckles. He glared at me again with eyes suggesting he would have those clenched hands around my throat shortly. Chills shot through me again, and I quickly made my way to Merman who was obviously elated. Thankfully, he waited until we made our way out of the courthouse to jump up and down emphatically and hug me to no end. He grabbed my face and kissed me violently on the mouth, the sort of kiss you see in an Italian mafia movie. I was still so shocked that I didn't even mind.

"Casey, what's the matter with you? It's over! You won."

"Well, it's not over yet, Merman," Don corrected.

"Whatever. This part is over, and we won! He can't come near you or Maddy."

"He's ordered not to go near you or Maddy," Don corrected again "but that doesn't mean he won't. If you even catch a glimpse of him, you find your way to a crowded place and call the police."

I could hear them talking, but I was still so shocked by the outcome that I couldn't respond.

"Casey?" They both said in sync.

"It's over?" I asked.

"This part is over," Don conceded. "The next difficult step will be minor's counsel. They need to see that life with you is nothing like Jerry claims, but rather, just as it should be. You will have to convince them of that through the distracting backdrop of a mortuary. But I think you can do it."

"We can do it," Merman assured Don, and me, though I was still mulling over the events in the courtroom.

"I need to get back to the office and type up this order. I'd like to have minor's counsel chosen and have this submitted by tomorrow. It would be good to get these evaluations done in the next month. It's not a lot of time. It typically takes at least two months, but I know someone who would be willing to start tomorrow if I asked."

"Okay," I mumbled.

"Okay," Don replied with a smile.

"Thank you. Oh my gosh!" I awakened from my shock. "Thank you! Did that really just happen in there? I mean…really?"

"Really," Don said laughing. "And you're welcome. Go home and relax. You've had an exciting morning, and you have a rough few of weeks ahead of you."

We parted ways, and though I knew he was right, I couldn't get past the relief and excitement to worry about the weeks to come. *I* would be the one picking Maddy up today, not Jerry or child protective services.

The sun was shining through the clouds and everything seemed brighter. As the shock wore off, the lack of sleep caught up with me again. I rested my head on the side of my seat as we drove home and felt at peace for the first time in longer than I could remember.

"Thank god for those chickens, huh?"

"You are ridiculous, Merman." I pushed him in his seat, and we both laughed. I did thank God for the chickens, but more so for the truth setting us free.

When we got back, Oliver was anxious to hear the news. Merman filled him in on all of the details, talking a mile a minute through his excitement.

"Thank god!" Oliver held my face with both hands and kissed my forehead. "You must be exhausted."

"I've been looking forward to being back in bed all morning. I wasn't sure I'd make it out of the courtroom alive with the way Jerry was glaring at me."

"Gerardo's the only one who didn't make it out of that courtroom today," Merman said through a pleased smile.

"Can I walk you upstairs?" Oliver asked. I agreed through a yawn, but first threw myself into Merman for a hug.

"Thank you. I don't know what I would do without you, my dark knight." He laughed.

"Dark knight? I like that. Do I get a cape or wings or something?" he teased, proudly.

"Don't push it, or I'll tell Oliver that you kissed me on the mouth."

Oliver cocked his head to the side with a confused smirk.

"Ah, do you feel left out, Oliver?" Merman grabbed for Oliver's face.

"Get off of me, dark knight." Oliver managed to avoid the kiss.

"Go sleep, silly girl." Merman hugged me and pushed me off down the hallway with Oliver close behind.

When we reached the inside of my apartment, he sat me down on my sofa and took my shoes off one at a time. He sat at the other end and pulled me down so that I was resting my head on a pillow in his lap. He didn't even talk, he just combed gently through my hair until I drifted to sleep.

Chapter Twenty-Two

Security Breach

Merman refused to let me go anywhere alone after the hearing. Considering how much Jerry had lost that day, and the rate at which he was beginning to lose his mind, Merman thought it best to have one of the four of them with me at all times. Though I didn't want anyone making a big deal over me, I was comforted by their presence as I didn't put it past Jerry to kill me if he had the chance. Throughout the following weeks, I couldn't stop picturing the utter hatred on his face in the courtroom, and waited most nights for him to break in and keep his promise.

Whether it was a trip to the grocery store or Maddy's school, one of them was with me wherever I went. I enjoyed the opportunity to get to know Celia better and especially loved the time with Oliver, but got the most entertainment out of trips with Eddie. He took the role seriously, and whether or not he could actually protect me didn't really matter since the amount of attention he drew in public made it impossible for Jerry to attack without multiple witnesses. He would peek around every corner we turned, back flat up against the wall, with a mirror. He even asked a few parents for their identification as they passed my car in the school parking lot. Some of them didn't know how to respond since his rented security costume looked questionably official. I would have to run over to apologize, forcing him back into the car before he could cause any more damage or humiliation.

A little over a week after the hearing, Don contacted me about minor's counsel. The attorney had been selected and wanted to meet with me the following afternoon. Don's voice alone sent my heart into a flutter. I had been anxiously anticipating the call for days. Whoever this attorney was would soon be making a recommendation to the courts on what was best for my daughter. Because of Jerry, I could no longer decide such things. A part of me hoped that he would be stupid enough to come near me.

Aside from the dead bodies drifting in and out of it, The Golden Oaks Funeral Home didn't seem such an awful place to me, but I also recalled with clarity my first impression. I had run silently screaming into the pouring rain and contemplated sleeping in a car before coming near the place. I vacillated frequently between feeling confident that God - as I now referred to Him in my prayers - would take care of us as He had so far, and the feeling of complete terror that the second minor's counsel saw the place, they would drag Maddy away kicking and screaming.

Don walked me through the whole process over the phone. The attorney would tour the facility and our apartment and interview everyone we kept in close contact with. The latter was the part that worried me. I knew that Merman, Celia, and Oliver would be a great testament to the loving life that Maddy had here, but Eddie and Uncle Stanley were another story. Though Uncle Stanley meant well, his abrupt demeanor and evident drinking habits could pose a threat to the harmony we presented, and Eddie…well, Eddie was Eddie. I wished we could lock him in the bell tower until we were finished.

We had our family dinner that night to discuss and prepare for anything that might come up while minor's counsel was on the premises. Don said it was best not to tell Maddy too much, or it might seem that we had manipulated her into saying the "right" things, so we waited for her to fall asleep on the sofa bed before we really began to plan.

"Eddie," Merman slapped his hand onto Eddie's shoulder "just answer the lawyer's questions directly. Don't add anything extra, okay?" Eddie stopped his dissection of the green bean on his plate. He had carefully cut it lengthwise and was attempting to remove each seed individually.

"Got it." He went back to his work.

"This is really important, Eddie. If we screw this up, Jerry could take Maddy," Merman reiterated. This fact seemed to bother Eddie. He looked carefully at Merman and then at me.

"Got it." Again, he refocused on his plate.

The rest of us looked at each other with apprehension, but realized this was as good as it was going to get with him.

"Don't worry, Casey. You're such a good mom. No one in their right mind would take Maddy from you." Celia had reached over to put her hand on mine. "Besides, it's not like you have her sleeping in a casket or something." She laughed at her own joke but didn't get much more than an obligatory chuckle from anyone else, and I was frozen trying to picture it.

"Who would do that?" I asked, disgusted. With that, Eddie looked up with a guilty face.

"Eddie, are you kidding me? Geez! Can you leave that part out tomorrow?" I was beginning to think the whole situation was going to be a disaster.

"What?" He looked around in sincere confusion. "They're comfortable. Have you felt the silk inside?"

"Eddie, seriously, you need to keep that kind of stuff to yourself. Especially tomorrow," Merman gently insisted with another pat on the shoulder. He seemed to have a way with Eddie that was neither insulting nor demanding, and Eddie responded well. He may have been the only person in the world that understood Eddie's eccentricities.

Oliver could tell that I was becoming tense and panicky about what was being revealed at the table. He gently rubbed my back, which nearly made my eyes roll back into my head. I had to focus on Eddie's pea pod to control myself.

"Better said tonight than tomorrow, right?" Oliver comforted with a smile.

"Definitely," I agreed. We decided not to overanalyze things and put in a movie instead. Once more, I fell asleep on Oliver's shoulder, having almost entirely forgotten about the next day's events.

"What was that?" Merman asked, sitting up abruptly and scaring me to death. Everyone sat up and listened carefully.

"I didn't hear anything," the rest of us said in unison. Out of recent habit and fear, I checked to make sure Maddy was still on the sofa. I logically knew that she would be there, but the threat loomed over me like a heavy cloud.

"I'm going to go check it out. Oliver, you come with me. Eddie, you stay here with the girls." Eddie nodded, and I looked to Oliver in a panic.

"I'm sure it's fine," he said, gently stroking my hair. "We'll be right back."

They left us there to wait and speculate. Celia and I sat close together and watched as Eddie paced back and forth in front of the door, or peeked through the blinds into the parking lot.

"Don't worry, Casey, Night Jock is here," Celia teased. I had to laugh, despite my terror.

"He couldn't possibly get in here, right?" I asked, seeking reassurance.

"Who, Jerry? I doubt it," Celia offered.

"Anything's possible," Eddie interjected "we don't turn the alarm on until eight when I leave."

"That's not helping," Celia said, throwing a ridiculing *what were you thinking* look at him. "The alarm isn't on, but the doors are locked on the outside. He'd have to be pretty handy to get into one of them," Celia reassured me.

"Not the garage door," Eddie corrected. "If he managed to get the garage door open, which isn't all that difficult, then…" Celia cut him off.

"Enough, Eddie! Are you *trying* to scare us?" She wrapped her arm around me. "Got that tazer handy? Jerry would beg for mercy if he saw that old friend." She laughed, and I tried to, but it came out as a whimper.

They hadn't been gone more than ten minutes. I knew because I checked the clock every thirty seconds. Just when I thought I might scream from the growing tension, Oliver and Merman came in through the door with a force that shot fear right through me. I jumped off of the couch.

"Is it him? Is he here?" I could feel the rhythm of my heart begin to escalate. The look on both of their faces made it clear that they didn't want to answer that question. They paused for an unusually long period of time.

"Just tell me!" I insisted. I walked to Merman and put my hands on both of his arms, shaking him. "Merman, just spit it out."

"I'm sorry, Casey. I should have been more careful."

"There's no way you could have known, Merman," Oliver assured him. Their cryptic dialogue was driving me mad.

"Could have known what? What is going on?" Merman couldn't get past his guilt to tell me, so Oliver finally conceded.

"It seems as though Jerry has been in your apartment upstairs."

He said this as he braced my shoulders with both of his hands. He must have been aware of the fact that I was tail spinning into another episode of palpitations. A rush of blood to my head had the room spinning. I broke free from his grip and made my way toward Maddy in a panic. I wanted to have her in my arms to make sure Jerry couldn't take her. The spinning room made my trek nearly impossible. I bumped into the sofa, the coffee table, and before I made it to her, I felt as though the ground had reached up and pulled me down to my knees.

I hadn't taken a single breath since I'd heard that Jerry had been in our home, and I was finding it difficult to keep my focus on Maddy through the black spots that were beginning to blur my vision.

I could hear muffled voices behind me and feel hands grabbing at me. I just wanted to have Maddy safely in my arms. I fought them off with what little energy I had and yelled at them to leave me alone, though my words came out in broken, breathless syllables. Before I knew it, I was on the floor, looking up at Oliver kneeling over me and saying something I couldn't make out. I watched him in confusion, his lips moving without sound. Then Merman was over me, mouthing what looked to be my name, again and again.

Slowly, the sound returned, and I could make out the panic in their voices.

"Casey, can you hear me?" Oliver maintained his focus on my eyes, while Merman looked back and forth between the two of us.

"What's the matter with her? Should I call an ambulance? Do something!"

"Just give her a minute. Her heart rate is starting to come down."

"Casey?" he tried again. Of course I could hear them. I was just too exhausted to get a single word out. I tried to force a response.

"Yeah…" was all I could manage.

"Thank god!" Merman nearly shouted and looked as if he had just avoided a train wreck.

Oliver didn't even crack a smile. He kept his fingers at my wrist and his eyes on mine. "Can you see me clearly?" He leaned in a little closer, and I nodded as much as I could make my head nod.

I felt like I was weighed down by a two ton blanket. I tried lifting my arm toward the sofa to feel for Maddy, but I couldn't get it higher than an inch or two off the ground.

"Just relax for a minute. Maddy is fine. She's still asleep if you can believe it." With that he smiled and stroked my arm. I happily complied with the beautiful doctor's orders.

I looked over at the white leather couch, suddenly remembering that there was quite an audience in the room. Celia had tears in her eyes and smiled when she noticed me looking. Eddie was watching us and checking his own pulse, for what reason I didn't know.

"You scared me to death," Celia said through a teary chuckle. "I was afraid you'd miss out on another shot at Jerronimo with that tazer of yours."

I was embarrassed that I had caused such a scene and that I had everyone so worried. I tried to sit up nonchalantly, but swayed when the blood hit my head. Oliver helped me and insisted I stay seated on the floor until I got my balance back.

I suddenly realized that no one had told me what happened with Jerry. Was he still there? What did he do upstairs? And even more frightening was the thought of how he got into the building.

"Is he here?"

"No," both Oliver and Merman said in sync. They both stared at me, unwilling to say anymore.

"I'm not going to die. Just tell me."

Merman refused, but Oliver gave in again.

"It looks like he got in through the door off of the stairwell."

"Ooh, I forgot about that one. Interesting," Eddie said with fascination.

"Eddie!" Celia yelled at him. "Can you go outside and keep and eye on things please." He shrugged and did as she asked.

"Anyway, the police are on their way, and we'll have that door secured by tomorrow," Oliver continued.

"You're sleeping down here tonight," Merman informed me.

"What did he do upstairs?" I could only imagine what he had been after. What if we had been in there? Was he going to kill me and take Maddy, or kill us…my heart was beginning to triple beat again. I cleared my head and tried to slow my breathing to avoid another scene.

Oliver looked at me with concern, having felt my rising heart rate through his fingertips.

"It looks like he just broke in. We couldn't find anything, and it didn't look like anything was missing. Of course, you'd know better than we would." Oliver continued to keep close tabs on my heart rate as he informed me.

"But you're not going up there," Merman insisted again.

"Will you help me up?" I asked as I held both hands out to Oliver. He helped me up slowly and kept both hands on me, making sure I was firmly planted before letting go.

"I'm sorry about that," I said, mortified.

"No, I'm sorry," Merman started with a deeply regretful tone.

"Don't be silly," I said, weakly punching his arm and then hugging him. He seemed only a little bit comforted from his guilt. He had seen the vengeance in Jerry's eyes too. I knew exactly what he was thinking. Jerry had clearly not been threatened by the restraining order and had taken things to a frightening extreme.

We kept our pow wow in Merman's living room as the police inspected the entire building. Oliver only left my side once to give his report. I showed them the restraining order, but they hadn't found any evidence linking Jerry to the break in. They had one unit already en route to Jerry's in order to question his whereabouts during the break-in, and another patrolling the neighborhood. I doubted they'd find him in either.

When the red and blue flashing lights cleared from the parking lot and the alarm had been set, there were still six of us remaining. Merman wasn't taking any chances. Eddie was camping out in the small chapel, Celia was on the white leather couch, Maddy and I were snuggled on the sofa bed, Oliver was on the floor next to us - close enough to hold my hand - and Merman was back and forth between his bedroom and the hallway. None of us, but Maddy, slept that night.

Chapter Twenty-Three

Judgment Day

At some point in the early morning, when the sky began to lighten with gray, I finally drifted to sleep. It was the kind of sleep I had needed all night to get through the upcoming day. Of course, it came just minutes before I would have to get out of bed.

Not only was minor's counsel coming to determine my future, but coming on a day with a family viewing in one chapel and a funeral service in the other. We were all getting up early to make sure everything was in order and ran smoothly. One slip and the whole day might unravel.

I was awakened by a door closing somewhere in the building and hugged my pillow, fighting the sleep that tempted me back in. While contemplating giving in to just ten more minutes, I suddenly remembered the sleeping arrangements that night and peeked over the edge of the sofa bed. Oliver and his sleeping bag were gone. My heart sank, but was quieted by the relief of knowing that I would be able to freshen up before seeing him again. I quickly slipped into the bathroom to rinse out my mouth and smooth down my hair before anyone could see me.

When I came back out, I realized that Oliver wasn't the only one missing. Celia had cleared from the couch, and Merman was nowhere to be found. Maddy and I were left alone, and it was quiet enough to hear the ticking of the clock in the kitchen.

I felt a little bit left out and wondered where everyone had gone. At that moment, I noticed a small post it note bending slightly upward on the coffee table. I peeled it off and read.

Good morning, beautiful!
I'll see you two this afternoon.
Oliver

I smiled uncontrollably as my heart rate sped. His handwriting was artful and legible, easily dispelling the stereotype of doctor scribble. I relished the idea of seeing him again soon. At least there would be one thing to look forward to that afternoon.

I attempted to wake Maddy, who groaned a little and hid her head under her pillow. After a few minutes of Maddy pretending to be asleep, and me calling her bluff with tickles, we eventually made our way upstairs to get ready for the day. Maddy had school, and I had two services before the dreaded evaluation. I would somehow have to work through the anxiety and perpetual butterflies until two-thirty when I picked Maddy up and came back to face judgment.

With worries swarming through my mind, I had forgotten who had been in our apartment the night before. The reminder hit me hard when upon opening the front door, a strong whiff of Jerry's cologne assaulted me. Chills shocked through me, and I shook, clinging to Maddy for precaution.

"What, mommy?" Maddy asked, trying to pull away.

"Nothing," I lied. "Go get dressed for school, honey." She skipped off, none the wiser.

I quickly but carefully inventoried each room, trying to figure out what Jerry had taken, if anything. I couldn't imagine what he would want, unless Oliver was right, and he was just trying to scare me.

I went back to the front door to find that someone, likely Merman, had replaced the lock. I could see the wood splintered where Jerry had forced it open. I recalled with dread what he had said outside of the delivery door the first day he found me. There was only a door between us, and it wouldn't stop him. Maybe he was proving his point.

I almost fell into a complete panic until I remembered, with comfort, that there was more than a door between us. There was Merman and Oliver, Celia and Eddie, and more importantly – everything that I now had to lose. My teeth grinded together as my resolve grew.

I decided to dress in the most confident piece of clothing I owned – a red sweater. I typically wore subtle colors, and had only worn that sweater once for Christmas years before. Bright colors drew unwanted attention, and I was careful to avoid it. Today had to be different. I had to wear my determination boldly. I looked in the mirror and was impressed.

After dropping Maddy off, I searched around for Merman. I knew that he would be furious with me, as I had left without an appointed security guard. He also had no way of getting a hold of me, and I was beginning to feel a little guilty for sneaking out. I had felt so emboldened in my red sweater and wanted to prove to myself that I could stand on my own. I guess I hadn't really thought it through.

I peeked into the small chapel to find Merman making the final adjustments to one of our friends in their casket.

"I'm back," I said nervously. He jumped slightly, but didn't turn. I could tell he was angry.

"Oh, you're alive," he said sarcastically.

"I'm sorry, Merman," I said, feeling worse by the second. "I'm just so tired of being afraid of Jerry. I wanted to prove to myself that I could do it alone."

"Oh, good. Here I was thinking that maybe you had forgotten that a sociopath had kicked your door in last night. But if you were just proving something to yourself, then that changes everything." His voice was rising, and he had turned to face me with his arms folded across his chest and his brows pulled together.

"I'm sorry," I said walking toward him, hoping for reconciliation. "I should have told you." He held his hand up to stop me.

"One minor oversight, and Jerry made it into your apartment, Casey! He could have followed you this morning! The police never found him last night, you know. He could have…I don't' even want to think of what he could have done!" He was pacing back and forth.

"I'm sorry," I tried again. "Please don't be angry. I need you today." He stopped pacing and looked to the ground, shaking his head. I held myself and fidgeted, playing with a loose string on my sweater. I had never experienced Merman upset with me. I didn't like it at all.

"I'm not angry at you…but could you please lose the wonder woman bit?" He seemed to relax his stance, and I was relieved that he was teasing me again. "You didn't even bring the tazer with you, for god's sake! I was going to start a man hunt, but Eddie saw you two leaving. Ten more minutes and I would have…"

I was so relieved that he wasn't as angry. I forced a hug on him, and he resisted momentarily before eventually giving in.

"So you're not mad?" I asked with a pleading tone.

"I can't be mad at you," he admitted. "But I would have killed you if anything happened," he teased. "Well," he changed the subject "I need to finish up in here, and Celia could use some help in the big chapel."

"Thank you for everything, Merman. For the door knob, for caring…for everything. I don't know what I'd do without you."

"Well, apparently you'd sneak out and put your life in jeopardy," he said sarcastically.

"Oh boy…I'll be in the chapel if you need me." I rolled my eyes, but took the hit with a smile, grateful that he had forgiven me.

I made my way down the hall, toward the chapel. As I passed the embalming room, I heard a high-pitched voice that I didn't recognize. I peeked in and jumped in surprise.

I didn't recognize him at first. Eddie was wearing a suit, which was unusual for Eddie since he typically didn't work around the families. His hair was combed neatly, though rigidly, to the side, and he looked…somewhat professional. He had his earphones in and didn't notice me. I watched, at first in amazement, and then with amusement.

He was dancing around while working on a body. He would dance over to the counter and grab something, and then dance back and touch up the hair or the lips. His level of informality around the body took me by surprise. Merman and Oliver were so focused and respectful around them. This was new.

All of a sudden, Eddie was playing a drum solo on the belly of the poor man on the slab. I was horrified, and at the same time I couldn't help but laugh out loud. I covered my mouth to muffle the sound, but it was too late. He had heard me. He pulled his earphones out.

"Did Jerry getcha?" he asked, seriously.

"No Eddie, Jerry didn't get me," I said, not sure if he was kidding.

"Oh. I should tell Merman." He started toward the door.

"Merman knows," I assured him. "Would I be here if Jerry did get me, Eddie?"

"Hmmm…well, that depends," he debated. "Did you bring the tazer? Because Jerry gotcha at your house, but you tazed him in the neck."

"Oh," I said, surprised by his logic. "I guess you're right." There was an awkward pause and then he put his earphones back in. "You look nice, Eddie," I said, loud enough for him to hear over the music. He simply gave me a thumbs up and continued working.

I made my way to the chapel and found Celia setting flower arrangements around the casket. She looked up and gave me a convicting smile.

"Busted," she said, dragging out each syllable.

"I know. I thought he was going to kill me himself!"

"It took an act of God to get him to wait a half an hour for you to get back. I couldn't calm him down. He called Oliver, and somehow *he* convinced him to give it a while."

The mention of Oliver's name had my heart fluttering. Then I was embarrassed. I'd have to hear from him too when he got back.

"I had my red sweater on…and felt like I could take on the world, and…" I tried to explain.

"You had your red sweater, huh? Well then, what were we all worried about?" she teased.

"I feel awful that you guys have to follow me everywhere."

"Okay, well feel awful while you check the tissue boxes would ya?" she said, jokingly pushing me.

By two o'clock, the viewing had concluded and the chapel was filling with families for the service. I slipped out to get Maddy at school, with Celia by my side. Leaving alone wasn't even a thought.

I had managed to keep the increasing anxiety to a dull roar by staying busy all day, but I could hardly contain myself on the way back. I considered drinking a bottle of wine to calm my nerves before the interview, but Celia reasoned that I would likely say something stupid, and they'd have to bury the lawyer in one of the departing caskets. I opted against the wine, and commented on the bad influence Merman was having on her.

Though terrified, I regained conviction whenever I thought about Jerry breaking in and threatening to sabotage everything I had worked so hard for. Somebody had to stop him, and it had to start today with the evaluation. As long as I could protect Maddy, I could figure out the rest later. Though the police hadn't offered much since the break-in, I hoped they would pin him down eventually. Yet, despite my hopes, I had a sick and sudden feeling that in the end, it would come down to Jerry and me, face to face, to the death. I shuddered and tried to shake it off.

When we arrived, the parking lot was filled. The service was beginning. Celia headed off toward the chapel, and Maddy and I went to our apartment to wait for the arrival of minor's counsel.

The thought of Maddy having a lawyer seemed absurd and inappropriate to me. She was far too young to be involved in legal matters. She was far too young to even know what a lawyer was. I prayed that whoever this person was, they would attempt to preserve her innocence and find a suitable explanation for a five year old. I had simply told her that a new friend was going to come and talk to us about what it was like to live where we were living and ask her other questions about school and friends and the like. She seemed excited about the idea. It broke my heart.

Just when I had settled us down to watch a movie and pass the time, there was a knock on the door. I jumped and closed my eyes to re-focus and say a quick but desperate prayer.

"Is that our new friend, mommy?" Maddy asked with a gleaming smile.

"I think so, honey." I kissed her forehead and made my way to the door with trepidation.

I hadn't asked Don for details about the person coming. I hadn't even stopped to imagine what they would look like, so when I opened the door to a young woman no taller than my shoulders, I was taken aback.

"Good afternoon. My name is Elisa Fredrickson." She stuck her hand out to greet me. I shook it and showed her in. She was uncomfortably serious and made no attempt at easing the tension in the situation. I immediately felt defensive and wanted her nowhere near Maddy. Something about her demeanor and authoritative voice was very threatening. It was evident that she knew the power she had in the situation - the power to take Maddy away.

I tried to remain focused on the objective, which was to convince this woman, and the court, that with me was where Maddy should stay. As she entered the doorway, I ran my eyes over her, hoping to get a better sense of who she was. Her posture exuded confidence, but was contradicted by her small stature. Her attire seemed to emphasize this contrast. A suit jacket, which appeared a size too big, hung just to her knuckles, while her suit pants were slightly bunched above her shoes. It looked like she had raided her parents' closet, though her face showed undeniable maturity through her serious eyes and small, pursed lips.

"Hello, Maddy, my name is Elisa." She forcefully smiled and held her hand out to Maddy, who giggled and shook it. "I'd like to talk to your mom for just a minute. Do you mind if we go in your room?" Maddy shook her head. I was surprised by the abrupt manner in which this woman was going about her process. Though I hadn't expected some long-winded introduction, I certainly hadn't expected someone so terse. Luckily, Maddy didn't seem bothered at all.

"Show her Hippo, mommy," she suggested.

"I will, honey," I promised. We made our way into Maddy's room, while she refocused on the television.

After Elisa closed the door, she sat in Maddy's chair and gestured for me to sit on Maddy's bed.

"Let's start with you telling me how we got to this point."

I had expected her to lead the discussion and didn't know where to begin. She pulled out a yellow pad of paper and a pen. The formality made me waiver. I was terrified of what she would do with what I divulged. I held Hippo close as I stumbled my way through the events that led me through the last six years and to The Golden Oaks. She said nothing while I spoke, but took copious notes. The lack of any feedback from her was making it hard for me continue with any confidence. Once in a while she would make a "huh" noise and take extra notes. She was effectively intimidating. I finished my debriefing and nervously stroked Hippo's head. She didn't miss a beat.

"So what are your greatest concerns about Maddy's father?" she asked matter-of-factly.

Where would I begin? I didn't want to sound like one of those women who demonize their ex-husbands, but she needed to know the truth. I described his limited interactions with Maddy over the years and the increasingly violent behavior of the recent weeks as objectively as I possibly could. I tried to avoid too many adjectives. I even mentioned the incident at the round-up and the suspected break in the night before in a journalistic, unemotional way. I needed her to understand and take me seriously, but still, she showed no emotion whatsoever, just more of the "huh" sounds and notes. It seemed as though she wasn't going to take my word for much.

"And what do you think about raising her here, in a funeral home?" she asked, looking me directly in the eye, with a hint of disapproval.

"Well...," I fumbled "It wouldn't have been my first choice." I laughed nervously, and she maintained a straight face, waiting to take notes. I felt the need to give all of the reasons why we had no other choice and to give the impression that we wouldn't be there long, but the thought of minimizing the beauty of what had transpired in this place made me angry. "It's the greatest thing that could have happened to us," I said with pride. At this her expression changed. She seemed almost eager to hear more.

"Really? Could you explain that to me?" Her tone was slightly sarcastic. This wasn't going well at all. She seemed to have already formed an opinion about me before she entered the apartment. I feared that saying much more would magnify that opinion.

"I think you'll conclude the same when this evaluation is over." The truth would have to speak for itself. Knowing me, I would just muddy it up with words.

She seemed to consider what I had said, slightly surprised by my vague answer.

"Huh. Well, it would seem that you have nothing further to add. I'd like to meet with Maddy now." Without warning, she stood up and headed for the door.

I had to resist the mama bear urge to wrestle her to the ground. She threatened the most basic part of my nature. She treated me like a criminal who had been stripped of their rights. Shouldn't she show some courtesy or ask permission, whether she needed it or not, from the mother? Apparently, I was guilty until proven innocent. I wasn't prepared for the overwhelming emotions that came with having my motherhood questioned by a stranger, even though I had questioned it myself from day one.

We both walked silently but deliberately into the living room. I watched her, wondering what had led her to this profession. She looked to be about thirty and didn't seem the type that had children, but rather focused on her career. It troubled me that someone without children could make such life altering decisions about parenting. She had no idea the lengths I would go to protect the little girl in front of her.

Without acknowledging me, Elisa led Maddy back to her room and asked for a tour. I could hear her showing Elisa around and introducing all of her animals, one by one. Shortly thereafter, the door closed.

I felt helpless and wanted to listen at the door, or what's more, tear the door down. I paced the living room in a panic, terrified that somehow she didn't fully understand the monster that Jerry had become. I felt sick at the thought of ever having been with him. I would kill him before I let him near Maddy. Wild thoughts played through my mind as I pictured Jerry trying to take her from me.

I sat back on the couch and tried my best to believe that no matter what was said in that room, one meeting with Jerry and one look at the police records would tell her all she needed to know. But, my mind argued, he was a rat and had a way of weaseling his way out of trouble, and she clearly had a less than positive opinion of me. I prayed again, that she would see him for what he was and that Maddy would be safe.

Every minute that passed dragged me deeper into fear. My stomach twisted into knots, and I remembered with dread that she still had the remainder of her evaluation to complete, including touring the facility and interviewing the rest. I pictured her walking in on Eddie playing drums on a body, and cringed.

I attempted to assure myself that, despite first impressions, Elisa would eventually see a glimpse of what I had come to find in The Golden Oaks. If nothing else, she would see it through Maddy. And no matter how wrong it all seemed on the surface, she would surely agree when she met Jerry.

After twenty minutes or so of sheer terror and violent plans, they both emerged laughing. She was a much different and much more amiable person with Maddy. Despite my increasing disdain for her, I appreciated it.

Maddy came over and jumped in my lap. I pulled her in close, grateful that it was over. I smelled her sweet hair as I kissed her forehead. Elisa observed even this small interaction. I fought to keep a friendly face, when in reality, I wanted her throat.

"I'm going to walk around the facility and speak with…," she looked at her notes, "Merman, is it?" Maddy giggled and I nodded. "So I will speak with Merman and a few others. It was nice to meet you, Maddy." Maddy giggled again and waved. Elisa collected her things, and I followed her to the door. She left with a simple and lackluster "Goodnight", and was gone.

I wanted to call Don and question his judgment. I was shocked that he thought she was the right person for the job. I sat Maddy back down with a movie and tried his office. I was desperate to hear what he thought, but there was no answer. I wanted to go down and find Merman and fill up on his reassurances, but I didn't want to run into Elisa and add to her already extensive notes. I was tempted to ask Maddy a million questions, but I didn't want to interrogate her after the interrogation. I was trapped with my discomfort, with nowhere to go and no one to talk to. I'd have to wait out the day.

Our part was over, and this fact allowed me to breathe a little easier, although the final judgment still loomed over me as I wondered if I had said too much or too little, and what Jerry had planned. Mostly, I prayed that she didn't catch Eddie dancing in the embalming room.

After about an hour of impatiently waiting to hear from someone, there was an abrupt knocking on our door. I leapt up and ran to it, desperate for answers. Merman stood in the doorway with his hands on his hips and a little bit of a disapproving look.

"You weren't even going to check to see who it was first? Just open the door and let him right in? What am I going to do with you?"

I couldn't believe that he was going to lecture me on safety protocol considering everything that had gone on in the last two hours. I felt like a warrior. I dared Jerry to come over and see what would happen. All I cared about was what had gone on with Elisa.

"Merman, if you don't tell me something in the next five seconds, I'm going to kill you." He smiled at my intensity and came inside. Maddy ran to him and jumped up for a hug.

"Did you meet my new friend, Merman? Her name is Elisa. She likes Hippo."

"I sure did." As he walked past me holding Maddy, he winked. "We all met her. And who wouldn't love Hippo?"

Although I appreciated that he was being careful not to get into details right away with Maddy there, I thought I might explode from the anticipation. I had prepared myself to hear the worst. I had waited for an hour to hear something. *This* was killing me.

"Merman, can I see you in the other room, please?"

He smirked and set Maddy down.

"I'm going to talk to your mommy for a minute and then I'll be back to hear more about your new friend."

Maddy agreed and snuggled herself back up on the couch. I practically dragged Merman into her room and sat him on her bed.

"So, what happened? Is she still here?"

"Nope, she left a few minutes ago. I knew you'd be up here writhing. She's quite a gal, huh?" He laughed, but could tell that I wasn't in a laughing mood. I just glared at him, wide-eyed, waiting for an answer.

"Well, I'll tell you that she seemed utterly uncomfortable being anywhere near the chapel and barely peeked into the embalming room. She spent most of her time talking with us."

"And?" I pried.

"Mrs. Personality is hard to please. I couldn't get much of a read on her. She asked me a lot of questions about what you do here and how much Maddy is "exposed" to," he said making quotes with his fingers and rolling his eyes.

"Oh, god! I'm doomed. She had it in for me before she walked in here." I had my head in my hands trying to keep it together. I didn't want Maddy seeing me upset. I felt bad enough about dragging her through the whole awful process. "She's my worst nightmare. Worse than Jerry." Merman moved in closer and wrapped his arm around me.

"She *was* pretty stiff. But I think she's just keeping a poker face to maintain the appearance of an objective third party. Either that or she was trying to keep from running out of here screaming. I'm sure this was a first for her." His attempts at humor weren't helping at all. I could just imagine the notes she had on that yellow pad of paper and how they could change my life.

"What was Don thinking with her? And of course, I can't ask him because he won't answer his phone!"

"I'm sure he knows what he's doing, Casey. You just have to trust the process, remember? You don't really believe, with all that's happened, that Jerry will win, do you?"

I didn't know what I believed anymore. She had me questioning every choice I'd made. I remembered the cold tone in her voice when she asked me about raising Maddy in a funeral home. I shuddered at the memory. This wasn't just a funeral home to me anymore, it was *our* home, but how would the courts see it?

"Casey, look at me." He lifted my face by my chin. I looked at him with hopelessness. "This can only end one way, and that way is Maddy with you, and Jerry out of reach." I wished I could believe him, but I had a gnawing feeling that it wouldn't be that easy. "Let her take her notes. You are a good mother, and whether or not *Elisa* likes the idea of Maddy in a funeral home, she can't deny that. Besides," he teased with a smile and a squeeze, "how could she resist the charm of that boyfriend of yours?"

"What boyfriend?" I asked through building tears.

"Oliver! She spent more time with him than any of us. She couldn't get enough of him."

"Oh, god, Merman, does she think I have a boyfriend?" That would be just great for her to report - I'm raising Maddy in a mortuary and shacking up with someone before I'm even divorced.

"Relax, no one said anything about the fact that you are madly in love with each other," he teased while gently nudging me, "which is probably a good thing, since Elisa was quite smitten. Hell hath no fury like a jealous woman…or something like that."

"That's not the saying, Merman" I informed him, completely bothered by the thought of Elisa flirting with Oliver. It brought back the protective rage I had felt while she was in the room with Maddy.

"Whatever," he said, brushing me off, "the good news is, Oliver won her over, so I think her report may have a more positive spin. It might cost him a miserable date with her, but hey, it's worth it right?" He had that smirk again.

"Are you kidding me? Did she ask him that?" I was standing up at this point, with my hands on my hips.

"I'm kidding. But the look on your face just now was hilarious." I punched his arm. "Ow! You're quite violent and edgy tonight. I hope you didn't get rough with Elisa." He laughed while rubbing his arm.

"Merman, quit messing with me, please. So, are you telling me that she left in a good mood? The woman actually cracked a smile, or showed some emotion at all?" I was on the verge of feeling some semblance of relief, but I needed confirmation before I could allow myself that.

"It looked like it to me, but you should ask Oliver. He's the one who spent quality time with her." He was smiling again, holding back a laugh. In some small way I appreciated his humor, though it made me want to punch him again.

Merman made plans for all of us to go to dinner and celebrate. I didn't really feel in the mood to celebrate, but he didn't let me argue. The five of us headed out, while Eddie stayed behind on call.

Oliver confirmed, over spaghetti and meatballs, what Merman had said about Elisa seeming to change her tone, though as I expected, he had no clue that she had been enamored by him. Celia had made sure to give her eyewitness accounts of Jerry's belligerent behavior and apparently, Eddie had somehow managed to be unusually normal.

By the end of the night, and after I forced as many details out of all four of them as I could through cryptic conversation to protect Maddy, I was left feeling less frantic. Though I couldn't completely rid of the fear that told me there was a possibility of losing Maddy, I was beginning to believe that Merman was right. There was no way Elisa could see things for anything different than they were.

A suddenly tripped beat reminded me that my heart hadn't triggered once throughout the entire ordeal with Elisa. I reasoned that it was my focused intensity and the instinctive, motherly aggression that had made the difference. Most of my episodes occurred during vulnerable moments on the defense and almost always involving Jerry. If only I could harness that aggression with him. The mere thought of fighting him to the death had triggered a new episode.

Chapter Twenty-Four

Agreements

The weekend passed without any word from Don. I had fought the urge to call him countless times, but my self-control was wavering. I needed an update on Elisa's visit. I needed to know if I was free to breathe or if I needed a plan to flee the country with Maddy.

The way Don had explained it to me - Elisa would meet with Jerry and at some point, give her preliminary findings and recommendations to both Don and Jerry's lawyer. She would then attempt to negotiate a resolution amongst the three of them, on Maddy's behalf, before presenting it to the court and letting the judge decide. I could hardly remain sane while the days dragged on.

All was quiet on the Jerry front as well. I expected an assault of some sort at every turn. Every time I opened the door to our apartment, I quickly turned on all of the lights and kept the tazer within reaching distance. I checked the backseat of my car before getting in and had developed a habit of looking in the review mirror twice as often as usual. A growing part of me hoped he would break the restraining order again so that I could sleep tight with him in jail…or should my haunting vision come to fruition, dead.

Another stipulation of the court that had yet to be addressed was the sale of our property and transfer of half of the money in our account. We had less than a week to get the house listed on the market, and Jerry had the same amount of time to remove himself and his things from it. As for the first part, Don had a real estate agent for me to work with but was waiting for approval from Jerry's lawyer. Apparently there had to be an agreement. As for Jerry moving out and paying me, I couldn't bring myself to believe that he would actually do it without being forced by the sheriffs. The thought was both thrilling and terrifying. I knew that he wouldn't leave or pay without a fight and certainly not without revenge.

Monday morning, the last week before the 30 day expiration of the court's orders, I sat by the phone in the kitchen. I had decided to give Don until 9 am before calling him and possibly showing up at his office. Maddy was already at school, and there were no services for the day, leaving nothing for me to do but focus on the phone.

I compulsively wound and unwound the cord from my finger, contemplating what news would be delivered through the line. I went over and over the possibilities, knowing that very soon, there would be a resolution to all of it. Our return court date was set just weeks away and so much would change. If Jerry was allowed anywhere near Maddy, I would have to make some decisions of my own. I knew that Merman would be more than happy to help me escape without a trace if need be, but we would have to disappear. We would be hunted by the law, and maintaining contact with anyone would be out of the question. The thought of living in a world without Merman or, my heart broke at the thought, without Oliver, seemed too high a price. Perhaps I would need another, darker strategy. The wicked possibilities had crossed my mind on more than one occasion.

The phone rang, breaking my sinister train of thought. I didn't even give it a chance to complete its first ring.

"Hello," I answered with breathless anticipation.

"Casey, it's Don. Do you have a few minutes to talk?"

"I've been waiting to hear from you all week. I have all day if you need it." There was a bit of resentment in my tone, though I tried to hide it.

"The hardest part is waiting, I know. But I have some interesting news that will make it worthwhile."

The wrenching in my stomach began, as did the accelerated beat of my heart. What had Jerry done? I could only imagine.

"What is it?" I asked, with more than a little reservation.

"I was contacted by a lawyer this morning. I actually got off the phone with him just five minutes ago." I wanted to scream *get to the point*, but I resisted. "He has an order to stay the sale of your property. Apparently, you and Jerry signed an agreement when purchasing the property. Do you recall doing that?"

"Yes, my mother had a lawyer involved during the whole process. She said it wasn't anything to worry about, but that we needed to sign whatever the lawyer had for us to sign if we wanted the deposit she was offering."

"Right. Well, do you have any idea what you signed, Casey?" I suddenly remembered having the same conversation with Merman. I had no idea what I had signed.

"No, I don't."

"It was a postnuptial agreement. Your mother must have had a hunch about Jerry from the beginning. Would you like to know what it says?"

"You're killing me, Don. Just tell me." The anticipation was unnerving. I couldn't believe my mother had the wherewithal to draw up a postnuptial agreement but couldn't get herself out of the nightmare she lived with my father.

"Should you and Jerry ever separate or divorce, for any reason under the sun, the property and everything in it become your sole property. Jerry signed this document in at least ten different places. He forfeited any ownership of this property the second he filed with the courts."

I couldn't believe what I was hearing. All of this time, I had lived in false dependence on Jerry. I had only imagined myself trapped. What was more - my mother had seen this coming. She had protected me from the life she couldn't escape. The revelation was too much to digest at once. I was speechless.

"Casey? This changes things. Jerry has ten days remaining to vacate the property, and then it's yours. He'll try to argue that he was unaware of the contents of the agreement, but he signed so many times. He'll never get around it. Well…one less battle to fight. Now we just focus on custody."

He was wrong. This only magnified the fight. Jerry would be livid. It was one of the only things he had over me. Now he would focus all of his rage toward stealing Maddy away. Maybe I could get him to take the house and leave Maddy alone.

"Do you think he'll give me custody if I give him the house?"

"What?" He sounded truly dumbfounded.

"I want to negotiate custody for property." I felt confident that Jerry would take the offer. After all, he had always been in it for the money.

"Why would we offer him anything when you're going to win everything? Casey, I can tell that your faith is wavering, but you have to believe me. All of the cards are stacked in your favor. Elisa's emailed me her preliminary report. It's good, Casey. She has some concerns about the mortuary, but overall, she feels that Maddy is better off living with you until Jerry has met all of the court's requirements of counseling, drug and alcohol rehabilitation, and anger management classes." I knew that this was supposed to be convincing, that I should feel relieved by this report, but I was anything but relieved.

"And then what, Don? So Jerry goes to counseling and rehab. Do you think he'll change? He broke into our apartment. He wants me dead. When he finds out about the house, he'll make it his only goal in life."

"When he slips up, we'll get him again. That's what the restraining order is for. You can't worry about what hasn't happened yet."

"The police still can't prove he was in our apartment. The next time he slips up, we might be dead. Please, just make him the offer."

"I don't advise it, Casey, but if this is what you want, I'll call right now."

"It's what I want."

He sighed. "Okay, I'll call you back." He hung up sounding utterly disappointed, but I had to try and resolve things in a way that would satisfy Jerry fully and keep him away for good. Money was the only way I knew how.

As I waited to hear back, I pondered ways that I could thank my mother. I had underestimated her greatly. For so long I had felt abandoned by her. She had given me money, but I had always wanted and needed her emotional support. In light of the day's revelation, I realized that she had done the best she could with what she had. She had known how to best protect me, and I was ashamedly grateful.

Again, I sat by the phone, waiting for an answer. I knew that Don would have to explain everything to Jerry's lawyer, at which point he would contact Jerry and call Don back with an answer, but I couldn't bring myself to leave the kitchen. I needed to know if I could let my guard down.

About an hour passed with me killing time by pacing the kitchen floor, fitting my feet into each square tile and pleading in prayer with each step. I knew Merman would want to be with me, but I needed to do this alone. I knew that Oliver would want to comfort me, but I feared that my ever increasing passion for him would jinx the possibility of a good outcome. I had been avoiding him for the last few days, terrified of the conclusion Elisa and the judge would draw should she see us together. I was completely helpless against the pull he had over me, and the only defense I had was to avoid him altogether.

The phone rang, and my heart stopped momentarily before exploding into a fit of palpitations. This was it – a small chance that this could all be over.

"Hello," I answered, more fearful than the first time.

"It's a no go, Casey. He wants to take this all the way." My heart sank deeper than I imagined possible. I didn't understand. He was never going to win – not in court anyway. "He wants the fight, Casey. You can't hold back any more."

I had fallen to my knees as the fear gripped me. I couldn't respond. I knew what he was after. It was me.

"Casey, this is all going to work out. Just don't go anywhere alone, and let me handle the rest. Oh, and one more thing…" he paused, and I didn't know that I could take any more news. "Elisa is going to make the recommendation that you move out of the funeral home within ninety days and find Maddy a suitable home, which isn't a problem since you'll have your house back before then. She will also recommend you keep Maddy away from the funeral home."

"Move out? But…this is the only safe place we know." I couldn't fathom living alone with all that was happening, or even worse, in that house.

"Well, if everything goes as planned, I will have the restraining order extended. I'm pretty sure that the judge will agree with Elisa. If you have another feasible option for housing, you should take it. She was pretty adamant about that part."

I had never considered that my stint at The Golden Oaks would end as abruptly as it began. All of the midnight conversations with Merman, family dinners, moments with Oliver, and the unmistakably fulfilling life that I had come to know flashed through my mind, and my heart ached. Of all the things Elisa would demand, the very security we had come to cherish was at the top of her list. She hadn't seen it, or hadn't cared. Don was right, the judge and any outsider for that matter, would agree with her. I tried to reason a way around it, but could think of nothing. "So we have three months to move out?"

"Well, three months after it is agreed upon in writing and signed by all parties or ordered by the court. It would be wise to agree to her terms before court. We want to appear the reasonable ones in all of this. It's really the only thing she's requiring on your end. The rest is concerning Jerry."

"I suppose I have no other choice." I felt defeated as our conversation ended, and I hung up the phone. I nearly cried at the thought of telling Merman and Maddy. Leaving was unimaginable yet unavoidable. I would have to make the most of the three months I had left. Some growing part of me feared that if I left, it would all end. I put it in the back of my mind and decided a call must be made.

I dialed the number of my childhood years and prayed that the voice that answered was the one I wished to speak with. After two rings, a voice answered, vaguely familiar and sober.

"Hello?"

I paused, unsure of how to proceed.

"Um, hello, I'm looking for Evelyn please."

"Casey, is that you? This is your mother, dear."

"Mom, you sound…great." I hadn't heard her sound that alert and clear since I was a child. I was pleasantly baffled.

"Well, thank you, dear. A lot has happened since we last spoke."

"That's why I'm calling. I got a call today. I know about the postnuptial agreement you had us sign when we bought the house. I don't know how to thank you enough. Jerry is coming after me for everything…he's coming after Maddy." I was beginning to well up with tears again. I so desperately needed her to comfort me. I had always needed that. I sucked in all of my emotions, knowing I would only be disappointed again. She didn't sound surprised by the news at all.

"Yes, I was notified of the pending sale late last week. I expected this day would come. I'm sorry to hear that it did, but I'm glad he can't get his greedy, dirty hands on any of it. Are you and Maddy alright?" She sounded genuinely concerned. I was shocked at the sudden change in character and didn't know how to respond.

"Um…yes, we're fine. I mean, we'll be fine." I was fumbling over my words. I didn't need to burden her with the details. I just wanted to share my gratitude for her loving wisdom.

"Is there anything I can do to help you two?"

"No, mom, please, I was just calling to thank you. We're doing just fine. How are you doing? You sound…so…happy."

"Well, like I said before, a lot has happened since we last spoke. The night you left, I realized that you had done something I had avoided for thirty years. You took a stand and did what you could to protect yourself and your little girl. I'm sorry that I never did that for you, Casey." Her voice quivered slightly, but quickly regained control and hardened. "I've left your father." She continued talking, but her last words hit me like an avalanche of long overdue absolution. The unshakable foundation of hypocrisy, tyranny, and submission that I had witnessed my whole life tumbled over me like a rush of crisp air. Mid-sentence, I interrupted her.

"You left him?" I wanted confirmation before I allowed myself the relief I felt inching its way up.

"Yes, dear, I left. I'm here getting all of my things together while he's away on business. I've been living on my own for nearly a month."

"What did he do? What did he say?" I could picture the tirade he had gone on when she told him and suddenly felt frightened for her.

"Oh, he did what your father does best. He threatened, berated, and stormed about, but in the end, I think he knew that it was useless. He's been surprisingly gracious in the last couple of weeks. I'm not quite sure what to make of it."

"So, now what?" The thought of my father being gracious to anyone made me laugh out loud.

"Well, I'm not sure, dear. I need some time to sort things out. I haven't had a drop of liquor in almost a month, and I've never felt clearer and more empowered in my life." She laughed thoughtfully. "He practically begged me not to file for divorce. He asked that I give it a year. I figure why not, I've made it thirty. In the meantime, I'm keeping myself busy." I was so happy to hear the life in her voice. I could hardly believe that my father had broken. Part of me wanted to tell her not to go back, not to give him another chance, but I had never seen him like this. Perhaps there was a small light at the end of that very long and dark tunnel.

"I don't know what to say, mom. I'm so happy to hear you happy. I want you to do whatever it is that will keep it that way." She laughed again.

"Me too, dear. Me too."

The conversation ended, and I hung up feeling like a very small thread in a larger tapestry of life. Somehow we were all woven together in a picture that I couldn't see clearly from where I was standing. I was humbled by the thought that my decision that night had given her hope for something better.

With the intricate and unpredictable tapestry in mind, I went to find Merman. I suddenly felt hopeful about the terrifying change ahead. I tried to picture Merman's thread and Oliver's thread, Celia's and even Eddie's thread somehow weaving together into something beautiful over time. I smiled on my way down the stairs as tears followed.

As I expected, Merman found the silver lining in the seemingly devastating news.

"How can you possibly be sad about leaving this old place when you have your house back? I mean, I always knew this would be temporary, didn't you?"

I had never seen it that way. I had never thought that far ahead, and I certainly didn't see that house as a trade up.

"I'd rather live here. I don't want to step foot in that house again." The thought of returning to that place of stagnation and servitude made me feel ill. I held myself to keep from shivering. Since the phone call with Don, I was beginning to feel extremely vulnerable, like the first time I took my training wheels off. I didn't believe I could do it on my own without falling and breaking something in the process. Merman was my set of training wheels, and I hadn't quite gotten my balance yet.

"So sell it," he said simply. "Move closer." He winked and sipped at his wine. I didn't know how to take his casual attitude about it all. Why was I so worried when he didn't even seem fazed? Maybe this didn't mean to him what it meant to me. After all, it was me on the receiving end most of the time. What had I ever offered Merman? I began to panic. I felt that fear that comes right before a break up. I imagined he and the rest would go on as if we had never crashed onto that hill. A hot flash came over me, and my palpitations came on with a vengeance.

"What?" He looked at me with concern.

"I don't know. I feel like once I leave, I'll never see you…any of you again." I held myself tighter hoping that I was wrong and dreading another casual response.

"What? You think you can keep me away? It's not possible, sweetheart. If you think Jerry's a stalker, he's got nothing on me. I'll find you wherever you go." He nudged me before hugging me tight. "Don't be ridiculous. Is that what this is all about?" He leaned back and looked at me. I was crying, though trying my best to make it stop.

"Yes," I managed to get out in a whimper.

"You don't give me much credit, do you? Though, I guess I can't blame you. I'd have trust issues after one day with Gerardo, and that father of yours…he sounds like a real piece of work." I laughed, but cringed at the truth of what he said. There it was, as plain as day, my dysfunctional past sneaking up on me and influencing my judgment. Seeing it clearly, I couldn't believe I had questioned Merman's loyalty. He had been nothing but loyal to me from the first moment I saw him through that breath-fogged window. That faint but insistent voice crept up from the center of my gut. This didn't bode well for a relationship with Oliver anytime soon. My perspective and judgment had been warped by years of manipulation and control. I couldn't trust myself to make decisions about relationships, not yet.

Just at that very moment of enlightenment, Oliver came in, his eyes piercing through any resolve I might have built in the last minute. He sat next to me, took my hand in his, and waited patiently to hear the news. Suddenly the thought of not being with him, one way or another, was too much to consider. I wanted him too much to ponder it any further. I pushed it back down, knowing it would demand my attention soon enough, and leaned in close to breathe him in.

Chapter Twenty-Five

Reckoning

In times of crisis, instinct overrides reason. It is the accelerated beat of a heart, allowing for a swift escape from danger; it is the enhanced peripheral vision to see the danger approach; and it is foremost, the beast of fight or flight, allowing the unthinkable and savage to surface for the preservation of life. It was in the dark hours of the increasingly rainy and bitter cold nights that my instinct took over, always in my sleep and always under the weight of Jerry's deadly grip. My dreams were becoming more violently foreboding and more difficult to shake.

The days passed, uneventful, yet increasingly ominous as such. There had been no movement forward with regard to Jerry moving out of the house or keeping with the court's order to divide our assets. I never imagined he would play by the rules, but was becoming concerned with what sinister plan he might be devising instead.

Don explained that Jerry would likely argue the validity of the signed agreement regarding the house, biding him time on the eviction front. But at some point, his time would be up, and it was this very time that had me most worried. Our hearing was one day away, and all would be decided.

Living around the unpredictable chaos that continuously circles someone like Jerry, my senses had sharpened, and I had become an expert at peering into the future to predict what might lie ahead, if only to avoid it. Lately, when I peered into the future, I saw nothing. I couldn't see a possible outcome to the hearing - I couldn't see us living back at that forsaken house, and I couldn't see what maniacal plan Jerry would unfold. The blindness was unsettling, and I figured that my senses had dulled, or worse…I didn't have a future to see.

I paced the hallways of The Golden Oaks with painful anticipation of soon leaving it behind, one way or another. Luckily, we had two new friends to prepare for services, and there was much to do to curb my gloom. I made a conscious decision to stay as present as possible in each waking moment, knowing that change was fast approaching.

I entered the large chapel to find Celia setting up for a service. She was swaying and humming to the music she had playing on the stereo. *Lean on Me* sang out as she straightened the clothing and hair of the woman in the pink, pearly casket. I tried to watch quietly, but the door gave me away as it creaked shut. Celia looked up and smiled, sauntering down the aisle and lip synching the words – a serenade. When she reached me, she took my hand and led me into a spin, which unfolded into a slow dance. It didn't last long before we were both giggling like silly school girls. I was going to miss her. I feared that outside of work hours, getting together with everyone would slowly become a thing of the past. I held back the tears that were fighting their way out.

A smooth and enchanting voice spoke behind me.

"May I cut in?" I spun around to find Oliver with a mesmerizing smile, holding his hand out to me.

"I was just warming her up for you," Celia teased and went back to her work.

When I put my hand in his, he pulled me in close. All of my haunting thoughts were replaced by warm electricity. I let my cheek press against his smooth jaw as I breathed in his intoxicating smell, and I cared about nothing more than moving in rhythm with him to the music.

With my days possibly numbered, I demanded of myself a final kiss. This was my justification. If I had no future, at least one that I could imagine, then I would make the most of every second. I pushed up onto my toes and faced him directly, with my nose touching his and my lips close enough to feel the warmth of his breath. He stopped swaying and stood still, careful not to initiate the forbidden. I entertained the possibility as I moved my lips closer and closer, and still he didn't move. Just as they lightly brushed over his, he spoke and awakened me from my delirium.

"Casey," he said in a struggled whisper. I suddenly felt embarrassed, realizing that he wasn't in on my life or death debate and would think me crazy if I tried to catch him up.

"I'm sorry," was all I could think to say. I pulled away, but he caught me by both arms.

"Casey…" He paused, considering something important. "I love you." The words shook me. I couldn't fathom why he felt the way he did, but it didn't matter. I had never heard those words ring with such genuine clarity. He continued before I could speak, "This," he pulled me in close so that our lips were barely separated, "this is what I wait for. Everything in me wants to sweep you up and make you mine, but I want it to be right. I don't want anything in the way when that time comes, because nothing will stop me."

His warm breath was stirring up wild desires and his words, wild images. I tried to focus on their meaning. He pressed his forehead gently against mine. I opened my eyes to find him looking right into them. I wanted to say it too. I was overwhelmed with emotion.

"I," I started, but he interrupted.

"You don't have to say it. I just needed you to know."

Before I could argue, Merman came through the double doors, blurting out a question before they had opened all the way.

"Has anyone seen Edd…?" He stopped when he saw our embrace and chuckled as we collected ourselves. "Well, I guess *you* haven't seen Eddie," he teased as he walked past us. "What about you, beautiful?" He headed toward Celia. It made me happy to hear the love in his voice when he spoke to her. He was becoming more comfortable with displaying his affection for her publicly. I could tell that this thrilled her and made it more real.

"I saw him out back hunting that raccoon that keeps getting into the trash cans." We all laughed, and she leaned over to kiss him on the nose, as she stood two steps above him. I wanted that freedom to love more than anything. There just had to be a future, and it had to be with Oliver, but he was right, there could be nothing in the way…not even me.

As we watched what I feared might be our last movie together on that white leather couch, I wondered how much time it would take for the past to be resolved and a future to be possible. I wondered what unforeseen obstacles would get in the way. I realized, as the images danced across the screen, that I had a lot of work ahead of me. The only way I could move on from the past, without it manifesting itself, unrecognizable and divisive, was to thoroughly inventory every choice, good and bad, and hold myself accountable for them all. I couldn't leave any room for the possibility of repeating such a ruinous past. It dawned on me, and not without sorrow, that a process like that could take time. I watched Oliver watch the screen and wondered how long he could wait…and pondered the depth of the love he professed.

Surprisingly, I slept that night. I had predicted that with court the next day, I would be wide-eyed and restless. The sleep though, was anything but restful. It was my first dream about a friend. The woman from the pink, pearly casket was in my apartment. She sat in the chair across from my sofa and said nothing, waiting for me to acknowledge who she was. When I realized where I knew her from, she smiled, stood and held out her hand. She didn't look like the waxy, pale, and soulless version of herself that rested in the chapel. She was beautiful with her silvery hair and pale, blue eyes. Her cheeks even had a healthy blush to them. I was confused, but trusted her implicitly. She waited patiently while I deliberated. Finally, I took her hand.

She led me into the kitchen and reached for a drawer. It was my junk drawer, a drawer that housed mail, clips, pens, coupons, and other miscellaneous objects. Despite the brief amount of time we had been there, I already had quite a collection. I was embarrassed and wondered if she was going to give me a lecture on being tidy.

I watched as she rifled through the papers and used two fingers to pick something up. I leaned in to see what it was. Her smile turned to a serious concern. She held up a gold key and looked at me, waiting for recognition. I didn't understand. She held it out closer to me, and her brows furrowed with deep distress.

"What is it?" I asked, wishing I could understand what she wanted, but she said nothing. I reached out to take the key, but it vanished from her hands. She held out her two empty hands, and the look of concern only deepened.

"What do you need me to do?" I asked, feeling sad that she couldn't communicate and that I couldn't help her. She shook her head in frustration, looked back at the drawer, and held out her two hands again. There was a knock on the door that seemed to startle her. She looked in that direction and then back at me. I feared that if I turned, she would disappear, but the knocking was persistent.

"Wait right here." I had the instinctive desire to hide her from whomever might be at the door. I felt almost protective of her. The knocking continued, but before I could reach it to see who it was, I woke up.

When the remains of the dream wore off, I realized that the knock persisted. I crawled out of bed and peeked through the hole, still shaken by my dream. It was Merman.

"Do you know what time it is?" He was in a complete panic, which quickly put me into a panic.

"Oh god, what time is it? My alarm didn't go off! Why didn't my alarm go off?" I ran to find my phone on the coffee table. I opened it to find that I had exactly one hour to get ready and be at the courthouse.

"I figured something was up when you hadn't come down. I'll take Maddy, you get ready."

"Thank you, Merman, thank you!" I hugged him and he indulged briefly.

"Go get ready! I'll be right behind you."

It didn't take me long before I was on the road, and luckily, traffic wasn't so bad. By the time I made it through the security line, I had three minutes to spare. As nerve wracking as it was to be rushed, I preferred it over waiting around the hallways of the court with Jerry lurking nearby.

I spotted Don immediately when I exited the elevator. He looked relieved to see me and gestured for me to hurry to him. I was so worried about what he might say that I didn't bother to look around for Jerry, but I stiffened when the smell of his cologne, the same cologne that had been in my apartment weeks before, passed over me. I decided not to look and continued on to Don.

"I'm glad you made it on time. We are first on the docket." The fear began to creep up, but I argued with it, reasoning that going first meant it would be over sooner. As I looked around, I saw Elisa sitting on a bench, reviewing paperwork.

"Apparently, Jerry agreed to none of Elisa's recommendations, so it's all up to the judge. He's planning on making the claim that he was tricked into signing that document for the property, but the executor of your estate is here to defend it." I looked around confused.

"The executor?"

"Yes, the lawyer you met with six years ago when you purchased your home."

"Oh." I looked around but didn't see any recognizable faces.

Without notice, the doors to the courtroom were opened by the bailiff. My knees wobbled, and I wondered if anyone could grow used to this process. Don led me in quickly, holding me by the arm. He seated me to the far right, all the way against the wall, and put his briefcase in the seat next to mine. I was grateful to see Jerry's lawyer sit on the opposite side of the aisle.

That's when I saw him.

Jerry was dressed in a black suit and a tie, and had cut his hair short. He looked alarmingly different, and I questioned whether or not I would have recognized him had he been lurking around or following me over the last two months. He looked thinner, and there was a faint bluish undertone beneath his eyes. When he saw me, he stared darkly. I shuddered at his soulless appearance. Before, he had been animated by anger and arrogance, but now, now he looked like pure hatred personified. It terrified me. It seemed as if he had shown up just to see it through, but with no concern at all about the outcome. Don sat between me and the vision of evil across from us.

"Don't look over there, Casey. It's no good at all." It seemed by his tone that even he was disturbed by what he saw.

I closed my eyes and prayed for peace, for some happy ending to this tumultuous story. I didn't want this to be the end. I so desperately wanted a future, a future with Maddy and Oliver and Merman and Celia...even with Eddie and Uncle Stanley. As I went down the list of the people I loved, a picture of my mother flashed by, and I smiled, trying to picture her lucid and happy.

Just then, another familiar scent wafted my way. I spun around, not sure what I would find, and saw my mother looking around the courtroom. She was radiant, the way she once had been. Her tall figure looked confident and strong. Her eyes were clear, and her wisdom shone through. She caught my eye and smiled, making her way over. I almost cried with happiness. She was there when I needed her most. I wanted to bask in her confidence. She looked over at Jerry, tilted her head in disapproval, and sighed. She sat behind me and leaned over to kiss my forehead.

"Don't you worry. This will be taken care of."

"Thank you for being here." I held back the tears that were becoming a far too frequent occurrence as of late. "Don, this is my mother, Evelyn. Evelyn, Don." They shook hands, and Don beamed admiringly.

"It's a good thing Casey had you there six years ago."

"Well," my mother said modestly, "I'm certainly glad I did this, but I wish I could have done more." She looked at me with a hint of sorrow and a lifetime of regret. I took and squeezed her hand. I wasn't afraid anymore.

A familiar looking man entered the courtroom, checked in and then nodded at my mother.

"Who is that?" I asked her, assuming it was the executor.

"That is Mr. Sheffield, dear. He's here about the contract." The name echoed in my memory. I knew it, yet it was just out of reach. He took the seat next to my mother and looked at me knowingly.

"Hello, Casey, I'm James Sheffield." He held out his hand and smiled. With the touch of his hand the memories flooded back, first to the small chapel with his mother May, and then further back to the day we signed those papers. I laughed at the irony.

"What is it, dear?" My mother's voice carried a slight hint of embarrassment. James winked at me, and I figured we could keep it between us.

"Nothing, I'm sorry. It's just been a long time, that's all."

The reunion was broken by the sound of the bailiff's voice calling the court to order. In walked the petit but potent Judge Oto. She sat down and was handed a thick manila folder by her clerk. She flipped through for minutes on end. She shook her head a few times and finally closed the file.

"Wheeler versus Wheeler," she called out, in what sounded to be an irritated tone. Don led me through the swinging doors and proceeded to introduce himself, and the three other lawyers followed suit.

"As of today, the property has not been listed, the assets have not been divided, and Mr. Wheeler has not complied with any of the court's orders regarding rehabilitation and counseling."

Jerry's lawyer began to give excuses, "Your honor, we've been dealing with the issue of a supposed postnuptial…" She cut him off.

"Mr. Oxman, am I correct in my assessment? Have any of the court's orders been followed?"

"No, your honor, but…" She interrupted him by slapping her hand down on her desk. I jumped slightly and prayed that her wrath didn't turn on me.

"I would like to see all four of you in my chambers immediately. The court will take a brief recess." She stood up and exited through the same door she entered.

The bailiff excused us and Don turned to me. "Casey, why don't you go down to the cafeteria with your mother? This could be a while." He held open the swinging doors for me, and I made my way back to my seat, hands trembling and heart racing. To my surprise and relief, standing at the back of the courtroom was Merman with his eyes wide in excitement.

The three of us made our way outside of the cold room while the four attorneys met behind closed doors with an unhappy Oto.

My mother and Merman stood looking at me, awkwardly awaiting an introduction as I replayed the last five minutes again and again in my mind. Hearing my mother's foot tapping snapped me out of my contemplation.

"Oh, I'm sorry. Mom, this is Merman. Merman, this is my mother, Evelyn." She held out her hand, and Merman shook it, before pulling her in for a hug.

"I'm so glad to meet you."

My mother stared at me in surprise over his shoulder. I giggled, knowing it would take her a while to adjust to someone as real as

Merman. I hadn't given her much information about the last few months, and I would have a lot of explaining to do. I attempted to quickly fill her in while Merman stepped away to take a call from Eddie. She looked at him with gratitude when I told her of how he pulled us from the wreckage, both literally and figuratively.

The two of them talked over coffee in the cafeteria while I busied myself with worry and dread over the discussions taking place in the judge's chambers. I was also preoccupied with glancing over my shoulder to look for Jerry. I was still shaken by his appearance and wanted to keep him in sight. Something in his eyes was reminiscent of my nightly terrors, and though the two sitting with me emanated confidence enough to quell the fear he evoked, I couldn't help but shake at the quiet rage I saw boiling beneath his surface. The irregular rhythm of my heart had begun a faint but steady rumble since I first saw him in the courtroom, as if preparing me to run.

After thirty minutes, Don came in and pulled a chair up to our table. We all quieted and waited to hear the news. My stomach wrenched with anticipation. I could only imagine the slamming of hands that had gone on in the chambers.

"Well, Jerry has about a half an hour to agree to the terms set by Elisa, and Oto has made it very clear that it is in his best interest to do so." I recalled Elisa's recommendation for Maddy to stay with me until Jerry completed his counseling. It wasn't enough, not by the looks of him in that courtroom. I panicked - terrified that he might accept the offer.

Don continued with a tone of half-surprise, "Oto is also inclined to honor the post-nuptial agreement. So, barring any new agreement between the two of you, the house is yours, and he will have forty-eight hours to vacate the property or be escorted by the sheriffs." At this, my mom nodded in relief, and Merman laughed in excitement.

Still, my mind fast forwarded to six months or so down the line when Jerry had fulfilled the requirements but not the intent of the order. What then? I couldn't stand the thought of Maddy anywhere near the darkness that surrounded him. I didn't care about the house or the money. I wanted to ensure Maddy's safety. The quiet rumble was beginning to roar.

"Casey." Don looked through me, it seemed. "If Jerry ever follows through with the counseling requirements, which I have a hard time believing he will, we'll reassess the situation. No one, not Elisa, not Oto, and certainly I will never let the monster that sat in the courtroom this morning anywhere near Maddy."

I couldn't hear his reassurances clearly through the drum beat in my ears. I looked around, hoping to catch a glance of Jerry. I couldn't breathe with him out of sight. The churning of my stomach began again - my sounding alarm in time of imminent danger.

"Casey, dear, this is all good news. Try to remain calm." My mother placed her hand on mine, like fire on ice. I hadn't realized how frozen I was until she touched me.

"Oto also made clear her intent to keep the restraining order in effect until he fulfills the court's orders and we return for a status hearing." Don seemed to wait for a sign of relief or gratitude, but I couldn't give it. Instinct had taken over, the purely animalistic adrenaline that had coursed through my dreams. As I sat frozen, grasping for reason, a warm arm slid around me.

"You're not going through this alone. There's an army of us behind you," Merman coaxed. "Everything that we could have hoped for today has been handed to you without question. No matter which way Jerry turns, he's lost."

Merman's words registered, but not as intended. Jerry was like a cornered animal. He had lost everything, which left him wildly vengeful with nothing to lose…and me, with everything.

"Nothing to lose," I mumbled. All three strained to hear what I had said. I didn't want to delve into more useless reassurances. I changed the subject. "How long do we have," I asked, numb with apprehension. Don looked at his watch.

"About fifteen minutes and we need to be back in the courtroom. We'll likely meet in her chambers again, so you can stay here. Just keep your phone on in case I need you. I'm going to check in with Oxman.

Hopefully Jerry has accepted his lot." He disappeared around the corner toward my fate. I hated that I was stuck in a cafeteria while decisions were made about my life.

"Worse things than this have resolved," My mother assured me. "I've just emerged from a thirty year prison of my own making and can tell you that there's no situation too difficult to be bettered. People like Jerry…like your father, they feed on power, whether real or imagined. You can't burden yourself with his moment of crisis, Casey. How well I know that now." She looked up, closing her eyes and taking a deep breath. "You just live your life, and if he wants to bring war to your front, then you stand tall and fight back." She sat up tall and leaned in just inches from my face. "Do you hear me, Casey? You hit him hard and without mercy. Show him there's no room for his wicked plans with you and Maddy."

The ancient warrior in her voice made me shiver. I had never seen her before. The quiet battle she had fought for so long had left her with wounds of wisdom. I knew that she wanted to spare me from all she had seen. I felt loved and brave even.

Merman seemed possessed by her too as he nodded respectfully. He squeezed me tightly and held my frozen hands.

"No matter what Don comes back with, you remember this."

As if responding to an introduction, Don came around the corner looking bemused. My recently adorned bravery quickly faltered. Again he sat amongst us, and again he considered his words.

"Jerry's nowhere to be found. Even Oxman can't find him."

Merman squeezed my hands and proceeded to ask what I couldn't.

"So what does that mean, Don?"

"That means everything we discussed will be order of the court. Jerry has forty-eight hours to be out of your house, and he can't come anywhere near you or Maddy."

"Says the court," I corrected.

"Yes," acknowledged Don, "says the court. He may try to bully you, Casey, but he can't play his games with the law. They'll get him eventually. Maybe things will look a lot different in forty-eight hours."

I played with the many possibilities of that statement.

"So that's it? It's done?" I was anxious to get out of there and get Maddy as quickly as possible. There was a madman on the loose, and although the school had safeguards in place, I wouldn't put anything past him.

"Well, we will go before Oto, and she will make the final judgment. I'll have everything typed and ready to sign and you can focus on moving forward.

"Thank you, Don." I mustered up gratitude from beneath the heavy blanket of frightened fatigue.

"I know you're scared, but this is all very good," Don concluded and exited the cafeteria once more.

We waited a while longer while Don finished up in court and verified the continuance of the restraining order. The judge had her clerk type up the order, which according to Don wasn't standard procedure. Apparently, even Oto didn't want the delay that comes with lawyers and their "dilly-dallying", as she called it. He assumed she meant Oxman. As long as the order wasn't official, Jerry was free to play.

All was signed, and we were gone by the time the court closed for lunch recess.

And there it was, the good news I had hoped for, morphed into my greatest vulnerability. The freer and more empowered I became, the more Jerry's hatred grew, as if one fed the other. I knew that the man I saw in that courtroom and this new version of myself could not co-exist. Either something would change or something would perish, but there would be reckoning.

Chapter Twenty-Six

Fight or Flight

Fear is exhausting, especially so when driven by its myriad forms. Anticipation is crippling, and together they are more caustic than any reality.

The irony of the situation hadn't escaped me. On paper I had won all of the freedoms a court can bestow, but I was enslaved by the fear that had resulted. I knew that I couldn't live in that state without end, but what I didn't know was how to go about my days as if he wasn't out there plotting revenge.

Reprieves from this insidious enslavement came in the form of my new and blessed family. Merman left my side only when replaced by Oliver, who only left my side when I insisted there was an entire world of sick people who needed his care. The truth was that I didn't like the idea of him being with me purely out of worry. It only reminded me of the complications inherent in our love. He humored me and left for a while, only to return as adorably worried as ever.

Celia was there to listen to my endless strife over it all, and Eddie was in rare form, double checking locks and the effectiveness of the alarm system. Though humorous at first, the false alarms were beginning to wear me thin.

My mother was planning on coming the following day to help me work out a plan for selling the house and finding a new one within ninety days, as ordered by the court. James would be with her to ensure I was legally protected. Everyone had come together, in their own unique ways, to care for us and help us through. I felt an overwhelming sense of belonging, and it was amazing.

At the close of that daunting day, I re-considered the meaning of family. Sacrifice and loyalty surrounded me in abundance, and in the unlikeliest of places. In life I had suffered a thousand deaths, and in the midst of death I had encountered true life. I had looked in all the wrong places, until there, on a hill of ivy, I was found.

I knew without a doubt that this funny little story had been authored by someone wiser than me. This God, as I called Him, the one to whom I had cast my numerous and desperate prayers, had seen me coming down that road and stopped me exactly where I needed to be. Perhaps, I thought, He knew where I was headed next.

It was this revelation that finally freed me. The fruitless struggle with the unknown was finished, and I looked forward to the next chapter, come what may.

With this mindset, I settled in for the night, peacefully sleepy for the first time in a while. After I washed my face and brushed my teeth, I stared at the reflection of a stranger. I looked tired, pale, and hungry. The constant anxiety kept me from ever being hungry, and worry had tattooed circles beneath my eyes. I wore the painted mask of my troubles.

I decided to shower, put on a little make-up, and eat some food to feel human again. I set Maddy up with some paper and crayons and felt at ease knowing that Merman and Eddie had some sort of security shift worked out downstairs. I had told them not to worry, but Merman didn't exactly concur with my new *come what may* attitude. Oliver didn't seem too convinced by my awakening either, and though he left to work a shift at the E.R., he insisted he would be back in the wee hours to check in.

It felt good to take a warm shower, free from the record of suppositions playing in my head. I took my time blowing my hair dry and putting on just a little make-up - enough to look somewhat human again. I stared back at my reflection and saw a hint of the strength I had seen in my mother.

After eating a grilled cheese sandwich with Maddy, she asked me to help her with a picture. She wanted me to draw the two of us with Merman at The Golden Oaks. I humored her, thinking the project might prove interesting and put to use what little sketching talent I had left over from my high school art classes. With plenty of eraser bits littering the table, there we were - the outline of the two of us standing in front of the building we would call our home for just a while longer. Maddy wanted Merman in the doorway waving to us, the leafless trees and ivy we saw everyday on our way to school, and on this particular night, rain. The image before me brought back memories of that first night. Little did I know that it would be a picture of hope and a picture of life. Of course, Maddy wanted a dozen more details, but I had maxed out my artistic skills and was tired enough to hopefully sleep through the night. I felt better than I had in a long time, and as I lay my head down, I fell asleep without struggle…the calm before the storm.

I woke up some time later with the feeling that someone was watching me. I sat up, startled to see the woman from my dream the night before. Her service was the next day and her name, I had learned, was Anne. She was standing over me and didn't greet me with a smile this time, but frantically reached her hand out to me, continuously looking over her shoulder as if something frightened her. The white dress she wore created a faint glow all about her. She was as lovely as the first time, and just as troubled.

I took her soft, frail hand again and followed as she led me back into the kitchen. She reached out and opened the same drawer, pulled out the same key, and held it for me to examine. I looked closely this time, hoping to find its significance.

I recognized it. It was the master key to the mortuary. Merman had given me a copy shortly after we moved in. I reached for it, hoping to better understand what she wanted from me, but it vanished once again. The look on her face as I stood there confused, was growing increasingly troubled. She strained and moved her lips, trying to speak. Finally, I heard her faint voice.

"Jerry." It came out as a ghastly whisper, sending chills right through me. His name confused me more. I tried to connect his name with the key again and again, until finally, it clicked.

"Jerry took the key?" The thought was terrifying as I said it out loud. She nodded tearfully and crossed the kitchen, looking for something. I followed her, trembling. I had never even thought to look in that drawer after the break-in. For weeks he had that key. God only knew what he had planned to do with it.

She reached into a dark corner of the kitchen counter. I leaned in to see what she meant to show me. A sharp pain twisted my stomach when I realized she had reached for the set of knives sitting on my kitchen counter, pulling one from the block. She held it out again, and my stomach wrenched with fear. The purpose of this I feared I already knew, but there was only one way to find out for certain. I apprehensively reached toward it, and to my horror, it disappeared.

"No!" I gasped.

She nodded frantically and once again struggled to speak.

"Casey," she rasped, "wake up! Wake up!"

I opened my eyes and sat up, completely drenched in perspiration. My heart was a mile ahead of me, as were my thoughts. I looked into the pitch black of my living room, but before I could consider the validity of my dream, I was instantly nauseated by the smell of sickeningly familiar cologne and sweat.

I didn't even have time to scream. His arms were around me, and a cold blade rested at my throat.

"Jerry, don't do this," I begged, careful not to move against the metal.

"Shut up." He spit at me with drunken breath. "You had your day of victory, now it's my turn."

"Jerry, please," I begged. He only pressed the blade closer to my throat. I felt it slice the surface of my flesh. I waited in terror for it to cut through, but it didn't.

"Do you think I care what the court says? Do you?" he growled, pulling my head back by my hair. "This is where real justice will be done. This is where I take you back, like I promised I would." I didn't say anything. I figured my chances of living were better if I let him do the talking. The silence provoked him to speak again, and the alcohol on his breath was nauseating as he labored over each word. "Did you really think you'd get away with leaving me? And taking everything?" He swayed and loosened his grip slightly. "And those losers downstairs, did you think they'd stop me?" He laughed with wicked drunkenness. "That one freak entered the alarm code so many times. He practically begged me to come in. And that Mer-man of yours," his laughter turned to gritted teeth, and the blade pressed deep again, "where's he now? Leaving you and Maddy all alone? Maybe he wanted to get rid of you."

My thoughts were immediately on Maddy. I didn't know if he had already gotten to her, or if he came for me first. The terror that was threatening to consume me was replaced by a surge of motherly rage. If she was already gone, then my life didn't matter, but if she was still alive, I would die to protect her.

Putting the threat of death out of my mind, I jerked my head forward, and then threw it back as hard as I could. I felt a piercing pain shoot across my throat and an intense ache swell at the back of my head. Both were drowned out by a loud and violent roar from Jerry. I had hit his nose hard, and both he and the knife were doubled over.

I turned and threw myself at him with wild fury. I clasped my fists together, as if I were holding a bat, and swung at his folded head.

He dropped the knife and stumbled backward, tripping on the coffee table and hitting his head against the wooden arm of the chair.

He lay motionless while I stood listening to myself breathe hard through my nose. I watched closely, looking for any sign of consciousness. I needed to see Maddy, know that she was alive. I knew that turning my back on him meant the possibility of a number of horrors, but I had to know. I ran to her door and quietly but frantically swung it open. Through the moonlight, I could see Hippo tucked under her chin, and the subtle rhythm of her breathing. She was alive and sleeping peacefully. The relief was euphoric, countering the adrenaline that had started an episode unlike any I had known. I had to get her out of there. I would take her to Merman's apartment and call the police.

The sound of the front door opening interrupted my planning and started the wild adrenaline frenzy once more. I spun around, ready to attack, only to find Merman in the doorway. He looked at Jerry on the floor and ran to me, looking me over in a panic.

"I'm fine. I'm fine!" I said, pushing his hand away and closing the door.

"He must have tripped the alarm somehow. I heard a loud noise and came up as fast as…" Before he could finish, he was hit by a savage force. Jerry had lunged at him and pulled him back onto the floor. He had Merman in a headlock and was using his legs to inch them both back toward the kitchen. I couldn't see in the dark, but I knew what he was reaching for. I jumped over both of them and kicked at the shining blade, hoping to get it out of sight and out of reach.

Mid-kick, something seized my ankle and all of my weight lurched forward, and before I could catch myself, I watched as my head fell toward the ledge of the kitchen counter, helpless to stop it.

A sharp pain led to black.

The faint echo of labored grunting taunted my consciousness. Images and memories pieced together told me where I was. I tried to open my eyes, but a piercing pain across my forehead made it almost impossible. Blurred images wrestled before me. One was on top of the other.

As my vision cleared, I saw that it was Jerry, mad with rage, slamming his fists into Merman. Again, the protective fury filled me, and I reached for the closest and deadliest object nearby. A sturdy handle filled both of my hands. I heard the echo of my mother's voice. *Hit him hard and without mercy. There's no place for his wickedness.*

I swung to put an end to it all, to make him stop. The pan connected with his head with a heavy thud. He wavered before falling limp to the side, hitting his head hard against the sharp edge of the coffee table glass.

I quickly rolled what remained of his body off of Merman and leaned over to assess the damage.

"Merman, are you okay?" I begged frantically. He wasn't responding. "Merman?" The tears flooded and the thoughts threatened. "Please, Merman, Please?" I brushed the sticky, bloody hair from his forehead. His face was swollen and unrecognizable. I leaned over and kissed his cheeks softly.

"I'm okay," he choked out, unable to open one eye.

"Oh God, oh God, thank you! Thank you!"

"Where is he?" Merman interrupted my praise.

"He's here." I leaned in close to see if Jerry was breathing. I jumped at the sight of his opened eyes, but they simply stared back at me. "I think he's…I think he's dead." Merman sat up and with his one good eye looked him over.

"I'd say so."

This revelation brought on grief I hadn't expected. I hadn't intended for him to die. I just wanted him to stop. He wouldn't stop.

I suddenly remembered Maddy.

"She can't see him like this, Merman. I have to get her out of here." I stood up, and like that cold blade that had rested against my throat, a dagger of pain shot through my chest. The pulse was coming so hard and so fast that I couldn't differentiate between beats. There was no steady rhythm.

I struggled against it, panicking and reaching around for something to hold me up, but the lack of oxygen was making the fight futile. I fell to my knees and watched as Merman helped me down to the floor.

I needed to tell him, to remind him about Maddy, but the pressure was crushing me.

"Mad…" was all I could get out.

"Maddy, I know. She'll be fine." He was holding my hand and brushing the hair from my face. He looked like he was at the end of a very dark tunnel that was beginning to close in around me. I was losing him.

As the darkness drew in, I heard another voice. It echoed of love beside me.

"Casey, we've got Maddy. She's going to be okay," it said. I could feel the warmth of his hand on my wrist and the velvet of his lips on my forehead. Oliver.

There was a low hum of commotion, though I could comprehend none of it. I fought to hold onto his voice in the sea of sounds. It was so close.

"Casey, I'm here. I'm here." I felt weightless, even under the pressure of my heart, as if I had been lifted. His arms were underneath me, and with every step he pulled me closer.

A red light pulsed through the darkness and colored his words. That too faded. I felt the warm pressure of his lips against mine. I wanted to press back, but I was slipping, and the dark was closing in. It was heavier than me, and I had to let go.

A tugging sensation on my arm, followed by a pinching pain, pulled me back into consciousness. My mouth was uncomfortably dry. I tried to swallow, but found that my throat was scratched and achy. I slowly became aware of a familiar pain across my throat and forehead, and an unfamiliar pain in my legs. When I opened my eyes, there was a woman busying herself with my arm. She noticed me watching her.

"You're awake. That's good. There are people waiting to see you." She untied a thick rubber band from around my upper arm and pulled a needle from my vein. I was momentarily confused, trying to pull together my last memories and form a reasonable explanation for my being in a hospital bed. I couldn't form a logical thought beyond the dryness of my mouth and throat.

"Can I please have some water," I managed to rasp into words.

"You shouldn't have any water for a while. The anesthesia is still in your system."

"Please," I begged. She paused and looked me over once, deciding.

"How about some ice chips, honey?"

"Anything, please." She left the room and was back surprisingly fast. She handed me a styrofoam cup with small cylindrical pieces of ice and a spoon. She helped me sit up, and the movement caused the pain in my legs and head to double. I winced.

"Slowly now," she cautioned, just a little too late. "Let me know if the pain becomes too much and we'll take care of it." I wondered what too much was and hoped I wouldn't find out. As long as I didn't move, the pain in my legs subsided.

I scooped up a small heap of ice and put it in my mouth. Never before had I cherished those little cubes of frozen water as much as I did in that moment. It soothed as it went down, and I scooped again and again.

"Don't eat too much of that or you'll be throwing up everywhere," she advised, and placed a small pink tray on my lap. I weighed my options. The dryness was too much to ignore, and I easily decided that I could handle a little vomiting. She placed a pillow behind my head and checked the bags of liquid hanging from a hook above me.

When the pain in my throat was tolerable, I asked her what I hadn't been able to guess just yet.

"What happened?" I realized after I'd asked that it was a rather broad question. "I mean, why am I here?" She smiled and sat at the end of my bed, patting my legs.

"I'll get your doctor, and he can explain everything." She got up and pressed a few buttons on a monitor that was attached to me by multiple wires, before leaving the room again. Her refusal to answer me was frustrating. The pinching pain in my legs struck again, and I lifted the blanket to investigate.

On both sides of my bikini line were gauze squares, seeped through with blood. I almost cried at the sight of it and considered any possible reason for what might have happened. A voice interrupted my panic.

"Hi," It was the deep and compassionate voice that I remembered clinging to in the darkness. My worry faded slightly at the sound. I looked up from the gruesome sight to see Oliver coming through the doorway. I suddenly became uncontrollably emotional. The tears spilt over in my confusion and pain.

"Oliver, I don't know what happened," I admitted in genuine distress.

He quickly pulled a chair up to my bed and took both of my hands in one of his, while the other brushed the hair from my forehead.

"Your heart wasn't pumping blood properly." He spoke slowly and soothingly, waiting for me to process. I remembered the crushing pressure in my chest and the darkness before the nothingness. "You have WPW or Wolff-Parkinson-White syndrome. Last night your heart rate exceeded three hundred beats per minute, and your ventricles couldn't keep up. They stopped working and you lost consciousness. The defibrillator was able to restart things, and when you got here, they were able to go in and fix the problem. They did what's called a catheter ablation. They killed off a concealed bypass that was causing the abnormal rhythm." He waited again. The drugs made my mind process things much slower than I was used to. Every one of his words traveled in slow motion, and I couldn't piece them together to make sense of much.

"And this?" I lifted the blanket and looked again, growing increasingly nauseated at the sight. Moving made it hurt. The pain knocked the wind out of me momentarily. He squeezed my hands and pressed a button on the side of my bed.

"They access your heart through the femoral veins in your groin. They feed a camera and the device that does the ablation along the pathway of the vein." Again, I struggled to comprehend completely. I was stuck on the fact that he had said groin and meant my groin at that. I didn't want to talk about my groin with Oliver anymore, though I was grateful to have a context for why I was in a hospital and why I was in so much pain.

"Did it work?" The idea of being rid of that troublesome beat was almost too good to consider.

"It's a wait and see kind of thing. You may have some residual, mild episodes, but if it worked, you will notice a significant difference. It has a rather high success rate." It was fascinating to hear him speak in such a formal and medical manner. I liked it, but then again, I liked hearing him say anything. I allowed myself to ponder the idea of a regular beat through the euphoric, drug-induced stupor I had awakened to.

The nurse came back in and smiled at Oliver. "Did you need something?"

"Yes, I think it's time for more pain medication. Has doctor Erwin been paged?"

"I paged him just before you came in. He should be here any minute," she said through a bedazzled smile. If I was lucid, I would manage an envious glare.

I gasped, suddenly remembering Maddy. "Where's Maddy?" The tears were beginning to spill over again as I recovered image after image. I shuddered at the thought of her having witnessed anything, and prayed that she had slept through it all.

"She's with your mom at Merman's place. She's showing her around." With this he flashed his beautiful smile and my heart warmed briefly before remembering the second half of my concern.

"Did she see…?" He shook his head before I finished the question.

"She slept through Eddie carrying her downstairs and the whole entourage of police and firemen." He smiled again, and I laughed, thinking about how she could sleep through anything, even our crash onto the ivy-covered hill. The laugh caused the pain to spasm.

"Try to stay still," he insisted.

"Try not to make me laugh then," I argued back.

He smiled. "Deal."

I lay back and sifted through the reel of memories from that night. The painful worry returned.

"Is Merman okay?"

"He's fine," he assured me. "Merman can take a few punches. He's got a couple of black eyes, but he's more worried about you." He gently brushed over the sore spot on my forehead and moved his finger down to my throat. I could see his jaw tighten and his eyes grow watery.

"Is he really dead?" Though the blank stare and morbid twist of Jerry's body on the ground was enough to know, I needed it to be confirmed.

"Yes, he's gone."

A wave of shame came over me and the tears started again.

"I can't believe I killed him. I didn't mean to kill him."

"Casey," he whispered, trying to console me again. "The autopsy report showed that he was pumped full of drugs. There was cocaine and other opiates, as well as an exorbitant amount of alcohol in his system. That combination alone might have killed him, but it's been determined that the cause of death was the trauma to his frontal lobe, which was determined to have been caused by the coffee table, not you."

I laughed morbidly through the tears. "So the coffee table killed him." I considered the illogical argument. "He wouldn't have been assaulted by the coffee table had I not slammed a frying pan into the side of his head." The violent ring to my words made me shudder, and the guilt welled.

"I don't think he intended on leaving alive, if he had any coherent intentions at all besides killing you…" he paused, and I watched as he ground his teeth again and fought back tears. "You saved your life,

Casey, and Merman's and Maddy's. Anyone would have done the same. There's no guilt in that."

I understood his perspective, but there was an awful heaviness that accompanied the knowledge of having taken a life…Jerry's.

The nurse came back in. "Dr. Erwin had an emergency call, but ordered pain medication and anything you might need for nausea."

"Great," Oliver approved, and she proceeded to prepare some sort of drug cocktail in a needle. I cringed at the sight of it. He smiled. "Don't worry, it goes in here." He lightly caressed just below the i.v. on my arm. "They'll likely keep you overnight to monitor your heart and your head," he said sweetly, brushing my hair aside again. I felt a cool sensation travel up my arm, and I was immediately dizzy, heart racing. I grabbed Oliver's hand in a panic. "It's okay. It's always intense at first."

"Don't leave," I begged.

"I'm not going anywhere." He sat beside me and held my hand as the pain faded, and it grew more and more impossible to keep my eyes open.

The sweetest voice beckoned me to wake. Another voice was trying to hush it, but I wanted to hear it again. I opened my eyes to see Maddy standing beside me.

"Hi, sweetie," I forced through my scratchy throat.

"Hi, mommy. Are you okay?" She petted my head and kissed my cheek.

"I'm okay, baby. Did you have fun with grandma?" I was so happy to see her. The tears threatened to return.

"I showed her all around, mommy. Except our house. We can't go in there. The police men are doing their work up there." She said it as if it were perfectly normal. I panicked, wondering if she knew. Had anyone told her? I scanned the room and found Merman sitting in the corner. His face was multiple shades of blue and purple, and one eye was swollen almost shut. I couldn't hold back anymore. Merman came and sat next to my bed.

"Am I that hideous?" he teased.

"Why are you crying, mommy?"

"I'm just happy that everyone's okay. That's all, honey."

"I'm okay, and Merman had an accident, but he can still see me through that eye." She carefully pointed to Merman's less beaten eye.

"I *can* see you," he said, turning his good eye to look at her. "So you better watch out." He tickled her and she giggled.

"I finished our picture, mommy." Maddy held up the picture we had started that fatal night, but it was much more elaborate than I had left it. "Merman colored the building, and Celia colored you and me, and Eddie made lighting, and Oliver made leaves, and… " she paused, trying to remember more and eventually gave up. "Isn't it pretty, mommy?" I held up the picture of the two of us standing in front of The Golden Oaks on that dark and stormy night. The added details brought it to life and flashes of the months inside that building – the life, the love…and the death – overwhelmed me. I shivered, reliving it all in a moment. Maddy probed again. "Isn't it pretty?"

"It's beautiful, baby." I pulled her in close and kissed her forehead. She took the picture from me and handed it to Oliver. He smiled at me, sensing the turmoil brought on by the drawing, and then turned to Maddy, letting her point out all of the details again.

Behind them on a shelf was a vase filled with flowers. Merman saw me looking at them and laughed.

"You'll never guess." He reached over and pulled a small card from the middle of them. I opened it and read. It was just signed *Uncle Stanley* with a generic get-well-soon greeting. I laughed too, but carefully as it caused the pain to spasm.

"He's a man of few words," Merman stated plainly. We both laughed.

I looked at Maddy, then back at Merman. "Have you said anything?" I asked, nodding toward Maddy, who was busy twirling around.

"No. I told her there was an accident, and she didn't require any details," he whispered.

"What do I tell her, Merman?"

"We'll think of something," he assured. "She doesn't see him often as it is, so we have some time." I appreciated that he included himself. I was so grateful that he was okay.

"So, I hear that you're coming home tomorrow," he said, changing the subject.

"That's what I hear," I responded without enthusiasm. There was a world of change to face when I got back.

The next day, after my heart proved stable and when I could hold down food and stand up on my own, I was released from the hospital. I had a hard time walking and was ordered to stay in bed for at least three days. I agreed, with my fingers crossed behind my back. I had never spent more than a day in bed. It wasn't in my nature. Besides, Christmas was coming, and I wasn't going to spend it in bed.

We pulled into the parking lot of The Golden Oaks and both Oliver and Merman helped me inside. Oliver insisted I use crutches to take some of the weight off of my legs and prevent the pain that came with every step. When they opened the front door, there was a small party waiting to welcome me home. Celia, Uncle Stanley, my mom, Maddy, and Eddie all clapped and cheered when I walked in. It was silly, but the sweetest thing I could have imagined. After gentle hugs and well wishes, I lamely made my way down the hallway.

Merman wouldn't let me past his front door, obviously keeping me away from the bloody scene upstairs. I looked at him suspiciously.

"You have everything you need down here. No stairs. Doctor's orders." He gestured toward Oliver, who smiled and confirmed with a nod.

"No stairs." He winked at me.

I complied, for the time being. I knew that at some point I would have to go back into that apartment and deal with what had happened. I knew that soon I would have to explain to Maddy that her father had died, and I knew that once again, the course of our lives had been altered dramatically. The great battle was over and yet, I felt that a new one had just begun.

Shortly after I settled in at Merman's, an investigator arrived to take my statement. He asked his questions as if he already knew the answers, but took copious notes. He informed me that based on evidence recently obtained, they had determined it was Jerry who had broken in previously and were sorry they hadn't detained him sooner. I wanted to applaud them sarcastically, but managed to control myself. I assumed the evidence was the missing key he had taken from my kitchen drawer, something I had overlooked myself.

I retold the events as I remembered them and barely made it through before breaking down. It was a nightmare I couldn't wake up from, and the evidence of it was right above me, sealed off by yellow tape. The investigator concluded with one final question.

"At any point during the altercation, did you fear for your life?" The question seemed absurd what with the stitches across my throat, but I knew the answer was significant.

"I feared for all of our lives," I answered angrily.

"Did you fear for your life, ma'am?" He stared at me, waiting for my reply.

"Yes."

That interview, along with the autopsy report and the testimonies of others, closed the case. It was deemed an act of self-defense and the D.A. had no intention of pressing charges.

That first night back at home, as the memories haunted me, I confirmed that I hadn't acted out of fear for my life. I had acted out of protection over the lives of those I loved. I recalled thinking that if Jerry had already killed Maddy, I would gladly let him run that blade across my throat. But he hadn't, and he was there, beating the life out of the one who had taken my hand in my darkest hour. Something savage had come over me, and I had swung hard, deciding that Jerry was done taking from me.

Chapter Twenty-Seven

Goodbye

No one claimed Jerry from the morgue. He had never talked about, nor had I ever met his family, and I could provide no further suggestions on whom else to contact. It seemed only fair to Maddy that I bring him home and give him a proper funeral. He was released to me without question as I was still legally his spouse. I suspected he would roll over in his body bag if he knew.

The five of us stood over his casket in the chapel, absorbing the enormity of all that had happened. I had already cried for days and was left with only a troubling numbness. I had cried for Maddy and what she would one day understand. I had cried over the life my hands had taken, and the self-condemnation that followed. I had cried from what Oliver claimed was the lasting effects of the anesthesia and pain, and I cried for the vulnerable uncertainty that loomed ahead. But standing there over

Jerry, despite the heavy finality of it all, I felt nothing. It was as if I was watching all of it take place from the outside, disconnected and indifferent, having run every emotion dry.

We put together an admirable service, for Maddy's sake. Though she was only five, I wanted her to have the opportunity for closure one day and a positive memory to rest in the place of a violent ending. Beautiful flowers surrounded his casket, which itself was not inexpensive. Besides the casket and flowers, everything was on the house, so to speak. My mom insisted on covering the remaining costs, as she too thought it was an important moment of closure for Maddy. The only difference with my mother was that she thought it was important for me as well.

Merman had worked wonders with Jerry's make-up, and someone would have to know where to look to see the fatal wounds on his head. I stared at them, knowing exactly where they were, and waited for some emotion to rise to the surface. Nothing came.

Unlike my dream of this very situation, there were no students of his or *any* mourners for that matter. Besides those of us whom he had intended to kill, he was utterly alone. I felt a passing sense of pity for him. Though he was a monster in the end, I imagined that at one point he was a small child like Maddy, and had probably faced countless abuses to become what he had been. I looked and saw no remnants of such innocence in his face. Even in death he looked disturbed.

The other four looked awkwardly my way for what I assumed was some insight as to what was going on in my head. They had asked me numerous times how I was doing. Merman had tried to explain to me the phenomenon of complicated grief, and Oliver had reminded me of all the contributing factors in Jerry's death, concerned that I still carried some sense of guilt. Complicated was an understatement, and guilt didn't respond to reason.

"Thank you for doing this," was all I could manage to say. "It means a lot to Maddy." The four of them looked at each other with concern and said nothing. Merman always said that when it came to offering solace to the grieving, silent presence was sometimes best. I could tell by his worried eyes that he struggled to practice this with me.

Maddy entered the chapel with my mom, both in black dresses. I watched as they walked up the aisle holding hands. Maddy smiled when she saw us.

Telling Maddy was more difficult for me than it seemed for her. I had explained that he had fallen and hit his head and that the injury was too bad for any doctor to fix. It wasn't a lie, just not the whole picture, and I wasn't sure she would ever need that.

"So we're going to bury daddy like we buried MacGuyver?" Once again, the simplicity of her perspective made me question the complexity with which I viewed life.

"Yes, honey, we're going to bury daddy…like MacGuyver."

"And like our other friends who come here?"

"Yes."

"Did Merman make him look handsome?"

"Very handsome," I added, hoping to salvage any positive memory she may possess.

I walked her to his casket and moved a stepping stool in place for her. She stepped up and looked over her father. She reached out to hold my hand, and then Merman's.

"He looks like he's sleeping," she whispered. "Can I touch him?"

"Go ahead, sweetie." It seemed like the best way to give her closure was to allow her whatever process she needed. Merman had once explained that the washing, preparing, and burying of the bodies was, at one point in time, the undertaking of the family. He said that it provided for a process of grieving and closure that some don't ever find anymore. I wanted Maddy to find it. She reached out her little hand and touched Jerry's. She pulled it back quickly and then reached again.

"He's cold," she said, sounding slightly troubled.

"Maddy, this is just your daddy's body. His soul isn't here anymore," Merman tried to explain.

"I know," she said assuredly. "He's really in heaven now, right mommy?" I felt everyone's eyes on me. What did I know?

"I'd like to think so, sweetie," for her sake anyway. It didn't seem like enough. She squeezed my hand and looked at me longingly. My heart broke, and I knew that my answer wasn't about me or Jerry. "He's in heaven, baby…with MacGuyver. And he's looking down at you right now thinking how pretty you look in your black dress. He doesn't want you to be sad."

"Really?" She giggled with delight.

"Really." I assured her. She squeezed my hand again and petted Jerry's.

"Goodnight, daddy."

"Goodnight, Jerry," I echoed.

The pastor Merman hired read from the bible and closed us in prayer. We decided to have a party to celebrate his life, for Maddy. I had put pictures of the two of them, of which there weren't many, around Merman's apartment, and ordered a whole feast of food. Everyone talked and said nice things about him, and Maddy seemed happy. This brought me peace, but could hardly break through the iron wall of numbness that had built itself around me.

I wanted to retreat. I felt as if I had lost my compass, and I was floating aimlessly at sea. The questions everyone had about what I would do now only magnified my utter confusion. I didn't know, and I couldn't produce a single feeling to guide me one way or another.

Oliver kept his distance, as I had retreated from him too. Even his smile and warm touch couldn't arouse a familiar feeling. As he talked to me, I held myself with my arms wrapped tightly around my chest. I didn't understand what was happening, but I was beginning to fear that a shift had occurred, from which I couldn't recover.

I quietly left the party and painfully made my way up the stairs, the crutches making for a precarious ascent. I stood in front of the door that sealed off a night that had changed everything. I waited for my old companion, the irregular flutter of my heart, to return, but it only continued its steady beat. That too echoed of an irretrievable past. I reached out and turned the knob, hoping that facing it would bring *me* the closure I had witnessed downstairs.

The room was still and contained traces of yellow tape and dirty shoe tracks. This was what Merman had hoped to clear before I came back. I was glad he hadn't. I wanted to touch, clean, and prepare the finality, like the body of a loved one. Maybe that would shock life back into me. I so desperately wanted to feel again.

Two assisted steps at a time, I moved into the living room. Flashes came back of Anne sitting over me on the now disheveled sofa bed. Another flash of a disappearing knife in her hands triggered a shortness of breath. Then it was a memory of cologne and liquor breathing from behind me, holding that blade to my throat. The rate of my heart increased, and I welcomed my familiar friend, though it disappointed me with its regularity.

The edge of the kitchen counter was spotted with blood. I felt my forehead. It still ached to the touch. I turned, remembering the sight of Jerry over Merman, hitting and hitting. Horror and rage worked their way through my blood as I recalled the fear of losing him. The feeling was so real and so intense. I moved closer, hoping to keep it. I stood there, over deeply soaked spots of blood. The cornered glass of the coffee table, the second and final blow, was stained with the same.

Emotions I thought gone, were rising quickly. The rage and horror were shifting to fear of loss as I remembered thinking Merman dead. And Maddy…I had to get Maddy out before she saw. I felt the dizziness from that night as my heart rate increased and the adrenaline pumped. I sat in the chair and scanned over the room again and again, replaying the terrible scene.

I held myself close, reveling in the flood of feeling, hoping it would awaken me. The tears came with swells of grief and remorse and pain. I rocked and cried.

It was freeing.

I sat in the chair and in the quiet of that room for a while. The tears were gone and replaced by the feeling that I couldn't stay there anymore. I had to move forward and continue in that direction. I pushed myself to a standing position and reached for my handy crutches when I heard the door creak open.

"Casey?" A soft voice spoke from behind me. I turned to find Oliver in the doorway. He wore a look of agony at the sight of me.

"I'm okay," I said through a completely stuffy nose and swollen eyes. He approached, holding his hand out. I took it, throwing myself into him. "I can't stay." The tears returned. "I just can't."

He held me close and whispered, "I know." I didn't want to let go, but I knew it would only get harder.

"I have to try and figure this out," I said, pulling away and touching my hand to my heart. "I don't recognize myself anymore. There's so much going on, and I need to sort it all out." I struggled to find the courage to say the hardest part. "I can't do this right now," I added, putting my hand to his chest.

The agony returned to his face, but he put his hand over mine and nodded. "I know."

The tears multiplied at the thought of leaving him. The irony of the timing was too cruel. He took me by both arms and pulled me closer. He looked over my face and stared into my eyes. I second guessed myself for an instant before he spoke.

"I need you to know something," he said intensely. "I'm not going anywhere."

It was everything I wanted to hear, but seemed so selfish. "I don't expect you to wait for me. That's not fair."

He shook his head in frustration. "I love you. I'm not going anywhere."

"But, I don't know how long…" I started, but he interrupted.

"You don't need to know. If you decide…if that time comes and you decide…," he fumbled over his words and the emotion in his voice and the tears in his eyes made me cry again. "I'm here if you decide that you want me here."

"I love you," I whispered, wishing it could all be so different. Being near him felt right, but there we stood, right in the middle of the chaotic context that made it impossible. He leaned in and kissed my forehead. And with that, he was gone, leaving me to absorb my decision.

A few minutes passed as I stood in the darkness of a room that no longer felt like home. A steadiness slowly replaced my shaky uncertainty, and I knew there was much to be done, and that maybe someday, I could have Oliver without reservation.

I headed back down the stairs and laughed at the predicament I had gotten myself into with my crutches. I decided to leave them where they were and make my way down on two feet.

Merman eyed me from across the room, a look of concern changing to a look of acknowledgement. He must have read on my face that a choice had been made. He sadly nodded and continued playing cards with Maddy. I went and sat on the arm of the chair Merman filled and put my arm around him, careful not to bump his badly bruised eye.

"You're leaving aren't you?" he asked solemnly.

"Yes."

"Oliver's gone," he added.

"I know."

"Are you sure this is how it has to be?" He looked up at me, like a wounded little boy, and my heart ached.

"I'm sure," I said over a growing lump in my throat. "But as soon as we're settled, we'll pick up where this game left off," I promised.

"Merman, do you have a…," Maddy paused and looked at me. I flashed her four fingers and she giggled. "Merman, do you have a four?"

"You little rascal," Merman teased and handed her his last card. "How much longer?" The sadness returned.

"As soon as I can find a new place. You don't mind if we sleep on your sofa for a few more nights, do you? For old time's sake?"

"As many as you need. You know that."

Jerry's party came to a close, and I settled comfortably into the sofa bed with Maddy, remembering our first night there. Soon we would begin a new chapter in our saga, and I would keep these people who loved us well a part of our story. I would make it a priority. Surely such friendships would survive beyond the walls of a funeral home. This was my closing thought before falling asleep, dreamless and restful.

Christmas came and went, and though we filled it with trees and lights and presents, something was missing. The void Oliver left was palpable to us all. Every room I entered brought with it a memory and a pang so strong I almost ran to the phone to call him every time. But there was so much to be done – so much that only time could sort out.

It wasn't long before James had multiple offers on the vacant house I once shared with Jerry. Its value had increased significantly in the six years we had owned it, and it was beginning to look like Maddy and I could buy a new home and have some money left over to get us by for a while. I agreed to the sale and was surprised by the ease of the process.

I spent days house hunting with my mother, and the few days borrowed time from Merman's sofa bed had turned into a few weeks. He seemed delighted by the extra time with us, but I was growing pessimistic about our prospects. I continued to work around the funeral home, as I wanted to contribute something, but Merman made even that difficult for me, insisting I should still be recuperating.

It seemed that despite my great declaration of a need to move forward, I had merely spun in circles in the same living room. The worst part was the obvious hole left by Oliver, not only in me, but at work. He had called a week later to let Merman know that he was back at the hospital full time and would likely not be back at The Golden Oaks Funeral Home anytime soon. The look on Merman's face when he answered the call made it obvious who was on the other end of the phone. Just hearing his name dredged up longing enough to make me second guess myself. I was discouraged, to say the least.

In the middle of a temper tantrum, where I nearly threw in the towel and moved back upstairs, I received a call from James about an unusual property just outside of the city. Location was important, as I didn't want to move too far away from either Merman or Maddy's school, and so far every available home had fallen outside of those parameters.

With forced optimism, I met James in front of large, worn building that looked out of place on the mostly residential street. It sat at the top of a steep hill and looked more like a business than a home.

"This is an interesting property, but I felt I would be remiss if I didn't show you everything within your search terms, considering there hasn't been much to see."

His use of the word interesting immediately dashed all hope I had mustered for the morning.

"But, you do live in a funeral home, so I suppose it couldn't get much stranger than that," he chuckled to himself. I wasn't amused.

He unlocked the door and led me through the tall entryway, and I immediately understood what he meant. It looked like a theatre of some kind. There was a small closed off area for what looked like a ticket booth and two entrances on either side into what I wasn't sure. To the left was a long staircase.

"The living area is upstairs," he said, pointing toward the staircase. "And in here," he led me through the red-velvet drapes to one side of the booth, "is what's left of a small theatre."

Sure enough, before me was a small stage and what looked like two hundred red-velvet seats. It looked very worn but very quaint, and I smiled, imagining all of the plays that had been performed in that tiny theatre.

"This facility hasn't been in use for over thirty years. The owner of the property passed away a couple of weeks ago, and the family has put it on the market, hoping for a quick sale."

I ran my fingers along the backs of the aged seats and tried to envision the person who lived in and ran this theatre, and then tried to envision *us* living there. What would I possibly do with it?

"This can be remodeled, obviously, and you could even rent this floor out to a business. With such little space in the city, these sorts of arrangements are made all of the time."

The idea of tearing any of it down made me sad for all of the hard work and life that had been put into it.

"Or," he joked, "you could open the theatre back up and make a living writing Tony-award-winning plays." He laughed and continued on through the curtain, but I stayed behind, staring at the stage and considering the possibilities. I felt an internal nudge, and I looked upward laughing.

"Really?" I hadn't even considered anything beyond finding a place to live. How I would make a living was next on my list, but this…this was beyond my imagination.

"Did you say something?" James asked, peeking back through the curtains. "The living space is this way."

"Coming." I took one last look at the theatre and followed James upstairs. The home upstairs looked immaculately kept. The hardwood floors were intact and the yellow paint was bright and framed by thick white baseboards and crown moulding. The whole space was open and airy. I was overwhelmed by its elegance. Every detail drew me in. It housed a lifetime of collected artwork, tastefully placed throughout. Its tattered outside hid its inner beauty, and I would have never imagined what was before me. The house was the entire size of the theatre below, and it was gorgeous. A lot of time, care, and money had been put into every detail. I couldn't even imagine its cost.

"It's well within your budget and far below market value," James added, following me across the long stretch of a living room.

I walked its length and peeked into all three bedrooms off of a hallway. The décor reminded me of my grandmother. It was bright and flowery, and I felt an immediate sense of belonging.

As I walked down the hallway, the pictures hanging from the wall caught my eye. I followed the family portraits and the story they told, landing on one of a couple, taken decades back. They looked madly in love with each other, literally standing cheek to cheek, his arms pulling her in close. They smiled back at me as I stared, remembering the feeling of being so close…once.

There was a glimmer in her eye that told me I knew her. I looked closely and could make no connection.

"The woman who owned the place was an actress and a playwright. She and her husband ran the theatre. She closed it down after he died. Beautiful isn't she?" James was now standing beside me, looking at the same picture that had enthralled me. "Ironically enough, she was recently in the Golden Oaks." I turned to him, slightly afraid to know.

"What was her name?"

"Anne Hardy."

My heart rate sped as I stared back at the picture. I looked closely again, and the glow around her shot recognition right through me.

"Anne?"

"Yes, she had her service just a day or so after…" He stopped there, leery of finishing his sentence and reminding me of that violent night. But it wasn't the thought of Jerry that disturbed me.

"I need to step outside for a minute." I excused myself and headed down the stairs and out into the fresh air. I paced in front of the steps, trying to comprehend the unlikely coincidence. I considered the possibility that perhaps I had lost my mind. Had I really seen her, spoken to her? Could it really be just a coincidence that I now stood in her home, a theater none the less?

"Really?" I shouted up at the sky. I laughed at the tapestry being woven just steps ahead of me. My God had a sense of humor, I decided. "You want me to write?" I asked out loud. "Here?" A woman walking by pulled her grocery bag in close and sped up as she passed me. I laughed again. I had always wanted to write. I would sneak it in like contraband whenever possible. It was something Jerry had always tried to keep from me. But was I any good? They were just my weird stories.

I imagined my weird stories playing out on stage. I imagined Merman and Celia and Eddie helping me with restoring the theater and with costumes and sets. I imagined family nights upstairs and for once, a place to settle and grow. I was giddy. I ran up the front steps and up the stairs to the front door and slammed into James on the other side.

"Oh, I'm sorry," I apologized breathlessly.

"Are you okay, Casey?" He looked startled as if he might call the police. I laughed and tried to catch my breath.

"I'll take it," I declared in between breaths. "I'll take it.

Chapter Twenty-Eight

Life through Death

I sealed up the last invitation with sweaty palms and unrelenting butterflies. I placed a stamp in the right hand corner and walked it down the street, dropping it into the blue bin. As soon as I let it fall from my hands, I considered reaching my arm all the way in and pulling it back out. It had been nine months, and I feared it would be tossed aside as soon as my name was read above the return address.

I walked back up the stairs, hoping. I smiled at the sight of the fresh paint and woodwork on the outside of my home. Between the four of us- me, Merman, Celia and Eddie - we had managed to bring the place back to life. A fresh new sign hung over the stairs declaring itself The Hardy Theatre, and in its front most windows hung posters picturing a black coffin covered in red roses, with the title *Life through Death* beneath it.

My first play would be opening in a little over a week. It was inspired by my life-altering crash onto a hill and into a real life. Names had been changed to protect the innocent, of course, but we were all there on the stage, portrayed by numerous actors. It had taken a while to figure out the complexities of theatre such as casting, costumes, lighting, sound, marketing, and set design, to name a few, but the story…the story came easily. The rest was waiting to be dusted off and put to use again. Everyone in my life had come together and contributed in their own way, and in just a handful of months, I was doing what I loved with the people I loved. Most of them anyway.

I opened the door to a hum of commotion. Rehearsals were running smoothly and the first show was almost sold out. I was ecstatic. I had stood at the edge, at the turning point, and I had stepped out in faith into a life I could never have imagined. It was that step, I concluded, that had been rewarded with blessing after blessing. There was only one piece missing.

"Did you mail it?" Two faces stopped their work and waited for an answer.

"Casey? Tell me you mailed it!" Merman and Celia now stood with arms folded and faces scolding. A bright reflection blinded me momentarily.

"Geez, Celia. That thing's dangerous." She laughed and held her hand out, admiring her dazzling engagement ring. She leaned over and kissed Merman's cheek. I chuckled and made my way into the theatre having dodged the question. I remembered the strenuous ordeal Merman had made out of finding the perfect ring and the perfect place to propose. It was on the stage in front of me now that he had knelt just a month ago, lights dimmed and soft music playing overhead, his palms and forehead sweating. Celia had swooned but caught herself in time to hear him ask for her hand, for a lifetime, with him. I had watched from the sound booth at the back of the room, which was now filled with busy hands preparing for the opening show. I cried by myself, with delirious joy for two of my favorite people and an ache of longing for someone else.

That time had passed quickly, and so much had happened since. The stage was now buzzing, an abbreviated version of my recent life unfolding on its surface. Maddy had insisted on a part in the play, so she played herself, though she had no idea since the character's name had been changed. The ignorant bliss of childhood protected her from the ugly truth of the story, for the time being. She had made no connection but loved being a part of what she ironically called "mommy's story." She was actually quite good, all thanks to Merman, who rehearsed with her day and night. I sat in the back row and watched with a smile as she said her lines.

As the days passed, I grew more and more anxious about opening night. But mostly the anticipation came when I thought about that invitation and whether or not he would come. I longed to see him, to hear his voice and to be close enough to breathe him in. But I wondered how long he had really waited before he had waited long enough.

That last night before the show, we worked into the morning hours, making sure everything was in place. I was too excited to sleep and after locking everything up, I pulled out a bottle of wine and sat beside Merman. Celia had gone home and Maddy was asleep. We both smiled at each other and toasted.

"I miss this," I said with immense nostalgia.

He laughed. "We'll have to make a habit out of it then." We both kicked our feet up on the coffee table and sighed.

"Do you think he'll come?" I asked, afraid to hear an answer.

"He'll come," he said with confidence.

"I wouldn't blame him if he didn't." It was true. I had considered it many times. "It's been a long time."

"Nine months is hardly a long time," he teased with a smirk. "Not when you love like that. I know now what that feels like, what I saw in him when he was with you, when he just mentioned your name." His smile grew. "He'll come."

Merman the romantic…I hoped he was right and was happy that he too knew love.

The morning came and kept me busy enough to stay focused on the tasks at hand, though I caught myself checking the pews and doors often, as if for some reason Oliver would be there hours early, if at all. Everything was running smoothly, almost too smoothly. I waited for the last second disaster, but it never came. Before I knew it, the seats slowly filled, and the backstage hummed with the excitement of cast and crew.

I locked myself into one of the dressing rooms I had converted into a business office. I was going through check lists and making sure everything was in order, obsessively. A knock on the door interrupted my mania. My heart jumped at the sound and I stood, straightening my dress and hair. I turned the knob, not sure what I would say, not sure who I would see. Disappointment hit hard when I saw that it was just Eddie.

"Fifteen minutes and we start."

"Okay, thanks Eddie." Behind him I saw my mother, looking as radiant as ever. I was happy to see her as her presence was rather calming. I remembered how she loved the theater, how my father would take her often when I was younger. I smiled at our shared interests. The smile faded when I saw my father behind her. I stiffened, and the frightened girl from my past made her debut. My mother left him about ten feet behind and approached the door.

"What is he doing here?" I snapped.

"He wanted to come, dear."

"Do I have to talk to him?" Before she could answer, he stepped up behind her.

"Hello, Casey." His usually hard and commanding voice was softened. It took me by surprise.

"Hello," I barely uttered.

"I wanted to, uh…" He cleared his throat before continuing. "I wanted to wish you luck." It seemed to take quite an effort, the words sounding unfamiliar to him. It wasn't life-changing, but it was something. My mother's facial expression begged for a polite response from me. What she was doing with him I didn't know. Whether or not he was capable of change eluded me further. But it wasn't my place to judge. The least I could do was be respectful and polite…for her sake.

"Thank you," was about all I could manage. It was a start.

"Well, we're going to get seated. Good luck!" My mother broke the tension and kissed my cheek. They left, hand in hand, to sit with the growing crowd. I watched them disappear through the curtain, feeling far too anxious about whether or not Oliver would come to trudge through all of the emotions my father had just brought to the surface. Eddie passed by again and held up ten fingers.

Trembling with anticipation, I closed up the office and walked through the crowd of costumed actors who were saying lines and finishing up with final touches. I found Merman and Celia, and together we looked around in amazement.

"I can't believe we've pulled this off," I said, still in shock.

"I know," agreed Celia, as she hugged me to her side.

"We'll see," Merman teased. "You should go sit and enjoy the show. We'll finish up back here." He shooed me off, and I made my way down the stairs from the stage and opened a side door that led into the seating. I peeked through the crack and scanned the crowd. I spotted my parents, Uncle Stanley, Don and Vivian, and Linda from Maddy's school. I recognized so many faces and felt abundantly loved. But there was one face missing. My heart sank, and I tried to reassure myself that whether or not he came, this night would be a success. I made my way to a seat in front where Merman and Celia would soon join me.

I could hardly contain myself. The anticipation and excitement were overwhelming. I felt Merman squeeze my hand as the house lights went out and the curtains opened. I watched as my words retold our story. It began with a doorbell ringing on a cold, rainy night. A woman held her daughter as she walked into a recreation of Uncle Stanley's office. I turned and saw him grinning. It was the first time I had seen the man truly smile. The crowd laughed, though not as loud as Merman, as the woman stumbled into the bathroom vomiting while the handsome mortician described embalming. They gasped when the "bad guy", as Maddy called him, attacked the heroine in the middle of the night, and when she fell unconscious into her lover's arms. Some cried when the two lovers parted, and most cheered in the final scene when they reunited with a kiss. I wondered if he was watching… wondered what he thought of the ending. I searched through the sea of faces but couldn't find what I looked for. The audience stood and cheered as the curtains closed once more. It was surreal. Besides the slight emptiness, I felt whole and happy.

I was greeted and congratulated by so many familiar faces. My mouth ached from smiling, and I welcomed the pain. We made our way backstage to congratulate the actors and celebrate. Everyone was thrilled by the success, though many were already discussing changes for the upcoming performances.

Merman had prepared the back room with champagne to celebrate. He gathered them all around and pushed me forward to attempt a speech. I didn't like the spotlight. I stammered before speaking.

"I… I just can't tell you how much this means to me. You have all contributed to my dream tonight and I thank you. You were brilliant."

"Cheers," everyone shouted, toasting their glasses. The revelry continued, and I tried to maintain a smile, but the more time passed, the deeper my heart sank. Celia came and sat beside me.

"The night's not over you know, and that was a pretty big crowd out there."

I stood up and patted her shoulder. I appreciated her optimism, but mine had run dry. "Thanks, Celia." I turned to go and lock myself in the back room, in case the tears that were building made an appearance, but I turned and stepped right into Oliver. My heart jumped, and I gasped. I could hear Celia giggling behind me. She had seen him standing there and let me walk right into him. But I didn't care. He was there. He held roses in his hand.

"Oliver!" Maddy shouted and hugged his side.

"These are for you. You were wonderful." He gave her the roses, and she giggled, hugging them into her. "You were both wonderful." He turned to me and stepped in close. We were eye to eye, wordless and waiting.

"I liked the ending," he finally whispered.

"Me too," I agreed, completely mesmerized and trying to catch my breath.

"Are you ready?"

My heart raced with wild anticipation.

"I'm ready," I whispered back.

With one motion he slid his arm around my waist and pulled me so that our noses were touching. He lifted me slightly off the ground and looked at me intently. We smiled and then our lips were one, the kiss I had waited for. The warm electricity returned stronger than I remembered. Everything about him was doubly amazing, and the longing I felt for him made me weak. All I could think, beyond his lips, was thank you, God – thank you. All I loved surrounded me. More than I ever dreamed of was mine. I had stepped out in faith, giving up everything, and this was His reward. I believed it. I felt it. The room around us broke into applause and cheering, but they were only an echoed backdrop to me and Oliver. When we parted, I was a bit embarrassed by the crowd that had gathered around us, but wholly overjoyed as I was still in his arms. He didn't let go, not once that night.

When the night had ended and the theatre had emptied, the six of us locked up and walked down the street to an ice cream shop I found shortly after moving in. Together we took up the entire width of the sidewalk. Merman and Celia walked hand in hand, passing loving whispers between them and glancing at me and Oliver with huge smiles on their faces. I didn't mind. It didn't embarrass me anymore. I wanted to shout out to the whole street how happy I was, but spared everyone the awkward moment that would surely follow. Maddy jumped from one line in the sidewalk to the next, trying to get Eddie to follow along, and he did, as amusingly as only Eddie could.

I couldn't stop smiling, my hand in Oliver's as the cool evening air blew against my face – my little family, together. He smiled back and leaned in, his lips close to my ear. His breath was warm and electric, and I looked forward to forever for the first time in my life.

"How's your heart?" he whispered, squeezing my hand.

"Full," I replied, and we both smiled, ready to start anew.